Unbroke Horses

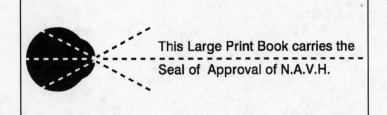

This Large Print Book carries the
Seal of Approval of N.A.V.H.

UNBROKE HORSES

D. B. JACKSON

THORNDIKE PRESS
A part of Gale, Cengage Learning

GALE
CENGAGE Learning·

Detroit • New York • San Francisco • New Haven, Conn • Waterville, Maine • London

GALE
CENGAGE Learning®

LIBRARY OF CONGRESS CATALOGING-IN-PUBLICATION DATA

Jackson, D. B.
    Unbroke horses / by D. B. Jackson. — Large print edition.
        pages ; cm. — (Thorndike Press large print western)
    ISBN-13: 978-1-4104-5655-7 (hardcover)
    ISBN-10: 1-4104-5655-2 (hardcover)
    1. Large type books. I. Title.
PS3610.A347U53 2013
813'.6—dc23   2013008697

Published in 2013 by arrangement with Cherry Weiner Literary Agency

Printed in the United States of America
1 2 3 4 5 6 7 17 16 15 14 13

This book is dedicated especially to my wife, Mary, and to Josh, Amy, Mateo, and Lucas whose love inspires these words.

With a special note of gratitude to Pat LoBrutto, whose literary vision, sense of character, and gift for storytelling make editing one of the most rewarding parts of this great adventure we call writing.

For the loveliness of my waters is crammed with corpses, I cannot find a channel to cast my waters into the bright sea since I am congested with the dead men you kill so brutally.

— HOMER, *The Iliad*

ONE

In those final days of a war in which there was no glory and the taste for killing was long past, multitudes of drawn and wasted soldiers set forth upon the battered countryside, their shoulders rounded and their clothes reeking of blood. They stepped over corpses twisted and decaying and some stopped to pick at the spoils while others, dull and thoughtless, threw down their weapons and shuffled ahead.

They wandered alone and in pairs and in loose companies of varying numbers, all afoot and oddly uniformed in tattered rags of gray and blue and many missing arms or feet or eyes. They bivouacked along the roadsides and in fields wherever darkness overtook them. At night they sat like mute beings wrought from nightmares, bent over small fires, unable to feed themselves and gazing out through hollow eyes.

Ten months before the Confederacy collapsed, field-commissioned Brevet General Ike Smith quit the army. He led the remnants of his battle-fatigued 12th Georgia regulars out of the Shenandoah Valley onto a rutted back road and summarily dismissed them.

"Boys," said General Smith, addressing the assemblage from atop a gaunt and leggy mount. "By the power vested in me by the Army of these Confederate States of America, I dismiss you from further participation in this war, which I do hereby declare to be over."

"Stand your posts," commanded a handsome young officer wearing captain's bars upon his shoulders. "This war is not over and the general has no authority to dismiss you. You men will form up in marching ranks. Sergeant, bring the company to arms, now!"

The general turned his head, hacked, and spat and looked back at the handsome captain through eyes shot red from alcohol and road dust. He un-flapped his service revolver and discharged a round between the buttons of the captain's field coat. Dust coughed out from the hole the bullet made and blood ran freely from the wound beneath it. The captain sat upon his horse and stared a blank stare past the general. He sat there a long time before he pitched forward, then fell from his horse, dead at the feet of the men who looked on but did not move.

The general regarded the sergeant with a dark and somber gaze. The sergeant threw down his weapon and threw down his ammunition pack, and when he did so, the others did so as well.

No one moved to aid the fallen officer, but one man caught up the reins of the captain's mount and lifted himself into the saddle. He wheeled the horse around and whipped it into a gallop with no direction and no plan other than to desert the war. No one moved, no one spoke, and they all stood mindlessly waiting for their orders and watching the lone horseman whip his mount ahead of the dust cloud that followed him as he shrunk from view.

The general holstered his revolver, and reached back and fetched a tarnished flask from his saddlebag. He uncorked it and tipped it back, then looked slowly at the tired and questioning eyes that stared up at him.

"Y'all are dismissed."

They mumbled and shuffled about, but none of them did anything but wait.

General Smith disregarded them all and nodded to a thin and pale private, standing at his boot heel. The general slipped his left foot free of the saddle iron and extended the private his arm. Private Raymond Smith took the arm, hooked the toe of his worn-out military shoe in the stirrup and swung up behind his brother. The general nudged the horse forward and tipped up the flask.

A mile down the road Raymond turned to behold the ragged company of gray-coated foot soldiers in poor marching formation as they followed behind.

By midday, the leggy gelding had out-walked the infantrymen until only the halo of dust that hovered above the trailing company was visible in the shimmering heat of the road. The general pulled the horse up sharply.

"Get off," said the general.

Raymond hesitated and the general struck the dull-witted private from the horse's back with a broad sweep of his thick arm and dropped him to the dirt. Raymond picked himself up and slapped the dust from his trousers with his hat.

"What did you do that for?" Raymond asked.

"Get yourself your own horse," Ike said.

Ike touched the gelding with his heels and the horse stepped out with Raymond trotting alongside to keep up.

12

"Where am I supposed to get one?"

"That ain't my concern."

"I got no money for no horse."

"You got a rifle."

"Well, I sure ain't trading off my rifle."

"Then, Brother Raymond . . . you can walk."

"Well, I ain't walking no more. I'll find me a horse."

Ike took another pull from the flask and continued riding. He corked the flask and hacked, then pointed off into the lowering sun as the private trotted alongside.

"Yonder's one that'll suit ye," Ike said, his voice raspy and airy.

Raymond shaded his eyes with his hand and squinted at a shirtless man clucking a big yellow plow horse in a freshly-turned field. He looked back to Ike for approval, but Ike ignored the dolt and took to hacking again.

"Well, I'm done walking," Raymond muttered as he left the road and crossed the field, stumbling across the furrows as he went.

Ike palmed the flask and watched the pantomime. Raymond circled the shirtless man and the big horse, then walked up to the man and doffed his hat. Raymond's mouth moved. The man stopped, talked

13

with his hands briefly, shook his head, and then turned away from Raymond. Raymond stepped up and spun the sun-darkened man around by his arm. The man threw off the reins and struck the dolt a powerful blow to the head. Raymond went down. The man advanced on Raymond, seized him about the shoulders, and dragged him off twenty yards, then cast him off onto a newly turned furrow.

The man turned and strode back to the plow horse. Raymond recovered the rifle and leveled it at the man's sunburned back. White smoke and flame exited the barrel along with the ball that ripped through the farmer's spine. The man arched backwards and fell dead upon the freshly plowed earth.

Raymond caught up the horse, loosened the harness, and let it drop. He left the headstall in place, removed the collar and cut the reins to riding length, then mounted bareback and trotted to catch up to Ike, who urged his horse forward and ignored Raymond as he approached.

"I got me one," Raymond said, as he gawked down at the general from his perch astraddle the Belgian.

"Put a pretty good knot on your head, didn't he?" Ike said as dust exploded beneath the footfalls of the horses, and the

14

column of soldiers behind them disappeared forever.

That night Ike and Raymond slept without eating. The next morning they robbed a farmhouse and, by the following night, the slow-witted Raymond had shot and killed another man and traded him horses.

They rode as two distorted images warped in the heat that ascended from the scorched roadway in shimmering waves. Week by week their appearance worsened. Their clothes hung like filthy rags, and they sat their thin and worn mounts like ancient warriors of the devil's brigade. They rode the plains and prairies into the sun. They rode through rain and the heat. They rode starless nights and days with nothing to eat.

The morning they rode up onto the banks of a great river, they heard music and boat whistles and the clank and clatter of deck chains and drayage wagons. All about them people chattered and hurried, and crowded the narrow streets. Long rows of docks jutting into the muddy waterway lay bobbing with smoking sternwheelers and all manner of skiffs and ferries and barges tied alongside. Sweaty black men transported burlap seed bags and wooden crates of various sizes onto waiting freight wagons. Dandies and women in uncommon finery strutted nearby

15

and heavily-spiced and greasy food smells swirled into the air from a steel chimney above a brightly colored dining hall where music played and women laughed and shrieked in disorderly good humor.

Ike and Raymond dismounted their boney nags and waited while a suited man turned to walk down the narrow alley in which they stood. The man hastened his pace and looked away as he passed by them.

"Excuse me, sir," Ike called out to the man, his voice thick and whiskey-slurred.

The man glanced back over his shoulder and paused, then turned and quickened his pace. Raymond trotted forward and detained the man while the ponderous Ike caught up, wheezing and out of breath.

"What can I do for you?"

"We just need a little money for food, that's all," Ike said.

"I see," said the gentleman as he cleared his throat and backed away from Ike. "A few pennies perhaps," he mumbled, and his eyes darted back to the alley entrance then furtively took in the rough appearance of the wretched-smelling man hulking before him.

The man reached inside his coat and withdrew a fine leather purse. His fingers fumbled inside the purse while he attempted to sort out the coins before exposing them. Raymond stepped behind the man, unsheathed a battered skinning knife, then moved in close and looked over the man's shoulder.

Raymond whispered through a crooked and toothy smile. "We're powerful hungry."

The man tilted his head and shot a backwards glance at Raymond, then drew his purse close to his vest as to conceal its contents from the trespassing eyes of the dolt.

"I'll take that," said Ike, and he snatched the purse from the gentleman's hand at the same time Raymond drove the skinning knife through the man's coat and slid it deep between his ribs.

The man slumped and Ike lowered him by his lapels to the ground, and then searched his pockets. He jerked the gold chain attached to the man's vest and withdrew an engraved watch from the pocket. He held the timepiece to his ear, then brought it down and clicked the cover open.

"Half past nine, Raymond. Time you and me got us some breakfast."

Raymond's expression brightened at the prospect and he stepped over the man's body and stood in the shadow of the general.

17

Raymond grinned and looked at Ike. "I want to get me some boiled eggs with runny yellers and some buttermilk."

Ike ignored Raymond and they left the elderly man where he went down. As they exited the alley, a dark-skinned stranger with the amber-colored eyes of a serpent watched them. He remained motionless and only his eyes tracked the approach of Ike and Raymond.

Raymond hesitated, but Ike walked on. When they were close Ike noticed the double-barrel ten-gauge hanging at the mulatto's left side where he held it with one hand, both hammers cocked and his long, delicate finger on the front trigger.

Ike stopped. Raymond fell in behind him. Ike regarded the mulatto with the air of his rank and tipped his head back in the direction of the still bleeding body in the alley.

"That ain't your concern."

The mulatto neither commented nor acknowledged the general's words and Raymond braced for trouble.

"When's the last time you ate?" the general asked of the expressionless mulatto who did not answer.

"Come on in, we'll get you something to eat," the general added, disregarding the mulatto's absence of response.

The mulatto measured Ike with his eyes, turned his head slowly to reassess the body lying in the alley, then slowly dropped first the left hammer then the right before moving his finger from the trigger guard of the ten-gauge.

Ike touched his hat, and when he stepped up onto the plank-board sidewalk that fronted the dining room, Raymond and the mulatto stepped up right behind him.

Two

Before Ike, Raymond, and the mulatto finished breakfast, a confused gathering of angry citizens congregated outside the dining room. The door swung open and a sheriff and two suited men entered with all the color drained from their faces.

"There they are," said one of the suited men as he pointed to the corner where Ike, Raymond, and the mulatto sat.

"It was those two," the other suited man said, waving a finger wildly about and gesturing toward Ike and Raymond.

The sheriff approached the table. His hand shook and his nervous voice was too loud for the circumstances. He held a cocked pistol in a reckless manner and aimed it alternately between the two brothers as he spoke.

"Don't you move. Put your weapons down slow on the table in front of you and stand up," ordered the sheriff.

"You," the sheriff said, looking at the mulatto, "get on out of here."

The mulatto rose without an argument and disappeared out the front door.

Ike and Raymond laid their pistols and knives out among the plates, and the sheriff pulled the two men out from behind the table.

"Let's go," he said, gesturing toward the door with his pistol hand while he collected the weapons with his other. "You boys are under arrest."

Out in the street the crowd that had gathered followed the sheriff and his two prisoners as they crossed the entrance to the alley and turned to cross the street. Someone screamed.

A shadow moved from a doorway near the alley entrance and the sheriff collapsed to the ground from the impact of a single shotgun blast. Then the shadow vanished and there was a great confusion of men running and horses fighting their riders.

Ike hunkered over the fallen sheriff and wrestled the sheriff's pistol from the dead man's grip on it. Raymond picked up the loose weapons lying at the sheriff's side and, in the disarray and confusion of the crowd, he and Ike fled deeper into the alley.

Two mounted riders wheeled their gape-mouthed horses and took up the chase, following the two fugitives around the corner and into the jaws of the narrow alley.

Raymond out-distanced his bearish brother and turned the corner at the other end of the alley as the horsemen bore down upon Ike. Ike, out of breath and wheezing, stumbled and fell, and the horsemen opened fire. Their bullets exploded the dust up all around the fallen general and bullets whined past him blindly missing their target and splintering the wooden walls of the surrounding buildings.

Ike's pistol shook loose from his thick hand when he fell, and he scrambled unarmed in the dirt of the alley awaiting his fate and cursing the two horsemen who fired wildly as they fought to control their mounts.

A shadow glided in behind him and, when he turned to look, Ike saw the dark figure of the mulatto then heard a thunderous explosion as hellish fire spewed forth from both barrels of the ten-gauge. The two horsemen lifted from their saddles and fell red and lifeless to the ground.

The mulatto stood over the general and offered no hand as the big man grunted and struggled to his feet.

"Ike," Raymond's shrill voice called out.

Raymond ran into the alley leading three unruly horses that fought the reins and tossed their heads.

At the other end of the alley, the entrance filled with angry citizens and indiscriminate gunfire. Ike, Raymond, and the mulatto grabbed at the reins and mounted the white-eyed horses in reckless haste then spurred the beasts until their rowels ran red with blood. They rode south out of town at a hard gallop and whipped the horses on until their lathered mounts had nothing left to give.

At a small farm set back off the road, they abandoned the spent horses, stole three fresh ones, and rode at a lope until the sun set, and twilight overtook them. They slowed the horses to a long walk and rode in silence. Ike looked over at the mulatto who rode beside him with his shotgun across his saddle and one hand on the stock. Ike read the hand-carved letters on the buttstock of the mulatto's shotgun.

"SAN . . . DO . . . VAL," he sounded out the letters. "Is that your name, Sandoval?" he asked.

The mulatto looked at him but did not nod or answer one way or the other.

"You ain't much for talk are you?"

The mulatto's eyes turned and, when they

met those of the general, they were void of response, and then he turned back to the road.

"Well, can't you say anything?" Raymond asked.

The mulatto ignored the remark.

"What's wrong with him, Ike?"

"Hard to say. Maybe he just don't have anything to say. It's not a bad trait in a man."

They rode until after dark, then stopped and made a cold camp. Ike lay back against his grounded saddle.

"Sandoval, you're welcome to ride with us if it suits you, or you can turn out in the morning if you want," Ike said. The mulatto did not acknowledge Ike, and Ike rolled over and slept.

In the morning Ike turned his horse west upon the washed-out road, and Raymond and Sandoval did likewise. The next morning and every other morning after that for the months that followed, General Ike Smith commanded his company farther and farther into the ancient wastelands to the west.

THREE

During the waning weeks of summer, the Montana weather was fair; the days warm and the nights cold. In those months of summer, J.D. Elder walked with an uneven gait that was no more noticeable than that of most men his age who have poorly mended those infirmities that come with the broken bones and twisted legs common to the rough-country horseman. However, in the cold of winter he would hobble about like a stove-up old man twenty years older than his age, and he cursed the Confederate minié ball that shattered his leg and left him among the dying at Chancellorsville.

A U.S. Army issue willow cane stood against the inside wall behind the door where it remained untouched since the day he put it there. On his good days, he had no need for it. On the bad days, his pride would not let him take it up.

In the strong sunlight, Elder's creased and

sun-darkened skin appeared as a stiff, copper-colored hide stretched over the bones of his face. He was a quiet man, gentle in his own way, but with a dark presence about him. In his youth, he was a man of handsome features. Time and circumstances weathered his appearance and features into those of a man of experience.

Singularity of purpose suited him. His wartime experience was a solitary existence he bore without regret. And he held no concern for the fate of the Confederate soldiers whose lives he surrendered to the Union Army when he tracked the rebels down through swamps and hardwood forests and across ground that left no sign of their passing.

He was a hunter of men, a profession in which he took no solace and no pride.

In his eyes, there was a shadow, distant and lonely, but there was no apology there, and no petition for forgiveness or consolation. His eyes were the eyes of age and wisdom, but they told you nothing of the man. The rash immortality of youth that once resided in them was gone, and in its place was fixed a quiet determination and an uncommon peacefulness. It was a peace negotiated and tendered in delicate balance. J.D. Elder's existence was a private withdrawal to the seclusion of the wilderness, a hermitage he preferred to the company of man.

In a small meadow surrounded by tall pines, the bent-over cowboy in his farmer's trousers and farmer's boots trod the plowshare furrow heavy-footed behind an unmanageable mule that pulled and quit, and finally let the plow stop and bog.

Elder thumbed the sweat from his eyes and took a certain pleasure in the musky fragrance of the freshly turned earth. The mule was uneasy, and it twisted in the traces and tossed its head as it reached for the swarm of flies that clustered just out of reach on its underbelly. Elder clucked the mule. The flies circled away in a small dark shadow of indignant buzzing then hovered back to the mule. Elder moved a calloused hand from the smooth plow handle to the thick reins that rubbed his sunburned neck, and he slapped the leather to the mule's rump. The mule lunged forward and the plow slipped free, turning the sod and leaving in its wake an imprecise row of clean, dark earth. Elder was no farmer and he took no exception to the crooked rows he plowed.

At the far length of the meandering furrows, a fence of lodgepole rails led to a sturdy log cabin chinked with river clay and sheltered by virgin ponderosa pine and Engelmann spruce that stretched skyward more than a hundred and fifty feet. Behind the cabin stood a barn and a corral with three young saddle horses and a mare heavy with foal, all switching flies in the shade of a steeply roofed lean-to.

On a lightly treed and gently sloping hillside east of the barn and house and corrals, twenty or thirty cows grazed; most with calves by their sides. A longhaired dog lay un-stirring on the south side of the cabin and watched with disinterest the hen and her chicks that scratched in the weeds near the front step where the grass had worn thin by the coming and going of Elder and the dog.

In this high mountain meadow, the late afternoon sun disappeared behind the ridge of granite peaks that commissioned its western perimeter. In the waning light, Elder watched his long shadow run out over the furrows and bend awkwardly trying to keep up with him as it encountered the fence and rose up to meet it.

At the end of the furrow, Elder stopped and turned to survey his work. He pulled off his hat and ran his hand through his thick hair and, for the first time, noticed the chill in the air. He looked back to the west and calculated another quarter-hour of daylight.

Elder unhitched the mule, drove it to the corrals, grained it, then put fresh hay out for the mule and the horses. All traces of daylight were gone from the sky when the dog followed Elder into the cabin.

The dog circled a spot near the door where it lay to watch the man build the fire that would light and warm the room. Wood smoke from the new fire back-drafted into the room and hovered about the ceiling beams until the flames heated up the air in the flue. The rising air drew back up the chimney taking with it the smoke, but leaving behind the smell of burning wood which Elder found pleasurable.

Elder prepared a freshly killed, young rooster then turned it slowly on the fireplace spit. The skin of the rooster beaded with fat that blistered and the fat dripped down upon the hot coals and burning wood, and crackled and sizzled. A new smell permeated the room, and the dog salivated and his eyes fixed on the rooster as it turned, and browned, and sputtered.

The man set out two plates. He piled them with boiled beans and molasses and hard biscuits. Then he tore the wings and neck from the bird with his fingers and arranged them loosely in a pile on one plate. On the other, he placed that portion of the rooster remaining, then sat down and reached for the rag he used to wrap the hot handle of the coffee pot.

As he did every night, Elder pretended not to notice the dog. The dog's eyes were eager with anticipation and its tail wagged, but it did not move from its spot. The dog stared. The man took up his fork, then set it back down and addressed the dog from the corner of his eye.

"Buck," the man said.

He set the dog's plate on the floor at his feet. The dog sniffed the plate, and quickly took up one wing then the other, chewing each in short, quick bites, breaking it up only enough to get it down. His tail did not wag. He lapped the beans and gorged himself on the dry biscuits. He sniffed the floor for morsels overlooked in haste, cleaned the plate, then returned to his saddle blanket by the door to watch the man and wait for scraps.

Elder took his time and slowly picked off the white breast meat with his fingers, forked in the beans, and soaked up the drippings with the biscuits. He settled back in the chair, sipped his coffee, and let the heat of the fire ease the soreness in his shoulders.

The dog and man felt drawn to the fire; the dog for the heat, the man for some primitive calling he could not describe that caused him to stare blankly into the flames in a nightly ritual he had never attempted to understand. His stomach felt pleasantly heavy and J.D. Elder turned his chair to face the fireplace opening. He poured more coffee from the cast iron pot then set his feet upon the river-rock hearth and crossed his boots before the fire. The heat of the flame soaked through the thin leather soles and burned the bottoms of his feet. He enjoyed the painful sensation and held the position until he could no longer tolerate the heat. He moved his feet aside and relaxed as the heat warmed his legs and soothed the damaged one.

In his sleep, the dog whined and whimpered. His legs twitched and he dreamed, and in his dream, he was running. Elder's eyes grew heavy. He set his coffee cup on the hearth, stretched back, yawned, laced his fingers behind his head, and eased the chair back on two legs. The fire crackled and hissed less frequently as the logs settled onto the coal bed.

Elder remembered his wife but forced from his mind the thoughts that still brought him pain and anger. His gaze followed the small flames that spiraled upward as they kindled the patches of dry bark in a triumphant blaze that was at once fierce and contentious then, as quickly, died down to become part of the indistinct flame that eventually consumed the log. Elder's thoughts escaped quietly from his head by the rhythmic flickering of the flame that lured him into another world.

The harsh and busy shadows that danced on the walls earlier were now soft-edged and lazy. Outside the night was quiet. The wind in the treetops was delicate and all but still. The only discernible sound was that of the horses as they nuzzled the soft grass hay and snuffled undisturbed in the safety of their shelter.

Elder set the chair legs down on the floor, and began to nod. He sighed. His chest rose and fell in a slow cadence, and his breathing was deep and heavy. He vaguely acknowledged the echoing of an owl and barely perceived the high-pitched, frantic yapping of coyotes far away in the night — then another sound — closer, unfamiliar, and out of place.

The dog raised its head and cocked its ears at the imperceptible shuffle of boot heels on the wood plank outside the door. A growl started low in its throat. Then, before the dog could utter a sound, the door exploded open, slamming with an awful clatter against the wall and scattering splintered wood across the room as two dark figures breached the shadowed entrance in a blinding blaze of shotgun fire.

Elder wobbled to his feet, confused and clumsy, like a character in his own nightmare. Muzzle-flash lit up the room and buckshot ripped into the dog, and the dog's hide was stripped from the ribs of its left side as it skidded back to the wall, streaking blood as it went.

Elder stepped forward into a double-barreled blast from the second shotgun and collapsed into a twisted and disjointed heap onto the floor, with blood running from his head and his shirt shredded and weeping from half a dozen red holes.

The two intruders, reeking of filth and whiskey, stood at the doorway and fired indiscriminately about the room, loading and reloading. Double-ought buckshot scattered coffee pot, dishes, and leftover food. Windows rattled in their wooden frames then disappeared altogether. The derelicts stopped to reload then hacked away inside the desecrated cabin until they could no longer tolerate the smoke-filled air.

In the corrals, a third man tied off the

three saddle horses, then gunned down the mule and the pregnant mare. The hen and her chicks lined out in a frenzied run from their roost and scurried for cover, a delegation of insignificant consequence disintegrated by a shotgun blast into an unrecognizable scattering of feathers, blood, and bone before they could cross the narrow stretch of dim light from the doorway.

Three dark figures re-entered the cabin and paid no regard to Elder or the dog as they packed their burlap sacks with bacon and beans and tins of peaches and the bottle of whiskey Elder kept in the cupboard. One took Elder's Henry rifle but they left the Sharps. Then they remounted, took up the leads of the fresh horses, and rode without conversation beneath a crystal-rimmed half-moon back into the night from which they came.

At dawn the three derelicts, outfitted in ragtag military attire and each leading a Rafter E horse, stopped in a wooded meadow and unsaddled their spent mounts. They swung their wet rigs up on Elder's fresh horses, fired double-barrel shotgun blasts at the wasted horses standing vacant-eyed with heads bent and cut them down at the knees leaving them to bleed and thrash about on splintered stumps of bone.

They rode the morning out and crossed the ridgeline before noon. At a narrow creek in a small clearing, they stopped to water the horses. The one named Ike grinned. Tobacco drooled from his cracked lips. He fetched a half-empty whiskey bottle from his saddlebag and, without wiping away the drool, sucked down two hard swallows. He offered the wet-mouthed bottle up to the others in a sweeping gesture. They shook him off and he took another pull from the bottle, corked it, and then coughed up a wretched plug of brown, viscid mucus the color of the tobacco wad that stained his un-kept teeth. Ike spat and then nodded toward a thin spiral of fireplace smoke rising from a sparse and poor farmstead in the valley far below. He motioned his company forth, and they descended the mountain like three scavengers devoid of territorial respect.

The cabin was makeshift and the livestock thin. The three men sat their horses out front.

"Hello inside," Ike shouted.

A young man stepped forth out onto the porch. He was fearful; he carried an old rifle but offered no threat to the three wretched horsemen in their filthy rags. Behind the door, a young but worn woman stood and revealed half her face. Two young girls looked out from the folds of the woman's skirts, their faces shallow and drawn and their eyes the eyes of uncertainty and fear.

"Morning," said the young man.

He waited for a reply. None came and he took one backward step to the echo of the ten-gauge, laid cross-saddle, that lifted him from the porch and set him, bleeding from the middle, against the wall. His tongue hung slack and his eyes rolled awkwardly back in his head, showing mostly white.

The three men dismounted without tying their horses. They trod heavily upon the porch, and paid no mind to the bleeding and twisted young man as they passed him by. They pushed through the door held in vain by the woman and imposed themselves upon the cabin and its occupants. The reeking degenerates descended first upon the woman then upon her young ones in a carnal frenzy, grunting and panting.

When they finished, one by one, they buttoned their fouled trousers and sat to the meagerly prepared breakfast table. They guzzled the cold gruel from the bowls and choked down the dry bread. They passed the pot and drank yesterday's coffee from it.

The arrogant and ponderous one searched

through the open shelves and modest pantry for whisky while the other two, stinking of blood and sweat, set the unclad corpses, gaunt and waxen, onto chairs and moved them to the table before bidding them good day.

The vagrants departed without ceremony, and passed without interest, the young man whose body had disengaged from his brain but who watched them with hateful eyes and who, in his mind, raised the rifle and squeezed the trigger, again and again. He cursed the vagrants but there was no sound. He wept but there were no tears.

The derelicts rode without concern, taking no precaution other than to travel below the line of the ridges and into the shadow of the valley. They followed a runoff creek that divided the mountains and flowed into a wide basin where aspens and cottonwoods grew in tall, green stands along its banks.

"She was purty, huh, Ike?" the thin, pale one called Raymond said.

"They all was."

The mulatto, Sandoval, rode mute and disengaged.

Raymond looked back at Sandoval and smiled a thin smile.

"Hey, Sandoval, did you like them?"

Sandoval did not answer and they rode in

silence, stopping only to relieve themselves and to tap the whiskey bottle.

FOUR

Ike, Raymond, and Sandoval rode the day down and by dusk, when the light grew gray and thin, they came upon a campfire attended by a young man in clerical vestments. The young clergyman looked up, surprised, but not fearful.

"It's not much, but you're welcome to share," said the young man motioning toward the fire and the bean pot.

"Obliged, reverend," Ike said. He stepped down from his horse, and the other two did likewise.

The cleric removed the bean pot from the fire. "Bring your plates and cups. I'll pour you boys some coffee."

"We ain't got none," said Ike. "Got no need."

He slammed the whiskey bottle down in the dirt and dragged the bean pot up between his thick legs where he sat. He coughed and spat, picked up the whiskey

39

bottle and took a long, hard pull, then reached in the pot and fetched out a handful of beans and ate them off his calloused and knotted fingers. He nodded, grinned, and fetched another handful.

Sandoval and Raymond hunkered up to the bean pot and pulled the dripping beans up on their dirty fingers. When they emptied the pot, Ike took the last pull off the whiskey bottle. He stood and threw the bottle into the trees and crowded near the young reverend.

He put his lips to the reverend's ear and whispered, "Where's your bottle?"

The reverend withdrew from Ike's grip and backed away from the putrid odor of Ike's rotted teeth. "I'm sorry, but I don't carry liquor."

"That sir is your misfortune," Ike whispered.

When the vagrants rode out in the morning, they passed by the lifeless body of the cleric and turned loose the reverend's horse to stumble and wander eyeless among the trees. They left the camp scattered with the clergyman's belongings.

They rode the sun around twice, ate the last of their provisions, traveled spare and sober, and gave no regard to the trail they left. On the third day Sandoval gut-shot a jackrabbit, and they devoured uncooked the fat carcass and its litter of six mucus-covered fetuses. On the fourth day, they shared a snake they could not identify and ate grubs from the wet heart of a decayed log.

By late afternoon on the fifth day, the itinerants descended the last mile of the trail. Sullen and drawn, they dismounted their fatigued horses on the rolling plain and entered the cow town afoot, leading their spent mounts. Their rundown boots raised small circles of dust where they walked and they reeked of old blood and vomit.

"We got no money, Ike," Raymond said.

"I know that," said Ike. "We'll trade for the Henry."

Ike surveyed the modest assemblage of buildings and led his company to the structure bearing a faded whiskey sign at its doorway. Inside, one man stood at the bar and four others turned cards at a small table in a dark corner lit by a single, overhead oil lamp.

The bartender regarded the itinerants suspiciously. "What'll it be?"

Raymond laid the Henry on the mahogany bar top.

"Whiskey and something to eat."

"Pickled eggs and crackers — that's about it," said the bartender.

"That'll do," said Ike. "We don't have no money, but this rifle ought to cover it."

"Sorry mister, but I can't pay my bills with that," the bartender said and stepped back.

Ike raised his hand to make a point but took a coughing fit instead and hacked brown mucus onto the floor. He turned it with the sole of his boot. Ike pushed the Henry toward the bartender and stared him in the eye.

"That ain't my concern. Set the whiskey here."

The bartender hesitated and the silence that followed was deathly still. The man standing at the bar hastened to the street. The card players folded their hands and waited with wet palms, waited for the roar of gunfire, and wondered if anyone among them would rise to his own defense.

Ike slid the egg jar down to Sandoval and pointed to the back bar.

"Give me that one."

If the bartender contemplated any resistance, he dismissed it without further thought. He reached back to the rows of bottles and brought forth an unopened fifth of China Rose.

Sandoval poked his blood-streaked hand

into the pickle jar, fetched out an egg, and carried the jar to a table near the door. Ike handed the whiskey bottle to Raymond, motioned the bartender for another, and the bartender obliged without protest.

The itinerants sat like vestiges of an ancient army of unknown origin, rancid and gagging on eggs and crackers and China Rose whiskey. One by one, the card players took their leave and sometime after midnight, the bartender slipped by them and took his leave without notice.

For all they drank the vagrants maintained a loud and dangerous court throughout the night. Then, just before dawn, Sandoval staggered outside and fell unconscious beneath the hitch rail where the horses stood the night, bridled and cinched without feed or water.

Raymond, with the undigested remains of a dozen eggs regurgitated upon his shirt, lay prone and wheezing by the legs of the chair from which he fell. Ike stood red-eyed and foul smelling and contemplated his fallen companions with contempt, then he himself tottered and fell.

The three awoke in their own excrement in a darkened cell with a barred window narrower than a man's head set high and out of reach.

"Wake up and take your breakfast," said a badged man from the shadows by the cell door. He slid bowls of gruel and cups of coffee on the floor beneath the bars, and the itinerants took them up without speaking.

Later in the day a tall, wiry man with a soft voice, a big moustache, and a sheriff's star pinned to the pocket of a black frock coat frayed at the cuffs, settled himself on a chair outside the cell.

"Them's J.D. Elder's ponies you boys rode in on," said he.

"No they ain't," said Ike.

"They're carrying his Rafter E brand."

"True enough. But they ain't his."

The sheriff sat quiet. His silence posed the next question, and Ike responded to it as though it came directly from the mouth of the sheriff himself.

"We traded him three of our own and give him ten dollars each to boot for them you see out there."

"You got a bill of sale?"

"Don't need one — we shook on it."

"That ain't likely. Elder ain't the kind to sell off his good saddle horses, money or no."

Both men bore the silence that followed with equal resolve. The sheriff's eyes narrowed. Ike Smith remained expressionless.

"Where you boys from?"

"Me and him's from southern Georgia," Ike said tilting his head in Raymond's direction. "I can't say about the negro."

The sheriff regarded the mulatto. "Where you from, boy?"

"He don't talk," said Ike. "Can't or won't."

"You got names?"

"We got 'em."

"Tell them to me."

"That skinny one's Raymond Smith. The other one's Sandoval Smith. I'm Ike Smith."

"You brothers?"

"Him and me is," said Ike pointing to Raymond, and then nodding toward the mulatto. "He ain't."

"Where you coming from?"

"Deer Lodge, most recently."

"Where you heading?"

"Maybe down around Bozeman."

"What brings you boys to these parts?

"Looking for work, mostly," Ike said. Then he dropped his gaze and examined the scuffed toes of his boots. When he looked up, the sheriff was on his feet.

"Hold out your hands where I can see them."

Ike stood and poked his meaty paws

through the bars. The sheriff took hold, one in each of his own, and turned them palm up. He looked at one then the other.

"Don't appear to me you found much work lately."

"No, sir, that's a fact," Ike said.

The sheriff returned to his seat and Ike remained at the bars, standing with his hands hung out over the cross rail.

"You didn't happen to see a young preacher man up the trail, did you?" the sheriff continued.

"We seen him, all right. Shared a fire."

"That's all?"

"Yes, sir. That's the long and the short of it."

"Well," said the sheriff, "his wife and boy are staying alone north of town. They was looking for him to be back two or three days ago."

"He was heading up the trail when we seen him. Nice fella. Didn't say anything of a wife though."

"You boys fight in the war?"

"Me and Raymond did."

"How about him?"

"The negro? Hard to say. We let him take up with us a while back."

"Is Smith his last name?"

"Don't know that for sure neither. We give

46

him that one."

The sheriff fell silent and regarded the vagrants with grave uncertainty. Ike took to hacking, coughed up a wad, and swallowed it with a grand show of distorted facial images that set Raymond to giggling under his breath.

"I got no further cause to hold you boys. I'm going to turn you out against my better judgment."

He paused and eyed them individually. "Don't let me see you around here again."

"No, sir," said Ike. "You won't even know we was here."

FIVE

In the cold, shattered remains of the cabin, J.D. Elder lay unconscious, shivering through the night and most of the day that followed. The late afternoon sun shone through the gap in the wall where the window once hung, and Elder raised himself up enough to behold the desecrated remains of the cabin. He could think of no reason he was still alive.

He put his hand to his left eye and found it swollen shut and crusted with blood from the deep crease where the buckshot ran a furrow from his eyebrow to his ear. Three clean holes in his arm, five in the skin over the ribs on the left side, and all clotted shut with blood. A sixth wound high on his arm still held the heavy lead pellet that caused it, and Elder cut the offender out with a boning knife.

Elder checked the dog, nailed the cabin door shut, and set out on foot in pursuit of the intruders. He moved slowly and with great stiffness. He carried with him his Sharps rifle, a pocketful of bullets, two biscuits, and a wool blanket.

He walked the trail trodden by the hooves of six horses: three mounted, three trailing. And when he came upon the meadow where the carcasses of two horses lay picked clean by buzzards and wolves, he saw the vagrants' third horse standing upright on front legs hacked off below the knees. The horse grazed a wide circle where it had eaten the grass to the dirt. It looked up at Elder.

Elder discharged a bullet into the horse's skull and moved on.

He slept that night far from the meadow but uncomfortably close to the presence of the itinerants.

In the morning, he arose before first light, built a fire, and waited. When the black sky split from the horizon in a thin gray line, he spread the fire cold and picked up the trail. He stopped only at night and the following afternoon he struck the homesteader's cabin.

The body of the young man lay near the porch, stripped by vermin of most of its edible parts and clad grotesquely in shredded work apparel. Elder opened the cabin door slowly, tentatively, and recoiled at the death stench that met him inside. He cupped his nose and mouth tightly with his hand and stepped farther inside. His gut wrenched. He quickly surveyed the single room, then stepped back out and leaned against the porch post.

Elder cursed the mindless trio, doused the cabin and the cadavers with coal oil from the barn, then struck a spark and watched until the structure was ablaze. He caught up a thin mare in the pasture, fashioned a rope bridle, and sat astraddle the bare-backed nag while the cabin burned. With the Sharps and the blanket slung across his shoulder, Elder put the mare to the trail.

Elder did not notice the harrier hawk that circled overhead on the warm air currents. He heard it screech, but paid it no mind. Two coyote pups, surprised by the sudden appearance of man and horse, slipped off into the trees and watched curiously. The tracks of the unshod ponies grew faint. Elder swung down from the mare and pressed forth on foot with the nag at his heels until darkness prevailed.

He built a fire and ate a rabbit he snared near the creek. He spat into the fire and thought about the trail he had lost sometime earlier in the afternoon. Tomorrow he would backtrack, maybe lose most of the day.

He tried to sleep and tried to understand the three men whose lives he would demand without explanation. He neither slept nor understood, and an hour before daylight he led the mare back up the trail. By mid-morning, he found the spot where the trail had played out. Elder rode circles and looked for sign until he picked up the itinerants' tracks. He pressed on, trying to ignore the burning pain in his arm.

Elder rode the sun, then the full moon, and stopped only out of consideration for the fagged mare and the poor terrain. He fumbled in the darkness, managed a small fire, and picked up on the wind a stagnant, cadaverous odor for which he had no explanation. He figured it to be the picked over remains of a wolf kill and gave it no further thought.

His sleep was only half sleep and, though he feared no intrusion, he slept with his hand on the forestock of the loaded Sharps. The moon hung low in the sky with a halo attending its perimeter, and the air bore ice crystals upon it that transformed his breath into smoky puffs. He brought his knees up and wrapped his arms about them to block out the cold. Elder tugged at the blanket, but the chill penetrated the thin wool shell and set him to shivering. He reached out from the blanket without rising, and clawed at the twigs and branches lying about, then tossed a handful onto the dying fire. He huddled close to the scant flame and turned back into his blanket, but found no comfort there.

Beyond the granite peaks, the moon slunk cold and distant and outlined the rumbling thunderheads in a framework of silver light. The wet smell of rain hung in the air, and Elder knew by morning the tracks of the degenerates would wash away in the impending storm. He gathered up his blanket, caught up the nag and, like a displaced exile, stumbled through the dark in search of better shelter.

Elder threw down his camp, hunkered tightly wrapped in the thin blanket and waited for daylight in a shallow granite cleavage among the boulders. In the dark he did not see the blackened coals of the cleric's dead fire, did not see the boot marks of the derelicts on the ground they trod, and did not attempt to further shelter himself from the light drizzle that sifted down from the pine boughs and swirled in upon him.

At first, only a fine mist eddied about in the frigid wind. Then the storm picked up and a torrent of pelting, whipping raindrops of enormous proportion drenched his blanket and pounded the nag as she stood her picket, head down, tail to the wind. Elder sat out the night soaked and convulsing spasmodically as he waited out his vigil.

Daylight was a long time coming and when it did come, it came thin and cold. Elder rose and the rain, which had subsided, threatened again with a steady drizzle.

Elder found the young cleric's body near the ashes of his cold fire, and he cursed the three men who left it there. He interred the remains in a crude grave of stone, marked with nothing more than a makeshift cross of dead wood. When he rode from the camp, he appeared, for all the world, as a missionary of poor account with the cleric's water-twisted Bible tucked beneath his arm.

There remained no further trace of the derelicts' tracks, but Elder reckoned their course by the nature of their habits, and set out as clearly as had they marked their trail solely for that purpose.

He rode blindly in the rain and set his mind to catalog the images of the three men. One was heavy and big footed. He wore high-heeled, government-issued cavalry boots and rode Elder's claybank dun gelding with the Rafter E jaw brand. The smallest man shuffled about in flat shoes, the left one absent a heel and both in disrepair. The third one walked smoothly with a long stride and wore straight cut, square-toed footwear common to the southern field hand. He now rode the bay mare. Elder saw them in his mind, knew their smell, and understood how they chose a trail and picked a camp. He would know them when he saw them, and that thought alone drove him onward.

In the afternoon, the rain blew in gusty bursts then settled to a chilling drizzle. Elder found an abandoned cave, deep and heavy with the smell of bear. He turned the nag out in a hard grass meadow and tied her with a three-legged hobble. He drank water from the creek and ate a biscuit then hauled his blanket into the cave and slept.

He awoke in the dark of night, shivering uncontrollably and burning with fever.

SIX

When there was light enough by which to see, Elder descended from the cave and wobbled up to the old mare who watched him with mild curiosity. Light-headed and weak, he steadied himself against the side of the horse. He led the mare to a rock upon which he stood to mount. He swung his leg over with no strength to spare and dropped his head to her thick, crested neck until he regained his equilibrium. His eyes burned. He tied the halter rope to his wrist then wove the mane hair between his fingers and touched his heels to her sides. His left arm throbbed swollen tight and red and the wound wept foul-and-yellow pus that soaked the makeshift bandage and ran out onto his trousers.

Elder caught himself nodding throughout the morning with hot eyes and only a dull awareness of the constant rain. He gripped the mane hair until his knuckles turned white, and his fingers knotted into a twisted and deformed claw no longer capable of feeling or movement.

In the waning light of late afternoon Elder fought delirium, and he resisted the urge to dismount the nag for fear he would not find the strength to mount her again. He raised his face to the sky with his jaw hung slack, and caught the rain on his parched tongue in a futile attempt to get water down his dry throat. He held his bladder as long as he could but finally wet himself and, for a moment, took pleasure in the warmth that blossomed about his groin and ran out onto the back of the plow horse and washed away in the rain.

Elder rode slumped on the back of the nag and let her have her head. The old plow horse navigated them out of the mountains and onto the plain through the darkness, her ears pitched forward and her eyes fixed on distant lamplights scattered before them, like a handful of yellow stars laid sparingly out upon the earth.

It was past suppertime when the mare plodded onto the muddy street and past the darkened buildings. She sloshed along and paid no mind to the two horses tied with slickers over their saddles and heads bent. She continued toward the light of the saloon and the sound of voices. She stopped at the hitch rail without being asked to do so, and she waited. Elder sat hunched and uninhabited like something unexplainable from out of the night.

First one man then another called attention to the deathly figure atop the old farm horse.

"Pull him down from there," said a tall thin fellow with a wide and fully grayed moustache and a star on his shirt.

"It's J.D. Elder," said another.

"Bring him inside my office and lay him in the cell. Clarence, go get a bottle of whiskey and a pot of hot coffee and something to clean him up with — fetch some broth too. He looks like he's hurt bad. Don't stand there gawkin' — go on."

Clarence wheeled about, clomped along the wooden walk, and disappeared into a dimly lighted doorway adjacent to the saloon.

Sheriff Milo Dunn pried Elder's stiff fingers from the mane hair and slipped the knotted bridle rope from his wrist.

"You boys bring him on in here," the sheriff said, leading the way into the narrow single-cell jail.

Elder's eyes regarded the room wildly, and his body convulsed, shook, and twitched as if he were fighting the devil for possession of it. Sheriff Dunn piled blankets on him and held his head cradled in his arm.

"Where's Clarence with that coffee?" he yelled to no one in particular just before the deputy appeared at the door, a pot in one hand, bandages and two small blue glass apothecary bottles in the other.

"Right here, Mr. Dunn," said the deputy as he set the pot on the hot stove and arranged the medicine and rags on the table.

The sheriff looked over his shoulder and nodded to the man nearest the stove. "Bob, get some of that coffee over here before this man dies of the chill."

"Here go," said Bob, extending the cup handle first. "Watch it, it's hot," he warned.

"J.D.," said the sheriff. "Take a little sip of this."

Elder pursed his lips and tried to gulp the steaming coffee. "Easy there," said the sheriff. "It's hot."

The sheriff tipped the coffee to the edge of the cup, and Elder sucked it down and closed his eyes as it burned its way down. He took another, then another. His breathing grew less shallow and the convulsions farther and farther apart. Some of the color returned to his face and the sheriff let Elder's head down gently on the pillow pushed up against the wall.

Elder looked about the room through narrow slits as he attempted to keep his eyes open. He felt the shirt tear from his left arm and the warm water dripping down his side as the sheriff dabbed at his wounds and recoiled at the offensive odor.

"Throw this in the fire," Dunn said as he passed the fouled bandage to the deputy and turned his head away in disgust. Clarence two-fingered the rag across the room and pitched it through the stove door opening.

"J.D., can you hear me?" asked the sheriff.

Elder nodded, but did not open his eyes.

"Your arm ain't too good. I ain't no doctor, but I'd say it's real bad."

Elder raised his head and it wobbled on his neck as though it were loosely connected. He steadied it some, then opened his eyes and squinted at the sheriff, his expression grave and distant.

"How bad is it, Milo?"

"Bad."

Elder looked directly into the sheriff's eyes but he said nothing.

Milo Dunn shook his head. "It's got a red streak halfway up it. I seen a few of them like this — arms and legs alike, laying in piles outside the surgeon's tent at Shiloh.

And I seen a few of them left on. But, I ain't never seen one like this left on and the owner of it live to talk about it."

"You can't take my arm," Elder said in a raspy whisper.

"There ain't much more I can do anyhow, and there ain't a doctor in a hundred miles of here."

"Mr. Dunn?" said Clarence in a voice just above a whisper.

"Clarence."

"Mr. Dunn . . . uh, Reverend Stanford's missus, she's a pretty good midwife. Reckon she could do anything with that arm?"

"I don't know, Clarence. I guess we don't have much choice in the matter. Come first light, you get on out there and see would she come lend a hand. We'll move J.D. over to my place. She's welcome to stay over if need be."

"Milo," Elder whispered. "The Bible . . . I had a Bible . . ."

"It's right here," said the sheriff.

"Open it," Elder said softly.

Sheriff Dunn wet his thumb and index finger and pinched apart the wrinkled and water stuck pages. He stopped on the family page and traced the words with a calloused and rough-nailed fingertip. His expression dropped and he looked fatigued and old about the eyes.

"This is Reverend Stanford's Bible, J.D. Where'd you get it?"

Elder adjusted himself up higher on the pillow and nodded his head vaguely to the north.

"Up the trail. He's dead."

The sheriff ran his hand over his face and shook his head slowly from side to side. "Who done it?"

"Three men — same as shot me up."

"Three? Did you get a good look at 'em?"

"Never saw them, but I'll recognize them."

The sheriff shook his head. His expression was distressed and blameful.

"They was here, J.D. I had them locked up right here in this cell and let them go. Didn't have no idea who they was. I knew in my heart they was no good, but I had no reason to hold them."

"We got to find them, Milo."

Elder took to shivering again.

"Here, J.D. Take another sip of this coffee. Bob, is that beef broth hot?"

Elder spoke in a weak voice, "Milo . . . they killed another man . . . and his wife and two baby girls up on Blacktail Creek."

Elder leaned back and closed his eyes and Sheriff Dunn slumped back in his decrepit desk chair and stared at the toes of his boots and contemplated, with grave regard, the unavoidable confrontation that lay before him.

Seven

The next morning, the deputy knocked on the door of the Stanford place with the backside of his knuckles and shifted uneasily from one boot to the other, then turned to look back over the road that brought him there. The door swung open unexpectedly. Clarence turned with a start, and there before him stood Sarah Stanford, radiant and speechless. She stared at the deputy and the light that shimmered in her eyes dulled, and she seemed to be looking through him. His face reddened and he snatched the hat from his head and looked down at his boots.

She excused her rudeness and invited him inside. He declined her offer to sit and chose instead to stand near the door. He stated his business and, when she inquired of news of her husband, his mouth went dry, and he averted his eyes and told her he knew of none.

The deputy explained the nature of his

visit, and Sarah questioned him for details concerning the severity of Elder's wounds. She listened for some evidence that would prepare her for what to expect and packed a small bag with strong smelling medicines and clean white linen rags. She made out a list of chores for her fourteen-year-old son, and promised to be back before dark.

When she bent over to kiss him she whispered, "You tell your daddy where I am if he comes home before I do—and stay close to the house." Her smile was warm and her eyes were soft and wet, but her voice sounded hollow and empty.

"Don't worry, I'll be fine," Matthew said. "Can I get me a cookie later?"

"Yes, of course. But only one, we don't want to spoil your appetite," she said, and then she hugged him tightly.

As Sarah Stanford and the deputy started down the road, she gazed back over her shoulder all the while until the small rough-hewn log structure was no longer visible for the trees. She turned and they rode in silence, and neither she nor the deputy observed the three dark horsemen outfitted in tattered military uniforms put forth in single file from the tree line and descend like a procession of malignant scavengers upon the cabin.

The ride into town was devoid of conversation. Sarah Stanford's instincts tugged at her, and she wished she had insisted that Matthew come with her. The deputy refused to risk breaking the protracted silence for fear that Sarah would somehow wrest from him the true state of her husband's misfortune.

Thirty minutes later, at Milo Dunn's place on the north edge of town, Clarence dismounted at the hitch rail and offered his hand to Sarah as she lowered herself to the ground. Inside the house, Sarah greeted the sheriff and his wife, and inquired again of news of her husband. Sheriff Dunn skirted the question and led her directly to the bedside where Elder lay fevered and failing.

Sarah pressed her palm gently to Elder's clammy forehead and put her ear to his chest. Elder drew each breath in shallow and labored cadence. His eyes opened and tracked the woman's movements as she removed the fouled bandages and winced at the condition of the wounds.

"Can you save my arm?" he whispered.

Sarah met his eyes with hers. "Mr. Elder," she said, "I'll try my best."

Elder nodded and tried to speak, but the sound was muffled and unintelligible. Sarah stood to her full height and moved across the room. She turned her back to Elder and spoke quietly to the sheriff and his wife. "I don't think he can make it. The infection is awful."

"You don't think you can save the arm?"

"I don't think I can save him. I'll do everything I know how, but I'm certain a doctor would want to amputate — it may be the only way."

"Can you do it?"

Sarah looked up at the sheriff and shook her head. "No," she said.

"Well that's that," said the sheriff.

"For the next two or three days we'll have to change those bandages and redress the wound every two hours . . . then there are the medications. I'll have to stay." Sarah's voice dropped off.

"You'll stay right here with us, dear," Mrs. Dunn said. "There's a comfortable bed in the next room, and I'll lay out a nice warm quilt for you."

"Mother," said the sheriff to his wife. "How would you like to take a little ride with me? We can go out and fetch Matthew and get whatever Sarah needs."

"Give me ten minutes, Mr. Dunn," said Mrs. Dunn. Then she turned to Sarah. "You come downstairs with me, dear. We'll make up a list of the things you need."

As the sheriff and his wife rattled off in the old one-horse buggy, Sarah waved, waited briefly, and then returned to Elder's bedside to prepare for her vigil.

The buggy-horse trotted out in an even jog, and Mrs. Dunn sat beside her husband, her hand hooked over his arm in the affectionate manner of a man and wife long past the period of uncertainty in their relationship.

"Milo, when are you going to tell that poor woman about her husband?" asked Mrs. Dunn.

The sheriff pushed his hat back and rubbed his forehead. "Tonight, I suppose. I wish I didn't have to tell her at all."

They rode the rest of the way; each in their own private thoughts, but when they drew in sight of the Stanford house Mrs. Dunn straightened and leaned forward in the seat, her hands to her mouth, her eyes wide and disbelieving.

"Whoa," snapped the sheriff as he pulled back the reins and braced his foot against the floorboard. He shifted the reins to his left hand and, with his right hand, pushed back his coat and squeezed his fingers around the wooden grips of the pistol at his side.

There, before them, lay the Stanford's old

mule. Its coarse head afloat like a crippled skiff run aground in a sea of black blood. Beyond the walleyed mule lay the Stanford's plow horse, its legs askew and its hide pockmarked with craters of proud flesh laid raw and ragged by buckshot. The dark house stared back at them through windows of shattered glass, its doorway choked with linen ticking, bedding, and the skeletal remains of a broken chest of drawers.

Milo Dunn took one wrap with the reins and climbed to the ground. His hands shook. "I'll look inside. Wait right here."

Mrs. Dunn trembled. Her eyes darted wildly about and she pressed her hands to her face.

"Matthew . . . it's Sheriff Dunn. Come on out if you can hear me."

The sheriff skirted the mule and pulled the chest of drawers out of the doorway, then slipped into the small house, his heart pounding and his eyes wide. His stomach tightened. The caustic odor of gunpowder hung like the scent of ancient graveclothes in the humble room. All about, the young family's accumulation of mismatched crockery, hand-me-down clothing, and dog-eared books lay scattered in a vile display of hatefulness. The old sheriff shuddered at the sight of it, and his knees weakened at the over-bearing presence of the perpetrators.

He staggered toward the door. "He ain't in here," the sheriff called to his wife. She dismounted the buggy and met him near the porch.

"You see if there's anything in there worth hauling out. I'll check the barn."

"My Lord, what in the world happened here?"

"I don't even want to guess, Mother."

In the barn, Dunn found a young black-and-white sheep dog tied and stretched to the end of his rope, hiding in a manger. He cut the dog loose and looked about for sign of Matthew, but found none.

Outside, near the calving shed, he found three sets of fresh, unshod pony tracks, long strided and heading into the trees, bound for the high country. Dunn followed on foot for a short distance, stopped and listened, and then continued up the trail. He walked almost a mile when an icy chill ran through him. He turned and started back. He ran and fell, and started up again. His aged lungs ached and his breath came shallow and sharp.

A volley of gunfire filtered up through the trees, distant and not real. Popping sounds dull and brief, then silent. Dunn forced his fatigued legs to move. He stumbled down through the trees, back toward the cabin. When Dunn wobbled out of the trees, spent and light-headed, he stopped, confused and unable to comprehend. Mrs. Dunn sat quiet and proper against the porch wall, her crisp, white dress wearing a bouquet of blood.

EIGHT

Ike and Raymond rode with burlap sacks laden with bacon, beans, coffee, and hard biscuits tied onto their saddles. Sandoval rode with the boy up behind. They rode with long-barreled shotguns slung crosswise on their backs, muzzles down, and saddlebags heavy with rifle cartridges and ten-gauge slugs and buckshot.

For more than three hours they rode steady then, when the trail leveled some and widened where a creek ran through, and aspen trees grew up in thick clusters along its length, Raymond dropped back and put his horse alongside Sandoval and the boy.

"Your daddy, he's a preacher ain't he?" Raymond said to the boy, his face twisted into a mocking smile.

The boy turned his head to look at Raymond, but he did not answer.

"You deef?" asked Raymond.

The boy shook his head.

71

"Well . . . is he? Is your ol' man a preacher?"

The boy looked away and nodded.

"I knowed he was. We killed him."

"You did not."

Matthew stuck out his jaw and looked Raymond in the eye. His throat tightened, and he felt the tears well up.

"He didn't fight back none — but he squealed like a pig."

Matthew's lips drew back in a thin line. "If you hurt him, I'll kill you," he said, his voice filled with hatred.

"Hey, Ike. This here boy says he's gonna kill us."

"Just you," Matthew said, and he pointed his finger in Raymond's face.

Raymond's eyes rolled white and vicious, and he backhanded the boy across the head with his clenched fist. The blow spun Matthew off balance, and he grabbed at Sandoval's heavy wool coat to pull himself back astraddle the horse.

"Leave him be, Raymond, or I'll whip you like a pup," Ike shouted.

Raymond wounded and vindictive, slunk away glaring at the boy. Raymond's bony knuckles reopened the clotted gash above Matthew's swollen and discolored eye, a disciplinary measure inflicted upon him earlier when he failed to sir Ike. Matthew pressed the wound against the shoulder of his coat to curb the flow of blood and peered about like a one-eyed deformity searching for a place to drop from the horse and flee into the cover of the thick brush. Raymond rode at the rear, and Matthew, knowing the depraved one would kill him given the opportunity, bode his time in contemplative silence.

The last of the dark thunderheads massed against the tall, granite peaks distant to the east. In their violent wake, they left an iridescent sky the color of a mountain lake, upon which drifted billowing white clouds and a pair of red-tailed hawks sunning themselves and riding the thermals high above the earth.

Below the circling hawks, like three mounted creatures of inconsequential significance, the itinerants advanced up country, their horses lathered and leaving deep tracks in the soft, rain-soaked ground they trod.

In a placid clearing where a creek of melting snow twisted through patches of wild berries and the sun glistened in refracted colors that appeared in the wet grass, as though the meadow had been scattered with pirate's treasure, the ragged company stopped to rest the horses. Raymond lagged back, standoffish and pouty. Ike swung down from his horse and took to a coughing fit, his brutish body hacking and unsteady. He leaned against the horse and snorted up great wads of dark mucus. He spat and snuffed, and let the brown drool remain wet upon his chin. He uncorked the whiskey bottle and took a long drink.

"Raymond, have a shot." Ike held the bottle out to Raymond, who stood off and looked up, but did not move.

Ike glared at the slight figure whose crumpled hat and loose-flapped shoes made him look like an ill-kept vagabond who, left to his own devices, could provide himself with neither food nor shelter. Ike again pushed the bottle into the air in Raymond's direction. Raymond shook his head.

"Private Smith! Front and center."

Raymond straightened and shuffled over to stand in Ike's towering shadow.

"Private Smith . . . did you not hear me offer you a taste of this fine China Rose whiskey?"

"Yes, sir."

"Then have you a touch."

Raymond took a long pull, swallowed, and had another.

"How about you Private Smith?" Ike said

to the mulatto.

Sandoval glided over mute and expressionless and tipped the bottle up, then handed it back to Ike and returned to his horse. The boy sat on the ground and watched through his good eye, and ignored the pain of the other, now shut tight, black, and blood encrusted.

They remounted and rode until dark. That night they made a cold camp and left Matthew unfed and tethered about the neck with a rawhide lace bound to the wrist of the mulatto, who never seemed to sleep.

"I gotta pee," the boy said to Ike.

"Stand up when you address me, soldier."

"I ain't no soldier."

Ike cuffed the boy hard across the head, slamming him to the ground.

"You call me sir when you talk to me."

Matthew got back to his feet and stood straight-backed before the ponderous man.

"Can I go to the toilet, sir?" The salty taste of a single tear ran into the corner of his mouth and he caught it with the tip of his tongue, but refused to acknowledge it or let another follow.

"Latrine privileges denied." Ike spun him around and put a boot to his backside and sent the boy sprawling, then coughed. He turned on his heel and walked a few steps and sat on the bare ground where he drank through the night while the others slept.

Matthew curled in the dirt against the cold and the cramps and waited out the night. In the morning, the men ate cold beans and hard biscuits and shivered. After they ate, they loosened the neck rope from the boy. Matthew stood and defiantly loosened the buttons of his trousers and relieved himself in their presence without turning his back or asking permission to do so. He shook himself off and glared at Ike.

Raymond stood to protest, but Ike shot him down with a stare. Matthew buttoned himself up and walked directly past Raymond and fetched up a handful of beans, then pulled a hard biscuit out of the burlap sack. He hunkered over his food and looked up at his captors through his good eye, like a scavenger of leftovers whose hunger surpassed his caution.

"Mount up," Ike ordered from high in the saddle. Matthew fingered more beans into his mouth, then reached up for the waiting arm of Sandoval and swung up behind.

They pushed on deeper into the wilderness, not hurried, but not stopping. Every time they did stop and Matthew looked over at Raymond, the feebleminded derelict drew a bead on the boy with his bony finger and let his thumb drop like a pistol hammer. Matthew could almost smell the gunpowder and hear the detonation. However, Raymond's expression communicated the threat far more effectively, and that alone sent a shudder through his body, for Raymond's eyes were those of an executioner, his thin and drawn face dispossessed of all virtue.

NINE

Sheriff Milo Dunn gently lowered the body of his wife to the two men who attended the horse and buggy out front of the jail office. A small crowd gathered. First one and then another, a collection of gawkers and the curious, their voices a babble of whispers spoken in rabid indignation and horror. The faceless voices whirled and spun around inside Dunn's head, a droning of unintelligible questions, growing louder and more urgent as more onlookers congregated and speculated.

The sheriff touched a rough knuckle to his eye. He caught hold of the buggy wheel with his free hand and tottered there a moment, then reached for the blacksmith's burly shoulder for support as he stepped to the ground. His face drained of color, his hands shook and his voice faltered. He stood shoulders hunched, and cleared his throat.

As Dunn struggled to compose himself, the blacksmith, Carl Swenson, put a huge, gentle hand to his shoulder. "Mr. Dunn, who vas it done dis terrible t'ing?"

Dunn looked up and scanned the crowd. He looked at the blacksmith. "It was them Smith boys."

"You mean those three we had in our jail?" a nameless voice asked from somewhere in the assemblage.

"Yes, sir, the same ones that shot up J.D. Elder — the same ones we had right here in our jail," Dunn said. He paused and cleared his throat again, and this time his voice rang with authority.

"They took Matthew Stanford with them. Headed up country. I'll need some help to go after them."

Men's voices, urgent and angry rose above the din. Women's voices, some supportive, others quietly cautious, added to the clutter of protests and threats against the perpetrators.

Dunn raised his hand to quiet the would-be mob.

"Be here in the morning before first light. Be armed. Be prepared to stay out as long as it takes. I ain't coming back without every one of them in the saddle or across it."

Dunn turned and walked toward the

house. His stomach knotted and his soul drained, he trudged along trying to control his palsied hands as he rehearsed the incoherent lines he would use to explain to Sarah Stanford. He did not hear Clarence shuffling up from behind.

"Mr. Dunn . . . wait up."

The sheriff turned and looked over his shoulder, then slowed.

"Mr. Dunn," said Clarence, now walking alongside the tall, old sheriff. "I'm going with you tomorrow. I borrowed me a gun from Bob Emory." Clarence pulled back his coat to reveal the butt of a battered pistol stuck in his pocket.

Dunn smiled a weak smile. "Clarence, I sure do appreciate that."

"Yes, sir, sheriff, you can count on me."

They walked along in silence, Clarence with a slight swagger and his hand on the pistol butt.

"Clarence, I'm going to need you here to take care of things while we're gone," said Dunn. "You know, in case them Smith boys slip back around us. Someone's got to be here."

Clarence did not like the idea of being left behind, but he said nothing in protest. The sheriff sensed his disappointment.

"You'll be the acting sheriff while I'm

gone," said Dunn. "You're the only other sworn lawman around, Clarence."

"Yes, sir."

"I'd feel a whole lot better knowing you were here as the acting sheriff in my absence."

Clarence smiled slightly. "Well . . . the acting sheriff, huh? Maybe you're right. I guess I better stay and look after things here. I'll just hang on to this 'til you all get back though," Clarence said, patting the butt of the pistol.

"Thank you, Clarence."

Clarence stopped and smiled, then turned back towards the jail.

"I'll look for you in the morning," Clarence said over his shoulder. "I'm real sorry about Mrs. Dunn."

The sheriff nodded, his eyes welled with tears. He just shook his head, and Clarence understood.

Dunn walked the short distance to the house and paused on the porch step before he entered. Inside, he hung up his coat slowly and carefully put his hat on the hall tree peg where it had set every night for as long as he could remember.

He started up the stairs and Sarah met him on her way down.

"Hello, Milo. Where's Matthew?"

Her voice was light, but her expression quickly clouded with uncertainty.

"Sarah, come in here and sit down," Dunn almost whispered as he led her by the arm to the soft chair near the fireplace. She refused to sit and her face drained pale and fearful.

"What is it? Where is Matthew?" Her voice was strained and impatient.

She pulled her arm away and stood facing the sheriff. His face was somber, his eyes red-rimmed and telling.

"Milo, tell me."

"They took him, Sarah."

"Who took him? Milo, what are you talking about? Who took my son?" Her voice trembled.

Milo Dunn's hands shook and his eyes watered up. He put his arm around Sarah's shoulder. "It was them three that shot up Mr. Elder."

Sarah Stanford's expression iced over with ghostly fear. She stared up at the tall, thin sheriff and waited for his next words, trying to wish away the horrible thoughts racing through her mind.

The old man's eyes watered up.

"They killed Mrs. Dunn." His voice choked. He stopped and pulled a handkerchief from his pocket and rubbed it into his eyes. "Sarah, they killed your husband, too."

Sarah collapsed down into the chair, and buried her face in her hands and sobbed. Milo Dunn stood beside her, put his arm around her shoulders, and gazed helplessly into the fireplace light. They stayed there for a long time. The old sheriff felt gutted of his pride and his manhood. He failed to trust his instincts and he allowed the derelicts to walk out of his jail. He let them ride out on Elder's stolen horses when he knew he should not have. Then he left his wife alone and unguarded in uncertain circumstances. Something he would never have done in his younger days, and for that, she lost her life. Milo Dunn questioned his worth as a sheriff and he questioned his worth as a man. He sat there considering the realities of growing old and useless; Sarah took his arm.

"It's not your fault Milo," she said, her voice betraying her feelings of guilt. "You did all you could, I'm sure of that."

"I let 'em best me twice," he said. "Now, my wife is gone and they've got your son." Then he looked down at her. His reddened eyes narrowed, and he put his hand over hers.

"I swear to you, we'll get Matthew back."

"Milo, I'm so scared. Why is this happening?"

Her voice shook and diminished to a whisper. She looked wistfully at the sheriff. "Milo, are you sure about Preacher?"

The old man nodded and drew her close to him and she sobbed. She cried until there were no more tears. She pulled back and looked up at the sheriff, her jaw set and her expression one of anger, her voice clear and deliberate.

"Milo, I want my son back. I want those men to pay for what they did to us."

The sheriff stood. "We'll do our best."

"Promise me you'll get Matthew back — promise me."

Milo straightened and looked down at her. "You got my word on it."

That night Sarah Stanford tended Elder's wounds and prayed for her son. She wept for her husband and fought the images that stole into her thoughts. Dunn packed his saddlebags, loaded his Henry rifle, and lay awake staring at the ceiling. Just past midnight, he looked in on Sarah and Elder, and then rode down to the jail to wait for the arrival of his volunteer posse.

Two hours before daybreak, Clarence slipped through the door.

"Hey."

"Clarence," said the sheriff. "You're early."

"Couldn't sleep."

"Coffee?" Dunn asked.

"Maybe later. Gotta get things in order here," the deputy said as he set about to tidy up the desk and straighten papers.

"How are you feeling, sheriff?"

The sheriff raised his head and in his eyes was the look of a defeated man. He shook his head. "Not good, Clarence. Not good at all. I'm not sure I can make it without Mrs. Dunn."

Clarence looked at the old sheriff and all he could do was pat him on the shoulder.

An hour later, two more riders pulled up, then three and four. Thirty minutes before dawn, twenty-two mounted riders stood their horses in the street, milling and talking and speculating. They came astraddle every manner of horse: good saddle horses, buggy horses, plow horses, and broken down, backyard horses. They came outfitted like a poor collection of schoolboys displayed with an arsenal of makeshift weaponry. Some had proper bedrolls, others did not.

Sheriff Dunn swore them in then, led his deputation of armed merchants and farmers clattering out of town, boastful, prideful, and unknowing. By the time the in-

85

nocents reached the Stanford place, the fractious horses in the group had settled down and, in the cold reality of daylight, the naive company of man-hunters got their first true measure of the enemy.

They circled the mule and gawked. They dismounted and surveyed the damage inside the house. They examined the broken furniture, and they stood in awe at the shotgun damage everywhere. Each man that trod through the spoils did so as though he were simply the spectator of an unrelated drama in which he played no role.

At the base of the trail, Sheriff Dunn called his company to order and addressed them gravely.

"Boys, it's all uphill from here. Spare your horses as best you can. You'll need all they got and then some."

Dunn set a steady pace and by noon, two horses, fagged and lame, fell out. By supper, four more horses gave out and would start back down first thing in the morning. Two or three more were questionable and, knowing their riders had no stomach for the chase, Dunn counted them out as well.

Dunn started the next day with twelve of the twenty-two and offered no consolation for those who dropped out. They pushed hard for the first part of the day, but by early afternoon the horses and men simply wore out.

Sheriff Dunn called for an early camp. The weary men turned the horses out to graze, some hobbled, some staked, some loose. The men fell to their blankets, most now depleted of all but the thinnest thread of motivation to continue. Dunn walked through the trees and sat upon a granite outcropping above the camp. He looked over the lot of them and figured three, maybe four would hold up.

Dunn had cowboyed with Tom Arbuckle before he died, and his two sons, Patrick and Tim, were among those resting below. They were both well mounted and, like their father, there was no quit in them. Carl Swenson, the Swedish blacksmith, was a gentle and religious man with an obsessive sense of justice that Dunn knew would bind him to the pursuit at all costs. As for the others, Dunn would wait and see.

TEN

Sarah Stanford, as though directed by a covenant of a higher order, set about to rescue Elder from the infection that burned him up with fever and fouled the air in the room. She soaked the arm, and reopened and drained the wounds. She cleaned the holes, snipped away the dead flesh, and teased the new and bleeding flesh with silver nitrate. Then she boiled bandages and redressed the putrid arm every two hours and, in between, she prayed for her son.

Elder's condition remained unchanged throughout the day. He took the broth and tea she brought him, but slept through and ate nothing that evening. During the night, the fever worsened and by morning, he lay burning and staring upward like a wasted corpse.

Sarah sat at his bedside and spoke to him, but he heard nothing. She kept cool compresses on him and changed the bandages on every even chime of the mantle clock. During the night, she refused to sleep. She sat by his side, and told him about her son and her husband and asked him questions he did not answer. She shared her hopes, fears, and feelings with him, but he did not hear and did not reply.

Just before dawn, she rose stiffly from the chair and walked over to the window, and gazed into the darkness. The moon was down and the few remaining stars hung in the black sky like pinholes in a velvet shroud. She wondered where Matthew was at that precise moment and hoped he had stayed warm. She wondered what he was thinking and she cried. She would not let her mind imagine her son harmed, as though if she did not think it, it would not be so.

She watched the sky fade from black to gray, and then turned when she heard the bed creak behind her. Elder stirred and mumbled. Sarah returned to his bedside and smiled at the cool touch of his face.

"Mr. Elder, can you hear me?"

Elder's eyes looked about the room as though the eyes' owner had lost all ability to control them. Then they slowed, focused, and stopped searching when they caught her intense gaze. He smiled a half smile and the deep creases that formed at the corners of his eyes brought life back to his face.

"Yes, ma'am . . . I hear you."

He tried to sit up, but Sarah put both hands on his shoulders, and gently settled him back.

"You stay right there. I'll get you something to eat. You've got to get your strength back."

Elder nodded, but did not respond.

When Sarah returned, she carried with her a cup of hot broth, which she set on the table near the bed.

"Can you sit up?" she asked.

Elder leaned forward, then fell back. She lifted his shoulders but he had no strength to help and the weight of him pulled her back. His eyes closed and she shook him. He grimaced, and the hot pain that shot through his body awakened his senses and he forced himself upright.

He faltered and gripped the mattress for balance, but held himself up. He expelled a long breath, and his head began to clear. Sarah watched and steadied him with her hands on his shoulders.

He looked up at her and nodded a thank you and his breathing steadied.

"You need to drink some of this," she said as she brought the cup of broth to his bedside.

Elder drank slowly and felt more sure of himself after he finished the beef broth.

"I still have both arms," he said, more as a question than a statement of fact.

Sarah smiled and, despite her haggard appearance, seemed to radiate an attractive quality that made Elder feel uncomfortably self-conscious.

"Yes, you still have both arms. The left one will be very sore for a while, though."

"Mrs. Stanford. Did they tell you about your husband?"

She dropped her head. "Yes," she whispered. "Sheriff told me."

Elder put his hand on her arm. "I'm sorry."

Sarah did not speak and Elder respected the silence. Sarah's hands shook, her eyes were red, and she reached deep inside herself.

"Clarence told me you buried Preacher."

"Yes, ma'am, I did."

"Will you take me to see him when this is all over?"

"Yes, ma'am, I will." Elder looked at her curiously. "Where am I?"

"This is Sheriff Dunn's home. It's the only place we had to bring you."

"Where is he?"

Everything caught up to Sarah at one time, and she collapsed into the big chair, buried her face in her hands, and sobbed. Elder sat up straight and leaned toward her.

"Mrs. Stanford? Are you all right?"

"I'm sorry. You couldn't know."

"Know what?"

Sarah cleared her throat. "Milo took a posse and rode up into the high country two days ago." She paused, took a deep breath, and put the delicate handkerchief to her nose. "The men who shot you and killed my husband — they killed Emily Dunn and took my son, Matthew."

Elder's back bowed and his eyes went cold. "Get my clothes."

"You can't get up."

"Mrs. Stanford, please get me my clothes. They don't know what they're getting into."

Elder stood with great uncertainty and he tottered without taking a step, then sat back down on the edge of the bed.

"You won't be much good to them dead," Sarah said as she laid his clothes at the foot of the bed.

"Mr. Elder. Let me help you get your strength back for a day or so. You are in no condition to be up right now. And please, call me Sarah."

"Maybe you're right," Elder said, as the

92

room spun around him. "I'm going to need your help, Sarah." He said her name gently and she felt her cheeks blush.

"Yes, of course, anything."

Elder rested his head back against the wall.

"How old is your son?"

Sarah looked surprised. "Why, he's fourteen. Why do you ask?"

"I need to know him, that's all. Is he big for his age?"

"No, not particularly."

"Is he a house kid or an outside kid?"

"Well, I guess you would call him an outside kind of a boy."

"Does he know how to handle a rifle or a pistol?"

"No. We never kept guns around the house. My husband was a preacher. He didn't believe in guns."

"Can he read?"

"Of course he can read."

"Does he carry a folding knife?"

"Yes, I think so."

"Did he ever get in any fights in school?"

Sarah paused and she looked at Elder with a quizzical expression.

"Mr. Elder . . ."

"Ma'am, I'd be more comfortable if you would just call me J.D."

"J.D." She felt uncomfortable saying it. "I

don't understand what you're getting at."

"Matthew's a preacher's kid. Preacher's kids generally spend a lot of time proving themselves to the other boys. I don't know exactly why, they just do, that's all."

"Well, as a matter of fact he has been in trouble for fighting. I had no idea it was because his father is a preacher — he never ever said a thing about that."

"I was a preacher's kid. Turning the other cheek never worked for me. It will go a long way with that bunch for Matthew if he's got some pushback in him."

Elder understood the perverse nature of predators. There are those who kill for survival, he reckoned, and those who kill for the sake of killing. Man is one of the few creatures on earth who find pleasure in the suffering of others, and those that do are the worst of the worst. For in them resides an absence of logic and honor, an absence of equity, and an absence of anything spiritual. That he believed without question. In Biblical terms, Elder thought of them as the equivalent of the anti-Christ and the embodiment of all that Satan embraces. Elder learned early that there is no middle ground with those possessed of evil, and he learned early that he who swings the sword must be swift and sure, for those who hesitate are bound to damnation. It went against the grain of everything he learned in his spiritual upbringing, and Elder never reconciled the difference.

Sarah studied him, the deep lines on his face, the troubled eyes. She felt his resignation to the cause that frightened her; at the same time it gave her an uneasy comfort that her son's life may well depend on this one, lone individual who she scarcely knew, but to whom she felt an uncommon closeness. She was sure it was desperation and nothing more.

"Will you get my son back?"

Elder raised his eyes and she looked directly at him. He wanted to lie. He wanted to give her assurance.

"I'll do my best," he said, sounding far less convincing than he wanted.

She touched his hand and her expression was tender.

"Please," she said in a whisper.

Elder nodded then lay his head back and closed his eyes. He thought of the boy, and he thought of the punishment the child must endure. He prayed the boy was up to it, and he prayed he himself would be up to it as well.

ELEVEN

The authoritative voice of General Smith reverberated through the morning air. "Left, right, left, right, left . . . platoon . . . halt!" Matthew stopped marching at Ike's command and glared at Raymond, who snickered and watched him over the rim of a dirty whiskey cup.

"A . . . bout face."

Matthew turned and faced Ike Smith.

"I can't do this good with my hands tied up behind me," said the boy.

Ike, the drillmaster, loomed over him, and then snapped to Sandoval. "Cut him loose."

The mulatto pulled from his boot a knife of Spanish origin, its blade tempered and honed in the forges of Toledo and its edge as sharp as a barber's razor. He appeared at the boy's side, gracefully moving from one spot to the next like a ghost floating upon the earth's surface, but never touching it. He reached forward without bending and, with one quick, upward motion, severed the rawhide lace.

The boy brought his hands forward and resisted the urge to rub the red welts that criss-crossed his swollen wrists. Sandoval moved back to the perimeter of the make-shift parade field where the horses stood tied. Raymond sat off alone with his whiskey, delighted to see the boy drilled and humiliated by Ike.

"You know what a private is, boy?" Ike asked.

Matthew shook his head.

"It's the lowest thing there is. There is only one thing lower. You know what that is, boy?"

Matthew glared up at the brown-toothed lout and shook his head again.

"It's a recruit. And you know what you are?" Ike said as he hacked up another foul wad.

"I ain't no recruit," said Matthew. "And I ain't no private, and I ain't no soldier."

Ike towered above the boy, and his mighty bear paw of a hand swung through the air at the end of his long arm like a great pendulum. When it struck the boy, it did so with a force that cracked loudly across the parade field and sent the boy sprawling backwards with blood spewing from his eye and red drool slinging from his mouth.

"You will call me sir," Ike said after the boy. Then Ike snatched the boy to his feet and put his reeking face very close to that of the boy. "Sir . . . you will address me as sir."

There were no tears in Matthew's eyes, and no sign of fear, nothing but a vast hatred from which Ike Smith took immense satisfaction.

"Now tell me, boy. What are you?"

"Nothing — sir."

Ike considered thumping the boy again, but changed his mind. "You are a recruit — that's less than nothing."

"Yes, sir."

Ike stood to his full height.

"Ten . . . hut. Fo . . . wad. Haw . . . tch."

Matthew stepped out . . . left, right, left, right, and executed Ike's commands without faltering. He marched in circles for more than two hours and never slowed or complained.

"Splendid," said Ike. "Fall out."

"Permission to use the latrine, sir," the boy said as he held a firm salute.

Ike smiled and returned the salute. "Permission granted."

Matthew double-timed to the edge of the trees, turned his back to the leering Raymond, and relieved himself. When he finished, he strode directly back to Ike who sat on a large boulder watching him.

"When do I get a gun — sir?"

Ike took a pull on the whiskey bottle. "Why do you need a gun?"

"If I'm going to be a soldier, I need to have me a gun. And I want a beltknife too, just like them other boys."

"You ever shoot a gun?"

"No, sir. Weren't no guns allowed in our house."

"Your daddy have a gun?"

"My daddy's a preacher. He don't believe in guns."

"You daddy's dead, boy. It don't matter what he believed."

Matthew's jaw tightened. He ground his teeth and his expression was no expression at all.

"I want a gun."

"You planning on killing Raymond there?" said Ike, tipping his head slightly in the direction of the frail one.

"Yes, sir. He's gonna kill me if I don't."

"Raymond! You tell this boy you was gonna kill him?"

"No, sir, Ike. I didn't."

"You lying to me about Raymond, boy?"

"No, sir. I ain't."

"Boy, you see that scattergun hanging from my saddle? Fetch it to me," Ike ordered.

Matthew hesitated a moment, then strode directly to the tall horse and took the long double-barreled shotgun in both hands and hefted the heavy weapon from the saddle horn about which it was slung. The weight of it surprised him, and the barrel dropped downward when he tried to level it. Matthew stood beside the horse and examined the gun, turning it in his hands and feeling the awesome killing power it possessed.

"Take it to your shoulder," Ike shouted.

Matthew braced the buttstock and leaned back to balance the barrels.

"Draw you a bead on Raymond."

The boy's expression was one of uncertainty and, as he looked into Ike's alcohol glazed glare, he swung the steel barrels around slowly. When they fixed on Raymond's position, he raised them by leaning his weight backwards. He stopped when Raymond's wasted and pale body appeared in the groove between the barrels.

Raymond straightened and he set the whiskey bottle in the dirt and watched gravely, the two dark holes boring into him. He glanced from the ten-gauge to Ike and back again.

"Ike? What are you doin', Ike?" He laughed weakly.

"Draw back on a hammer, boy."

Matthew let the gun drop to his knee, caught the hammer with the palm of his hand, and drew it back until it clicked twice.

"Take aim."

The boy raised the gun again and Raymond squirmed as the boy sighted in on him.

"This ain't funny, Ike."

"Get up on that front trigger and squeeze."

Matthew's arms shook from the weight of the gun, and he steadied it the best he could while his finger made contact with the trigger.

"Pull it!" Ike shouted.

The ten-gauge spewed forth thunder and fire, and Double-ought buckshot chewed up the brush around Raymond. The explosion deafened the boy and the recoil sent him sprawling in the dirt.

Raymond wet himself and stood trembling. Ike raised his whiskey bottle and laughed until he took a coughing fit, then took a short pull from the bottle.

"Raymond," Ike said when he stopped laughing and coughing. "Fetch a biscuit and some beans for Private Matthew Smith."

TWELVE

Wind and rain drove Milo Dunn's posse to a standstill on the fifth day, and that night they stood their horses on the leeward side of granite breach, and hunkered down cold and wet without the benefit of shelter. Talk was spare, but when there was any talk at all it was hollow and given by some to abdication.

By the gray light of dawn, those who lost the will to continue rode or walked their horses out of camp, leaving only three to ride with Sheriff Dunn: Patrick and Tim Arbuckle, and Carl Swenson.

"Boys," said the sheriff to the remaining three. "If any of you all want to head back down with the others, there won't be no hard feelings."

Patrick rolled the brim of his hat in his hand and slapped the water off it against his leg. He put the hat back on and adjusted it low over his eyes.

"Me and Tim signed on for the duration. You say ride up country — we ride up country. No need to ask."

"Tim?" the sheriff said, addressing the younger brother.

"You heard Pat — same goes for me."

"Yah, same t'ing for me," the big Swede agreed.

"Well then," said the sheriff. "Let's get on with it."

By mid-morning, they topped out and rode just below the ridgeline, traversing slick trails of mud and shale rock. When they came upon the cold camp of the itinerants, they saw no evidence of the parade ground it had been and could not have known of the initiation rites of the general's new recruit. The campfire ashes stood cold. A handful of leftover beans smeared a nearby rock, and shards of glass from a broken whiskey bottle reflected brown and brilliant in the sunlight.

"They went this way," Tim Arbuckle said at the point where the milling tracks lined out of the tree-covered camp and entered the gap in the granite wall that opened onto a narrow trail. He waited for the sheriff, who rode back from the west side of the camp, and together they sat their horses in the trees while Patrick and the blacksmith returned from the heavy brush on the east side of the clearing.

Dunn slid his rifle free of its scabbard and laid it cross-saddle. The others eyed him with uncertainty and did likewise. With Patrick in the lead, the thin delegation of lawmen rode blindly forth into the gaping yaw of the granite mountain.

The trail twisted downward for more than a mile, then entered a flat meadow undulating with magnificent wild grasses and spotted with native pines growing among a careless scattering of immense granite boulders. At the edge of the meadow, Sheriff Dunn called forward to Carl Swenson.

"Carl. Tell them boys to hold up in the trees."

Carl did, and the Arbuckle brothers sat their horses and searched the trees and the clearing with their eyes. Dunn led his horse forward and Swenson dismounted. Patrick swung down and Tim leaned forward, resting his arms on the saddle horn to listen to what Dunn had to say.

Dunn pointed to the three sets of tracks where they entered the clearing and disappeared into the buckbrush.

"It's a little too easy, ain't it?"

"You suppose they're waiting for us?" asked Tim, his voice hushed, but steady.

Patrick nodded in the affirmative and Dunn seconded.

"It's as good a place as any. Ain't no way to go but ahead or back."

"Yah," Swenson agreed. "But we must proceed."

"I'll stay up front," Patrick said. "You all spread out in the trees as best you can and give me cover if I need it."

"I don't know, Patrick. It's risky," said the sheriff.

"We got no choice, Milo. If we ride out together it just makes it easier on them."

"I'm with Pat," said Tim.

"Yah, me too," said the Swede.

Dunn nodded and rubbed his knotted knuckles into his tired eyes.

"All right," he said. "Tim, you and me will follow wide about forty, fifty yards behind. We can't give them time to get a good shot off at Patrick. Carl, you stay far enough back so's they can't get us all in range together."

Patrick and Tim exchanged a handshake, and Patrick turned his horse about and entered the clearing riding straight up in the saddle and resting his finger along the sideplate of the cocked Henry rifle in front of him. Milo Dunn and Tim Arbuckle waited, and then rode cautiously out left and right to flank the meadow. Swenson nudged his horse forward and followed Patrick and thought of all the things he wished he had told his wife, but never did.

THIRTEEN

Thunder shook the ground he rode upon and lightning discharged smoking, white-hot bolts of fire that smelled of sulfur and streaked down from the sky like cannon shots from an armada of ghost ships among the black clouds. Then the misty, swirling ghost ships exploded into great thunder-heads that swelled and heaved and ran aground, and stalled against the granite peaks where they massed overhead and cast the meadow in darkness. Below the clouds a ridgeline of tall pines tilted and creaked and leaned, and some twisted and splintered, ravaged by the wind as it moaned and spiraled upward along the cleavage of the barren breach where nothing grew and nothing lived.

Patrick's horse tossed its head, rattled its bit, and trotted out stiff-legged and tense, its neck bowed, its nostrils flared wide and red. He checked the horse lightly with the bridle reins and spoke gently to it, but his voice was uncertain and the horse jigged and pulled at the bit. Patrick rode anxious and uneasy. He resisted the urge to look back, but let his eyes explore the shadows of the woods, and he held the horse in a troubled walk.

Patrick reckoned the sheriff to be nearby as agreed, riding off to his left in the brush-choked tree line, watching and covering him. But all that traveled there was the wind, for Milo Dunn rode the rock and tangled brush and impassable deadfall to a standstill, then watched helplessly as Patrick Arbuckle proceeded farther into the clearing alone.

Patrick's insides were a tight knot as he glanced to the darkened woods to his right where he presumed Tim to be riding, out of eyeshot, but somewhere close by. He expected to catch a glimpse or some small sign of reassurance, but there was none. An empty feeling clawed at him. For the first time since he entered the meadow, Patrick Arbuckle felt the completeness of his vulnerability. He navigated the lightning-streaked clearing like a thief trespassing with uncertainty through forbidden territory, a dark and brooding place presided over by unseen demons and invisible gatekeepers. He imagined the feel of a bullet ripping through him, and every sound and every odd movement in the brush set his nerves on edge and made him wish for a fight if there was to be one.

Carl Swenson started into the clearing and, despite the cold, rivulets of perspiration trailed down his back and his mouth went dry. His big-knuckled hand, like a crudely sculpted appendage of leather and bone, gripped the forestock of the rifle cradled in the fork of the saddle. His eyes darted from rock to rock and tree to tree and paused at the shadows, then moved on. All the while, he stayed his course and held his distance behind Patrick.

He watched and he listened, but he neither saw nor heard the quiet disturbance in the trees behind him at the edge of the clearing. He did not hear the muted sound of pine needles and layers of decayed aspen leaves swelling upward from the ground, shuffling, rising, falling away, and finally revealing the tall shape of a dark man ascending from beneath the cover of the ancient forest floor.

The dark man stood to his full height and methodically brushed the leaves, stems, and needles from his nappy hair. He raised a long barreled rifle to the light, checked the receiver and bore, then braced it against a sturdy sapling and cradled it in the notch of his thumb and finger. He limbered the long, delicate fingers of his right hand, lined the front blade sight on the centerline of the Swede's back, and raised the barrel slightly to adjust for the distance, moved it a hair's breadth to the left to adjust for windage. He took a slow, deep breath, exhaled part of it, and then gently squeezed the trigger home.

For the mulatto, time stood suspended in a silent dream state clouded by the smoke and fire of the muzzle blast that seemed muted and far away. The rifle bucked and settled and he imagined he could see the bullet. He glorified in its majestic power as it spiraled, traveled in a graceful arc, and hissed across the long clearing, buffeting the air with perfect precision before it mushroomed on impact and shattered the Swede's spine.

Swenson stiffened. The dark hole in the Swede's shirt grew red and large. He remained upright, as though suspended in place. The rifle roared again and the second shot exploded a fist-sized cavity from the side of the blacksmith's skull, scattering bone and gore and loosening him from the saddle.

At the sound of the first shot, Patrick quit his horse, dropped to the ground, and scrambled hand and knee for the cover of the brush. The horse came undone. It reared and pivoted and, when it put all four feet to the ground, it became a blind and mindless runaway. Wild and reckless, the horse answered the instincts that drove it to return at all costs to the place from which it had come. The horse collapsed mid-stride under a volley of rifle shots that opened its sides with bleeding holes. Its head furrowed into the dirt, and red froth bubbled at its nostrils and it thrashed with legs that only went through the motions of running.

Patrick looked back for Swenson, but saw only the Swede's riderless horse stumble forward under a fusillade of lead that ripped through the saddle leather, slapped against its hide, and plumbed holes deep into its lungs.

Patrick squeezed into a dry granite flume and listened for Swenson to return fire and, when he did not, the cowboy rested his head back against the rock and contemplated his situation with sober concern. He rose up to look about, but could see nothing but thick undergrowth and the trees and boulders and small white and yellow flowers that grew in clumps near the rocks. Except for the wind, the meadow was devoid of sound. The grass bent and swayed, and the silence itself was the silence that screams inside the heads of madmen.

He shuddered. His stomach knotted. He shouted out.

"Timmy!"

The word echoed back to mock him in his own voice, and repeated itself over and over as it eddied away in the wind.

Patrick cursed his indiscretion, and he stood and ran for the trees. Three hundred yards back down the trail gunfire popped. First six or seven rapid fire shots, then two and two again, then a single shot and silence.

Patrick flattened up against the rough-barked, mossy side of a ponderosa pine and waited for the whine and sputter of the derelicts' bullets. None came.

He ran in a crouch with his arms dangling, appearing for all purposes like an alien warrior lost from some other time. He crossed the thirty yards of open ground and took cover in the brush on the far side of the meadow. He plunged headlong into the dark undergrowth, swung his arms up to protect his face from the thorny vines, and slogged through a boggy break, penetrating deeper and blindly into the muted thicket that smelled of sweet decay and stagnant water. He ran and stumbled, then ran until there was nowhere else to run. At the edge of a steep creek-bank, he lost his footing and tumbled down its muddy incline. Half in and half out of the water he lay on his back, his chest heaving and the air coming and going in raspy gasps.

Off to his right another short volley of gunfire popped slow and methodical, a deliberate and unhurried sequence of shots like target shooters sighting in on old bottles. Patrick rose to his feet and ran toward the sound. He ran for a hundred yards or more, climbed the creek-bank, and then stopped to listen. His heart hammered so that he could hear it thumping against his ribs and, except for the throbbing in his ears and the wind, there was no other sound about him.

He leaned forward, and his weight urged his heavy legs into motion, and he entered the unknown stillness with great trepidation. His mouth was dry and tacky. His tongue felt large and unfamiliar. His lungs ached and demanded more air than he could give them.

He carried his rifle in both hands and slunk through the trees. A phantom shot became a multitude of shots as it broke the silence from across the clearing and echoed away from one granite relay to the next. Patrick ran to it.

At the edge of the meadow, he found Tim's bay horse where it lay in grotesque repose, twisted and gut-shot, and staring out from a cloudy eye with no life left in it. The saddle was wet and blood-soaked, and a trail of fresh blood puddled in dark pools on the damp, hard ground in an irregular line that bore deeper into the woods.

Patrick looked about, took in the trees, the clearing, the trees on the other side of the clearing and the brush and rocks. No sign of the gunmen. No sign of anyone. He thumbed back the hammer on the Henry then turned and trotted the bloody trail.

Fifty yards before him the branches of a serviceberry bush lurched and jerked counter to the wind. Patrick cut a wide circle around the bush, gained high ground on it, and came down upon it making no sound. He stopped, raised up to sight the area, and then dropped flat, as a wheezing and coughing sound emanated from a blind spot in the swale beneath the serviceberry. He checked the impulse to leap forth, and waited and listened. The broken rattle of an injured cough issued weak and labored from the concealment of the low spot. Patrick, less cautious now, arose and shouldered his way through the brush in the direction of the sound.

When he could see, he saw Milo Dunn before him, his coat soaked black-red and sticky from blood that seemed to come from everywhere, and his leg pinned beneath the carcass of his head-shot horse.

Sheriff Dunn rolled his tired, drained eyes, and he looked up at Patrick.

"Get him off my leg," he said to the cowboy.

Patrick unsheathed his belt knife and laid the latigo back with one sharp upthrust. The center-fire saddle loosened and Patrick braced both feet against the horse's back while he pulled at the saddle leather and pushed on the deadweight of the animal. The sheriff hissed as he sucked in air and grimaced at the pain. Patrick pulled harder and the sheriff's leg slipped from beneath the horse as it followed the smooth stirrup leather out.

He laid the sheriff gently in the meadow grass, pulled off the wool coat that smelled like wet dog, and then unbuttoned the frayed shirt. He counted four holes in the old man's parchment-like skin.

"How am I?" asked the old man.

"You're shot up some."

"I figured."

Dunn turned his head a half turn and looked at Patrick. "Am I gonna die?"

Patrick did not answer. He rolled the old man onto his side and counted three exit wounds. He rolled him back over and shook his head.

"I don't think so. Four went in. Three came out. Don't look like any of them hit anything real serious, but I can't tell where the one is that didn't come out."

Patrick rolled the old man onto his back and took the blanket from beneath the saddle, then spread it over the sheriff, who looked frail and bony and out of place.

"Where's my brother?"

"Back that way, maybe," said the sheriff as he tilted his head to the left. "I heard lots of gunfire. I never saw Tim at all."

Patrick gave the sheriff a pat on the shoulder and disappeared into the thick brush. He picked up the blood trail again. He followed the line of crimson puddles as they pooled closer and closer and finally stopped at the boot heels of his brother. Tim lay before him face-down with a gaping, large-caliber bullet wound that sliced cleanly through the pant leg with a wide incision that severed the femoral artery and left it running unchecked until the young cowboy ran out of blood.

FOURTEEN

Ike and Raymond Smith rode the meadow trail down the middle with the boy up behind Raymond. They passed Patrick's horse with its legs twisted and its head bent under it. They rode by the blacksmith's horse and then by the blacksmith, both with red holes in them where they lay in positions of unnatural disarray.

At the lower end of the meadow, Sandoval waited and sat his horse quietly. He neither smiled nor showed concern in his expression and if he felt remorseful or prideful, it did not show. Nor did he acknowledge, in any discernible way, the arrival of Ike and Raymond and the boy when they approached. Like an ancient legionnaire, tattered and poorly kept, Sandoval stood ready to receive his orders and it mattered not what they be, for the mulatto had no opinion.

The boy sat sullen, his eyes grave and

hard. His hands clasped full of Raymond's coattails and his heart full of malice.

"Ike, they's still one of 'em back there we didn't get," said Raymond.

"Don't matter," said Ike.

"Well, yeah it does."

Ike's eyes went icy, he turned his head slow, and his eyes bored into Raymond.

"Don't it?" Raymond asked as he sat back in the saddle and retreated from Ike's glare.

"I said it don't."

"Well then, it don't," Raymond mumbled under his breath as he whacked one of the boy's hands loose from his coattail.

They turned their mounts about and with Ike in the lead, followed by the mulatto, then the imbecile, they descended the trail single file. Ike rode with the whiskey bottle between the fork of the saddle and the crotch of his legs, and every now and then, he tilted his head back while the others followed behind.

Their descent of the mountain continued at a lazy pace, and before long, they were strung-out over a two-hundred-yard stretch. Raymond watched Ike's head go back and his arm go up and he knew it would be a long day. Before long, his own head weaved and bobbed, and he dropped slack in the bridle reins and dozed.

They rode through the day, and at dusk long shadows crossed the trail, but they did not stop. Ike tottered in the saddle some, but showed no sign of calling for camp.

Night came and the trail lost its features to the darkness, but still they rode. The horses rocked along with lowered heads, and Ike and Sandoval had the appearance now of only shapes riding up ahead.

The boy leaned out to the side and looked up into Raymond's face and, when he saw the imbecile's closed eyes, he gathered his courage and slid quietly down the horse's rump. The horse maintained its steady rhythm, and when the boy's feet touched the ground, they did so without a sound.

He stood frozen where he alighted and dreaded what was coming next. He held his breath and did not utter a sound. The three derelicts rode on without him, and there he stood thin and small against the mountain, a speck of human insignificance attended only by his moon-cast shadow.

The moon that cast the shadow was more than a half-moon, but what light it shed was unreliable. Dark clouds with white outlines reworked the night sky into a broken and patched canopy with gaping holes flooded with bright stars. As the clouds passed over the sky, the holes moved with them and stars poured through the new apertures at some other place in the overhead blackness. The moon itself was at first clear and bright, then appeared opaque, then disappeared altogether. When full darkness befell the trail, Matthew Stanford ran.

He abandoned the shale rock trail on the spot where he quit Raymond's horse, and where his feet fell, he left no footprints. Matthew scaled the smooth granite-rock escarpment above the trail where no horse could travel, and he did so driven by the images of dead men, mutilated horses, the vile smell of whiskey breath, vomit, unwashed filth, and the hollow glare of Ike Smith's blood-streaked eyes.

When Matthew Stanford stopped, he was more than a mile above the trail. In the light of the now cloudless moon, he saw the shapes of half a dozen trees, heard the splashing of a small stream, and felt a cushion of soft grass beneath his boots. He walked the flat bench in the moonlight and, when he came to the stream, he straddled it and dropped to his knees. He lowered his face, touched his dry lips to its moonlit surface, and drank.

When he finished he crawled into a rift between two great boulders where grass grew and stunted alpine brush tented one end. Storm clouds swept across the night sky and once again obliterated the moonlight. The boy curled up overcome by fatigue, and he slept. But his sleep was fitful and restless and filled with hideous images of distorted faces and agonizing sounds. He sat up, and embraced his knees and hunkered in the darkness, fearing the uncertainty of wakefulness and terrified of his dreams. Matthew Stanford wept silently, stared out into the dark, and listened for the sounds of the derelicts he expected to come grinning to him in the night.

Morning was a long time coming and, just before the gray dawn light outlined the mountain ridgeline, the temperature dropped to near freezing. Matthew drew his knees closer and shivered. His breath rose before him as though it was white smoke, and he buried his face against his legs and re-breathed the warm air he exhaled.

The trees and boulders began to take shape and, as the weak sunlight gradually brought a new day into focus, the boy crawled to the edge of the escarpment and gazed as far down the trail as his line of sight would allow. And there he saw, in the muted colors of the morning sun, three horses tied and waiting. But he saw no sign of the derelicts who tied and left them there.

The muscles in his back stiffened and he sat up higher and stretched his neck for a better look. In the early cross light, he saw the shapes and movement of the horses as they tossed their heads and switched their tails, but he could not make out their colors or markings. He squinted his eyes and shifted his head about, trying to see beyond the brush and into the uncertain light.

When Ike's horse sidestepped into the slanted rays of the cold sun, the boy's stomach twisted into a hard knot, and he retreated as far back into the rift as his small body would fit, but his instincts told him to run.

Then, from the trees below, voices shattered the still morning air.

"I seen him!" Raymond's shrill voice shouted. "He's right up there."

Three rifle shots cracked before Raymond's words faded. Matthew cringed and he held his arms over his head.

"Cease fire!" Ike's angry voice ricocheted off the granite escarpment and withered in the pines. "I want that boy alive."

The voices sounded low and muffled, and Matthew could only hear the unintelligible drone of talking. Then the voices disappeared all together . . . and Matthew waited. He looked up over his arms crossed on his knees, but his line of sight was limited to the narrow slit of sky above him and the ten feet of passageway that made up the rift between the granite walls that protected him and held him captive.

Thirty minutes passed. Matthew's legs went numb and his back cramped. He turned slightly to relieve the pressure on his legs and a voice startled him. The voice close, familiar, and angry.

"I thought you said you seen him," Ike bellowed. "But he ain't there. Ain't nothing there, Raymond. Take you a good look . . . nothing."

"I swear, Ike. I thought it was him, for sure. Maybe he up an' stole down that-a-way."

The voices carried on the wind, bounced off the cliffs, and came at him from all directions at once. Matthew barely breathed. When the voices grew weak and distant, Matthew leaned forward and rubbed his legs. He crawled to the rift entrance and looked out. He crept forward and used the heavy brush for concealment, and then he stood and peered down the trail where the derelicts left their horses. They were gone.

Matthew sighed. He closed his eyes for a moment and took a deep breath. He regained his courage, trotted in a half-crouch to a water hole, then dropped to his knees and drank. When the boy arose, a large shadow stood beside his. The boy spun around wild-eyed, his heart pounding. There stood the dusky mulatto, his facial features indiscernible in the dark shadow of the backlit sky. Matthew choked and froze. Sandoval came down off the rock like a panther, smooth and deliberate, and quiet. His amber eyes glared at the boy and did not falter as he bent at the water's edge and shifted the rifle to his left hand. He cupped his free hand into the cold stream, touched it to his lips and drank slowly, watching the boy all the while. Sandoval dried the hand on his shirt and switched the rifle back to it. He stood for a moment, and his eyes bore into the boy and weighed some private thought. Then the mulatto turned and, with the same suddenness in which he appeared, he disappeared from sight over the side of the barren escarpment.

Matthew stood bewildered and, when he chanced to look down after the mulatto, he saw no sign of him and heard no sound but that of the wind upon which the dark man vanished.

FIFTEEN

Patrick Arbuckle stood over the two shallow graves piled with rocks and marked with crosses made of deadwood and tied with saddle strings. A light rain fell and his face was wet. He looked up to the clouds, haggard and spent, and angry. He surveyed the graves, considered the wolves and coyotes, and stacked more rocks on each one.

With the final stone in place, he dropped to one knee. He could not find the words to say to his brother. He tried to swallow the hurt in his throat, tried to feel right about leaving his brother and his friend in this desolate place. Nothing made sense to him and nothing felt right about it.

By the time Patrick found his way back to Sheriff Dunn, the rain had subsided and small patches of sunlight began to spread out upon the wet ground. Columns of steam rose from the trunks of fallen trees as the sun warmed and dried the saturated bark, and all around him birds twittered and ground squirrels scurried about. For all the violence that shook this high-mountain meadow, it was as though nothing had happened.

Patrick hesitated when he crested the small rise and looked out across the shallow swale to see the old white-haired man lying still and pale. The old man's eyes stared heavenward from beneath half-closed lids that did not move, and the young cowboy looked across at him as if he was someone he no longer knew. The Sheriff Dunn that Patrick knew was tall and strong, the idol of his boyhood games, not the aged and broken stranger that lay before him.

Dunn moved an arm and Patrick ran to him, down across the draw and up through the brush on the other side. When he reached the sheriff he was out of breath and stood there puffing while the sheriff looked up at him.

"Tim and Carl?" the sheriff asked in a low voice, his eyes not hopeful.

Patrick shook his head. The sheriff looked away, defeated and lost.

"We gotta get off the top of this mountain, Milo. You think you can sit up?"

"I done tried, son. There just ain't no go

left in me. You're gonna have to get down on your own."

"I'm not leaving you here, Milo . . . and I don't want to argue about it."

"Son, you got no choice."

Patrick considered the distance, the time, and the old man's condition and he knew the sheriff was right.

Patrick thought about it, and then nodded.

"It's the only choice we got."

The sheriff nodded in agreement.

Patrick checked the old man's wounds and redressed them as best he could, then he started back down toward the meadow.

"I'll be back in a couple of hours," he promised over his shoulder as he descended out of sight beyond the serviceberry and buckbrush.

Patrick returned to the twisted carcasses of the shot up horses and retrieved canteens, saddlebags, and the catch ropes he and Tim had tied to their saddles. He packed up what ammunition he could carry and cached everything but the ropes alongside the trail, and marked the spot with three flat rocks.

When Patrick returned to the spot where he left the sheriff, he built a makeshift lean-to, wrapped the sheriff in the extra saddle blankets and left him with food, water, and ammunition.

He looked over his shoulder. The old man smiled slightly and nodded, and Patrick Arbuckle left with grave misgivings.

Sixteen

When the mulatto walked away and left him that morning, Matthew Stanford turned and ran without thinking — up through the granite split above the grassy shelf and over the first steep ledge where no horseman could follow, and when he stopped it was only to regain his breath, then he ran again and kept running. He clawed his way up the side of a mossy cliff to the summit and fled blindly over boulders, rocks, and deadfall, stumbling and falling. He had no sense of the distance he covered or the direction he traveled. When the sun passed overhead in its short arc from ridge to ridge and darkness came, the preacher's son stood small and insignificant upon the damp forest floor, and looked about at the towering trees and indistinct terrain and wept.

Like an animal, he fell to his knees and pawed at the decay and debris beneath a stand of pine trees that grew in a crude row at the base of a sheer precipice and formed a shelter against the wind. He scratched at the hard soil until his fingers bled, then he burrowed into the shallow hole and pulled what he could of the diggings over the top of himself.

The moon hung nearly full and clear, and stark, ringed in a halo of crystal light in the starless sky. The wind died, the night was still, and the rain froze on the leaves, pine needles, in small puddles and reflected the moonlight back like diamonds strewn carelessly about. Halfway between midnight and dawn, white frost covered the ground of that immense and vacant wilderness. The small boy lay huddled and shivering with his threadbare wool coat pulled up over his face and his eyes squeezed tight against the images of madmen that waited in the dark and came to him staggering and cursing and bloody. His bones ached from the cold, but it was fear that trembled within him.

If he slept at all during that night he did not remember it, for when the light of dawn burned a thin gray line along the eastern ridges, exhaustion overcame him and he fell into a deep and troubled slumber.

He awoke with the midday sun warming his face. For a brief and fleeting moment, he imagined himself beneath the thick quilt of his own bed. He lay on his side and stretched his cramped legs without opening his eyes.

A red ant scurried across his face. He reached up, brushed it away, then turned onto his back and stretched again. He felt another inside the leg of his trousers, and he reached down and squeezed it between the folds of the course cotton material. Then he felt a bite on his back, another on his neck, and two more on the soft flesh beneath his arm.

Matthew screamed and jumped to his feet. Ants, dark and fast, covered his hands and face. He clawed at his clothes, swatted madly, and ran. With one hand flailing at the crawling insects and the other tearing at his clothes, Matthew threw down his coat and pulled his shirt over his head. His skin burned from the bites and the swelling red welts. He sat, pulled off his boots, and tugged at his stale socks as great numbers of ants dropped onto the ground and as many sought cover beneath his clothes. Matthew stood and hopped about and pulled off his trousers.

He looked down at his feet and his legs, and when he saw the swarm of insects crawling and advancing upward he bent forward, flailed, and swatted at them. When he felt them in his hair and his ears, he knew to do nothing but run. He ran through the trees and down a gently sloping gully. He ran through brush at the bottom of the gully, and then crossed a narrow clearing toward the rushing sound of the river. He stumbled over its rocky banks and plunged himself into its freezing water. The shallow bank where he entered the water dropped off into a dark swirling pool that drew the boy deep beneath its surface. He thrashed and shook, and trembled as the icy water seized his breath.

He scrubbed his hair and face, then scratched at the persistent insects that, despite the water, bit and clung to his skin. His lungs ached and felt ready to burst, but he kicked his way up toward the light of the surface. He broke into the bright sunlight with a gasp, then dropped from sight beneath the roiling, frothy water and rolled under in the swift current as he clawed the crawling insects from his hair with his fingertips. When he came up the second time in a quiet, swirling eddy, the water was dark with ants and Matthew's limbs were numb and stiff, and slow to respond.

The boy's muscles quivered and twitched uncontrollably. His arms and legs refused to respond as he willed them, and he found himself tumbling in the current, rolling against the rocks and unable to navigate the short distance to the riverbank. His pale, blue body washed about in the froth, then floated up onto a shallow shelf at a bend in the river course. Matthew threw out a wooden arm. His numb fingers gained purchase on the rocky bottom and held him against the current.

For a moment, he lay shaking and gasping, and then he gathered what was left of his strength and leveraged himself into shallow water. He crawled like a waterlogged creature up onto the grassy bank and collapsed. His body convulsed violently as he lay in the sunlight with his chest heaving. For more than an hour, he lay without moving, the sun warming him slowly, and finally quieting the muscle cramps and spasms.

He was like a stranger to his own body and re-introduced himself gradually, first moving a toe, then a foot, and a leg. He tried his fingers and his arms and, when they began to respond, he sat up and examined himself for more ants. Three of the dark and lifeless insects hung from vice-like mandibles locked in death upon the soft skin beneath the boy's arm.

Matthew stood, angrily picked them off, cast them to the ground, and stomped them with his bare feet. He looked around and realized he had no idea from which direction he had come and no recollection of where he had discarded his clothes. He squinted upward into the sun. Its slanted rays angled in from the west and dropped low in the afternoon sky.

Then he glanced back at the river. It appeared somehow different. He knew he had drifted downstream, but he was certain it could not have been far. He turned full-circle and surveyed the steep terrain that attended the river on both sides. Nothing looked familiar. Nothing felt right. Matthew's heart raced as he turned around and around, looking up at the steep mountains and dark forests. He ran to the river's edge and leaned out as far as he dared, trying to see beyond the upstream turn where a wide-reaching growth of scrub willow and tall cottonwoods obscured his view.

He walked upstream toward the grove of trees and, when he reached a straight stretch below the bend in the river, he caught a glimpse of the brilliant green, narrow cut in the mountainside that led up and out of the meadow. The boy's eyes brightened and his pace quickened, then he suddenly felt sick to his stomach.

When he rounded the bend, he saw before

him the meadow and beyond that, the green slash in the tree line and in the foreground, his trousers, boots, and shirt crumpled in a pile in the tall grass. The river raged loud and unceasing between him and his clothes.

With his wiry arms wrapped about his pale and unclothed body, he stared at the unremitting water and his insides knotted. He ran tender footed and stumbled over the rocks at the river's edge. The river roiled and frothed and hissed at him where he stood, and sprayed icy white water high into the air, defying him to enter.

Matthew dropped his head and cried, then ran downstream and back up again. He paced and tested the water and backed away. Then he screamed and ran at the river, ignoring the rocks and charging blindly toward the roar of the crashing water. When he reached the river's edge, he closed his eyes, held his breath and threw himself into the churning blue-black water. The cold hit him first. Then the strong current caught him and pulled him under. He bobbed to the surface paddling like a small puppy as the torrent swept him away.

The boy kicked his legs and clawed the water, but the current turned him sideways and carried his body over the rocks and boulders. He fought for a handhold or a foothold, but there was none, only the ache in his ears and the sight of the sky and the trees flying past him as he sped downstream. Suddenly the water eddied into a backwash and drew him into a whirling pool where the powerful current spiraled downward. He sucked in a deep chest full of air and watched the lighted surface of the pool ascend above him in the darkness as the spiral drew him downward.

His eyes hurt and his lungs begged for air. He exhaled and large bubbles escaped upward before his face. Then, almost as quickly as it pulled him under, the whirling current released him, and he floated to the surface where the water lay calm and gentle among the boulders.

Matthew sputtered, gasped, and paddled for the gravel riverbank. When his hands touched bottom he pulled himself out, then stood and ran. He ran from the water and tried to run away from the cold. He found a narrow game trail that ran parallel to the river and followed it for a quarter of a mile or more, then stopped to catch his breath.

He stood bent over with his hands on his knees and, when his breathing slowed, he raised his head and looked upstream. There it was, the meadow, the green cut of the sloping gully, shining like new spring grass in the brassy sunlight. Matthew laughed aloud and his laugh was like the laugh of a stranger, uncertain, and close to hysterical. His voice quivered, but he did not weep.

Matthew was on the right side of the river, standing there thin and pale, and naked in his brief moment of victory. He felt triumphant and strong. When his eyes set upon the pile of clothing he abandoned earlier, Matthew's heart soared.

He reached the worn-out socks and underwear and filthy trousers, and he scooped them up in a bundle, and held them close to his chest and grinned. No treasure could have been more welcome. He placed the bundle on the ground, then carefully picked up one piece at a time and shook it and examined it before he put it on.

After he dressed, he started up the gully in his stocking feet. Fifteen yards up the trail, he found his lopsided boots. He sat in the dirt and forced first one foot then the other into the wet leather tops. When he stood, he stomped his feet. It felt good to have his boots on, and Matthew looked around for his shirt and coat. He found them ten yards farther up the hill. He buttoned the shirt with clumsy fingers and slipped into the tattered wool coat, then set out walking.

Matthew ran his hand over the rough surface of the wool coat. He rubbed the soiled legs of the trousers, and looked down at the familiar run-over boots. These were his clothes. They were who he was, and in his nakedness he felt that he had lost the only thing he had left. Now, back in his clothes, Matthew stepped forth with renewed vigor.

He walked the rest of the day without eating and, when darkness fell upon him, Matthew curled up on the ground, shivered, and tried to sleep. Each time he drifted off, he was back in the icy river with the water swirling and roaring about him. He tucked his face down inside the wool coat, breathed in its familiar scent, and tried to trick his dreams into letting him beyond the river and into the quiet void where sleep awaited him.

An hour before daylight, Matthew arose to the light of the waning moon and walked the cold out. He struck a line high above the river and followed its course by the sound it made. When the sun lit up the eastern ridges, he climbed a boulder the size of a trapper's cabin and stared into the variegated darkness of the skyline. And there he waited until the sun came up fully and the shadows among the dark trees and tangled underbrush turned again the colors of daylight.

Matthew had ignored the hunger in his belly during the night when it was cold, dark, and lonely, but now it was light and the sun was up and Matthew needed food. He gathered about him a collection of smooth stones, round and uniform in size. He stacked them in a pile atop the boulder where he sat and waited.

When first one squirrel, then another and another ventured forth, Matthew pretended to ignore them, but watched them closely. The squirrels watched him back, standing steely-eyed and motionless. Matthew targeted the nearest one, let loose a stone, and grunted as he fired it down from his perch atop the boulder. The stone flew straight and true, but missed its intended victim by more than two feet. Each of the squirrels, as though commanded by a universal order, stood at attention with gazes fixed upon the stone, where it lay spent and harmless.

Matthew selected another stone the size and weight of the first and fired it with the full swing of his arm. This time the stone found its mark and caught a waiting gray squirrel broadside and crushed its bony frame, then bounced against a hollow log, sending the other squirrels scampering for cover.

Matthew was unsure of his shot, and he kept his eyes locked on the animal lying on its side with one leg waving wildly. When the leg stopped, the boy climbed down from the boulder and hurried to claim his kill.

He picked the squirrel up in his small hand. It hung limply with its head drooping on one end and its tail and hind legs swinging at the other. He stuffed it into his coat pocket then set about to gather up kindling and dry wood for a fire. When he had an armload, he hauled it back to the boulder top.

Matthew had no flint or steel. He tried for over two hours to ignite the kindling before he gave up and his hunger drove him to accept the prospect of eating the squirrel uncooked. He dug into his trouser pocket and fetched out an old folding knife his father gave him on his eighth birthday. He tested the edge with his thumb, and then pressed the point against the soft underbelly of the squirrel. His first cut was too deep and he wrenched back at the foul odor of the severed entrails. He held his breath and finished gutting and skinning the rodent. He removed the head and forelimbs and held the gaunt carcass in one hand as he

141

contemplated his next move.

He sat for a long time before he closed his eyes and took the first bite. He tried to swallow, but gagged and spat. The taste of flesh aroused his hunger. Matthew took another bite and another, until it became easier to swallow and he began to tear the raw meat from the bones like some ravenous and primitive predator. When he finished, Matthew felt his strength begin to return. He picked out another stone and went in search of a better place to hunt.

Matthew followed the course of the river. He had his clothes. He had food in his belly. He clung to the smooth stone, and the look in his eyes was hard and deliberate.

Seventeen

On the third day after his fever broke, J.D. Elder carried his left arm in a sling and walked from Sheriff Dunn's house to the saloon. It was early afternoon and the town showed no signs of the sheriff's absence or any noticeable concern for the circumstances that called him away. He pushed open the batwing doors with his good hand and stepped inside. The light from the doorway shone across the front half of the narrow room, but the rear portion lay cast in a murky shadow and Elder waited for his eyes to adjust to the dim light before he addressed the bartender.

"Bob, I hear you rode out with Sheriff Dunn and his posse."

The bartender hesitated. He looked somewhat embarrassed.

"Well, J.D., that's right, I did. I had to turn back though." Then he added quickly, "My old saddle horse broke down the first day out. Had to walk him most of the way back down. He just wasn't up to it."

Elder offered no consolation.

"How many more of you wasn't up to it?"

The bartender rubbed his chin, and then wiped his hands on the towel he picked up from behind the bar.

"Truth is, J.D., a lot of us wasn't up to it."

There was a defensive tone to his response, and Elder did not like the sound of it. He glared at the bartender.

"Come on, J.D. We ain't lawmen. That's what we pay Dunn for."

"How many, Bob?"

"I don't know — most of us I guess."

"Most of you? How many men does Milo have with him?"

"I don't know for sure — enough, I think."

Elder slapped his good hand down hard on the flat surface of the bar. The bartender flinched and backed away.

"How many?"

"Three," the bartender said looking down at the floor. "Patrick and Tim Arbuckle, and Carl Swenson."

"That's it?" Elder said. "That's the best this town could do? How long they been gone?"

"Five days, going on six. They left the day after you rode into town all shot up."

"They find a trail?"

The bartender resented taking the brunt of Elder's implied accusations and now, in the clear light of day, safely back in his own element, he felt ashamed.

"Yeah, J.D.," he said softly. "We picked up a clear track at the Stanford place. It headed straight up into the high country. The Smith brothers were still riding your horses and carrying the Stanford boy double; looked like they were striking for the summit."

Elder's sense of urgency heightened.

"I need a rifle and a good horse. Can you help me out?"

The bartender reached under the bar. "The Smith brothers left this one behind the night they were in town." He set the rifle across the bar and Elder picked it up, turned it over, and read the serial number. He shook his head.

"They took this from my place," Elder said.

The bartender read Elder's determined expression, then pointed down the street.

"Sam Fry's got a couple of good young horses over at the livery."

Elder slid the rifle from the bar and turned toward the door. As he started toward the street, the bartender called out to him.

"J.D.," he said, hesitating.

145

Elder turned his head and looked back without answering.

The bartender agonized over some inner thought, and then his voice trailed off.

"Nothing," he said, shaking his head slowly and looking down at the floor.

Elder stopped by the mercantile, spoke briefly with the owner, charged two boxes of .44-40 cartridges, then limped across the street and down two blocks to the livery. Fry loaned him a stout gelding and wished him good luck, but did not offer to go along. Had he asked, he would have been refused, and he knew not to ask. When Elder returned to Sheriff Dunn's place, Sarah was waiting for him. She opened the door, and he looked pale and tired as he stepped inside with his uneven gait that told her the leg was bothering him.

"J.D., are you feeling all right?"

"I'm fine, Sarah," he said smiling weakly.

"Come in and sit down. I've got lunch almost ready."

Sarah had grown accustomed to helping Elder since he became her patient, and she put her arm around his waist more out of natural reaction than anything else and walked him to the table. Elder did not need the help, but he liked the closeness of her and he put his arm around her shoulders. As they approached the table, a sense of mutual embarrassment overcame them and they dropped their arms awkwardly, as though attempting to change the subject of an inappropriate conversation.

Sarah busied herself at the stove. Elder wrapped his hand around the cup of coffee Sarah had set on the table for him.

"I'm going after Matthew today."

The words fell out blunt and sent a chill up Sarah's back. She turned quickly to face Elder, her emotions whirling in a confusion of joy and trepidation. His words renewed her hopes and, at the same time, left her with the empty realization that she would now be completely alone, not knowing if she would ever see her son or Elder again. She covered her mouth with her hands. Tears rimmed her eyes. She prayed for this moment and now it was here and all she could do was tremble.

Elder stood and walked to her. He held her in his arms.

"I'm so afraid," she whispered.

"I know," Elder said. "It's all right."

Sarah looked up at Elder's craggy face.

"Please bring Matthew back to me." Then she looked away and whispered, "And please, J.D., don't let anything happen to you."

By dark, Elder was three hours up the trail from the Stanford place when he stopped and made camp in a protected stand of aspen trees where a small stream ran and the wind did not blow. He redressed his wounded arm with medicine Sarah had given him, then built a concealed fire and ate. Elder rubbed the aching knee and stretched the muscles that had grown lazy while he lay bedridden. It was good to be up and out again. Elder felt his strength returning and he breathed deeply of the crisp mountain air.

When he tried to sleep, he found himself lying awake with thoughts of Sarah Stanford running through his mind. He was uncomfortable with the feelings he had for this woman he scarcely knew. The awkwardness of it bothered him. The untimely inappropriateness of it caused him concern. But the simple reality of his distraction could get him killed, and Elder understood the high cost of being caught off guard. He dismissed Sarah from his thoughts and concentrated on everything Clarence and the bartender told him about the three derelicts and the fourteen-year-old boy who, for the time being, were the only ones on his mind. Elder gazed past the stars and beyond the endless black sky as he replayed the quiet night in the cabin when three strangers invaded his life. He saw the images of the preacher and the corpses that comprised the violated young family he encountered. He saw mutilated animals and mindless destruction that marked the path of the derelicts, and he cursed.

Elder awoke angry, ate a cold breakfast, and started up into the wilderness before dawn. The young gelding was fit and strong and by the second day Elder had pushed him high into the timberland, but found no sign of a trail left by the lawmen or the derelicts. Rain and wind had washed any tracks clear and, if they had passed this way, their passing was no longer evident on the earth upon which they trod.

With no trail to follow, Elder judged his course by the terrain and trusted his instincts to guide him. He rode the day with no sign, and the second day he rode from sunup to dusk before he found faint tracks of three shod horses traveling back down from the high country above. Elder recognized the tracks of the derelicts' horses, and he knew they flanked Dunn and his men, but he could only imagine the circumstances under which they did.

Elder followed the tracks, lost them in the rocks, then found them again where the riders put their mounts on a westerly course along the upper rim of a deep ravine. Elder smiled.

The deep ravine appeared to lay a navigable route over the ridge and out of the wilderness range. Surely, the outlaws hoped to follow the trail through the ravine. And just as surely, they could not know the ravine and the trail played out at a dead-end canyon of impassable granite cliffs at the end of a two-day ride.

Elder's pulse raced. Two days in, he calculated. Two days back out, and no other way for them to go but back to this point. He searched the tree line with his eyes and scanned the broken and clear patches of brush for movement or sign, but there was none. He massaged his bad knee for a moment, then dismounted and walked the tracks up the trail from which they descended for more than a mile, carefully examining and calculating and looking for the smallest detail to tell him what he needed to know.

There was too much uncertainty, no clear sign. Elder had to decide. He promised to bring Matthew back to Sarah, and that was now more important than the revenge that burned inside him.

Elder contemplated his choices. He could choose to continue up the trail in search of Dunn and his men, or he could follow the deep ravine. His first inclination was to connect with Dunn to ride in-force against the derelicts. His instincts, however, urged him into the unknown of the deep ravine where he knew Ike and his delegation to be riding.

Before committing to the deep ravine, Elder chose to continue the ascent on the trail traveled by Dunn and his men. Another mile up and the trail widened out into a flat meadow eighty yards across, where the earth was soft and the tracks of the derelicts' horses stood out in three-abreast formation less than a day old. Elder assessed the marks of each set of hooves with painstaking detail. He measured them with his eye and gently outlined each impression with the touch of his fingers. He stood back and viewed the length of the stride of each horse, moved up the trail, and then measured the balance of each horse's gait. One set of tracks he determined earlier to be carrying double, now showed signs of carrying a lighter load. The tracks of the other two horses remained unchanged, as they had been farther down the trail.

Elder dismounted and studied the tracks

with great intensity. He limped along, bending and searching and leading the young gelding. Elder stepped back to the horse. It skittered, rolled its eyes, and pulled back from the cowboy.

"Easy now," Elder said as he caught up a handful of mane hair, mounted and turned back up the trail at a trot, reasonably certain the boy was no longer with the derelicts. That left three possibilities. The boy was dead, he was lost, or he was with Dunn. He prayed it was not the former.

Night descended with no moon and no stars, and Elder made a cold camp at the entrance to the deep ravine. He picketed the gelding, then hunkered nearby wrapped in his wool blanket. He fetched a dry biscuit from his saddlebag and set his canteen at his feet. The still air grew cold and wet, and the dampness settled onto Elder's blanket and saddle. He ignored the chill and he ignored the damp, but he could not ignore the frustration he felt.

Elder's concerns ran deeper than his comfort. He stared out into the dark and tried to make sense of the circumstances he faced.

J.D. Elder pondered questions with no answers, but he knew one thing without a doubt. He could not let the three derelicts come down off the mountain alive. He catnapped throughout the night, and when morning came, he spurred the young gelding farther up Dunn's trail at a killing pace, stopping only to let the horse blow. By midday Elder followed a clear trail preserved in places where the damp earth held the tracks undisturbed by weather or the cover tracks of other animals.

Seven horses ascended the steep climb up the mountain before him. Three sets of tracks coming down matched three of those going up. The three coming down Elder recognized as those stolen from him. Elder had nailed on the old shoes four nails to a shoe instead of six. A make-do job until he could pick up a supply of nails and new shoes in town.

Elder concluded that Matthew, whether dead or alive, was still somewhere up ahead. He rode the strong and willing young gelding hard for the next three hours.

He pulled the gelding up in a narrow clearing flanked by a steep granite escarpment showing the signs of horses and men on foot in a confusion of tracks in a manner suggesting disorder and uncertainty. Elder dismounted and tied the gelding. He slowly walked the area checking the tracks and searching the brush where the derelicts left their horses tied. He walked up the trail, lost the tracks on the long stretch of shale rock, and then picked them up again a quarter-mile up.

Three sets of tracks coming down single file with one riding double. Elder followed them down until they disappeared on the rocky section of the trail. He found them again when they came off the rock. Three clear sets of tracks, and no one riding double, Elder concluded.

Elder returned to the trackless shale rock and stood looking about as though waiting for a vision that would reveal to him the whereabouts of Matthew Stanford. No vision came, but Elder felt certain the boy and the general's army parted company here. Whatever his fate, Elder found no sign of the boy at this point.

Elder walked out the area in continually widening circles. He identified tracks made by the cavalry boots and the field shoes and a pair of worn out low-quarter shoes, but he found no tracks belonging to the boy. Elder turned his gaze upwards to the escarpment, and started up the granite surface, following the lateral and vertical fissures that afforded him footing. When he reached the spot where the rock shelved out, he found where the boy took refuge. Elder found two sets of tracks, those of the mulatto and those of the boy. They lay before him as clearly as though written upon a document awaiting his arrival.

The larger set of tracks came down from above and descended from the ledge to the trail below. The smaller set of tracks, cast in the soft earth by a child's foot, scampered hither and yon, and then led out and over the top of the escarpment heading for the ridge. Elder tracked the boy for nearly an hour before he returned to take up the trail in search of the sheriff.

EIGHTEEN

Patrick Arbuckle descended the trail into the evening and stopped only when there was no light by which to travel. His sleep was fitful and consumed with thoughts of Sheriff Dunn lying alone and dying and waiting for his return.

On the second day of his descent, Patrick met Elder on his way up. Patrick told him of the killing and of the sheriff's condition.

Elder offered the bridle reins of his horse to Patrick.

"Take the gelding. You'll make pretty good time on him. Fetch Milo and get him back down as quick as you can. I'm going after the boy," Elder said.

"The Stanford boy?"

Elder nodded. "I don't know how he did it, but he's out there on his own and, judging by his trail, he's heading into some mighty rough country, and he's on foot."

Patrick looked sideways at Elder, regarded

the tattered bandage with doubt and asked, "You fit enough to go it afoot?"

"Don't have a choice. That boy was smart enough to strike out where no horse can follow. That's why the Smith boys didn't go after him. Anyway, I gotta find him and bring him back no matter what."

Patrick sensed something deeper in Elder's conviction than his concern for the boy, but gave it no further discussion.

"What about the Smith boys?"

"They left a set of clean tracks heading up Big Bear Creek. I reckon it'll take them another three days before they get turned around and make it back out to the trail. I plan to be there when they do," Elder replied. Then he thought for a moment. "But, I guess that all depends on the boy," he added.

Elder stood and gathered up his saddlebags and rifle. He slung the saddlebags over one shoulder and the rifle over the other. He extended his hand to Patrick, who stiffly rose and shook it.

Elder squinted with one eye at the gray sun. "Better part of an hour's daylight left. We best not waste it."

Patrick stepped up into the saddle, his expression grave and resigned. He turned to look over his shoulder at Elder, who had already started down the trail.

"Leave me some sign," he said. "I'll be back unless them three show up in town."

NINETEEN

What moon there was hung cold and watchful at the edge of the world, and those few stars that appeared on that black canvas sky did so with great reverence, as though their presence might offend the moon. The sky itself was broken and uncertain, its shadowy clouds hurrying across the moon path borne on a wind that never touched the earth.

High up near the summit of those scarred and barren peaks, a timber wolf raised its soulful voice to the moon in a ritualistic homage as old as its ancestors who paid tribute to another ancient moon thousands of years before the wolf came full born into this empty wilderness. And when Matthew Stanford stood completely still and didn't breathe, he was certain he could see the eyes of that ghost wolf and those of its ancestors, yellow and glaring in the night, their jaws dripping, their hides stretched tight over frames of bleached bones, and the smell of death about them.

Matthew shuddered and turned full circle, searching the trees and the black void of the underbrush and backing to the center of the small clearing. The wolf raised its voice again and another wolf voice answered it from a distant source that was at once everywhere, and at the same time nowhere at all. Then, close by in the darkness of the tree line at the backside of the clearing, a third wolf reached out to the moon, its head outstretched and its hellish wail as evil as the mourning cry of any mortal ever condemned to the night eternal.

A chill knotted the boy's insides and his hands trembled. He spun to face the sound. His eyes tracked blindly among the trees. He stared into the blackness and tilted his head like a blind man, as though to see where there was nothing to see. He backed away in short, uncertain steps and his left hand dug deep into the front pocket of his trousers for his folding knife. His fingers were clumsy and thick, but when he got the blade open, he held the knife out, as though the sight of it might be understood by the wolf.

Then he remembered the squirrel and he knew the wolf would pick up the scent of it. He groped about in the deep pocket of his tattered wool coat and found the gutted and half-eaten carcass he had put there earlier in the day. He fished out the hide-less rodent and pitched it in the direction of the wolf. Then as he backed away, he bent over and clawed up from the forest floor a great handful of humus and scrubbed it between his fingers and on his bloodstained trousers and between the layers of his coat pocket, then he rolled about in the darkness on the ground itself, hoping to conceal the blood scent from the wolf. Then he stood and faced the dark woods.

"Hey," he shouted out to the wolf and to the night, and to no one at all. "I'm leaving you this squirrel."

His voice rang small and insignificant, but it echoed and amplified through the clearing and when it came back to him, he called out again.

"You all see that wolf?" he called to an imaginary companion nearby. Then he ran to that spot and answered himself.

"I seen him," he replied to himself in a voice lower than his own, then he crossed to another spot.

"I seen him too," he said in a different voice that sounded much like the others, and they all echoed together and clashed in confusion, then they were gone and Matthew stood more alone than ever.

Overhead the clouds left only faint traces of their earlier presence, and the moon lit up the remaining wisps of the thinning clouds and swirling smoke trails like silver lines scratched upon the surface of the black sky. Stars shone in great numbers from skyline to skyline and the light from the moon and the stars was enough for Matthew Stanford to see the outline of a gaunt and haggard she-wolf trot out from the dark cover of the thicket and into the clearing.

The yellow eyes of the wolf burned from deep within, unchanged by a thousand years of procreation, unchanged by a thousand frozen winters, a thousand years of survival. They were the eyes of her ancestors and the eyes of her future, and there was nothing soft in them at all. But when the boy looked into those eyes as they grew nearer and larger, he swore he saw himself.

The wolf trotted toward him slowly, methodically, and with measured calculation, her undercarriage heavy with milk and swinging from side to side in rhythm with her silent footsteps. She put her nose to the ground, and then tested the air with her head extended and her nostrils flaring, but all the time her eyes never left the boy, and she never altered her pace.

When she was so close Matthew could smell the musky scent of her den and the odor of her litter on her, he saw the hind-quarter of the gutted squirrel clamped in her jaws. Matthew stood frozen, clenching the folding knife in his hand and daring not to move a muscle. The wolf stopped fifteen feet away, and Matthew dropped his eyes from hers. A low growl rumbled deep in the throat of the wolf and she bared her teeth.

Matthew tensed. He choked the knife in his hand, and watched the wolf sideways and stood his ground, but in his mind, he ran. The she-wolf watched the boy, he watched her, and they regarded one another with great apprehension. Then, as though summoned by a silent calling, the wolf turned and trotted off, her breath smoking from her gray muzzle in the cold night air and the moon lighting up the silver hair on her back.

Matthew waited a long time before he moved, and when he did, he collapsed to the ground where he stood, his body trembled, and he was exhausted. He sat in the same spot for more than an hour, and then he crawled beneath the low canopy of a serviceberry. He checked carefully for ants, covered himself with a blanket of damp humus, and lay there wide-awake until he began to feel warm, and then he slept.

When he awoke, he was shivering and it was dark and the mist from the ground fog swirled slowly about, transforming the clearing into a place he did not recognize. He pulled the wool coat over his head and tried to sleep, but yellow eyes glared in at him from everywhere in his dreams and all he could do was wait for daylight, and daylight was a long time coming.

Dawn arrived gray and cold, and Matthew arose from his makeshift lair with the appearance of a wallowing creature excavated from a graveyard, his hair matted and tangled, his face stained the color of the forest floor. He stretched and looked about and, were he full-grown, he would have presented a fearsome sight, but he only looked small and pitiful.

In the opening light, Matthew could see where the clearing rolled out into a narrow trail below, but for the ground fog, he could see no farther. He looked back up the direction from which he came, and then sat cross-legged and waited for the fog to clear. He crossed his arms over his knees, laid his head upon his arms, and closed his eyes. He listened to his stomach grumble and felt waves of hunger ripple through it, and he thought about the squirrel.

Matthew did not remember falling asleep, but when he raised his head the fog had lifted and slanted fragments of early morning sunlight cut through the trees and lay long shadows across the clearing. Birds twittered from high in the tops of the pines, jays squawked and scolded, and a multitude of insects and tree frogs cluttered the air with a barrage of strange sounds unlike any the boy had ever heard before.

The woods came alive with activity and the boy rose to his feet as if he had overslept. He brushed himself off and looked about for the wolf, half expecting her to be waiting for him. He saw no sign that she had ever been there, and he wondered if she had. He started down the trail, walking briskly and eyeing the ground for squirrel rocks. Ahead of him, the trail, which was no trail at all, narrowed then widened and turned up a gently sloping incline, then disappeared into the open sky. When the boy cleared the crest he stood in awe at the sight he beheld, for there, stretched out before him and rising up into the clouds, loomed a spectacular vista of rugged mountain peaks as far as he could see, and he could see to where the earth curved and beyond. Matthew could not remember ever feeling so small or so alone.

There was no more trail; no more right way to go, only the broken granite and shale rubble and centuries of deadfall left in the moraine of some extinct glacier that passed through there before the time of man. Everything it broke stayed broke, and fifty-million years later, the scarred earth still had not mended. What the ancient glacier left behind was forbidding and inhospitable, and the boy knew he would go no farther. His insides twisted and knotted and his hopes dimmed like the last flicker of a candle flame before it sputters and dies.

His small fingers curled into fists that clenched the lining of his coat pockets and he wanted to cry. He wanted to close his eyes and feel his mother's arms holding him as she smoothed the hair on his head. He longed to hear her soft humming and to be a baby again.

He looked down at the boulders and crushed rocks, and piles of gravel and shale. Then he looked all about as though to confirm what he already knew. His jaw tightened.

"I ain't quitting," he shouted to the mountain and to the sky. "I ain't giving up."

He turned back the direction from which he had come, tight-lipped and grinding his back teeth. Before he got to the clearing, he picked up three good squirrel rocks, put two in his pockets, one in each side for balance, and held the other in his throwing hand.

As he entered the clearing, three or four young squirrels chittered and scampered out of range. Matthew regarded them with a cold eye and walked on. Halfway across the clearing, a fat squirrel sat upright on his haunches, nibbling rapidly and filling his cheek pouches. Matthew approached within a dozen feet of the squirrel and the squirrel did not move. Matthew cocked his arm and let fly the stone. It hurled through the air carrying with it Matthew's anger and disappointment, and when it struck, it was five feet off target and the squirrel did not move.

Matthew took two steps closer, loaded another stone, and let it fly with calculated precision, and when it struck it broadsided the squirrel and carried it into the brushy undergrowth. Matthew ran to retrieve it. When he reached the spot where the squirrel should have been, the squirrel was gone, and there was no blood, and no sign it had ever been there.

The boy picked up his stone, fetched the first one nearby, and continued up the trail, ignoring the entourage of squirrels that mocked him from out of range as he went.

In the heavily treed area just above the clearing, Matthew stepped into the shadows and surprised a young squirrel that sat motionless and watched him with measured curiosity. Matthew walked directly toward the squirrel without breaking stride, and the squirrel watched the boy cock his arm. Matthew watched the stone as it flew through the air with perfect accuracy and toppled the rodent where it sat.

The squirrel lay where the rock hit it and Matthew squatted to skin and gut it. His hands shook with hunger and he ate it while the blood was still warm. The meat was difficult to chew and hard to strip from the bones, and it was stringy, but that did not matter. Matthew ate each bone clean, and then he crushed them with his back teeth and sucked out the sweet marrow that tasted of blood and tasted of something wild. When he stood, he did so with the stiffness of an old man. He ran the back of his hand across his mouth and tossed the last of the chewed bones onto the scanty offering of hide and offal at his feet.

"Hey, wolf. Here's some for you," he said loud enough for his echo to repeat itself. Then he turned and started up the trail, backtracking as best he could remember, and every now and again, he looked over his shoulder for the wolf.

TWENTY

By the time the morning sun shone red and fully shaped above the eastern ridgeline, J.D. Elder had already found and studied the place where Matthew spent his second night on the trail. He praised the boy to himself. The boy had the good sense to find decent shelter and had the good sense to cover himself against the night cold, but most of all he had the will to survive. That pleased Elder. "Good lad," he said aloud, even though there was no one to hear.

Elder hardly acknowledged his bad knee. He set forth on the boy's trail, tracking him and reckoning he had to cover twice as much ground as the boy if he was to overtake him. For all his good sense, the boy did not attempt to cover his trail and, if he had, Elder would have tracked him anyway. As it was, the trail was clear and Elder smiled each time the boy had a choice to make and made the right one.

By late afternoon Elder reached the river. For most of an hour, he trod the ground upon which the boy had made such a commotion. He pondered what he saw there and, for all his tracking skills, Elder could not conclude what had transpired. He picked up the trail and tracked the boy until after dark, then, when there was nothing more to see, he stopped and made camp. He laid his rifle down and dropped his pack beside it, then set about to gather wood by the light of the waning moon, just up and barely visible for the trees. The fire he built was a good one, and the light from it lit up the trees around it from base to tip, dancing on the branches and sending burning embers from the flames spiraling upward into the night sky.

Across the narrow gap and on the facing slope of the next rise, Matthew sat in a cold camp and watched the dull orange light flicker in the distance. He could almost feel its heat, smell the smoke from it, and taste the hot coffee he imagined simmered in a pot blackened by it.

Matthew sat for a long time and watched the fire, and imagined Ike Smith sitting before it, whiskied up and vile.

While Elder sat and nursed his aching knee by the fire, Matthew found two dry and sturdy sticks as long as a man's arm and as big around as a buggy whip handle. He set the first as deep into the soft ground as the weight of his body could drive it. He moved back four or five feet, and eyed and adjusted the second one until it lined up on the first and they both lined up on the firelight across the gap. He tapped it into the ground, then moved back to recheck it. He sighted the fire on the sticks, then realigned the back one slightly to the left, gauged it to be online, then stood and drove it deep into the ground until the tops of both sticks pinpointed the location of the fire.

Matthew did not sleep much that night and when the first light of dawn arrived, he was hunkered near the sighting sticks waiting for it. He waited until there was enough light to get his bearings, then dropped to one knee behind the sticks and sighted on the spot where the campfire had been. There were no signs of man or horse. He studied the terrain all about, and when he set out on the trail, he set out to skirt high above the tracks he left. For all his reckoning, the boy believed surely that the fire he saw belonged to no one but the general and his company.

The boy crossed into the gap from one

direction while Elder crossed into it from the other, and by midday they passed one another without knowing it. They both proceeded with great haste, Elder thinking to be closing in on the boy, the boy thinking to out-distance the general's company. And, thusly, they paced themselves throughout that day.

Elder's leg slowed him some, but by late afternoon, he discovered the boy's camp from the night before, he discovered the sticks, he discovered the boy's tracks, and he cursed. Elder stood behind the sticks where the boy had stood and cursed himself for the fire. He took a pull from the canteen and took a biscuit and a piece of dried beef from his pack. Elder ate and tried to figure the boy. One side of him admired the boy. The other grew impatient.

For the next two days Elder pursued the boy and the boy traveled like the devil himself was after him. Matthew was a half day ahead of Elder when he reached the main trail. Every place he had been ran together in his mind, every rise in the trail, every clearing, every fallen tree and every turn, but when Matthew stepped out onto the trail amidst the tracks of shod hoof prints ascending and descending, his spirits soared. He could feel the blood course

173

through his heart as he started down the trail at a trot and, for the first time in days, he let himself think about home.

The going was easy for the most part, and the boy covered nearly five miles before the light began to give out, and the sky took on the scarlet colors of evening. His insides gnawed at him and his mouth was dry, his spittle like cotton. He looked back over his shoulder and turned off the trail at a shale rock table where his boots left no prints.

He entered a flat meadow of tender sweet grass grazed to the ground by whitetail deer. A shallow, spring-fed creek split the meadow down the middle. The upper edge of the meadow rolled away into a high plateau of boulders and gravel. A thick row of spruce trees stood between the plateau and the meadow at the lower edge.

A horse snuffled in the shadows of the spruce and a whiskey-riddled voice cracked from the same shadows.

"Private Smith. We been huntin' you, boy."

Matthew stood frozen in place, his face drained of its color and his heart wrenched as though it had been torn from his chest. He turned half to his right to face the sound.

"I been hunting you too," he called out in a loud voice that sounded steadier than it was.

Ike rode forward followed by the dullard. Sandoval hung back in the shadows, only his outline and the outline of his horse visible in the dark shadow of the brush.

The boy stood his ground and Ike approached, looking more wretched and wasted than the boy remembered, and every bit as terrible as his worst nightmares.

"How's come you to leave me?" the boy asked.

Ike stared down at the boy from the thin and glassy-eyed horse. "Seems to me it was the other way around," said Ike. "You wouldn't try to play the old general for a fool, now would you, boy?"

"No, sir," said the boy. "I was about to wet my britches and asked Raymond if I could get off."

"And what did Raymond say to you, boy?"

"He said set yourself down, so I did. When I finished, you all were gone and I had to do the best I could for myself."

"Raymond," the general shouted. "Is this boy lying to me?"

Raymond straightened up in the saddle, his droopy eyes now wide and attentive. "I never told him nothing like that, Ike."

"Yeah? Then how come you didn't stop me when I got off a your horse, if you didn't say nothing about it?" Matthew shot back.

Ike glared at the boy then his eyes went red, the veins in his thick neck swelled, and he glared back at Raymond.

"Are you lying to me, Raymond? I do not tolerate a liar in my camp, brother or no," Ike shouted. Then his voice got quiet and only the rough edge of the whiskey kept it from being a whisper.

"This boy makes a point, Raymond. If you're lying to me . . ."

"I ain't, Ike, he's the one who's lying, not me."

"I ain't neither," the boy said.

"You are so."

"No I ain't."

Raymond opened his mouth to respond and Ike withdrew the pistol from his belt. He ratcheted back the hammer, turned, swung the barrel and looked over the sight at Raymond.

"That'll do!" Then he turned to the boy. "Swing up behind Raymond. There will be no more trouble — from either of you, or I assure you I will take harsh disciplinary action as befits a deserter and a fool."

Ike pushed the pistol back into the holster, sawed the horse's head around, and rode back into the shadows where the mulatto waited. Raymond kicked a stirrup loose and hung an arm down for the boy. As he pulled

Matthew up, he put his face close to the boy's and held him there for a moment, his little eyes drawn tight and his lips a thin line of hatred. Raymond's putrid breath fouled the air about him and he whispered, "I'm going to kill you for that," and Matthew believed him.

They rode a short distance in the dark, the mulatto leading the way and Ike in the rear. When they stopped to make camp, it was a meager camp with no fire. They threw down their rigs, hobbled the horses, and sat in the dark. They ate strips of burnt deer meat, fouled with ashes from an old fire and dirt from the bottoms of their saddlebags. Ike was out of whiskey and his mood was bad.

"Sandoval," he said. "I am entrusting this boy to you. If he gets away I will commence with your field execution and, I assure you, we will roast your heart for supper."

In the dark, Matthew could not see Raymond's expression clearly, but he knew he was grinning. He knew Sandoval was not.

The general and the dolt gathered their blankets about them and lay in the dirt to sleep. Sandoval motioned the boy to a narrow rift between the boulders. He looked into the boy's eyes and the boy into his and, though they exchanged no words, the boy knew he would not get a second chance from this one, whose expression was as deadly as that of the wolf whose amber eyes and drooling jaws tracked him in his sleep each night. Sandoval followed the boy and nodded him into the small space between the boulders, and then the mulatto spread his own blanket across the opening, rolled up in it, and slept with no concern that the boy would be anywhere other than where he left him.

The boy dropped off just before daylight and slept lightly until he felt himself dragged from his dirt bed by the leg. He got his eyes open and, in the dark lost track of where he was. His head cracked against the side of the boulder, where Sandoval deposited him near where the horses stood tethered.

"Get them horses saddled and be quick, boy," the general's raspy voice boomed low and mean. Matthew, confused and disoriented, rose to his feet and the general sent him sprawling with a boot to his backside. Blood ran from the boy's head when he hit the ground and opened a wide gash alongside his jawbone.

The obese general puffed over to the boy and jerked him up by the collar.

"Quickly now," he ordered. "Quickly."

They saddled and mounted, and rode

steady all that day, staying off the main trail, but backtracking just the same. At night, they camped with no fire, and the next day was like the first and the third was like them both. They had no food, and when the rancid deer meat ran out on the second day, they stopped eating and did not attempt to trap game or take a varmint, and Ike would not risk a shot, so they went hungry.

They rode the fourth day from before dawn to past dark and when they entered Milo Dunn's town they did so with no regard for their welcome there. Like the wasted remnants of a company of misused infantrymen, they rode slouched and indifferent through the streets, their clothing tattered and flagging, their horses hollow-eyed, bony-hipped and gaunted up, and their own faces drawn and lifeless. They proceeded down the middle of Front Street, with the general leading the way past the false-fronted mercantile and the darkened dentist's office with its oversized molar sign swinging and creaking from its signpost, past the sheriff's office and directly to the bar where Ike's horse stopped, and the others did likewise.

Ike dismounted and dropped his reins over the hitch rail without tying them. He fetched a rawhide string from his saddlebag, and jerked the boy down from behind Sandoval and tethered the boy about the neck with the string, and then he lifted the saddlebags, a lever action rifle and the ten-gauge from his own rig. Sandoval dismounted and Ike held the end of the string out to him, then Ike stepped up onto the boardwalk. Raymond and Sandoval followed suit, and when they entered the saloon, they did so with the boy in tow, and arms and ammunition to make a long stay of it.

TWENTY-ONE

Ike Smith stepped inside the saloon and stopped just past the doorway of the dim and narrow room that smelled of lamp oil and cigarette smoke. He surveyed the room and each of its occupants who, to a man, stopped what they were doing and shifted uncomfortably under his gaze. The long barreled shotgun swung loosely at his right side where he held it with one hand. He made no attempt to conceal the big gun nor did he present it as a threat but, as he stroked the knurled surface of the double hammers in a gentle and loving manner with his thumb, the weapon took on a life of its own, like something fearsome and short-tempered.

A young cowboy, on his way to the door, stopped when the general entered, then continued with some uncertainty and excused himself as he approached Ike Smith.

"Begging your pardon," the cowboy said

to the general. The general did not budge and he did not bother to look at the cowboy.

"Excuse me," the cowboy said as he tapped the general on the shoulder.

Ike Smith moved with extraordinary quickness and swung the heavy ten-gauge upward in a furious arc driven by one hand on the buttstock, the other on the forestock and all his ponderous weight behind it. The steel-plated butt of the shotgun struck with such force as to lay open a wide gap in the cowboy's head from temple to jaw as his head snapped back with the sickening sound of broken vertebrae. Whole teeth and tooth fragments spewed forth from the cowboy's bloody mouth and he slumped to the floor, all the light gone out of his eyes.

The proprietor stood sober and disbelieving, his hands flat on the bar top. Two of Milo Dunn's posse-quitters stood at the bar opposite the proprietor. One locked his hands around the beer mug before him; the other cleared his hands slowly and placed them on the bar without being asked to do so. A young cowboy and a well-dressed patron sat at a nearby table below the single oil lamp in that part of the room.

The eyes of all five fixed on the blood-spattered general and each of them weighed his private thoughts carefully. None moved and none spoke, and only the well-dressed man held his gaze as the others looked away. The general stepped forward.

Sandoval entered behind him, bandoliered with a double row of shotgun shells and tethered to a bruised and filthy child creature that followed bent and swollen so that none recognized the lad nor thought him anything more than the unfortunate, feral offspring of some dark and deranged wilderness liaison. The boy kept his head down and neither spoke nor looked about.

The mulatto slipped into the shadows near the wall and the boy moved with him like a heeler, leaving the general hulking over the center of the room, his pig eyes burning like fire coals set deep in sockets gouged in clay and sculpted beneath a thick brow of bone.

Raymond entered last. He pushed the door closed with his foot and stood off to the bar side of the room and watched Ike and Sandoval, his expression doubtful and grave. He alternated between a nervous smile and a scowl, and his fingers drummed rapidly on the stock of the shotgun he held up to his chest in both hands.

The well-dressed man at the table rose slowly and stepped clear of his chair, a pistoleer of some experience, judging by his outfit and his manner. He finished the whiskey left in his glass, and then set the glass among the wet rings on the tabletop. He acknowledged Ike with a nod, not asking for permission to leave, but clear on his intent to do so unmolested. He looked about the room and back to Ike.

In the uneasy silence that ensued, no one in the bar moved or made a sound or showed any sign of irreverence, as though they stood witness to the forging of a sacred covenant signed in blood and witnessed in blood.

"Gentlemen . . ." the pistoleer said at the same time the blast from Ike Smith's ten-gauge shook the room and smoke belched forth amidst the fire from the muzzle holes that lit up the place. The pistoleer jerked back loosely as though he had no bones to hold him together, and he collapsed to the floor, his satin vest running freely with blood that bubbled and whispered as it pumped from the holes in his chest. His gun hand lay close to his still holstered pistol and his fingers fluttered, spastic and gripping, out of control and with no linkage to the brain of the gunfighter to whom they belonged. His eyes darted about the room in the same disconnected manner, blind and wild and crazy. His mouth moved and the words that came out of it were incoherent babbling that rose and fell for only a brief moment, then his hand stilled, his eyes calmed, and he stared blankly up at nothing.

"You," Ike said to the man seated at the table. "Get them two out of here." He nodded toward the cowboy then toward the pistoleer floating in his own blood.

"Yes, sir," the man said.

"Set 'em out front then get yourself back in here. Raymond, go with him. If he attempts to desert, kill him."

Ike addressed the proprietor. "Show me the back door," he said.

The proprietor kept his hands in full view and pointed to a dark doorway in the corner at the rear of the room. "It's through there," the proprietor said without vacating his position behind the bar.

Ike pointed toward the door with the muzzle of the shotgun. "Show me."

The proprietor hesitated. Ike advanced half a dozen steps and looked over at the immobile bartender. The proprietor's face was void of color, his hands shook, and he watched Ike with grave misgiving.

"Do like I told you."

Then Ike drew back the second hammer with the solid double click like the sound of an iron bolt on a heavy door.

"There's nothing back there," the proprietor said as he stepped from behind the bar and led the way.

Ike slammed the muzzle of the shotgun into the middle of the proprietor's back, sending him stumbling forward.

"I didn't ask you if there was anything back there," Ike said, as the proprietor arched and gasped for air.

The proprietor hesitated and Ike caught him up by the collar and hauled him like a puppet to the back room.

"Where's the lamp?" Ike asked.

"Over there," the proprietor said softly, pointing to a small table stacked with wooden crates and empty bottles.

"Light it."

Ike waited until the dim, yellow light crept into the dark corners and revealed an outside door with a flimsy latch bolt. Six full cases of cheap whiskey were stacked in the corner with a partial case on top. Several bottles of good whiskey stood on the shelf above. Beside them stood a collection of tinned peaches, two jars of pickled eggs, a small barrel of crackers, salted beef, coffee beans, and sacks of sugar, flour and dried pinto beans. On the other side of the small room, hanging on the walls and scattered about upon the floor, were utensils of the trade and an odd assortment of hand tools, rope, wire, nails, kerosene, and rusty iron brackets and buggy parts.

"Take them boards there and nail the door shut," Ike said.

The proprietor shuffled forward, nursing his hurt back and breathing in short draws. "Yes, sir," he wheezed. Then he fetched a hammer from a shelf, and drove a handful of sixteen-penny nails into three cross boards and secured the door thereby from intrusion or escape.

Ike reached forward and took a hard pull on each board. "That'll do. Now get yourself back out there and don't give me no reason to lay you out front with your friends."

"No friends of mine," the proprietor whispered.

Ike backhanded him a severe blow, splitting his mouth and splattering blood across his face.

"I didn't ask you if they was your friends."

The proprietor glared at Ike, but dropped his gaze when the general turned back toward him. Then he wiped his mouth on his shirtsleeve and shuffled back to the safety of the bar.

Ike pulled back the tattered coat he wore and withdrew a gentleman's gold watch from his vest pocket. "Half past eight," he declared. "Raymond, you and Sandoval sit up here," he said motioning toward a table in the corner at the front of the room. "Bring the boy with you."

Raymond gathered up his rifle and reached for his saddlebags wedged between Matthew and the wall. The saddlebags refused to budge. Raymond released his grip on them, grabbed a fistful of Matthew's hair, and jerked the boy onto the floor.

"Stay off my stuff," Raymond said, and then he backhanded the boy across the side of the head.

Matthew covered his head with his arm, awaited a second blow, then pushed himself to the end of the leash and glared out at Raymond from under the table through dark and swollen eyes hard with hate. His face was dirt streaked and caked with dried blood. His bottom lip lay split and scabbed.

Raymond feigned a lunge at the boy as he walked past the table, but the boy did not budge.

"Boo," Raymond said, and then he smiled toothy and crooked, and laughed.

"Sandoval, bring the boy," Ike ordered.

Sandoval moved, without a sound, toward the table at the front of the room. The slack tightened in the leash. He gave it a harsh jerk and the boy lurched forward and followed, scrambling forth on his hands and knees, trying to get a grip on the string to keep from choking.

"Tie him," Ike said, nodding to the brass foot-rail at the bar.

Sandoval tied the boy off with five feet of lead and returned to the table to sit with Ike and Raymond.

Ike stared across the room at the wall. Raymond crossed one leg over the other, picked at a scab on his face, and nibbled the pickings he held between the long nails of his fingers. He looked about the room, silent, unfocused.

Sandoval regarded Raymond with a cold, wolf-eyed stare that unsettled the dullard, who shifted uncomfortably and turned to Ike.

"What are we going to do now?" he asked, more to fill in the silence than out of concern.

Ike's eyes never moved from the wall. He brought his hands together slowly, his elbows propped on the table as though to pray and his index fingers extended on either side of the bridge of his wide nose in a contemplative pose.

"We're going to stay, Raymond," he said. "We're going to stay."

Raymond turned to Sandoval in time to see what he took to be a fleeting look of disagreement on the dusky and expressionless face of the mulatto and for the first time since they left the war, Raymond felt a knot of fear well up inside him.

TWENTY-TWO

With great concern, J.D. Elder knelt and pressed his fingers to the wet earth, traced the boy's boot print, and looked up the trail. Above him, a granite wall rose to the clouds, and water trickled down from the boulders and ran along the fall line of the escarpment, and seeped out onto the ground. The trickling water gathered in shallow pools, and the pools, linked by slender rivulets, converged and gained momentum, and became a small stream. Farther down the trail the water tumbled into a rocky streambed, now slow and quiet, but growing wild and turbulent where it became a full borne white-water river below the tree line. Along its edge grew tender new grass, translucent and emerald colored and starkly brilliant against the soft lavender stream orchids that bent upward, delicately beautiful and conspicuously out of place among the deadfall and shale rock.

Elder let his fingers feel every detail of the boot print as though perhaps his fingers would show him what his eyes could not see, as though they would somehow confirm what he already knew. Elder's instincts told him the boy outflanked him. His head told him to confirm it. Elder rose and continued up the trail for nearly a mile before he turned back upon his own tracks and upon the tracks of the boy and followed a new set of the youngster's boot prints as they descended the loose gravel and the granite switchbacks heading back down the mountain.

Elder cursed under his breath. He cursed the wounded arm and the defective knee. He cursed his slow pace, he cursed the derelicts and he pressed on.

In two days time he crossed the first tracks of the horses. A day after that Elder stopped at a clearing and studied the intersection of the tracks of the derelicts' roughshod horses and the boot tracks of the boy. He followed the tracks into the clearing and back out again and, when the tracks departed the clearing, they did so with one horse carrying two riders and the boy's boot prints no longer in evidence. Elder cursed the boy's misfortune.

When Elder put to the trail he did so with

doubtful concern and a vacant feeling that left him cold, and threatened to let his emotions override his judgment. He knew not to rush, not to get careless, but he also reckoned the derelicts would now be less inclined to keep the boy alive.

Elder contemplated his options and those of the derelicts, and he gambled they would keep the boy alive. There could be no more mistakes, and Elder let his instincts take over. He studied every sign and pursued the trail with unshakable intensity. He trod the shale rock and gravel, picked his way among the immense boulders and thin strands of lodgepole pine and aspen. He walked the sun across the sky without stopping, and he walked the moon came up. When the stars appeared, they did so in a brilliant display of uncommon clarity and contrast, like a black velvet alpine meadow in bloom with a shimmering cover of stark-white ox-eye daisies. He searched the sky and watched his breath float upward like great puffs of smoke and, when he found the pole star, he set his course by it and followed his moon-cast shadow into the night.

An hour past full dark Elder felt a presence about him but saw nothing. He listened and heard nothing. He stopped and waited. He listened a long time. When he stepped out again his eye caught an imperceptible movement in the woods above the trail, and he turned to see the silver outlines of a pair of timber wolves following him, trotting silently with yellow eyes reflecting the moon and a thousand years of predation, gliding lightly across the night and glaring down on him narrow and cold. Elder watched the icy breath of the wolves hang in the moonlight. A cold chill ran through him and he chambered a round.

Throughout the night, the wolves watched him, and he watched them back. Methodical, calculating, and unhurried, the wolves appeared to measure Elder. They paced him step for step, then he would look up and they would be gone. Then, as suddenly as they left, they mysteriously reappeared an hour or two later, then disappeared again only to reappear at some unexpected place along the trail in the shadows of the moonlight, where they awaited his arrival before trotting out again.

Sometime before dawn, the wolves vanished for good and the man shivered as the moon and stars set and the dew set in dripping wet and cold, and frost crystallized the moisture on the ground and turned it white. In the belly of that hollow predawn he hobbled along, bent over, lumbering down the trail, favoring his bad leg and missing the wolves and wishing the sun up.

An hour later the first indication of sun appeared and backlit the eastern ridges with a thin, red line, and the gray sky above the chiseled peaks took on the muted colors of morning. Elder's breath smoked in the air and he stepped out stiff-legged, trying to shake the cold. He traversed the rocky slope until midday, then sat down beside a glacial creek, pulled off his boots, and soaked his feet in the icy water. He fetched a strip of salted venison from his pack, tore off two pieces, and chewed them into wads, one in each cheek, for the rest of the afternoon.

He followed the trail signs with ease, for they lay before him with no intent of concealment. As Elder feared they would, the tracks bore down through the wilderness, descending heedlessly back to town, and nothing he could do would change that.

When night came, darkness closed in about Elder with no moon and no stars and, when he made camp and got a small fire started, the insignificant light it made confirmed the absolute darkness about him. Elder pulled his blanket around his shoulders and lay with his bad knee to the heat of the flame. The leg ached, his arm throbbed, and the half-healed buckshot wounds itched and pained him.

His eyes burned. His body felt used up. He lay first on one side, then the other, but it made no difference. He pondered his circumstances with random thoughts that turned and twisted in his head, and he tried to sleep. Finally, he lay on his back, locked his fingers behind his head, and stared upward into the endless, dark universe where here and there a distant star shone through the cloud cover like celestial islands, unchartered and uninhabited, but somehow inviting, inspirational, lonely. He liked the way the stars made him feel, the way they made him think, the way they made him forget.

He could not forget Matthew Stanford and his stomach twisted. To Elder, the boy was as unknown and as distant as the stars. In his own way, Elder felt he knew the stars and in the same way, he felt he knew the boy. To Elder, each star, like a child, was born of purity, innocence, and anonymity, shining in its own glorious light, waiting for its time of discovery.

Elder thought about the promise he made to the boy's mother, and he couldn't be less sure of what lay ahead for the boy who, like a star blazing across the heavens, was bound for a destiny that couldn't be more uncertain.

Elder wondered what it was that brought him to this place at this point in his life. Maybe it was simply time and circumstance, and nothing more. Or, maybe it was fate. There was no reason for him to be here that he could see, and he could not imagine a less likely situation for himself. Everything seemed to have a place in the grand order of the universe, the mountains, the trees, the stars — everything, except him. If he had a rightful place on earth he did not know where it was, but his own day of reckoning was upon him, of that he was certain. For the first time he could remember, Elder had no idea what to do about it.

Three men he did not know imposed themselves upon him, violated the sanctity of everything he held valuable, and now the same derelict men with their child captive rode back to town, deliberate, bold, and careless. The unpredictable nature of that act alone disturbed his sense of order, set him off-balance, and stole from him the hunter's edge.

Elder had been bested. As he lay searching the bare sky, his anger choked him. His anger transcended his wounds and his fatigued muscles. It displaced his uncertainties and drove him to his feet.

Elder paced and circled the fire. If his leg bothered him, it did not show. His gait was smooth and strong. He was a tracker, a hunter, a warrior. His instincts arose within him. Ancient callings suppressed by a thousand years of civilization lashed out at his senses like a primitive creature raging in the night. His chest rose and fell, his jaw muscles tightened, and he shuffled around the fire, calculating and measuring in his mind Ike Smith and Raymond and the amber-eyed mulatto. All three men were dangerous, unfeeling, and unpredictable. Above all else, they were unfailingly consistent.

Of the three, the mulatto concerned him most.

For more than an hour Elder and his shadow danced around the fire until the cold and damp urged him to his blanket. He stoked the fire, banked it with an armload of deadfall, then wrapped himself in his thin wool blanket, and slept until dawn.

By the end of the next day the steep mountainside trail angled down to a gentler slope and the going was easier as the sharp granite gave way to grassy meadows and parklands where scrub willow, aspen, and cottonwoods grew in thick bunches alongside creek banks and bogs. Lowland birds twittered and flocked among the treetops. Ground squirrels flagged their tails and darted about. A mule deer raised its head, pricked its long ears, and watched undecided as Elder passed without making eye contact.

Elder walked the day into late night, skirted the trail to the south, leveled out of the foothills and slipped unnoticed into town two hours past midnight.

At the far end of the street a dog barked back at the coyotes yipping in the hills and, but for that, there was no other sound. Elder made his way across Front Street at the south end of town and stole along between the dark, unlit buildings until he could see the sheriff's office. A single lantern burned inside casting a weak, yellow light out onto the boardwalk and into the street.

On the other side of the street and down several buildings from the sheriff's office, the light from the saloon and its attendant shadows flickered in the long, narrow block of light that lay across the walk and halfway across the rutted street. He watched a solitary shadow lumber into the yellow patch of light, then out again.

Elder moved down the row of buildings and stepped into the fire gap between the dry goods store and the apothecary shop. In the shadows, he waited, pressed up against the rough-sawn siding of the store building, and watched.

He saw a shadow cast by the oil lamp. Through the panes of the narrow front window of the saloon the ponderous, dark shape of Ike Smith interrupted the light and stood there gazing out into the night and looking directly at Elder. Elder stood fast and did not move and soon the massive head turned to the right, then to the left, but saw nothing but the darkness and the detail of the street where the small stretch of light fell across it.

Elder raised his rifle, quietly chambered a round, flipped up the Vernier tang sight and placed the blade of the front sight in the center of the outline of Ike's monstrous head. He aligned the back sight with the front sight and felt his heartbeat quicken. There would be an instant of muzzle flash, a loud report, shattering glass, an explosion of human gore, then the big man would totter and fall crashing to the floor.

Elder's jaw tensed, his finger tightened on the trigger. His thumb gently released the hammer and let it settle back delicately in place and he lowered the rifle.

"Not yet," he whispered.

The figure moved away from the window. From inside the saloon, Elder heard loud coughing and sporadic talking. Somewhere up the street, a dog barked for the sake of barking.

Elder slipped quietly out of the narrow alley and crept along the shadows toward the sheriff's office. Not knowing what to expect, he stalked the night like a panther and, when he approached the edge of the pale yellow light from the window, he chanced a glance and saw there was no one attending the small office.

Elder pushed the old wooden door, and it creaked on unoiled hinges and he stepped inside and quickly surveyed the room. No one was there, but the oil lamp burned on a short wick and Milo Dunn's desk had a busy look of disarray about it that suggested someone had been working there.

Elder closed the door quietly behind him and moved toward the back of the room, staying close to the wall and out of the line of sight of the window. He extended his hand toward the bolt on the door to the jail cell at the rear of the office and, as he did so, the door jerked open and Elder saw the black holes of a ten-gauge swing down at the same time he heard a voice echo forth from the darkened hallway.

"Don't even move," the voice said soft and menacing.

The door swung inward and bumped the wall and, when it did, the light from the office reflected back from Patrick Arbuckle's narrowed eyes. The eyes turned up some and wrinkled at the corners.

"You come close to getting shot, J.D."

Patrick looked Elder over as they moved into the light.

"You all right?"

"I been worse."

"They're here, you know," Patrick said.

Elder nodded, "They still have the boy with them?"

Patrick leaned the shotgun against the wall near the desk and sunk into the wooden chair.

"They got him. He looks real rough, but he's still alive."

"Milo?" Elder asked, with some doubt clouding his expression.

"That old man's tough, but he ain't doing all that good."

Elder wrung his face in his open hands. His eyes looked tired, his expression hollow. He turned and gazed through the window into the darkness in the direction of Dunn's place, even though he could see nothing beyond the streaked panes of glass.

"How's Mrs. Stanford holding up?" He asked, still staring into the night.

"About as good as you could hope, I expect," replied the cowboy. "I don't know how she does it. She's doctoring the sheriff off-and-on around the clock, and camping out in here, and wondering why we don't just march right in there and get her son back."

Patrick stood and shuffled over to the gun rack on the wall behind the desk. He checked the lock on the chain running through the levers and trigger guards of the weapons. He turned back towards Elder and Elder looked over at the cowboy.

"J.D., if we don't do something to get that boy of hers back soon, I'm afraid she's going to do something crazy."

Elder looked puzzled. "Like what?"

"I don't know — something."

"What about the Smiths?"

Patrick shook his head. "They're holed up in the saloon. Got the boy, got Cyrus Tull, Bill Nichols, and Tommy Clark."

"Anyone hurt yet?"

Patrick nodded. "Yeah . . . they killed Bobby Thompson straight away."

Patrick looked over at Elder. "You know Bobby Thompson? Eighteen years old. Just started peelin' broncs for us last fall. Broke his neck and lined him out on the street in front of the saloon. Then they shot up someone I didn't know, a gambler I think, and lined him out on the street too."

Elder fell silent. He limped around and slumped into the hardwood visitor's chair in front of the oak desk.

"How do you know they haven't already killed the boy?"

"They got him tied on a string by his neck. Every so often, they put him out the door and let him stand there. Then, after a while they drag him back in. The big one, calls himself General Smith, says they'll shoot the boy if he tries to run, or if anyone tries to get him. Then they ask for food, or whatever they want, and someone gets it for them. Then, once in a while Ike . . . the general, will get out there by the doorway and carry on like a preacher."

"What do they want here?"

"I don't know. They don't say. Near as I can tell they plan to stay a while. They don't seem to want much. Cyrus Tull's family offered the general five-hundred dollars to let Cyrus and the others go. The general turned them down. Said he wouldn't need money where he's going. He said this was Armageddon and the time had come for atonement."

"What do you think he meant, Pat?"

"I don't know. I guess I'm not exactly sure what he meant."

Elder closed his eyes and took a slow, deep breath. "Well, if you ask me, I believe he means to make a stand of it right here."

"A stand of what? There isn't anything here for him. Hasn't he already done enough damage to this town?" Patrick snapped back.

Elder stood. He shook his head, and started back toward the cell. "I'm going to catch a couple hours sleep."

When Elder was in the doorway, Patrick called to him.

"J.D., what do you think he wants?"

Elder turned. His expression was grave and his voice tired.

"I think he wants to die."

TWENTY-THREE

Ike Smith coughed, hacked, and drank until just before dawn, then he fell into a stupor and slept an uneasy, fitful sleep. When he came to, it was mid-morning, and Tommy Clark argued with Raymond in a loud and desperate voice.

"I can't stay in here anymore," Tommy protested. "If you're going to shoot me, then you'll have to shoot me in the back, because I'm not staying."

Tommy's hands shook and his voice quivered. Bill Nichols and Cyrus Tull tried to quiet Tommy, but Tommy pulled away and took half a dozen steps toward the front of the saloon.

"You better sit yourself down right now," Raymond said.

Sandoval sat off to the side of the room with the boy. Ike Smith stood over the bar with his back to the door and the ten-gauge lay up before him on the glass-ringed mahogany bar top.

"You don't need me," Tommy said. "I'm too old to do you any harm and too poor to do you any good . . . please, I just can't stay in here."

Tommy turned and walked slowly toward the door.

Raymond looked over at Ike, but Ike leaned over the bar and stared into his whiskey glass. Then Raymond looked to Sandoval, and Sandoval looked back at him with no expression and no opinion on the matter.

"Ike," Raymond said as Tommy approached the door.

"Ike," Raymond said again as Tommy pulled the door open, then stepped outside, and gently pulled it closed behind him.

The general turned and watched Tommy Clark turn to the right and disappear from the doorway. He heard Tommy's boot heels on the plank boardwalk and watched Tommy come into view as he crossed in front of the window. Tommy glanced inside, his parchment-skinned face rutted with deep furrows, his eyes red and wet with relief. The corners of his mouth turned up in a tight smile. He nodded his gratitude and touched his hat brim at the same time glass and wood exploded from the window frames. Double-ought buckshot ripped through the old man's frail carcass and sent him skidding into the street.

Patrick Arbuckle positioned himself inside the dry goods store where he stood watch. By the time Tommy Clark closed the saloon door behind him, the cowboy was on his feet and headed for the doorway. When Patrick stepped out onto the wooden sidewalk, the street was empty except for the twisted body of the old man lying with one leg bent under him and his hat folded in the dirt beneath his head. Tommy Clark's shirt ran red and the ground around him ran red. The dry earth soaked up his blood, and all that remained was a black stain and a slight body that appeared to be much smaller than the man who previously occupied it.

"Ike Smith," Patrick shouted. "I'm coming for the old man. Hold your fire."

"Permission granted," said a tired and gravelly voice from inside the saloon.

Patrick dashed across the street and dropped to his knees at Tommy's side. He pressed his fingers to the old man's jugular and cursed under his breath. Then he stood and, in one smooth motion, hefted the old man's body up onto one shoulder and hauled him up the street, where Elder and

Clarence, and two other men met him halfway to the sheriff's office.

"They killed ol' Tommy Clark, Mr. Elder," Clarence said as Patrick approached. "Why did they do that?"

Elder shook his head and stepped forward to help Patrick carry the body inside the jail. "No reason, Clarence. Here, let's get him inside."

They laid the old man out on the bed in the cell and covered him with a blanket. Elder turned and looked directly into Patrick's eyes. "Pat, did you see anything of the boy?"

"Couldn't see anything, J.D. It's too dark in there. Except for the general, no one gets up near the door or the window."

"Who's left inside?"

"The boy, Cyrus Tull and Bill Nichols."

"We going to wait them out?" asked one of the two men, neither of whom Elder knew by name.

No one answered. Finally, Clarence spoke up. "Waiting don't seem to be doing any good," he said as he looked down at his boots.

Elder laid a hand on his shoulder. "No, it sure doesn't, Clarence."

Then he looked over at Patrick. "Pat, Clarence is right."

Patrick glanced at Clarence then back to Elder. "Course he's right — but what do we do about it?"

Elder shrugged. "Is Milo at his place?"

"He's there. Mrs. Stanford is there, too."

Elder lifted his gun belt from the back of the desk chair, swung it over one shoulder, then he picked up his rifle, and walked toward the door. "Take a walk with me, Pat."

Patrick fell in with Elder and together they headed up the street toward the edge of town and the well-kept house where Sarah Stanford tended to the old sheriff.

"What are you thinking, J.D.?"

"I think I need to get face-to-face with Ike Smith."

"Head-on? J.D., are you thinking straight? There's no such thing as facing that one head on. He'll do you just like he did Tommy Clark and all the others."

"Well, I know he'll try."

"J.D., he won't just try, he'll do it. Him or one of the other two. It don't bother them none to shoot a man in the back."

Elder was quiet as they approached the steps of the front porch at the Dunn place.

"You know, Pat . . . the way things are laid out now, everything's going their way. If we don't change that fast, then we got no say in what happens here on out."

Elder's expression turned grave and sober. "I can't let anything happen to that boy and that's about all there is to it, pure and simple."

"I understand," Patrick said. "But, what do we do?"

"Come on inside with me. We'll talk it over with Milo."

They opened the door and stepped inside. The hallway opened up into a small sunny kitchen where Sarah Stanford stood at the table over a tray with her back to the door.

"Ma'am," Elder said softly.

Sarah whirled around, surprised that anyone else was in the house. She stared at Elder and her expression softened. "Mr. Elder," she said, showing every bit of the strain of the last few days.

Elder nodded and pulled off his hat. Patrick did likewise.

"Please. Sit down. Let me get you two something to eat."

"Thank you," Elder said.

"Yes, ma'am," Patrick replied.

Elder and Patrick sat. Sarah poured them coffee in big, thick, round-handled cups. She sliced bread and cheese, and slabs of smoked ham and put the plate on the table, and then she sat across from Elder and caught him in her intense gaze.

"Mr. Elder, they have Matthew."

"Yes, ma'am, I know they do."

"We have to get him out of there. Those men are insane. They're worse than animals and I will not let my son suffer another day with them." She put her face in her hands, but she did not cry.

"Ma'am — Sarah," Elder said as he arose and put a hand on her shoulder. "We're going to do everything we can. We just need a little time, that's all."

Then he gently turned her face up so he could see her eyes. "Promise me you won't do anything to try to get Matthew back on your own," he said, his voice soft but firm.

Sarah looked up at Elder. Her eyes teared up and she set her jaw.

"Promise me."

Sarah nodded. "I promise, but please, I don't want my boy to spend another night there," she said.

"I understand — just give us some time."

Sarah regained her composure and she took a deep breath. She dabbed at the corners of her eyes with her finger.

Patrick stood. "Mrs. Stanford, would it be all right for us to go up and see Milo for a few minutes?"

Sarah smiled a small smile. "Yes, of

course. I was just going to take him his lunch. Please, come on up. He will be very happy to see you both."

Elder and Patrick followed Sarah up the stairs and into the old sheriff's room. Milo Dunn lay propped up on two goose-down pillows, the sheet pulled up around his shoulders and his eyes closed. His big white moustache moved, and he pulled his good arm out from beneath the sheet and scratched his nose.

"Mr. Dunn," Sarah whispered. "You have company."

The sheriff's eyes opened and it took him a moment to focus, then he smiled. "Well, ain't you a pair."

"Morning, Sheriff," Patrick said.

"How you feeling, Milo?" asked Elder.

"A lot better since I got me a real doctor," Dunn said, as he winked at Patrick.

Patrick smiled and looked over at Sarah. "Well, I hope he don't complain as much to you as he did to me."

Sarah smiled and turned back toward the door. "I'll be right downstairs if you need me, Milo," she said, as she left the room.

The three men exchanged small talk for a quarter of an hour before the sheriff finally leaned back against his stacked pillows and closed his eyes. He rubbed his eyes with his good hand and yawned. Then he opened his eyes and looked back at Elder and over at Patrick. "You boys didn't come here just to pass the day."

"No, fact is, we didn't," said Patrick.

"Milo," said Elder, as he sat on the edge of the old man's bed, "I want you to swear me and Patrick in as deputies. This situation isn't going to get any better, and I think it's time to look the devil in the eye."

"You mean Ike Smith?"

Elder nodded.

Milo rubbed his forehead; his expression appeared strained and tired. "J.D., I don't know about that one. He ain't like no one you or me ever went up against before. I seen a bunch of them in my time, but he's a first for me."

"You think about what you would do in my place, Milo. You know I don't have any other choice."

Milo shook his head and he waited a long time before he said anything. "No, no, you don't. I wish you did, but you don't." He looked up at Patrick. "Son, go over there to that top drawer," he said pointing to the tall dresser against the wall. "There's two or three badges in there, I think."

Patrick walked over to the dresser. He pulled the top drawer open slowly, and began to rummage through its contents.

"Over on the right side," the sheriff said. "Underneath that pile of papers, I believe."

Patrick moved a stack of papers, withdrew two badges, and handed them to the old man. The sheriff took them, checked the pins on the backs, and rubbed each one on his blanket.

"Raise your right hands," he instructed. Patrick and Elder did.

"Do you swear to uphold the laws of the Territory of Montana to the best of your ability, so help you God?"

"I do," said Elder.

"I do," said Patrick.

"You are hereby appointed to the office of Deputy Sheriff. Good luck to you both."

He handed each one a badge, then gazed out the window and watched the clouds billow up white and grand against a sky as blue as glacier water. "You know I'd be with you boys if I could."

He looked ancient and distant.

Patrick touched the old man's arm. "We know you would Milo."

"There isn't anyone we'd rather have," Elder said, then he and Patrick collected themselves and walked toward the door. They stopped at the doorway.

"J.D., you can't meet one like him halfway," the sheriff said. "Not ever."

"I'll remember that," Elder said.

Milo nodded and they left.

Elder and Patrick stopped on the porch and pinned on their badges, then they started down the street and neither spoke until they were away from the house.

"Well, what's your plan?" Patrick asked.

Elder looked over at Patrick. "I don't have one."

Elder's expression was uncertain and he thought for a moment before he continued. "Look, Pat. I need to get inside with the boy. I've got to talk to him and find a way to get him out of there."

Elder studied the dust on his boots. His voice fell to a whisper. "They're going to kill Bill and Cyrus and the boy, Patrick."

Elder raised his head and looked at the young cowboy. Patrick dropped his gaze and turned his head up the street in the direction of the saloon. "Yeah, I know," he said. Then Patrick turned and regarded Elder with serious concern. "But, you can't get in there, J.D. They'd shoot you quick as a wink and not give it a second thought."

"I don't have any doubts about that," Elder said. "They don't have any reason to know me by name, do they, Pat?"

Patrick thought. "Maybe they do," he

216

replied. "Milo said he asked them if they got those Rafter E horses from J.D. Elder, and they said they did. I reckon by that they know your name. But then, I suppose they probably think you're dead, by the way they left you."

"I suppose," Elder said. "It just wouldn't do any good for them to know who I am when I get inside — they may decide to finish the job early."

When they got inside the sheriff's office Elder laid down his rifle. He slipped his belt knife into his boot and pulled his pant leg down over it.

"Patrick, I'd like you to be watching the front door. Send two men around behind the saloon to keep an eye out there. We won't know what to expect, so just be ready and don't let them get to their horses under any circumstances, you understand?"

"I'm with you J.D.," Patrick replied. "But, try to give me some kind of sign if you can."

"I will, Pat," Elder said, then he walked out the door and started down the plank board sidewalk toward the saloon, favoring his bad leg.

TWENTY-FOUR

Ike Smith spoke slowly but firmly. "Raymond, bring me the boy." His voice sounded thick and tired, and he began to hack and cough until his eyes watered, then he spat and turned toward Bill Nichols and wiped his wet mouth on his coat sleeve.

"Reach me that bottle," he said pointing in the general direction of the back bar with its rows of flint glass whiskey bottles lined up one-deep before a hazy mirror that made the selection appear greater than it was.

"This one?" Nichols asked.

Ike nodded without looking up. "That'll do." He took to hacking and spat another wad, red with blood, onto the floor where he stood.

Cyrus Tull sat at a table near the bar. He glanced at the bloody wad and looked back up at Ike. Ike saw the questioning look on Tull's face.

"Don't get your hopes up."

Tull turned away to prevent the expression on his face from betraying the hate in his heart.

Nichols set the bottle on the bar in front of Ike. Ike took it in one hand, pulled the cork with the other, then tipped the bottle back and took three long swallows. He set the heel of the bottle on the bar, but did not take his hand from it. His eyes watered up again and he wheezed.

Ike's voice rasped from the whiskey. "The boy, bring him here like I told you."

He slapped his bear paw of a hand down hard against the bar top and sent an echo ringing through the high-ceilinged room. "Now!"

Raymond jumped from his chair and sent it crashing behind him as he scurried to the back room where the boy lay tied alone in the dark. Raymond untied the boy's hands and unhitched the tether from a thick eyebolt buried in a wall-beam.

Raymond jerked the boy forward. His voice was troubled and urgent. "Come on."

"Don't pull on me," the boy said and he jerked the tether free from Raymond's hand. "I heard him."

Raymond reached for the loose end of the tether. The boy snatched it from the dullard's reach, then strode past him, and into the dull light of the bar. He narrowed his eyes and kept walking.

"Hey," Raymond said, but Matthew ignored him.

When he got up alongside Ike, Matthew stood looking up at the immense bulk of the man whose tattered rags hung upon him, filthy and reeking. Ike stood with his eyes closed, pinching the bridge of his fleshy nose between his thumb and his index finger.

Matthew waited and Ike disregarded him.

"What?" Matthew finally said, his tone impatient and disrespectful.

Ike dropped his hand from his face, opened his eyes, and turned his massive head slowly. His small, red eyes bore into the boy. "What? Is that what you said, boy?"

"Yeah . . . what?" Matthew said again, then he waited for a crashing blow to follow, but none did.

Raymond's face drained of its color and he shrunk to the far wall. Sandoval straightened up in his chair, and they both watched Ike with great intensity. Tull and Nichols tensed and Nichols shook his head side to side, hoping to get the boy's attention without drawing notice from Ike Smith.

"What." Ike weighed the word and his eyes narrowed. He cleared his throat and spat. He then reached down, grabbed up the front of the boy's shirt in his enormous hand and lifted him off his feet. He set the boy down roughly, like a rag doll upon the bar.

Matthew swung his fist at the heavy arm and, when he connected, it had no impact and Ike held him there until the boy felt like his chest would collapse. When Ike released his grip, the boy wheezed and sucked in a deep breath. He watched the general with a tentative look, but said nothing and sat perfectly still.

"You could have made a soldier," Ike said with a hint of regret in his voice. "You had the makings of a good one."

Matthew glared at him, tight-jawed and apprehensive.

"As it is now, you ain't no better off than the rest of them." Ike picked up the whiskey bottle, tilted it back and forth slowly, and looked down the throat of it with one eye closed. "You know, boy, you had the opportunity." He paused. "You had the opportunity and the guts to be a real soldier."

Then Ike opened the closed eye and his gaze was hot and wild. He turned his massive head to the boy and Matthew's resolve turned to fear. He felt his courage leave him and he felt sick in the pit of his stomach.

His insides trembled and tears welled up hard and demanding, but he held them back. His eyes locked onto the bloodshot, pig eyes of the general, and he dared not, could not, divert them.

"Why did you desert us, boy?" The general's raspy voice pitched halfway between rage and disappointment as he slammed his fist to the bar.

Matthew flinched and shuddered. "Because you ain't real soldiers," he blurted out against his better judgment. "And I ain't no private. You're just drunks that kill old people and ladies and little kids — and I hate you all."

Then he leapt from the bar and bolted for the door. He had the door open and headed for the street before Ike could turn around. Sandoval and Raymond stood at the back of the room, and Raymond ran for the door at the same time Sandoval fired a blast from the ten-gauge. Matthew cleared the doorway and rounded the corner by the shot-out window when the door slammed shut behind him from the impact of the slugs. The rawhide thong about his neck fouled beneath the closed door and when he reached the end of the leash, it jerked him down.

The thong tightened and pulled him back toward the doorway and choked off his voice. Matthew's eyes bulged in his head and his tongue swelled too big for his mouth. His eyes rolled and he could barely see the dark shadow reach for him at the same time the door swung open and Raymond stood there with the other end of the rawhide gripped in his hand.

J.D. Elder was in the street and headed for the saloon at the same time Matthew made his exit. He reached the boy the same time the boy reached the end of the slack in the rawhide leash knotted about his neck. Elder caught the boy up, lifted him to his feet, and pulled enough slack in the string to give the boy air. Matthew gasped and coughed, and his hands shook as he tried to get his bearings.

"Well, looky here," said Raymond, waving the muzzle of the shotgun at Elder and the boy. "Ike, come take a look. We got us another one."

"Kill them both," Ike ordered from the shadows just inside the doorway.

Raymond grinned, his brown, tobacco-stained teeth showing like faulty snags in the bright sunlight. He ratcheted back the double hammers and giggled like the idiot he was. When he did, Elder stepped forward and, in one quick motion, slapped the muzzle of the shotgun around, seized him about the neck, and wrestled the weapon from him.

"Run," Elder ordered the boy as he jerked the rawhide string from Raymond's grasp. He gave the boy a push and the boy ran. For every part of him that wanted to pull the trigger and watch Raymond die, Elder could not exchange the temptation of that moment of revenge for the lives of those Ike held hostage inside. He shouted to the dark doorway.

"Won't no harm come to your man here unless you bring it on him."

A calm voice, raspy and deliberate, spoke from the darkness. "Let him be. Consider him a fair trade for the boy. We got no more business here. Turn him loose and we'll be on our way."

Elder pushed Raymond toward the doorway and kept the shotgun. Raymond stumbled inside and, when Elder turned to follow the boy, he looked up in time to see the mulatto step out into the sunlight and snatch the boy up and drag him into the alley. Matthew screamed and Elder hesitated for a brief moment. Before Elder could take his first step, a whiskey-soaked voice behind him caught him up short.

"Drop the scattergun," it said. "Then turn around nice and slow."

Elder dropped his eyes to the breach of the shotgun Ike held. The hammers were still back and set. Elder bent forward with Raymond's shotgun held in front of him as he gently reached to place it on the plank boardwalk.

"Easy now," Ike said.

Then, Elder dropped to the ground and swung the muzzle around as he did so. He squeezed both triggers at the same time, and a swarm of shotgun pellets ripped into the thick body of Ike Smith, scattering cloth remnants and bloody flesh onto the wall behind the general. Ike tottered, but did not fall. His clothes ran red from his mid-section to his thighs and he tottered back and forth, like a great tree cut away but balancing on its stump before it falls to the earth.

Ike blinked his small red eyes, and the eyes looked out past Elder, past the street, past the town, and past his own life. Then he smiled. He slumped slowly and gracefully to the plank boards, and he leaned up against the wall of the saloon. His shotgun lay next to his unfeeling legs and he looked down at the wet holes in his coat and in his trousers.

"Raymond," he said in a clear voice, "I been shot."

Raymond stood in the doorway, the large bore of a rifle trained on Elder. Behind him, the mulatto held the boy with the muzzle of his shotgun pressed against the boy's back. Raymond's hands shook.

"What should I do, Ike?"

"Get me inside," Ike whispered. "Bring him too. I want him kept alive." Ike nodded toward Elder.

"Help me get him in," Raymond screamed at Elder.

Elder threw down the shotgun and kicked Ike's weapon out of the way as he hefted one massive arm and shoulder while Raymond lifted on the other side. They managed to get Ike inside and laid him out on the floor near the door.

Ike gestured with his finger, and Raymond stepped forth and kneeled at his side. Ike gestured him closer, and Raymond placed his ear close to Ike's face. Raymond stood, walked to the bar, and returned with a fresh bottle of whiskey. He held Ike's head and Ike drank until the amber liquid overflowed, gushed out, and ran down his chin, his neck, and onto the floor. Ike coughed and whiskey ran from his nose and, when it stopped, he made no attempt to clean himself, and no offer was made by Raymond or Sandoval.

Raymond stood by the boy and watched

his brother bleed. "It's your fault," he screamed at the boy, and then he struck the boy on the side of the head with his closed fist and sent the boy reeling to the floor.

Elder stood in the boy's defense, but Sandoval backed him down with the shotgun and Raymond turned on him with the rifle. Raymond's hands shook and he waivered in indecision. Only Ike's command stood between Elder and the explosion of muzzle flash from the rifle held by the dullard.

"Don't you move," Raymond warned.

Then he turned to Bill Nichols and waved the rifle wildly about the room. "Help him," he ordered, gesturing toward Ike's bleeding carcass.

"I'm no doctor," Nichols protested.

"I don't care if you ain't no doctor, just do something to make him stop bleeding."

"What do you want me to do?"

"I don't know. Shut up. Just shut up for a minute."

Raymond appeared confused and frantic. His eyes darted about the room, looking for something. His confusion turned to desperation, and his expression turned wild with no reason about it. As his composure deteriorated, he began to breathe heavily and his hand twitched.

"Raymond," the gravelly voice from the floor said just above a whisper. "Come here."

Raymond chewed his tongue and his head stopped its jerky movements. "Ike?"

"Come here," said the gravelly voice again.

"Here I come, Ike. Here I come."

Raymond dropped to his knees beside his brother and put his ear close. Ike spoke, but only the dullard heard him. Raymond nodded and kept nodding, and then he stood. Sandoval stood as well. He waited for what he knew would be the calling-down of fire and brimstone, and the extermination of every man in the room, including the boy.

Both men stood and surveyed the room. Elder moved to a position that put himself in a crossfire between the two. Tull and Nichols edged over to the bar for cover. Matthew slid unnoticed along the floor to a chair that held one of the spare shotguns he knew to be loaded.

Sandoval looked at Raymond then over at Ike and back to Raymond. If he had a preference for staying or leaving, it did not show. And if he had a preference for killing or sparing the lives of those he was about to execute, that was equally undetectable in his eyes or his demeanor.

In that brief interlude where time seemed

suspended and there was no clear course to be taken save that of the dolt, upon whose next move would determine the fate of every man in the room, Ike rose to his feet.

Blood ran down his shirt and pooled at his feet. For all the outward damage to his ponderous body, Ike stood with great authority and a frighteningly cold expression. He commanded the attention of everyone in that half-lit prison, and the eyes of those in attendance never moved from him.

He held up one hand with his finger extended to make a talking point and, as his lips formed the words, a thunderous explosion of smoke and fire shook the room and he fell back into a mass of gore that had once been his midsection. His blank eyes stared at the ceiling and his expression was soft and restful. They never saw Matthew standing there with the smoking shotgun in his small hands. And they never saw the hatred in the eyes of the boy when he discharged the second unspent barrel.

Raymond stared in disbelief as Ike's body convulsed and his legs shook, then all was quiet. Elder lunged at Raymond and wrestled the rifle from his grip and took him to the ground. Sandoval fired a single blast from his ten-gauge. It missed Elder and a portion of the spreading load struck Nichols and sent him to the floor.

Sandoval bolted for the back door with no regard for Raymond or Ike and no regard for those who stood immobilized by the sudden turn of circumstances.

TWENTY-FIVE

The gunsmoke that filled the room coiled upward and hovered about in the stale air, and rose to the cracked and yellowed ceiling. Shafts of brilliant sunlight split the smoke and cut across the room at an oblique angle and, for a moment, the silence that ensued was that of a mute kaleidoscopic dream in which no one spoke and nothing moved, and when something did move, it made no sound. And the red of the dreamscape that was blood was only a color wildly splashed about and it had no significance. And there was no significance to the blank stare of Ike Smith, whose eyes were the eyes of a corpse, no more and no less dead than those he himself dispatched without regard.

Though his ragged coat ran wet and dark with blood and his flesh was badly torn, he lay composed in a manner of one of great authority and fearsome coldness, as in his own death he might at any time rise to command his derelict detachment to arms. His eyes, rendered hollow and empty, and devoid of color, saw blindly into another dimension, and his expression revealed nothing.

In the smoky haze, J.D. Elder wobbled on his knees and Matthew Stanford let the long-barreled shotgun sag in his grip. Both he and the enormous gun seemed suspended in time.

Then, from some deep and primitive place within the dull-witted brother, a chilling wail stabbed the silence and Raymond rose to his feet, knife in hand, and descended upon the boy, hacking the air and slashing wildly and cursing through his own drool.

Matthew reeled wide-eyed and threw his arm up to protect his face and took three furious lacerations before Elder hurled himself into Raymond. Raymond staggered off-balance, but recovered with the strength of a mad man and turned his blade on Elder. Raymond plunged his knife downward and Elder raised his hands up to protect himself. The sharp edge of the blade slashed through Elders forearms, and the knife-edge burned like fire and the cuts in his flesh ran wet, warm, and red. Elder gripped the wrists of the dolt and pulled him down into his arms. Raymond pulled back and the blade of the knife slid through the fingers of Elder, who held on.

Raymond hesitated. Elder rose to his feet, released the knife with his right hand and delivered Raymond a powerful blow to the head that sent the dolt to his haunches. Raymond tottered and Elder dealt him another and another until the fight was out of him and he slumped backward onto the floor in a dark pool of his brother's blood.

Elder turned toward the boy. The front door of the saloon exploded open, and Patrick Arbuckle crashed into the room, his eyes wild and his rifle searching out a target.

"J.D.," he yelled into the half-light.

"Patrick. It's over. Don't shoot." Elder shouted back as he stood and covered the boy.

Patrick stood full-height and looked about the room. He surveyed the confusion before him with disbelieving eyes. The room smelled of blood, and the immense carcass of Ike Smith was afloat in it. Blood ran from Elder's hands and blood soaked Matthew's coat sleeve, and Patrick Arbuckle staggered back a step.

He laid his rifle on a table and rushed to Elder and the boy. He looked back toward the bar.

"Cyrus, run get us some help in here,

fast," he ordered. Cyrus Tull headed for the door. Bill Nichols' wounds were minor and he grabbed a handful of rags and a half-empty whiskey bottle. He handed Patrick the bottle and dropped the rags on the chair next to the boy.

"Here," Nichols said to Elder. "Take this and wrap those hands."

Elder took the rag that appeared to have been a man's muslin shirt at one time. Then, he reached down, and caught the boy by the collar and lifted him to his feet.

"You all right?" he asked.

Matthew nodded. "Yeah I'm all right."

"Sit here," Elder said, motioning to the chair behind the boy.

Matthew sat back in the chair, but held his bleeding arm up against his chest.

"Let's get that coat and shirt off of you," Elder said as he helped the boy shed the tattered and filthy clothing.

He looked at the boy's arm and dabbed it with a clean rag until the blood ran freely.

"Could have been worse," Elder said.

"Could have been better," the boy said, looking Elder directly in the eye.

Elder looked back at the boy and smiled a half smile. "It could have been better."

Elder wrapped the wounds and stopped the bleeding.

Raymond rolled his head and moaned.

Elder glanced over at Raymond then looked directly at Patrick. "Patrick, take him back to the jail and watch him close. That yellow-eyed one is still out there. He might come back. I'll take the boy to his mother."

When Elder and the boy were halfway to the door, Cyrus Tull and four or five other men crowded into the saloon, some armed with rifles, others with nothing more than curiosity. They conversed among themselves and all talked at once to Elder as he excused himself and walked with the boy past them and into the street.

Elder put his hand on the boy's shoulder and they walked in silence down the plank boardwalk, past the sheriff's office and the hotel and the dry goods store and the blacksmith's shop. At the end of the walk they turned right and strode past the school-house, then stopped at the bottom of the steps of Milo Dunn's place.

The boy looked up at Elder. "Why we coming here?" he asked.

"Your mother's here taking care of the sheriff and waiting for you," Elder replied. "You ready to go in and see her?"

"She's gonna be mad," Matthew said. "I'm a mess."

Elder smiled. "Yeah, you are."

When they stepped onto the landing, Elder reached out and slowly opened the door. The boy stood behind him as Elder stuck his head in to announce their presence.

"Hello," he said. "Mrs. Stanford. Anybody?"

"Mr. Elder," a female voice said from the kitchen followed by Sarah Stanford as she rounded the hallway corner wiping her hands on her apron.

Elder stepped aside and Matthew stood in the doorway. When he saw his mother, he ran and threw his arms around her and she embraced him, and wept and held him tightly and rocked him back and forth.

"Oh my baby — Matthew — sweetheart. I can't believe it. I can't believe you're here."

Her tears streamed and she kissed his head, and dropped to her knees and kissed his face. She looked at him and dabbed at her tears with the corner of her apron, then laughed as she held him at arm's length.

"You're a mess," she said from behind her tears and smile.

Matthew looked back at Elder. Elder shrugged.

"What?" Sarah asked. "What is it?" She smiled.

"It's nothing Momma," Matthew replied.

His voice sounded old and tired.

Sarah's smile faded to a half smile and, for a moment, she felt an uncomfortable sense of loss. She saw in it his eyes. Eyes that looked hard around the edges. Eyes that had seen too much. Elder noticed it and Matthew felt it.

Then, Sarah stood, brushed the apron smooth and put her arm around Matthew's shoulders.

"Your arm, it's bleeding. Come in here and let me look at that. Oh, Mr. Elder, you're bleeding too. Both of you come in here now."

She pulled her son to her breast and kissed him on top of his filthy head. She dressed the wounds and never stopped looking at her son.

"It's so good to have you back home," she said. "Now go on upstairs, first door on the left, and get out of those disgusting clothes. I'll be right up."

She turned to Elder.

"Mr. Elder." Her eyes teared and she smiled warmly. "How can I ever repay you?"

"No need, Sarah," Elder said softly.

"I'm sorry, J.D.," she said as she shook her head and held her arms tight around herself. "I didn't mean to sound so formal — it's just that my head is reeling. I haven't slept three hours straight through since you left and it seems like you have been gone forever."

Elder turned a chair from the table. "Here, sit down for a minute."

Sarah sank into the chair, closed her eyes and sighed.

"I've prayed for this moment so long it seems like a dream."

She opened her eyes and turned her head towards Elder, who sat on the table edge and watched her. She reached out and took both his hands in hers. She looked at the blood-soaked bandages and back up at Elder.

"Thank you so much," she said, her cheeks running wet and her smile quivering with uncertainty.

Elder stepped closer and held her head against his chest.

She closed her eyes and whispered in a soft, unsteady voice. "J.D., I don't know what I'm going to do."

Sarah began to weep openly. She sobbed and the tears rushed forth and she held his arm tightly to her.

"Preacher's gone." The words choked in her throat and fouled on her lips. "Mrs. Dunn . . ." her voice trailed off. She shook her head. "I don't know if Milo's going to make it or not, and I don't know what else to do for him."

Then, like a spiritual cleansing of saving grace at the altar of redemption, Sarah Stanford set her tangled emotions free and her body racked with deep sobs as she gave in to the outpouring of her soul and doubts and fears.

Elder held her. His fingers smoothed her hair and he searched for the right words to say, but could not find any so he just held her. He looked down at her soft hair and strong hands and felt as though his heart lay open.

For what seemed a very long time, she remained with her head against his chest and he with his hand on her hair, long after the tears stopped. Elder wanted to hold her close to him, wanted to take her in his arms. He turned his head to the window and in the glass saw their reflection. His face flushed.

He stepped back and she turned her face up to him. She blinked and smiled.

"I'm sorry. I didn't mean to embarrass you."

"It's not that. It's just, well — I don't know if I have any right to feel what I'm feeling right now and I don't want to be . . ."

"Mr. Elder," she interrupted. "I don't

know if you know what it feels like to have everything in the world that means anything to you taken away. I lost my husband and it broke my heart. There were times when I thought I would never see my son again. I didn't know if you were alive or dead. There were nights when I was sure Milo wouldn't make it until morning. And those long nights I listened to him barely able to take a breath I stared at a picture of Mrs. Dunn and wondered if she would have done anything differently if she knew how fleeting her life would be."

Sarah paused, took a deep breath and spoke more slowly. "She was a wonderful, proper woman, J.D. But, I truly believe that if she could have even one day back she wouldn't waste a second of it fretting about what may or may not be proper."

Elder shifted his weight from one boot to the other.

"Sarah, I buried a wife and child who meant more to me than life itself. I came here wanting nothing more than to be alone. To find a quiet place where I fit into and wouldn't feel I had to explain myself to anyone. Something changed all that and I'm still trying to understand it."

Sarah stood, faced Elder and held his

hands in hers as she looked up at him and smiled.

"Friends?"

Elder smiled and nodded and he wrapped her in his arms and held her and she held him.

"Better get that water going," he said finally. "That boy of yours could sure use a bath."

"No offense," she said, as she backed away, "but a hot bath wouldn't hurt you any either."

She laughed. Elder grinned.

"Is it all right if I go on up and look in on Milo?"

"That's fine, but if he is sleeping, please don't wake him. He's so weak and frail I want him to get all the rest he can."

"No ma'am, I won't."

"J.D.?" she said as Elder started for the stairs. "Is the killing over?" Concern lined her face and her expression reached out for his reassurance.

Elder weighed his answer then broke eye contact before he spoke.

"It's over."

He set a boot on the first step then turned back toward her to tell her what he truly felt; but when she looked up at him with uncertain eyes he lied to her again. "It's all over."

TWENTY-SIX

Milo Dunn's condition improved over the next week, and he appeared to have taken a turn for the better. On Sunday morning, a bank of cirrus clouds piled up in a brilliant, white drift against an aquamarine sky while the old sheriff napped outside on the porch in the warm sunlight. He awoke and sat quietly, his eyes taking in all the old familiar sights about him. He tilted slightly, his frail body propped in Mrs. Dunn's rocker and held up with pillows on each side.

Sarah closed the door softly behind her. She smiled and asked how he was. Then she gently tucked the blanket up under his arms. He said he was fine. Then he smiled and thanked her. She left, and when she returned with his tea, his head lay tilted to the side and he was dead.

The next day she stood alone over Milo Dunn's grave, long after the others paid their respects and left. She wept and placed upon the freshly spaded ground wild flowers picked from the meadow behind the Dunn house. Upon the next grave, where the mounded earth had not yet settled, Sarah arranged a small bouquet for Mrs. Dunn. Sarah smiled faintly behind her tears as she laid the flowers just so. These were Mrs. Dunn's wild flowers; picked from those that grew along the oft-traveled path from her back porch to a sitting place beneath a wind-twisted chokecherry tree. A place where Mrs. Dunn and the sheriff sat in the evenings and told each other about their day and sometimes just held hands and watched the sunset or the clouds roll up against the mountain peaks. Now the two old wooden chairs sat starkly vacant and cold.

Sarah crossed the graveyard to an unkempt corner where a mound of freshly turned earth, presided over by a temporary wooden cross, held the body of Ike Smith. She read his name and her anger flared. She paused. Her breathing turned rapid and shallow, her hands shook, and she clinched her teeth. In her heart, her feelings raged. She cursed and rebuked him, but no words came from her lips, and she cried no tears for him.

She stood there a long time, staring at the

cross and searching her soul for grace and mercy and some way to forgive Ike Smith his trespasses, but she found no compassion there and her heart filled with malice and for that, she felt ashamed. She turned and strode quickly away. In her heart, she wished the soul of Ike Smith condemned for eternity to her worst visions of a hell in which tortured souls found no quiet and no rest.

Sarah Stanford walked alone for hours along the wooded creek that ran east of town and skirted the cemetery. She attempted in vain to reconcile within herself the feelings of guilt and hatred, feelings that she never before permitted herself to have. Now, she had them all, and the right and wrong of it overwhelmed her. She stopped where the creek turned gently and the current eddied around large boulders casting their shadows across the water. Lichens grew close and thick on the north face of the giant rocks and white flowers no larger than a bird's eye crowded into a pocket of sunlit soil just above the water line.

She stopped and gathered her skirts up about her legs. She sat in the tall grass with her knees held in her arms and her chin propped up as she listened to the fast-moving water lap at the rocks and the rush of the wind as it hissed across the treetops. She sighed and closed her eyes in the palms of her hands. She sat there a long time as she attempted to put her thoughts in order.

She had no misconceptions about her relationship with the Reverend Stanford. In her own way, she loved him very much. It was a love without passion, a marriage of respect and practicality, maybe even admiration. It was a marriage filled with consideration and good intentions. A marriage that produced a son and gave Sarah a sense of fulfillment in the absence of the emotional intensity she desired but never acknowledged openly.

She remembered the many nights she had wept and the guilt she felt for wishing the reverend to be something he was not. It made her ashamed. She prayed for strength and forgiveness, and the guilt made her work harder to convince herself that what they shared was enough. The reverend was good-humored and kind. He did not deny his higher calling to her, but he knew in his heart that if forced to choose between his marriage and his work, he would have no choice at all. While Sarah refused to think about it, she knew he had unconsciously made the choice long ago.

Sarah mourned her husband's death, but

came to terms with it quickly in the face of almost losing Matthew. She missed him dearly and never let a day pass without telling Matthew to remember his father. She told him to be proud of his father's courage, and his commitment to his faith. Sarah reconciled herself to many things that changed her life in those long weeks since Clarence appeared at her door, but she could find no reconcilable grounds upon which to explain other feelings that stirred deep within her.

For a long time, as she sat there, Sarah agonized over uncomfortable feelings she tried to force back into some secret part of her mind. As though to think them was to say them, and she was not ready to confront them just yet. She shook her head and raised her face from her hands. She stood and walked to the water's edge. She paused, then walked downstream a few steps and bent to scoop up a handful of the cold water. She sipped it and the coolness of it stilled the anger stuck in her throat. She bent over, fetched another and held her wet hand to her cheeks and forehead.

Sarah looked skyward. "Preacher," she said. "Please help me find the strength."

She turned back toward the long shadows and started for town with thoughts of J.D.

Elder spinning in her mind.

Matthew was there to meet her on the steps when she got to the house just as the last light of day hung in a pale red glow along the western ridgeline.

"You all right?" he asked as she took his hand.

Sarah looked down at him, smiled, and they sat on the top step together. She pulled him close, hugged him, and kissed the top of his head.

"I'm going to be fine," she said. "How about you?"

He pulled away gently and sat on the steps. Sarah sat beside him.

"Sweetheart, what's wrong?"

He opened his hand for her to see.

"Can I have this?" he asked.

Sarah felt the tears welling in her eyes.

"That's your father's old watch — it doesn't even run."

"I know. Grandpa gave it to him."

He paused and looked back up at her.

"I'd just like to have it."

His eyes were wet, but he did not cry. Then, Sarah put her arms around the boy, and he put his around her and they both wept quietly.

"Your father would want very much for you to have it," she whispered.

Sarah rocked Matthew in her arms, and he felt like a little boy again. She rubbed his back and patted him the way she did when he was a baby, and he buried his face against her shoulder. She felt his tears soak her dress, and she held him tighter.

She held him like that a long time, and then he pulled back and wiped his nose on his shirtsleeve. He looked down at his feet and spoke softly.

"Momma, you know I done something really bad, don't you?" He sniffed and caught his runny nose on the back of his hand.

"Shhh . . . that's all right, sweetheart. You don't have to talk about it."

"I need to," he said. "I can't keep it in me no more, and I know daddy would be ashamed of me if he knew."

"Matthew, don't say that. Your father would never be ashamed of you. He loved you so much."

The boy stared down at his boots, then up at his mother. His eyes went cold, his expression grave.

"Momma, I killed General Smith. I shot him. And when he just stood there I shot him again. I watched him bleed and I was glad I did it."

Sarah's stomach twisted into a tight knot.

The young boy's expression was one of uncertainty and guilt, but his eyes held a coldness she had never seen before. She chose to dismiss it.

"Matthew," she said, as she took his hands in hers and looked into his eyes. "Mr. Elder told me what happened. What you did was a very brave thing. It's something you will never forget, but you must always remember that what you did saved your life and Mr. Elder's life and maybe the lives of lots of others. Ike Smith was an evil man, sweetheart, and he would have gone on killing. I'm so sorry you had to be the one to stop him, but at the same time I am very thankful you had the courage to do what you did."

"Do you think Daddy knows?"

"I don't know, but if he does, I'm sure he would feel the same way I do. I think he would be very, very proud of your courage."

"You do?"

"Yes, I do."

Matthew laid his head against her shoulder and neither spoke. They watched the stars come out and the moon come up and, though neither said it, it was as if that night, the Reverend Stanford looked down upon them from the heavens beyond the stars and the moon and the darkness.

Sarah shivered and stood, pulling Matthew up by the hand. "Come on, let's get inside. It's too cold out here."

The light from the doorway spilled out onto the porch and when the mother slowly pulled the door closed, the last of the light shone across the small meadow casting a fleeting luminous reflection in the cold, yellow eyes of the mulatto. He watched the door cut off the last sliver of the light as he rose from his haunches. He paused and contemplated for a moment, then he turned, and slipped ominously back into the woods.

Mother and child stood in the hallway, the mother looking for strength, the boy reliving his first taste of mindless violence.

TWENTY-SEVEN

Patrick Arbuckle and J.D. Elder looked at one another from across Dunn's old desk in the sheriff's office, their expressions drawn and their faces tired.

"J.D., we got a telegram back from the marshal this morning. He says it may be a week or two before he can get anyone up here to take Raymond Smith back to stand trial." Patrick Arbuckle stood and leaned against the doorframe.

Elder rose and walked unevenly to the window. He put a hand against the sash for balance and looked down the street as though he were expecting someone.

"Two weeks is a stretch," he said, and he paused a long time. "Where do you suppose Sandoval is right about now?"

Elder turned to face Patrick.

"Sandoval? I'd like to think he's a long way from here."

"Is that what you think?"

Patrick shook his head. "No, it ain't."

Elder waited. Patrick thought for a moment.

"You know he didn't have a horse," Patrick said. "A man afoot's got a lot working against him in this country. It bothers me some we never found a sign of him anywhere."

"It bothers me too. You know, there was no love lost between Sandoval and Raymond. I watched them two together, and I don't think Sandoval would throw water on Raymond if he was on fire. But, you know something else? I think Ike had a hold on Sandoval that might make Sandoval do things he ordinarily wouldn't."

"What are you saying?" Patrick asked.

"I'm saying I think Sandoval will be back for Raymond out of pure respect for Ike. Anyway, we got to expect it. If Sandoval looked to put distance between him and this place, he would have picked up a horse first thing. And we know he didn't do that — at least we don't think he did."

"I don't know, J.D. Sure seems he would have made a move by now if that were the case. You sure you ain't just a little spooked not knowing where he is?"

Elder looked at Patrick over a weak smile. "Could be," he said. "Could be."

"On the other hand," Patrick said, "you could be right. No reason not to be expecting it, I suppose."

"Can you keep three guards on Smith for the next couple of weeks?"

"I think so. Nobody's resting too easy the way it is with him in there and the other one out there somewhere," Patrick said, nodding first toward the cell and then broadly toward the mountains.

"Let's take a walk," Elder said. "We're going to need a plan."

Elder and Patrick walked out the back, past the cell, and into the alley behind the jail.

"You can put one man out here. He can cover the back door and both sides of the alley from right over there." Elder pointed to a doorway beneath a stairwell that offered some protection and reasonably good visibility up and down the alley.

"One man can cover the front door from the street and the other can stay inside and keep an eye on Raymond," Elder added.

"That should do. Might as well get started," Patrick said. "I'll get things lined out with the volunteers; give them time to get ready for tonight. This is not going to set well. Everyone's nervous enough as it is."

"I expect they have a right to be. They been through a lot," Elder said over his shoulder as he proceeded down the alley, leaving Patrick to tend to matters at the jail.

Elder walked slowly and thought about Sarah and Matthew, uneasy knowing they were alone at the edge of town in Dunn's big house with no one to watch over them. He reached over and carefully rubbed his mending arm with his bandaged hand and touched the ribs that felt raw and tender. He remembered waking that first night to see Sarah standing over him, vigilant, tired, and beautiful. Every feature of her face stuck in his mind like a photograph. Her eyes honest, warm and direct, her high cheekbones and her hair pulled back, not tended to, but somehow alluring as long, loose strands fell in a soft frame at the sides of her face. Her smile, restrained but given easily, made her face radiate a captivating image that compelled Elder to gaze at her.

Even now, each time Sarah smiled, Elder found himself awkwardly unable to keep from staring. He knew she was aware of the effect she had on him, yet she made no effort to let him off easy. Elder pictured her looking up at him through the corner of her eye and smiling as she often did when conversation ran thin. In his mind, he was certain she did it just to watch him fumble for words, for when he did so she would look away and laugh, and squeeze his hand playfully.

Elder climbed the front steps and knocked on the front door. "Sarah. It's me, J.D. Elder," he called through the bolted door.

"Coming," he heard Sarah's voice say from inside.

She opened the door and invited Elder in with a smile.

"What brings you here tonight?"

Elder's expression was serious and concerned.

"I need to talk to Matt."

Matthew entered the room and looked at Elder but did not speak.

"Have a seat, Matt."

The boy weighed the name and the sound of the name in his mind. No one called him Matt, and his initial reaction was to correct Elder, but he said it to himself and it felt like it fit, and it felt like a man's name, and the boy pulled the chair closer and sat. He crossed his boots under the chair, and rested his chin in his hand, as he looked Elder directly in the eye.

"Matt, we got a problem and I'm going to need your help," Elder said, taking the chair across from the boy.

"What kind of problem?"

"It's Raymond and Sandoval." He paused while the two names sunk in with the boy, and the boy's expression paled.

Sarah stood near the stove and watched the conversation but remained silent, her arms wrapped about herself. Never had she witnessed the reverend engage Matthew man to man. It was always father to son or preacher to boy, but never man to man, and it awed her to see how quickly and easily Matthew responded to Elder. She smiled and her face radiated admiration for J.D. Elder.

"The marshal can't come for Raymond for another week or two," Elder said. "That means we have to keep him in our jail here. It also means Sandoval may come back for him."

Matthew dropped his eyes to stare vacantly at the table, and he folded his hands in his lap.

"Sandoval won't let anyone take Raymond," the boy said in almost a whisper.

A chill ran down Sarah's back and Elder sat back in his chair.

"You don't think so?" Elder replied.

"No, sir," Matthew said. "I don't."

"Why's that?"

"Just 'cause General Ike wouldn't allow it."

"But, Ike is dead," Sarah interrupted, as though perhaps her protest would make a difference.

"Don't matter."

"Matt's right, Sarah," Elder said. "Sandoval has no feelings for anyone or anything, but he has a loyalty to Ike Smith, dead or alive, that I believe he will honor."

Elder looked over to Matthew.

"Is that the way you see it, Matt?"

"Yes, sir. That's the way it is."

"Well then, we'll have to expect Sandoval to be back. When he does show up we can expect trouble," Elder said. "And Matt, that's why your mother was worried about where you were tonight. You understand that, don't you?"

Matthew nodded. He stood and walked over to his mother. He looked up at her and put his arms around her, and she pulled him close to her.

"Sorry," he said.

"That's all right, you didn't know," Sarah replied.

Sarah looked up at Elder and extended her hand to his.

"Thank you, J.D."

Elder squeezed her fingers gently and smiled.

The soft light of the oil lamp reflected its image in the kitchen window glass. Its flame flickered and danced, and Elder, from the corner of his eye, saw his image in the glass and watched his shadow move behind him on the wall as the flame of the lamp flared and twisted. In the dark glass of the window, he saw the reflections of Sarah and the boy and the mirror image of the room. Behind the images, for but a fleeting moment, there was a man Elder did not see. The man watched Elder and the woman, and the boy, through narrow amber eyes and he was invisible. Then, without a sound, without any sign that he had ever been there, the man vanished into the moonlit shadows of the night.

TWENTY-EIGHT

"Hey, can anyone hear me?" Raymond wailed from the corner of his cell with his face pressed against the bars and his eyes searching the narrow patch of light from the half-closed doorway. "Is anybody there?"

Patrick Arbuckle sat with his legs crossed and studied the spur on his boot as he spun the rowel with his finger and tried to ignore Raymond's incessant pleading. Patrick checked and rechecked the ammunition and the rifles, read the wanted posters again, then paced about the small office. All the while Raymond kept at it.

"My slop bucket's full — y'all want me just to use the floor?"

Patrick turned his head in the direction of Raymond's voice and shouted back.

"You make a mess on that floor and you'll sleep in it," Patrick answered as he swung the hall door full open and approached the cell.

"Put the bucket by the door, and then put your face up against the back wall."

Raymond nudged the bucket forward with his foot and waited beside it for Patrick to open the cell door. Patrick looked up from under his hat brim, his expression cold and short of patience.

"Do like I told you."

"Yes, sir."

Patrick glared at Raymond and Raymond backed against the wall.

"Turn and face the wall and put your hands flat above your head."

Raymond did so and over his shoulder he said, "Kinda touchy, ain't you?"

"Don't push me."

Patrick turned the key in the lock. The iron tumblers clunked into place and he edged the door open.

"If it was up to me, you'd be laying up beside your brother right now."

"Yeah, well, if Ike was here you wouldn't be so smart."

Patrick backed out, his voice barely a whisper, "Is that so?"

"Yes, sir, it is so," Raymond replied. "My brother ain't through with y'all yet."

"Your brother's dead."

"Don't matter none. You'll see."

Raymond turned and sat on his mattress

with one foot up. Patrick glanced back at him then turned away, unnerved by Raymond's smile and the mindless look in his eye. When Patrick stepped out into the alley, he heard Raymond shuffle across the cell.

"Can you hurry it up with that slop bucket — I'm about to bust," Raymond shouted.

Patrick emptied the bucket in a ditch at the end of the alley and refilled it up a quarter of the way with clean water and returned to the cell to find Raymond standing with his trousers hanging dark and heavy and a puddle at his feet.

Patrick's face went red and he clenched his jaw. He took a breath and shook his head. "Have it any way you like it. Now back against the wall."

Raymond complied and Patrick set the bucket inside the cell. Patrick's eyes bore into Raymond's eyes, and Raymond grinned at him like some mute creature inbred and aberrant, with no past and no future.

"I'm hungry," Raymond said.

Patrick locked the cell and double-checked it. "You can stay hungry," he said over his shoulder. Then he closed the hallway door behind him and sat down at the sheriff's desk.

"Coffee and a bisquit'll do me," Raymond's muffled voice said through the closed door. "Sheriff . . . y'all hear me? Sheriff? Sher . . . riff. Hello. Hey, someone. It ain't fair you not giving me no supper."

Patrick ignored Raymond's whining and more than an hour past midnight the complaining stopped. Patrick listened at the door. He heard the sound of heavy breathing and Raymond mumbling in his sleep. He sat out the night with his boots on and his pistol before him with the hammer cocked. He checked on the front and rear guards every hour. He napped in between, and the night passed without incident. In the morning, three volunteers relieved Patrick and his men. At midnight three more, J.D. Elder among them, took over the night shift, and those dark hours passed cold, strained, and slow.

The next four days and nights were the same, and by the fifth night, the volunteers lost their taste for the mission, and their talk, which early on was bold and conceited, degenerated to criticism and doubt. One by one, they dropped from the roster until only Elder and Patrick and two others remained. Those that defected did so in a boastful manner and everywhere they congregated they criticized Elder's over-cautious concern and whispered behind his back, but when they met him on the street, they nodded, touched their hats, and said good morning.

At noon Elder gathered about him the last of his small force. Patrick Arbuckle attended with a conviction of purpose no less committed than that of Elder himself. Clarence stood there stark, rigid, and humorless, his expression distant and vacant, his resolve unshakable. At the back of the office Oliver Swenson, barely eighteen, straddled a chair. In the slanted rays of the window light, he could have been mistaken for his father. His hands and arms were the hands and arms of a blacksmith, thick, burly and coarse. His face was the face of a child, innocent, expectant, uncertain. But it was the boy's eyes that fixed on Elder, and in those eyes Elder saw the full burden of hatred they bore.

"Oliver," Elder said. "There's no need for you to be here."

The boy looked down and his cheeks reddened. He cleared his throat but did not speak.

"What I mean to say," Elder continued, "is that your ma and little sisters need you now. It won't help matters none for you to get yourself hurt."

Oliver pulled off his hat and scratched his

head, his eyes avoiding those of the older man. He put the hat back on and pulled it down as he might in a storm. He looked up at Clarence. Clarence nodded. He shifted his gaze to Patrick and the cowboy looked at him straight on.

"It's your call, Oliver," Patrick said.

"I'm staying," Oliver said. He looked up at Elder. There was no compromise in him.

"All right," Elder said.

"Clarence?"

"I'm staying too, Mr. Elder."

Elder reached down into the front pocket of his trousers and retrieved a folded telegram. He unfolded it and laid it upon the desk with a kind of reverence that gave it great importance and drew Patrick, Clarence and Oliver in close while they waited for Elder to speak.

"What's it say, J.D.?" Patrick asked.

"It's from the marshal. Says he will be here on Tuesday. He's bringing the district court judge with him. They're going to try Raymond Smith right here."

"Well, that's two days from now," Patrick added. "Does he say how long the trial will last?"

"Says here, they will stay until Friday morning. The trial and hanging to be completed by then."

Patrick looked doubtful. "We could save everybody a lot of trouble, J.D."

Elder shook his head. "I promised a fair trial. I stand on that."

"I don't see why," Patrick said. "That boy's going to hang for what he done."

"And I hope he dies slow," Elder added. "But it will be done right."

"In the meantime," Elder continued, "we've got to keep a close eye on him."

He turned and unlocked the chain at the gun rack, drew out a ten-gauge, and handed it to the boy.

"Oliver, you keep this with you. Get yourself a pocketful of shells from the bottom desk drawer."

Elder looked over at Clarence and Clarence looked away. His cheeks flushed red and he put his hand over the old pistol stuck in his belt. Elder pulled down another ten-gauge.

"Clarence, you'd better have this," he said. "Get yourself some shells too."

"Yes, sir, Mr. Elder," Clarence said as he smiled at Oliver, then turned, and smiled at Patrick.

"How do you want to work this, J.D.?" Patrick asked.

Elder sat in Sheriff Dunn's oak chair behind the desk, pushed the chair back against the wall and rubbed his knee. He turned his eyes to the young cowboy.

"Twelve hour shifts, six to six. Three of us take the night shift, one the day shift. No other good way to do it."

Patrick thought it over. He agreed with Elder. It was far more likely for Sandoval to come at night if he was going to make a move at all. He nudged his hat back and sat in one of the chairs near the window. He did not count on Clarence for much and the youngster was questionable. That left just him and Elder.

"All right," Patrick said. "I'll take the night watch."

Elder looked up from the papers on Dunn's desk.

"Pat, if it's all the same to you, I would just as soon be here at night."

"Well, J.D., it ain't all just the same to me." He sat forward in his chair, his jaw tightened, and Elder saw in his eyes the same smoldering hatred he had seen in them up on the mountain, and Elder understood.

"Boys," Elder said to Clarence and Oliver. "Better get on home and get some sleep. Be back here at six and Pat will get you lined out for the night."

"Right, Mr. Elder," Clarence said. "I'll

just get me some shells to take with me."

Then he reached in the desk drawer, pulled forth a handful of loose shells and stuffed them in his jacket pocket, which bulged and hung heavy to one side. He smiled and reached for another handful.

Elder stood back. "Well, Clarence, that ought to do you."

"Yes, sir," Clarence said. "That'll do it."

Clarence headed for the door. He balanced the heavy shotgun in his right hand and, with his left hand, supported the overloaded pocket of his sagging jacket.

"Oliver?" Elder said, as he nodded in the direction of the open drawer. Oliver stepped forward, fetched out a small handful of shells, and stepped back.

"I reckon this'll do me," he said.

Patrick watched the two through the window until they walked out of his field of vision, then he turned to Elder.

"What are we going to do now?"

"They're all we got, Pat. Best we can do is to set them both up in the alley tonight and hope they can look out for each other. I'll make a bed in the empty cell and stay right here in case you need me."

"Fair enough. In the morning we can send them home for the day, and I'll catch a little sleep back there while you tend to the front," Patrick said. Then he added, "We should be okay during the night, but that's going to leave us with no one in the alley or out back during the day — all we can hope is that Sandoval won't do anything in the light of day."

Elder's expression grew darker. "It's not like we got any options."

Then, as he considered the circumstances, Elder looked over at Patrick.

"Pat, do me a favor and stop by and check in on Sarah and the boy. It bothers me, them being alone out there like they are."

Patrick pulled a shotgun out of the rack and headed for the door.

"Will do."

Elder watched Patrick jerk the latigo tight and step up into the saddle. The young cowboy turned the stocking-footed sorrel gelding away from the hitch rail with the ten-gauge slung crosswise over the pommel.

Uneasy and restless, Elder wobbled slightly as he walked over to the wall clock, opened the pendulum door and picked the brass key out of its holder. He wound the clock until the spring was tight, returned the key to its place, and then started for the cell to check on Raymond.

Elder pulled the door open, letting his eyes adjust to the darkened hallway. He gazed into the dim light and saw the outline of the cell bars and the rim of the slop bucket backlit from the shaft of light from the high window in the cell. Midway to the cell door, his gaze fell upon a dark shadow, settling first on the cold eyes of the mulatto, and then upon the black circles of the shotgun's double barrels.

TWENTY-NINE

Patrick Arbuckle rode straight for the Dunn house. In the morning light, the main street lay cast in soft shadows on the east side and the sun lighted the upper edge of the false-fronted buildings where it struck them on the west side. A dog slept against the buildings where the sun warmed it. A horseman dismounted and nodded. Patrick nodded back.

He nudged his horse into a trot and looked back over his shoulder. He turned the horse down the street where the Dunn house set among the trees and there were no houses beyond.

An uneasy feeling nagged at him and he could not let it go. Patrick doubled the horse with a quick jerk on the reins. The horse snorted and tossed its head and, when Patrick stuck it with his spurs, it bolted white-eyed down the center of the street at a full gallop with dust flying up around its striking hooves.

A block from the jail, Patrick heard a shotgun blast and watched as the glass from the jailhouse window flew in slow motion from its frame and fell in broken pieces upon the plank boards and onto the street. He heard a pistol shot, leaned forward over the horse's neck, and spurred it harder. When he approached the scattered glass shards, he already had one foot free, and swung from the saddle as the horse slid and bounced to a stop.

Elder exited the building as Patrick approached him at a run.

"Around back," Elder shouted. Patrick went right, Elder went left. When they met at the rear of the jail, Raymond and the mulatto had vanished into the brush.

"Were they on foot?" Patrick asked.

"I'm not sure," Elder replied.

Elder walked to the edge of the clearing and called to Patrick.

"They're on horseback," he said to the young cowboy. He pointed to the tracks where they left the horses tied, then looked out over the direction in which the two escapees departed.

"It looks like they're heading up country."

"That's what it looks like," Elder agreed.

"Do we go after them?" Patrick asked.

"If we do, it will just be us."

They were tired. It showed in their faces, and it showed in their voices. They stood silent, each weighing thoughts of his own.

"We both got reasons to bring them down," Elder offered. "But I expect they'll ride hard and try to get as far away from here as they can."

Whether it was the exhaustion or the futility that drove his response, Patrick looked at his boots then back up at Elder, and he spoke in a slow, quiet voice. "I'm ready to let the marshal take it from here."

Elder took a deep breath and let it out slowly. "That's it then," he said. "Let's try to get things back in order around here. We got a lot of things that need to be repaired."

"It doesn't feel right giving up, does it?" Patrick said, more as a statement of fact than a question.

"No, it doesn't. But we did what we could. It's just a damn shame they bested us at every turn."

Patrick and Elder walked straight for the telegraph office.

"I wouldn't say they got us at every turn," Patrick said.

Elder looked at him questioningly.

"Ike Smith paid. Eventually, them other

two's bound to run out of luck," Patrick added.

He looked over at Elder and there was no certainty in his expression.

"You think we've seen the last of them?"

"They got no reason to come back here now. We better make sure everyone around town stays alert until the marshal and his men get here, though."

"What happened in there?"

"Apparently Sandoval was already in the back — the rear door was still open and he just walked right in. He must have waited for the three of you to leave. I was out front and on my way back in to lock up. I noticed the keys missing off the desk and, when I opened the door to the cell, I saw someone in the shadows. He fired, I rolled back toward the front door and got one shot off — missed. Next thing I knew, him and Raymond was gone. That's when you rode up."

"I reckon he was watching us the whole time," Patrick said.

Elder nodded. "I reckon he was."

"Patrick, can you get the word out to everyone? I want to get out to Dunn's to check on Sarah and the boy."

"I'll do it now," Patrick replied.

Elder closed up the office and rode out to

Dunn's place. Before he dismounted, he rode the streets and the undeveloped area behind Dunn's house. When he was satisfied everything was in order, he tied the horse and climbed the steps. He paused a moment and then knocked.

"Who's there?" asked Sarah through the bolted door.

"It's me, Sarah — J.D."

The door opened and Sarah looked at Elder with some concern. "Is everything all right?"

"Sandoval broke Smith out not an hour ago. It looks like they headed up country, but we can't be sure."

"How in the world did he get him out?"

Elder's expression was apologetic.

"He caught us when we weren't expecting it."

"Are you okay?" Sarah asked, as she looked him over, half expecting to see blood.

"I'm fine. Patrick and I decided to let the marshal and his men take it from here. Aside from Clarence and Oliver, there ain't a man in town that would lift a hand to go after them."

Sarah understood and she held no ill will for any of them. But, in her heart, she harbored a vindictiveness she could not reconcile. She wanted to challenge Elder and she wanted to know it was over.

"So, what do we do now?"

Elder walked to the table, pulled out a chair, and sat down. His face looked worn and his posture showed the weariness that was catching up with him. He looked past Sarah, through the window, and past all the killing.

"I think we need to let this all heal and get on with our lives." Then he looked directly at Sarah, and she waited. Her expression was unsure, but hopeful. Her eyes searched his and he chose his next words carefully.

"I don't have much to offer you, Sarah. But I think you and I and the boy could make a life of it if we — if you are willing." His voice was tentative and it was clear he was not comfortable with the words.

Sarah smiled and she moved to the chair across the table from his. She sat and held his folded hands in hers.

"I am willing," she said, with a tone of great conviction. "Matthew just worships you and you would be so important to his life. And mine."

Elder smiled back at her and he then took her hands in his. "We can make it work."

Sarah nodded in agreement. "We just need to take it slow and give it time to make sure there is no doubt, ever. I owe Preacher the respect of a proper mourning, and I will honor that, and I will always honor his life and the fact he is the father of my son."

The feelings she shared with the preacher and those she felt for Elder were different on every level, and she followed her heart through that dark passage without reservation.

They stood and embraced and it felt right. Elder resisted his desire to take the embrace further. He looked down at Sarah, and she up at him, their eyes communicated that which their words would not permit, and they both smiled.

"Where's Matthew?"

"He's at the school," Sarah answered. Then she asked, "So, what is next?"

Elder was formulating the plan as he spoke.

"Well, I think you and Matthew need to stay here in the Dunn house for a while. It's close in and I wouldn't feel comfortable with you being as far out of town as you would be at your place."

"I agree," Sarah said. "The Dunns had no family, so I don't know what's going to become of this place. I suppose there's nothing inappropriate with staying on here a while longer."

Elder nodded, "I'll stay on at the hotel until I can get my place livable again. There is a lot to fix there. I'll start back up there tomorrow or the next day to see just how bad things are."

"Well," Sarah said. "When you leave, I'll get Clarence to take Matthew and me back to our place to gather up some things. We left everything back there."

"Let's give it a couple of days until the marshal arrives and we're sure those two Smith boys are a long ways from here," Elder said.

Elder walked to the window, stared out at the brush-covered ravine behind the house, and back up into the mountains where he imagined Sandoval and Raymond to be riding hard to put as many miles as they could between themselves and the town that interred General Ike Smith. He could not have been more wrong.

THIRTY

Sandoval and Raymond rode their horses until the beasts had nothing left to give, then they watered and rested the used-up animals near a small spring where no trail ran. Sandoval left a clear track where they entered the wilderness area, and the course he set marked a predictable route to the south. They rode south throughout the day, and when they reached the sprawling, treeless slope of the granite escarpment that rose to the summit, Sandoval turned the horses into the rushing waters of a wide creek. When they exited the water, it was on a gravel wash where they would leave no sign of their having been there.

The mulatto turned his horse into the darkness of the thick timber and reversed course back the direction from which they had come, and the slow-witted Raymond followed.

"We're going back 'cause of Ike, ain't we?"

Raymond said softly.

The mulatto nodded and they rode until dark. They stripped the rigs from the horses, then hobbled the weary nags, wrapped themselves in the saddle blankets, and waited for daylight.

When daylight came, they blew into their hands for warmth and then threw their rigs onto the matted backs of their horses. The horses grunted when the tightened cinches cut into their thin hides. The breath they exhaled smoked out into the chilled air and the horses, with the ghostly figures upon their backs, appeared like some terrible apparitions of the night.

They rode slow and deliberate and made a trail where there was none, and Sandoval covered their tracks with great skill. Raymond rode clumsy and unaware, and Sandoval eyed him with contempt, but never checked him or let it show.

"So, why are you doin' this, Sandoval? Ike was no kin to you."

Sandoval turned around in the saddle and looked at Raymond. He turned back without acknowledging the question.

"I guess you feel like you owe him."

They rode until dark and made another cold camp where they waited out the night.

At mid-morning, they stood the ridge

above the Stanford place and watched it a long time. They watched the road and they watched the house, and when they were certain there was no one there, they descended the steep grade and turned out the horses in a wooded pasture down from the barn and the house. They kept to the woods and shadows and approached the homestead with great caution. They packed their saddlebags and shotguns with them and left the saddles and riggings where they left the horses. They came to stay, and Raymond realized it had nothing to do with Ike. It would be vengeance for the sake of vengeance — a mission even Raymond understood.

Sandoval motioned Raymond to check the barn and the house, and he waited in the brush where he could see up the road until Raymond returned.

"Ain't no one here anywhere," Raymond reported, as he slipped back into the tree line with the mulatto.

They found a place in the barn and settled in as they shored up the doors and barricaded the breezeway. Sandoval gained entrance to the locked house and filled an empty grain sack with provisions from the pantry and the root cellar. He filled a crock with water from the well and placed everything neatly in the barn near the wall of the horse stall. Then he checked his ammunition and sat with his back to the riser.

"We just going to wait?" Raymond asked.

The mulatto nodded and Raymond laid out a blanket from his trip to the house and they waited.

Streaks of afternoon sunlight cut across the interior darkness of the barn from holes and cracks in the old wood, and Sandoval reckoned them to have an hour, maybe an hour and a half before the black of night descended upon them. They would hunker in the night with no fire and no lantern, waiting like untamed creatures that inhabit the darkness of the unknown.

Sandoval stared across the dim light at nothing at all. He neither blinked nor moved his head and Raymond studied him a long time before he spoke.

"You're a negro, ain't ya?" It was neither a question nor a statement, but more a thought that carelessly escaped the indiscriminate brain of the dolt.

Sandoval never moved his head and only his eyes shifted to Raymond. Raymond gave no indication he recognized the contempt in the mulatto's gaze, and Sandoval went back to staring across the dark expanse of the barn.

"You got yellow eyes, but you look like a negro." Raymond could feel his superiority rising, as though the power vested in Ike now resided in him; a genetic legacy he accepted without question.

Sandoval reached for the ten-gauge and Raymond shrunk back as though Ike had backhanded him. Sandoval re-positioned the shotgun and let it lay. Raymond sat up and busied himself looking at his shoes. He looked a sideways look at the mulatto, as though Ike's power did not vest itself fully in him.

"You'd kill me if it came down to it, wouldn't you?" Raymond asked.

The mulatto nodded he would, but he did so without paying Raymond the respect of a direct look.

"It don't matter," Raymond said. For that brief instant, the weak flame of insight or resignation caught the mulatto off guard. For that same brief instant, the mulatto sensed there might be more to the dull brother of the general than he reckoned there to be. As quickly as it occurred, Sandoval dismissed the thought. His contempt for the dull-witted Raymond carried with it no provisions for exoneration.

Darkness made the barn feel colder than it was, and the vastness of it made Raymond uneasy. He wrapped the blanket about him, curled up on his side, and slept deeply.

Halfway through the night he awoke abruptly, startled by nothing, but aware of a presence hanging heavily over him. He opened his eyes wide without moving and, in the truncated light of the moon showing through the cracks, he looked and Sandoval sat staring blankly ahead and showing no sign of life.

"You okay?" Raymond whispered.

Sandoval did not respond.

"Sandoval?"

The mulatto turned his head and nodded. Raymond lay back down, wrapped himself tightly in his blanket, and slept facing the dark figure whose presence caused him grave concern by the very nature of his cold unpredictability.

Just before daylight, Raymond sat up and stretched. He looked about, and the mulatto was gone. He sat there without moving until the pale light of early dawn began to fill the cracks in the wall. He tried to remain calm as he walked the barn from end to end and side to side. He checked the stalls and the hayloft and found no sign of the mulatto. The doors remained bolted from the inside, and Raymond felt a flush of panic begin to swell within him.

Everything felt wrong and Raymond was unable to summon a clear thought. His breathing was shallow and fast and he tried to think. The horses. Sandoval took the horses, he said to himself. He slipped out the back of the barn on a dead run for the small horse pasture where they had turned out their mounts and left their rigs the day before.

Raymond crossed the yard between the house and the barn and just before he entered the woods, he spotted Sandoval coming up from the cellar of the house. He stopped, crouched, and turned to watch the mulatto from the cover of the brush. In this moment of indecision, the slow-minded Raymond considered quitting Sandoval and riding out with both horses. He decided to stay and crept quietly back to the barn.

When Raymond slipped back into the barn, Sandoval was waiting for him and the loathing in the mulatto's eyes caused Raymond to cower and slink back to his blanket. Sandoval stood over him, and Raymond stammered.

"I wasn't going nowhere. I thought you quit me and I was checking on the horses."

Sandoval took a step closer.

"You didn't tell me you was going. When I woke up, you was gone."

Sandoval ignored Raymond and dropped a burlap sack filled halfway with jarred chokecherries, an onion, and an old potato with runners growing from its eyes. Then he turned and took his post at a knothole in the wall that looked out upon the side of the house, and he waited.

Raymond ate the potato raw and picked at the jar of chokecherries and he too waited.

THIRTY-ONE

Elder rode the highland trail with great apprehension. That terrible night the three horsemen descended upon his cabin felt like a nightmare, and nothing in his memory of it remained clear beyond the sound and smell of it, neither of which he would ever forget. When the trail turned and the ridgeline of the cabin rose above the boxelder and scrubwillow, he stopped and sat his horse a long time.

I don't know that I have it in me to start over again, he said to himself. Then he touched the horse with his heels and rode in, knowing that starting over was the only thing he knew to do.

It was worse than he imagined it would be. The dead mare and her foal picked clean with nothing but their hides and bones left to the flies lay in the corral where they died. There was no sign of the hen and her chicks, but the cabin was a horrifying reminder of the mindless mission of Ike Smith and his delegation of misfits.

Elder tied his horse and went to the barn for a shovel and an axe, and when he entered the cabin the smell of death hung over it like a hellish nightmare. Elder buried what remained of the dog and set to work separating the lost from the salvageable, and he knew he would be there much longer than he had guessed when he discussed the trip with Sarah.

Sarah Stanford tried to make life as normal for Matthew as she could, but the boy began to withdraw and Sarah grew concerned. He did not cry, and he did not ask about his father. He was neither curious nor interested in Elder's activities and never engaged his mother in conversation. He responded to her, and he did what he needed to do in school, but he remained detached and quiet.

Sarah sat on the edge of the boy's bed to talk to him before he went to sleep.

"Matthew, sweetheart, I know you've been through an awful lot," she said, as she put her hand to his forehead and gently brushed his hair back. He looked up at her and, for just an instant, she thought she saw him reaching out for her by the softening expression and the wanting in his eyes.

"It may help to talk about it," she said, desperately trying to draw him into a conversation. "Can you please tell me what you're feeling?"

Matthew's eyes shifted their gaze to the ceiling.

"I'm okay." His voice was neither weak nor searching, and it was not hard. It was no more and no less than the voice of a boy who could never again be a child. When Sarah heard it, she heard the voice of a boy lost in that great, dark abyss that lies between childhood and adulthood.

In that dark void, the child wandered lost and searching. The mother could only linger on the outside, unable to enter and unable to help. She extended her heart and she extended her hand, and she helplessly watched the abyss slowly begin to consume her son.

She tried to be understanding and she tried to be strong, but the longer she stared at the expressionless face of the child, the more she felt a growing hatred for the three derelicts for whom she could find no forgiveness.

She stood and turned to look back at the child over her shoulder as she moved toward the door. The boy did not acknowledge her, and she sensed he seemed more preoccupied than withdrawn. The coldness about him was unsettling and it made her uncomfortable. When she closed the door behind her, she felt as though she no longer knew the child on the other side of it.

Sarah sat at the kitchen table. She buried her face in her hands and she cried.

As he did each night, Matthew lay in the dark staring at the brown teeth of General Ike Smith, waiting for the crushing blow of the general's enormous hand. He watched Raymond come to him in the dark, grinning and menacing. He felt the constricting rawhide about his neck and he dreamed, as he did every night, that he was unable to breath and unable to call out. He ran and his legs moved but he remained at the end of the tether and when he did escape, it was always into the waiting arms of the mulatto, who was never in the dream but existed only as a force the boy knew to be him. Then the dream would start over and he saw it again, and again, until it became a part of who he was.

The child eventually lost his fear of the dream until the dream became the gatekeeper to his sleep, which was always fitful. The dream collected its toll and the boy stumbled through the gateway nightly, like a man broken and resigned to his fate.

He awoke at the first light of day, his only thoughts were the countdown until dark, and his hatred for the three men who rode out of that dream before it was ever a dream.

Sarah had no plan and she had no one in whom to confide. She got Matthew off to school, and she walked over to the sheriff's office where she found Clarence busying himself keeping the small office in order.

"Good morning, Clarence," she said as she let the door close behind her.

"Hey, Miss Stanford," Clarence said. He stood up straight. "How are you doing this morning?"

"Oh, not real good, Clarence. I'm just so worried about Matthew."

"Well, he sure did go through a lot," Clarence offered as a gesture of some understanding.

"I know he has. But, I'm afraid it's affecting him far more seriously than we know. He won't talk, and he just seems so distant and unreachable."

"Is there anything you can do to help him?" Clarence asked.

"I thought if you could take us out to our place after school this afternoon, we could bring back more of our things so the Dunn place would feel a little more like home to him. I think it may do him some good to go

291

there — you know, just to have him get involved with the changes being forced on us."

It seemed to flatter Clarence that she came to him just as she would have gone to Sheriff Dunn were he still alive.

"Yes, ma'am, that's a good idea. We'll borrow a team and wagon and bring back whatever you want."

"Thank you so much, Clarence. Matthew will be back right at noon, if that's okay with you."

"That's fine. I'll pick you up at the Dunn house then."

"How did things go with the marshal?" she asked.

Clarence took his seat behind the desk and leaned the chair back.

"He and his men left yesterday. Said they had a clear trail leading upcountry and they would push hard to make up as much time as they could. He was a good one. He said we could rest easy because they wouldn't quit until they had 'em both — one way or the other."

Sarah wished it would be the other, but she only smiled a weak smile and said, "We'll see you at noon then."

Clarence pulled into the yard of the Dunn

place at the same time Matthew entered the house.

"What's he doing here?" the boy asked his mother.

Sarah gave him a gentle hug, which he did not return.

"Clarence offered to take us home for a couple of hours so we can get more of our things and bring them back."

"Aren't we going to stay at our own place?" There was an edge to Matthew's voice, and it made the question sound like a challenge.

"We are, sweetheart, but not until they get those two men in jail. It's just not completely safe right now."

Then she added, as a shallow attempt at minimizing Matthew's concerns, "They're probably a long way from here by now. We're just being extra careful."

Matthew looked at her and his expression was sobering and cold.

"They're not a long way from here," he said, and she believed him.

Sarah turned away and her hands shook as she gathered up a blanket for the seat of the wagon.

"You need to be thinking about what you'd like to bring back," she said, and she hurried to the door and waited for the boy.

Clarence helped Sarah up and onto the narrow seat, and Matthew climbed into the back without being asked to do so.

The deputy clucked the horses and reined them down the road to the Stanford place. He sensed Sarah's uneasiness and he sensed the boy's detachment, but he said nothing. And so they rode, each deep in thought, none related to the other.

Every instinct in Sarah's nature protested, but she refused to let fear control her and she resisted the urge to tell Clarence to turn back. The familiar road she had travelled so often before now seemed foreboding, and she could feel the emptiness of the house to which the preacher would never return. She wondered if this was the right thing to do for her son, and she had grave doubts there was anything in the house that would somehow restore the sullen child to the one General Ike Smith had stolen from her. But she knew nothing else to do and she left it at that.

The road to the Stanford place was not on the way to anywhere and the state of it was poor. The ruts and rocks made for a rough ride, and Clarence did his best to avoid those he could. For the next three-quarters of an hour they bumped along in silence. At the last bend in the road before they would see the house and barn, the boy stood and addressed both the deputy and his mother.

"Can I get out here and walk the rest of the way?"

Clarence looked at Sarah and she at him, then to the boy.

"Wouldn't you rather just ride to the house?" she asked.

"I want to check the small pasture to see if the cows are okay. It's closer if I walk from here."

"Well, I guess that will be all right, just be sure to come straight to the house from there."

"I will."

"Be careful, sweetheart."

The boy looked at her and nodded and he stepped out onto the rear wheel and climbed the spokes to the ground. She waved, but the child did not turn to look.

"What do you think, Clarence?"

The deputy shrugged. "I think he'll be fine. We can keep an eye out for him from the house."

Sarah smiled, but the smile was weak and no smile at all.

The deputy pulled the wagon as near the house as the small yard allowed, and tied off the team. He stepped around to assist

Sarah and when she stepped down, she stood at the foot of the steps, stared at the door and the small windows, and back toward the barn. Nothing felt right.

Sarah stood before the door and held the key clenched in her hand in her pocket. When she inserted the key in the door lock, she held her breath as she turned it. The solid click from locked to unlocked was a comfort and she pushed the door open and allowed the deputy to enter first. The repairs made to the outside of the house misrepresented the state of the interior and Sarah cringed when they stepped inside.

Clarence paused and waited for his eyes to adjust to the low light and his nerves were on edge. Sarah followed Clarence in and together they stood there silently waiting. Finally, Sarah went to the window, pulled back the blinds, and let the light in. Everything looked to be in order, but the destruction she saw reminded her of the presence of the three men who stole her son and murdered her husband. Sarah quickly began gathering up the things she needed.

"I'll just put whatever we need here on the table so you can load it into the wagon, if that's okay with you, Clarence." Her voice betrayed her lack of confidence and that made the deputy uneasy.

"That's fine," the deputy said. In his mind, he was pleading for her to hurry, but he said nothing of it.

Matthew kept to the brush and trees and avoided the clearing as he made his way from the road to the pasture. He approached the small pasture from the high-country side where he would see the horses before he would see the worn saddles and thin saddle blankets partially concealed beneath the branches of a serviceberry that offered them little protection. When he saw the horses and when he recognized the one Raymond rode, his insides twisted and he vomited.

He spat, looked about, and his eyes were wild, his breathing rapid, and his hands trembled. He found the rigs where the derelicts dropped them and went to them. There were no saddlebags and nothing left with the outfits.

The boy removed the cinches from both saddles. He drug them off with the bridles and buried them all under leaves and dead wood, then started back for the house. He wanted to run, he wanted to scream, and he wanted to warn his mother and the deputy. But he knew Sandoval and he knew Raymond, and he knew not to do anything that would give them an edge.

He stayed low and moved under the cover

of the brush and deep into the shadows. The same way they would do it in the general's army. He tried to get his mind to work the way Ike's mind worked. In so doing, he stopped at the wooded edge of the clearing and watched the house and the barn. He considered Ike's careless but devious thinking.

They'd stay in the barn, he said to himself. It was too late for warnings, it was too late to run, and the boy knew the best he could do for his mother and the deputy was to avoid capture.

He tried to understand why they returned. He heard Elder's concerns and he heard the speculation from the others. The derelicts might come back for revenge or they might even come back for Ike Smith's body. They could only guess, for none knew the true nature of their intent. When the boy watched the mulatto, then the slow-witted one exit the back of the barn, he knew.

They came for me.

THIRTY-TWO

Clarence watched nervously as Sarah piled the last of her things on the table and looked about the room, anxious to leave, but wanting to be certain she would not have to make a return trip.

"Okay, I think we have it, Clarence. I'll call Matthew and we can go."

She moved to the door as the deputy followed her with his arms loaded. When she pulled the door open, the late afternoon sunlight obscured the presence of the two men waiting on the other side of it.

Sandoval kicked the door from Sarah's grasp with his heavy boot; the door slammed hard against the wall and set her back off balance. The deputy staggered back as well and when he did, Raymond and the mulatto descended upon them with great violence. Raymond struck the deputy a fierce blow to the head with his pistol and disarmed the stunned, bleeding man as he held him to the floor with his foot. He threw the deputy's pistol near the door and pressed his worn shoe hard against the deputy's chest.

"Where's the boy?" Raymond asked.

"That's none of your business," Sarah shouted at him.

He looked at Sarah, then back at the deputy. "Where is he?" Raymond asked, his voice now more insistent.

"You leave my son out of this," Sarah screamed.

Before the words fully crossed her lips, Raymond hit her full on the face with his fist and she went down with her head twisted to the side and her face bleeding.

"Last time," Raymond said, now addressing Sarah. "And if you don't tell me, Sandoval here's gonna kill this deputy."

He looked at Sarah and asked very quietly, "Where's the boy?"

Sarah sobbed and held her bleeding face in her hands. "He's in town staying with friends," she lied.

"That boy belongs with us," Raymond said. "They took Ike. We're taking him."

"My son has nothing to do with this," Sarah said through the blood and tears dripping from her hands. "You leave him alone."

The mulatto leaned the ten-gauge against the wall near the door. He jerked Sarah back by the hair and dragged her deeper into the room. He stood over her in the half-light, slipped his trouser braces off his shoulders, and looked down at her. He slid her skirt up with the toe of his boot. She slapped at his leg and attempted to cover her legs with the skirt.

Clarence rose to his knees and when he lunged for the mulatto, Raymond struck him a slashing blow across the back of the head with the barrel of his pistol, and the deputy collapsed in a heap at the feet of the mulatto.

Raymond's expression was one of confusion as he looked from the deputy to the woman and back to Sandoval. He tried to think and he tried to imagine what Ike would say.

Then he addressed Sandoval. "Not now. We need her to get the boy."

The mulatto backed off and Raymond's brush with authority encouraged him to push it further. "Now tend to him," he ordered as he pointed his thumb at the deputy. "We need him alive too."

Sandoval stood to his full height and glared down at Raymond as he pulled his suspenders up over his shoulders, ignored the order, then turned and took a seat at the table.

Raymond bent down and shook the deputy. "I don't mind doing it," he said under his breath, as though Sandoval's insubordinate refusal was a minor infraction not worthy of his attention.

The deputy stirred and raised himself up on one elbow, then managed to get himself up to a sitting position. He gazed about the room and there was no reason in his eyes as they took in the surroundings as though they were the eyes of a newborn.

Matthew's hands trembled as he slipped into the barn and waited for his eyes to adjust to the darkness. With his back to the wall, he dropped to his knees and it was like the game he had played a thousand times. He crept around the perimeter of the breezeway and entered the stall where Sandoval and Raymond stored their weapons, food and ammunition; it looked as though they planned to make a long stay of it. He gathered up Raymond's extra handgun and filled the empty saddlebags with the shotgun shells and pistol cartridges, then he hauled his bounty to his secret hiding place and stashed everything save the pistol and a pocketful of cartridges.

He slipped quietly out the way he came in and took the long way around the yard under the cover of the brush and trees, which grew sparse where he approached the house. He stopped to wait, and while he did so, he checked the pistol. Each chamber of the worn cylinder housed an unspent round, and he pushed the cylinder gate into position until he heard it click home, then he carefully let the hammer back down.

The gun felt heavy in his hand, but he liked the feel of it and he imagined the thunderous explosion it would make and it excited him. He remembered the power their weapons gave Ike, Raymond, and Sandoval. He remembered how badly he wanted to see Ike's shotgun spew its venom when Ike told him to shoot Raymond, and he remembered how badly he wanted to see Raymond suffer at the wrath of the shotgun. But mostly he remembered the absolute power he felt when he watched the buckshot rip into Ike. A power he summoned by the mere act of lining the big man up in the weapon's sights and squeezing the trigger. He remembered the surprise he experienced when Ike bled but did not fall, and he remembered how easily the second shot came. He felt the power of the weapon in his hand and the boy knew, beyond question, the third and the fourth shots would come easily as well.

He watched the window but could see no

movement. There was no light inside the house, and the fading light of day caused shadows to cross the yard and the porch in such a way it was difficult to distinguish the real from the imagined.

The boy waited, but when he heard his mother scream, he ran low and fast to the side of the house next to the porch. From there he could see Raymond and Sandoval through the partially open door, and he could hear their voices. He heard his mother weeping and pleading, but he heard nothing from Clarence. He moved low around the front of the elevated porch and when he gazed upon the slightly opened door, he saw Sandoval's shotgun leaning unattended against the doorjamb. The carved letters stood out clearly and Matthew's eyes locked onto the prize. He wanted to take away the mulatto's power, and nothing was more important to him at that moment.

He slipped quietly up onto the porch and crept closer to the doorway. He heard heavy footsteps inside, near the door and, when he did, the boy retreated to the cover of the front steps. Raymond's voice was loud and his mother sobbed. The boy waited until Raymond's voice moved deeper into the room and away from the door, and he made a quick move to mount the porch and grab the shotgun. As he stepped forward and extended his hand, the mulatto's long arm reached out of the darkness, took up the shotgun by the forestock, and disappeared back into the room.

The boy spun back off the porch and crawled back around to the side of the house. His breathing was rapid and shallow, and he waited there until he was sure no one saw him. He knew Raymond and he knew Sandoval. Most importantly, he knew his mother and Clarence would live or die because of the choices he made. The weight of it overwhelmed him. His mind raced and he tried to think as he moved into a better position.

Matthew slid on his back into the crawl-space beneath the porch and stopped. When he located himself directly beneath the front door, he held the pistol in both hands, the barrel pointing upwards, the hammer cocked, and his finger on the trigger. He watched through the spaces between the boards and knew he had one shot. He knew he would take the shot and he had no plan beyond that.

He lay there until the light was gone and the cold began to settle in, and he listened. The sounds that emanated through the partially opened doorway were few, but when he heard his mother's soft voice asking Clarence if he was all right, he knew he had time. He laid the pistol across his chest and began to shiver.

A light grew from the window where an oil lamp sat. The flickering light from the burning wick caused shadows to dance out onto the porch and reflect across the boy's legs through the cracks. He withdrew from the reflection and grew colder as he waited.

Raymond's voice ordered Sarah to cook them something to eat, and the boy could hear the familiar sounds of dishes, pots, and pans against the tabletop and the stovetop. She asked Clarence to go out to get wood for the fire and the boy imagined the mulatto's disapproval as he heard Raymond's voice above the other sounds.

"Let him get the wood," it said to Sandoval. Then to the deputy it said, "If you try to run, we'll kill her, then we'll come get you."

"I ain't gonna run," the deputy's voice said, with all the fight whipped out of it.

Matthew slipped out from beneath the porch and ran to the back of the house where the woodpile stood. He waited, concealed behind the small outhouse, and watched to make sure Clarence was alone.

The mulatto stood on the porch and

watched as the deputy shuffled toward the woodpile. Clarence bent over to pick up kindling and the boy could see Sandoval watching, so he made no move and he made no sound. Clarence stood with as much kindling and starter wood as he could handle, then he turned and carried it back to the house. On his second trip, the deputy returned for cordwood, and the mulatto sat on the porch rail looking up the road with no regard for the deputy.

Clarence picked through the split wood and Matthew whispered to him from the shadows.

"Hey — Clarence. Don't look up. It's me, Matthew."

Clarence nodded slightly and kept picking through the wood.

"I got all their stuff and I got a gun. Is my ma okay?"

The deputy nodded again. Then he moved down the woodpile closer to where the boy hid. With his back to the mulatto's position he whispered, "Give me the gun." He looked in the direction of the boy, but turned quickly and moved away when he heard the mulatto walking across the yard toward the woodpile.

The boy cocked the pistol and pressed up against the wall of the outhouse. At the same instant, Clarence dropped the arm-load of wood to divert the mulatto's attention from the sharp click of the hammer settling into place.

Clarence looked up at Sandoval, and Sandoval waved him back to the house from midway across the yard. Clarence gathered up his wood and walked back across the yard with Sandoval at his side. The boy stepped out from behind the small building and lined the front sight of the pistol along the spine of the mulatto. Just before the pressure of his finger on the trigger released the waiting round, the mulatto stepped in front of the deputy. The boy backed off his shot, turned back into the shadow of the outhouse, and trembled. Then he slumped to the ground with his head between his knees and he began to weep.

When he heard the door of the house rattle shut, he looked out around the corner and rose to his feet. Across the yard on the other side of the house, the borrowed team stood hitched to the wagon and tied to the rail where Clarence left them. He thought about unhitching the team and running them off — they would surely return to town and that would alert someone. It would also alert Raymond and Sandoval that they were not alone and he could not risk that.

He thought about it a long time and dismissed the idea of riding one of the horses out for help. He reckoned his best option to be to untie the team, point them toward town, and hope they headed back to the barn from which they left earlier in the day.

The boy circled the yard and came up to the waiting team from the blind side of the house. He pushed the heavy pistol in his belt and fumbled with the knot at the hitch rail. He watched the house, and he prayed the horses would remain quiet. When he loosened the knot, he slowly led the team away and walked them as far down the road as he dared, then he slipped off into the brush and the two Belgians plodded quietly away into the night.

THIRTY-THREE

Raymond and Sandoval sat at the table and ate bacon and beans, while Sarah and the deputy looked on.

"Git us some more coffee," Raymond ordered as he pushed his cup toward Sarah. Then he looked at Sandoval and pointed his fork in the mulatto's direction as he assumed command much as he had seen Ike do.

"In the morning, you ride in with him in the wagon," he said pointing to Clarence, "and fetch the boy."

By Sandoval's expression, it was clear he did not like Raymond's plan. Raymond continued.

"You can lay in the back with a canvas over you so no one sees you."

"The deputy here won't do anything wrong, 'cause I'll be here with the woman and I will kill her and he won't let that happen."

Sandoval did not like the plan, but what little of Ike's authority Raymond did muster was enough to command his compliance, and he nodded his approval.

As the two men ate, Sarah and Clarence sat out of the way on the floor. Sarah looked at Clarence through the side of her eye as she watched the two men eat.

Matthew? She mouthed in pantomime to the deputy.

The deputy nodded a subtle yes, and Sarah sat back with a great sense of relief.

In the dark, Matthew found his way back to the barn and, once inside, worked his way back to his hidden outpost where he covered himself with hay and waited for daylight with the pistol clenched firmly against his chest.

The child lay on his back with his eyes staring blank and empty upward with the full realization that his nightmare had become his reality, and he cared not whether he slept or stayed awake — either way, his day of reckoning had come, and he couldn't have been less prepared for it.

Matthew tried to sleep and, when he did sleep; three terrible apparitions rode into his dream as they did every night. This time they rode gaunt horses with no saddles, and the horses breathed fire, their eyes were red, and the ground trembled where their black hooves struck the earth. The men that rode them grinned and they smelled of smoke and sulfur, and called his name. Their voices were airy and frightening and he saw himself in the dream, tethered about the neck, too spent to flee. He stood and braced himself for their approach. The thunder that followed them shook the sky and the red eyes of the horses grew large and vile. He tried to turn away, tried to run, but all he could do was watch, as the stench of them grew nearer.

When the thunder sounded again, his eyes opened and he heard the door of the barn swing slowly on rusty hinges as it opened. He looked through the slats of his outpost that was now both a refuge and a trap. A dark figure slipped in carrying an oil lamp and moving toward the stall where the two derelicts had left their ammunition and supplies. When the light cast its soft glow onto the empty space, Raymond's voice echoed loud and angry.

"What the hell? Sandoval — someone took everything," he yelled back toward the house.

Sandoval came to the porch and looked out to the barn then across the yard. Raymond met him halfway between the two buildings and the mulatto indicated with his hands that the team and wagon were gone, and Raymond's fury exploded.

He ran up onto the porch and into the house. He pulled Sarah up by her hair and jerked the deputy to his feet by his shirt collar.

"The boy got our things," he screamed. "Where is he?"

Sarah shook her head and Raymond dealt her a crushing blow to the face.

"Where is he?"

In the dark, Matthew stopped to look at the pistol. He liked the heavy feeling of authority about it, and he knew without it he was but a helpless child. The thought of not having the weapon reaffirmed its power and, above all else, it affirmed his blood tie to it.

As he stood there holding the pistol, he thought about his father. He remembered the sermons his father preached on violence. He remembered passages from the Bible his father quoted so many times the boy could recite them from his memory.

"Let us turn in our Bibles to Matthew 5, verses 38 and 39:

"Ye have heard that it, hath been said.

An eye for an eye, and a tooth for a
    tooth:
But I say unto you, That ye resist not evil:
but whosoever shall smite thee on thy
    right cheek,
turn to him the other also."

His father would pause and look out over
the congregation. Matthew listened and he
believed every word his father spoke. He
remembered the raised hands and the
amens that accompanied those sermons.
And he remembered believing that the
words alone protected those who spoke
them.

Now his father, the leader of that forgiv-
ing flock, lay dead and in Matthew's
troubled reasoning he could only conclude
that his father's death was the outcome of
one simple fact.

He did not have a gun.

THIRTY-FOUR

Matthew Stanford chose not to suffer meekly as his father preached. He chose not to passively stand by and let fate dictate his circumstances. For that, he felt great shame and he felt he dishonored his father. When he squeezed the trigger and watched the unstoppable Ike Smith crumble before him, he felt as though he had signed an unimpeachable pact with the devil that condemned his life forever. With his soul laid to waste, the boy vowed from that day forth he would take an eye for every eye, and a tooth for every tooth.

The boy crept through the darkness and, when he reached the house, he heard voices and, though they were subdued, one belonged to his mother and the other to Raymond. The boy moved around to the front of the house, just off the porch, and listened through the partially opened door.

Inside, the deputy lay tied and tethered

about the neck, and Sandoval stood over Sarah. Raymond's voice was high-pitched and excitable as it was each time the boy witnessed the dullard at the edge of losing control.

"We want that boy," Raymond yelled. Sarah sobbed and she rose to plead with Raymond when Sandoval struck her a vicious blow and sent her reeling back to the wall. The ten-gauge with the hand-carved stock lay on the table and Sandoval stood near it as he slipped the suspenders from his shoulders and he knelt before the woman as he lifted her skirts.

Sarah begged and she resisted, but Raymond held her down as Sandoval dropped his trousers and forced himself between her legs. He hovered above her on his knees and forced her knees apart. She fought and screamed and the mulatto showed no concern.

Clarence frantically twisted and kicked at Raymond. Raymond turned and casually discharged a round from his pistol that entered the deputy's face just above the jawbone and the deputy stopped kicking.

Matthew knelt at the entryway and slowly pushed the door open far enough for him to locate Raymond and Sandoval. They had their backs to him, and only his mother saw him breach the opening with his pistol held in both hands and fixed on the back of the mulatto.

The boy moved forward with great restraint and was inches from the mulatto when his finger closed down on the trigger and the fire from the barrel blackened Sandoval's shirt where the bullet entered his back. Sandoval lurched forward and fell next to Mrs. Stanford, and he did not move. Raymond rose to his feet and was out the door when the boy's second shot ripped through the dullard's trousers, sending blood and flesh spewing from his upper leg. He ran without stopping, and Matthew knew he would head for the horse pasture.

Matthew turned and, without hesitation, leveled the pistol again at Sandoval and squeezed off another shot. The bullet slapped into the dead flesh of the mulatto and the body twitched only from the impact, for there was no life left in it.

He pulled the mulatto's body from his mother, and she lay there shaking with the color drained from her face. She tried to speak but could not. She tried to reach for the boy, but her hands trembled and she was unable to do anything but sob.

The boy put his arm around his mother. "Are you okay?" he asked. She continued to sob uncontrollably and he shook her. "Ma, please. Are you hurt anywhere?" He began to sob, and his mother's arms went about him and she held him close and shook her head, no.

All she could do was call his name and they remained like that until Matthew pushed away.

"I have to go after him."

"No, no, no, no," his mother pleaded. "Please Matthew, let it go, please."

The boy looked at her and his eyes were hard. At his feet lay the bleeding body of the mulatto and the face-shot body of the deputy. He helped his mother to her feet and guided her out onto the porch.

The first hint of dawn provided daylight enough for Matthew to see Raymond's blood trail headed straight for the horse pasture.

Matthew reached for the deputy's pistol where it lay on the table, placed it in his mother's hands with the trigger cocked, and he went back into the house for Sandoval's shotgun. He broke the breech, found two unspent shells in the chamber, then locked it and returned to his mother where she sat on the porch.

"If he comes back, point the pistol at him and pull the trigger."

She looked at him, her eyes resigned and she nodded, yes. In that fleeting moment the parent had become as the child and she obediently listened.

"Please be careful," she said, and it was the mother speaking to her child.

"I will."

Matthew turned and set out on the trail of blood, knowing Raymond Smith would be waiting at the end of it. The part of him that feared what was to come was, driven by that part of him that had waited for this day from the first night he lay awake in the forbidding darkness that became his life after they bound him in rawhide and tied him out to sleep. The killing of Ike and Sandoval fed that hunger inside him to vanquish those demons whose presence filled him with unrelenting fear. Pure hatred drove him to Raymond.

Raymond moved quickly. The bullet that grazed his leg left a gaping hole where it ripped the flesh, but the bleeding slowed and he was able to use the leg despite the pain. Raymond had heard the blast of the pistol and saw Sandoval drop as he fled the house, running for his life, and with no clear idea of the identity of the intruder.

When Raymond reached the small horse pasture and found the disabled saddles, he

319

turned and searched in circles, confused and panicked. He looked over the fence and the horses stood waiting, and all he wanted was to be astraddle one of them heading for the high-country. He hobbled to the fence when a small voice from the trees halted him midstride.

"Hey, Raymond."

Raymond spun around and his expression was one of relief and skepticism. He smiled but the boy did not smile back.

"You little son-of-a-bitch. Was you the one shot Sandoval?"

The boy looked at him from the cover of the trees and when he stepped forward, he ordered Raymond to sit down, and he did.

"I see you got Sandoval's shotgun. Is he dead?"

The boy nodded, and he leveled the shotgun at Raymond as he moved in closer and sat down himself.

"What you planning to do with that big ol' gun, boy?" Raymond asked in that taunting voice Matthew heard each night in his dreams.

"I aim to shoot you with it."

"You got no cause. You know it was all Ike and Sandoval. I was just along with them."

Matthew was calm and that, more than anything, disturbed Raymond.

"Tell me about my pa."

"What do you want to know?"

"I want to know how you killed him."

"There ain't no good can come from that."

"Tell me."

Raymond's hand moved slowly toward his holstered pistol.

"Take it out with your other hand and throw it to me," Matthew said as he lifted the big double barrel up and pointed it at Raymond.

"Easy, boy — that's a touchy trigger on that gun."

Raymond paused and deliberated.

The boy's voice was calm and deliberate. "I don't mind killing you."

Raymond believed him and he slowly slipped the pistol free and threw it. Matthew picked it up and checked the cylinder. "Four good ones left," he remarked.

"Now tell me about my pa."

"There ain't that much to tell," Raymond offered.

The boy cocked the pistol and leveled it at Raymond.

"Every time you lie to me, I'm going to shoot you," the boy said. Raymond could see Ike in the boy's eyes and he started talking. Matthew stopped him.

"I just want to know what you did. Did

you cut my pa with your knife?"

Raymond dropped his head and nodded.

Matthew pulled slowly on the trigger and a round exploded through the bottom of Raymond's shoe, splattering blood, bone fragments, and shoe leather along the man's trouser leg and across his shirt. Raymond screamed and twisted where he sat.

"Tell me what else you done," Matthew screamed.

"We cut off his legs," Raymond screamed back. Another round blasted through the other shoe and Raymond began to plead for his life.

The boy stood and approached the bleeding Raymond. He stood over him, leveled the pistol first at one knee, fired a round, and did the same with the other knee, and Raymond whimpered, pleaded, and cursed. Matthew threw down the empty pistol next to Raymond and went back for the shotgun. When the boy returned, Raymond had the barrel of the pistol in his mouth. He fired one empty chamber after the other, and his eyes pleaded for one live round.

Matthew stood over him a long time and watched the desperate actions of a man who wanted to be dead. The boy fired the first barrel, and the slug ripped into Raymond's right arm rendering it limp and useless.

"Kill me, damn it. Kill me!"

Matthew crouched down with the shotgun across his knees and watched Raymond die as his life ran out of the holes in his body.

Whatever the boy expected, satisfaction or guilt, it was neither. A primeval calling from some ancestral place dark and brooding within the child stirred his instinct for something more than bare survival. And, without knowing it, the boy found himself catapulted onto that plane of existence where only those willing to die are chosen to live. The kill-to-live terms of harsh survival now resided in the boy, and nothing he could do could change that.

He stood to his full height and discharged the remaining barrel into Raymond's still chest. He looked down at the grotesque body, twisted and neutralized as it lay before him, and a sense of power and control rose strong and bold within him. He gripped the shotgun as though it was an accomplice in his conquest, and he kicked Raymond's dead foot as he turned and surveyed all about him that was no longer a place of comfort or shelter. This was now his kingdom and the universe over which he ruled. He accepted his role as payment for the soul he rendered for it.

Matthew Stanford, fourteen years old,

trod forth from the valley of death with a contract, signed in blood, and a taste for killing.

THIRTY-FIVE

Standing before the desecrated cabin, J.D. Elder could only stare in disbelief at the carnage that was once his sanctuary. For everything that was in him that wanted to leave and never return, he set about the task with deliberate effort and conviction. He cleared the rubble from the damaged cabin and piled it in the yard. The front door lay with the window casings and broken furniture and, when it was all out of the cabin, the pile looked small and the bare cabin looked small as well. He stood back, assessed the pile of rubble and the smallness of the cabin and shook his head. *There ain't much to a man's life when you measure it in material things,* he said to himself.

Elder leaned on the shovel and looked about. He spat, tipped his hat back, and pressed the sleeve of his shirt to his sweaty brow and contemplated whether he wanted to rebuild his cabin or his life. He thought about Sarah and he thought about Matthew. They needed him. He was just not sure he wanted to be needed by anyone.

He stayed there for the better part of three days and, when he stood back to measure his progress, he was satisfied with its outward appearance. It looked livable and did not betray the damage done to it. Inside, it felt hollow and empty, as though the heart of it was missing and the shell that remained was without life or promise.

This place had been his refuge and he had been at peace here. The delicate line between isolation and seclusion was an imaginary one that existed in the mind and could be crossed at will. Elder was a private man, but he was not a recluse, and he did not cross that imaginary line. His need for human companionship grew less as he adapted to the serenity of being alone, and that suited him.

Elder looked past the split rail fence to the meadow beyond. The cattle grazed there as though Ike Smith and his men had been nothing more significant than a thunderstorm, loud, brief, and then gone. Standing alone in the warm sunlight and listening to the sounds of the wind and the birds, Elder regarded that dark night as little more than a memory, like so many other memories that resided within him.

Then he remembered the preacher's truncated torso swinging and twisting gently in its grotesque and unthinkable state. He could see Ike Smith, gut shot and smiling, and waiting for the next shot. He watched a child executioner, exempt of remorse and devoid of guilt, pull the second trigger out of revenge and retribution, and Elder saw the look of the condemned in the eyes of the child, and he knew the decision to stay or go was no longer his to make.

He had no plan, but feelings long since repressed and remote now stirred within him. He wanted to sit with Sarah, he wanted to know the boy and, in a way he could not express, Elder felt there could be more to his life than simply waiting it out in the undemanding comfort of his own small world.

Elder stood up straight and it was impossible for him to dismiss the fear he had of failing again. Nevertheless, the consequences of not trying weighed more heavily than the cost of failure, and Elder felt himself putting the pieces of a plan together that not even he clearly understood.

He walked back to the porch, sat on the top step, and leaned back against the big corner post. It needs doing, he said half aloud.

He was still thinking about Sarah and the boy as he saddled his horse. When he stepped into the stirrup and swung his leg over, it was like the final signature on a contract in which there were no provisions for cancellation. Elder felt good about his decision and, when he turned his horse back down the trail, his plan began taking shape. It was a plan constructed of broken pieces that he was not at all convinced would fit.

He would give it time, and he would help Sarah and Matthew settle in. He would spend time with the boy and try to help him come to terms with the taking of Ike Smith's life. He would not try to replace the boy's father, but he would work at being a father to the boy.

The late morning sun followed Elder and his horse, and the horse's pace was deliberate but not hurried. Elder sensed the horse, like himself, knew that leaving the mountain was the beginning of a new journey with an unknown destination that, left to their own choosing, neither would have chosen.

When Elder rode out of the last of the timber and entered the north end of town, he saw Patrick and several men gathered around the livery wagon, and he urged the horse into a trot. Patrick saw him first and waved him over. Elder dismounted as one of the men threw back the canvas sheet and exposed three bloodied bodies that, at first, all looked alike.

"What is it, Pat?"

Patrick shook his head. "It's a long story, J.D. You men take care of Clarence first," he said to the three men on the other side of the wagon. Then he looked at Elder. "Better come inside, J.D.," he said as he motioned in the direction of the sheriff's office.

Elder looked over the side of the wagon, recognized all three bodies, and his mind was wild with speculation.

"What about Sarah and the boy?"

"They're okay. Mrs. Foster, the banker's wife, is with them at the Dunn's place."

Elder followed Patrick inside and Patrick explained as much of the story as he understood. Elder sat back in his chair, his face drained of color and his expression one of confusion and disbelief. He stood up and started for the door.

"I'll be at Dunn's. We can talk later."

Elder mounted the waiting horse on a run and spurred the animal away from the crowd and down the street toward the edge of town. He dismounted in front of the Dunn house and dropped the reins on his way up the steps. He tried the door and it was open. He burst inside.

"Sarah, are you here?" The kitchen was empty. "Sarah!"

"She's up here," a soft voice answered from the top of the stairs.

Elder negotiated the stairs as fast as his bad leg would allow, and when he turned the corner Sarah lay on the bed, where Mrs. Foster tended to her wounds.

The swollen, bruised face and labored breathing caused Elder to look at Mrs. Foster with eyes that asked the question.

"She'll be fine," she said. "It looks worse than it is, but she does need to rest."

Elder nodded.

"And the boy?"

"He's in his room."

"How is he?"

Mrs. Foster did not answer immediately. Elder waited.

She looked up at him.

"Well, he's not injured." She paused again.

"But?"

"I'm not sure. He was tired when they brought him up, and he was hungry. He sat at the table and ate, but never said a thing about what happened. I don't know what I expected, but he didn't seem at all bothered

by anything except how his mother was doing."

Elder waited and Mrs. Foster just shook
her head.

"It just seemed strange to me," she added.

"You know he shot two men to death up
there, don't you?" Elder asked.

"Yes, I know. That's why I expected him
to be upset, I guess."

"Sometimes it just takes a while for something like that to catch up to a person,"
Elder offered. "Can I see him?"

"He's been asleep for less than an hour.
Let's let him rest."

Elder nodded towards the stairs.

"Can we go down and talk?" he asked.

THIRTY-SIX

Mrs. Foster sat across the small table from Elder with her hands resting against the hot sides of the coffee cup before her. Elder stared into the cup he held, then lifted his head slightly and looked at Mrs. Foster with grave uncertainty in his eyes.

"Sarah?"

"She's fine, Mr. Elder. I know she looks bad, but she'll mend. She's just mentally and physically very tired."

She raised her eyes and studied his face. There was no anger there, but his expression was troubled and she could not reconcile the circumstances with his demeanor.

"What is it, Mr. Elder?"

Elder shook his head but did not respond.

Mrs. Foster weighed her thoughts and did not press the question. They sat in silence a long time. Elder pushed his cup away, then stood up and positioned himself behind the chair as he rested his hands on the arch of the back of it and leaned forward.

"I'll be back this evening to check on Mrs. Sanford and the boy. Thank you for the coffee — and for looking after them."

Mrs. Foster paused. She looked up at Elder then she looked away and spoke softly as she stood.

"I expect they'll both be up and around by supper time. Would you like to join us?"

"Thank you, ma'am, I would."

He carried his hat and paused at the door looking down at his boots before he opened it. He turned and Mrs. Foster stood at the table watching him as though she anticipated his next question.

"Did the boy seem okay to you?" he asked softly.

Mrs. Foster shook her head. "No, Mr. Elder, he didn't."

He raised his eyes to hers and his expression was one of deep concern.

"Physically, he's tired, but he's not hurt. I'm no authority, Mr. Elder, but there's a kind of coldness about him that I find very unsettling."

"Well, ma'am, he's been through more than most and, no doubt, more than any boy his age."

Mrs. Foster again studied Elder's face, and this time she weighed the value of

333

continuing the conversation before she replied.

"Look, Mr. Elder, it's not my place to say, but this boy killed three men. I know he's been through a lot, but he's not upset, he shows no remorse, and he won't talk to anyone about what happened."

Elder nodded but did not speak.

Her voice shook slightly. "His eyes look old and hard. It gave me the chills when he looked at me."

"Well, I'll try to talk to him when the time is right. Let's see how it goes this evening," Elder said, without speculating on the boy's condition.

Elder closed the door and stood on the porch staring up the street, more conflicted than he had ever been in his life. He shook his head and walked slowly to his horse. He leaned both elbows across the saddle and stood like that a long time, looking off into the darkness that had become his life.

Elder found Patrick at the sheriff's office with two of the men who had helped off-load the bodies earlier. He left the door slightly ajar and addressed the men with a nod as he moved to the empty chair near the gun rack. "Leo, Johnny."

They nodded back. "J.D.," they said in unison.

Patrick looked up at Elder from the chair behind the desk. "Well?"

Elder sat down, pushed his hat back and stretched out his legs.

"Sarah and the boy are resting. Mrs. Foster says they're doing as well as can be expected."

"Meaning?"

"Sarah's bruised up some, but nothing serious. The boy ain't hurt none."

"Did you see them?"

"No. They were both resting up. I didn't want to bother them. I'll go back at supper time and look in on them."

Patrick leaned back in his chair. Leo and Johnny stood.

Johnny tilted his head in the direction of the door. "We need to be getting back. You boys let us know if you need anything."

The two men started for the door and Leo looked back over his shoulder. "It's a damn tragedy is what it is," he said.

The door closed behind them and Elder looked back at Patrick.

"What is it?" Patrick asked.

"The boy."

"What about him?"

"I'm not sure. Mrs. Foster said he seems different now."

"That kid's been beat, kidnapped, lost in

the high country, drug around on a leash, watched people die, then killed three himself. I reckon that would make anybody different," Patrick replied.

"That's what I said, but Mrs. Foster seems to think it goes a long ways past that."

"How so?"

Elder rubbed his chin between his index finger and his thumb, and looked up at Patrick. "He just acts like it never happened. No remorse, no fear, no hatred — nothing."

Patrick looked over at Elder then leaned forward with his elbows on the desk. "You know, J.D., funny thing, the only gun we found at the Stanford place was the one Clarence had. We know the boy used a handgun and a shotgun on Raymond and the mulatto, but there was none to be found."

The cowboy leaned back in his chair. "But then, we ain't had a chance to talk to the boy, but don't it seem strange the guns to be gone like that?"

"It does. Both Raymond and Sandoval were always well armed," Elder replied. "How close did you all look?"

"Well, we didn't search the place. But we looked around a fair amount just expecting to find the weapons to be with the bodies."

"Maybe the boy just threw them into the brush."

"Maybe," Patrick replied, with no conviction in his voice.

They sat there in silence a long time. Patrick appeared to be wrestling with a thought. He measured his words carefully when he spoke. His expression was grave and Elder watched him with concern.

"Sandoval was shot clean, but Raymond died slow. He was shot up bad, like the kid took his time and took pleasure shooting him."

"Don't sound like a kid, does it?" Elder replied.

"What it sounds like, J.D., is an executioner."

Elder tensed. He was thinking it and Patrick said it, and the sound of it left him feeling cold and empty. "Where do you think that leaves the boy?"

"I've seen full grown men broken by less," Patrick said as he looked down at his boots.

Elder's expression was devoid of answers and it betrayed the defeated spirit within that threatened to draw him back to the hermitage that had become his refuge from those things he could not control or influence. He sat without speaking, and Patrick did not breach the silence.

Elder took off his hat and placed it on the desk. He ran his fingers through his graying hair and wrung his face in his hands. When he did speak, his voice was quiet and thoughtful.

"I feel like an old man. I don't know how much usefulness I got left in me."

Patrick watched and listened.

"A lot of things I tried to do, I never got done." He looked directly at Patrick and shifted in his seat.

"Now there's a young woman and a boy who need help, and I'm not sure I got the kind of help they need." He tilted his head as he looked over at the cowboy, who was struggling for a response.

"Dammit, J.D., you ain't no different than the rest of us. We don't know what we can do, and we don't know what we can't do — we just do what we can and hope for the best."

"And what happens when that's not good enough?"

"I don't know. I was just taught you keep trying."

"I reckon that's right. It just gets harder when you get older and you got more behind you than you do in front of you."

"Well, there is one thing I can tell you for

sure, J.D., ain't none of us exempt from that."

Elder smiled a half smile. "I suppose."

THIRTY-SEVEN

Elder knocked on the door of the Dunn house and stepped back. The door opened slowly and Sarah stood in the entryway. She smiled a crooked smile and began speaking.

"Before you say anything, I know how bad it looks, but Mrs. Foster promised me I would be back to normal in a few days."

Elder smiled and studied her face. The swollen lips looked painful. One eye gazed back at him beneath a badly bruised and puffy eyelid. She had a small laceration at the corner of her mouth and a larger one across the cheekbone on the right side of her face. When she attempted a smile, the smile itself was awkward and distorted her features even more.

"I was expecting worse," Elder lied. "How are you feeling, Sarah?"

She reached out for his hand and led him into the dining room. "Much, much better now that I've had a little rest."

At the bottom of the staircase, Sarah called up to her son. "Matthew, Mr. Elder is here to see us, and it's time to eat."

There was no response, but Elder could hear the boy shuffling around upstairs.

"Okay," the boy's voice drifted down the stairwell.

"How's he doing?"

Sarah turned and looked at Elder and shrugged her shoulders.

"I don't honestly know, J.D. He seems okay, but there is a void I can't explain. He went through so much. I saw what he did — what he had to do, and I'm not sure many men could have done it."

Elder nodded his agreement and turned to the sound of the footsteps coming down the stairwell, slow and deliberate. When they reached the bottom, Matthew turned the corner. Elder studied the boy's appearance and demeanor with great intensity. The boy glanced at Elder and then diverted his eyes to his mother.

"Matthew, say hello to Mr. Elder."

Matthew avoided eye contact. "Hello," he said.

Elder watched the boy take a seat at the table. "Good to see you, Matthew."

Matthew nodded and Elder took the seat across from the boy. Mrs. Foster entered the small dining room from the kitchen with a steaming pot of stew she placed on a hot pad in the center of the table. "I hope you're all hungry," she said, her voice friendly, but somewhat uncomfortable.

"Yes, ma'am," Elder said as he shook the red, cloth napkin out and placed it on his lap.

"That smells wonderful," Sarah said as she put her hand on Mrs. Foster's arm. "Is there anything I can help you with?"

"No, no — you just sit down and enjoy your supper. I'll bring the biscuits and coffee and we'll eat."

Conversation was polite and, by their silent agreement, no one brought up anything to do with the events of the past couple of days. Matthew neither spoke nor attempted to draw any attention his direction. His motions as he ate were perfunctory and deliberate and, if he was grieving, he showed no signs of it.

Elder was the first to engage the boy. "What do you think of that stew, Matt?"

Matthew nodded his head up and down and continued eating, as though the act itself was a satisfactory answer to the question.

Sarah straightened in her seat when Elder asked the question, and she stopped her fork in midair waiting for the boy's answer. When none came, she looked over at Elder and raised her eyebrows then continued eating.

The awkward silence that followed was punctuated by the repeated sounds of fork against plate and cup against saucer until Matthew looked over at his mother and said, "May I be excused?"

Sarah smiled. "Yes, of course, sweetheart. What are you going to do now?"

"Just go outside for a while."

"But it's dark out there."

"I know. I'll just be on the porch."

Sarah looked worried. She glanced at Elder and back to Matthew.

"Well, I guess it's okay. Just don't go anywhere else."

Matthew excused himself and no one spoke until they heard the door open, then close.

Sarah turned to Elder. "I am so worried about him. What do you think?"

"I don't know what I expected," Elder said. "Has he talked at all about what happened?"

"No, and I didn't think too much of it after we got him back the first time. But now . . . after all that happened out at our place, it's like he's a different person."

Mrs. Foster nodded in agreement. "I've known Matthew since he was a baby. This is not the same boy."

"You weren't there, so you can't know," Sarah said. "But what Matthew did to save me was the bravest and most frightening thing imaginable."

She paused a long time. Elder and Mrs. Foster hung on the silence. Tears formed at the edges of her eyes and her fragile expression betrayed her defenses.

"But . . ." she cleared her throat and took a deep breath. "But what he did to the other one was . . ." She buried her face in her hands and wept openly, unable to finish her sentence. Mrs. Foster rose, put her hand on the weeping woman's shoulders, and patted her back without speaking. Elder gazed blankly at the pair, his expression robbed of any consolation, and his mind searching helplessly for something to say.

He stood and moved to Sarah's side. He placed his hand on her shoulder next to that of Mrs. Foster, who looked at him with pleading eyes.

Matthew stopped at the doorway and went through the motions of opening and closing the door. He remained quietly in the shadows of the foyer to hear the conversation he was sure was about him. He listened until the talking stopped, then slipped silently outside.

Sarah regained her composure, but chose not to continue the conversation. Elder picked up his coffee cup and turned toward the door.

"I think I'll see how Matthew's doing."

Sarah looked up at him, smiled her awkward smile, and whispered, "Thank you."

Elder picked an apple out of the bowl on a small table in the foyer on his way out.

THIRTY-EIGHT

Outside the air was soft and warm and the boy stood on the porch, his arm holding on to the corner post and his eyes staring blankly off into the darkness. He heard the door and he heard Elder's footsteps behind him, but he neither turned nor spoke when Elder approached.

"I brought you this," Elder said, holding out the apple.

The boy glanced over his shoulder and turned back to staring out into the night.

"No thanks."

Elder moved to one of the two old chairs that attended the porch on either side. He set his coffee cup down on the railing and pulled his folding knife from his pocket, then took a seat without further addressing the boy. He opened the blade, wiped both sides against the leg of his trousers, and began methodically slicing the apple as he leaned back in the chair.

There was annoyance in the boy's voice as he turned to face Elder.

"What do you want?"

Elder sliced carefully through the apple without looking up. He studied the boy before he spoke. He was tempted to skirt the issue, but decided against it.

"How does it feel to kill a man?"

The boy stepped back and looked at Elder. He checked himself before he spoke and he chose his words with care.

"Don't you know?"

"Well, I know how it feels to me, but I'm not fourteen years old."

"You think it feels different for an old man than it does to me?"

"I reckon it might."

Elder sat back, ate apple slices, and did not breach the silence that followed. The boy moved to one of the chairs and sat down, and neither of them spoke for a long time. Finally, the boy looked down between his feet and his voice was steady, but softer than it was earlier.

"I know it wasn't right," the boy said. "And I know I'm going to hell for it."

The boy stuck out his chin and clinched his jaw. The look in his eyes was one of resignation and defiance and, for his tender age, he gave the appearance of one condemned for eternity. In the boy's attitude, Elder sensed a frightening awareness of one who accepted his ill-fated destiny with no intention to go meekly to his end. Elder looked over at the boy.

"You think you're going to hell because killing is a sin?"

"I know I am."

"What do you suppose would have happened if you hadn't done what you did?"

"I know what would have happened. I'd be dead and so would my ma. But that don't make it right."

"No, it doesn't. What you did, you did because of the circumstances you were in and because that chore, as bad as it was, fell to you. You did what needed doing."

"Thou shalt not kill. It's one of the Ten Commandments, and I broke it."

"But you did it because you were protecting innocent people. You did it out of courage, and you did it because, for whatever reason, you were the only one that could get it done, however that came about."

Elder avoided treading into the fundamentals of Christian doctrine, where he was sure the boy was better equipped than he to make his point. They were both the sons of preachers, but Elder had no clear recollection of the last time he sat in a church, and he knew this was a personal struggle for the boy, not a philosophical one.

The boy remained silent, for within him slunk a disturbing realization he could share with no one. He let Elder's words find their rightful place, but he weighed his desire to believe them against his own dark reality. His fate fell irrevocably into condemnation when the first hammer dropped and he watched his own innocence bleed from the shirt of Ike Smith, of that he had no question.

As he contemplated that thought, he also understood that the total of the sin he committed was far more than the killing of Ike Smith. He reconciled himself to the reasoning of killing Ike Smith, and he had no question that killing Sandoval was for the right reason. Killing Raymond was an indulgence, and the pleasure he took with every pull of the trigger he took with a lustful disregard of the right of it.

"Look, Matt. No one can tell you how to feel, and no one can make it better for you. I can tell you, you will never feel good about killing a man. That is the good in you talking. I can also tell you that letting it get to you can break you."

Matthew sat hunkered with his elbows on his knees and his face cradled in his hands.

Despite Elder's consolation, killing Raymond did feel good — Elder was wrong about that. His eyes turned up to look at Elder.

"How can it break me?"

"If you let it, killing can turn you into something you don't want to be."

"Like the Smiths?"

Elder nodded. "Like the Smiths."

Matthew sat back in his chair and, for just a moment, he looked like an innocent boy again. As quickly as the innocence appeared, it vanished. There, before the older man, a damaged boy sat on the threshold of ruination and beyond his reach. Elder wanted to believe his talk did the boy some good, got him to open up and, maybe, reached the boy on some level. The look in the boy's eyes told him otherwise.

THIRTY-NINE

The Arbuckle Cattle Company included twenty sections of lowland grazing where good mother cows produced the calves that earned Patrick's father, and his father before him, success where others had failed. In the high-mountain summer ground, they raised yearlings on an additional thirty sections of grass-rich land where they competed with wolves and mountain lions and the calamitous effects of an early winter if their timing was bad.

Patrick and Timothy, the last two remaining in the family, carried on the Arbuckle tradition in the same hard-working manner of those who preceded them. Timothy understood operations and finances. Patrick understood cattle and horses. Together they kept the ranch on track. Now with Tim gone, Patrick found himself struggling with the loss of a partner as well as the loss of a brother. The weight of it hung heavily upon his shoulders and he immersed himself back into the business with relentless determination.

J.D. Elder rode with Patrick to check the springs in the lower pastures, and they talked as they headed out from the corrals.

"I talked to the boy the other night," Elder said, as he closed the last gate and stepped up into his saddle.

"How'd that go?"

"I'm not sure."

Patrick looked at him and furrowed his brows.

"I mean, the talk went fine — I'm just not sure anything I said made any difference."

"The boy have anything to say?"

"He told me he was going to hell."

"He mean that in the Biblical way, or did he mean his life was just turning to shit?"

"No — he meant in the Biblical way. He believes he's beyond redemption."

"He get that from his daddy?"

"He did. Everything that preacher ever said stuck with the boy. Now he can't get it out of his head that his soul is lost."

"What do you think?" Patrick asked, as he turned the horse down a trail that led to a thicket of trees.

"About his soul?"

"No, about the boy."

"I think there's a lot going on inside that head of his that he ain't telling us."

"I suppose you're right about that."

"Well, it gets more complicated from there."

"How's that?"

"Me and his momma are talking serious about marriage — not right away, but eventually."

Patrick sat back in his saddle and laughed, then looked over at Elder, who was neither smiling nor amused.

"J.D., for a damned ol' hermit you sure did find your way into a family situation in a hurry."

"I wasn't looking for it, it just happened."

Patrick pulled his horse up sharply and Elder stopped with him. The cowboy looked at the older man, and there was no humor in his expression.

"I've known you a long time, J.D. There's something bothering you. What is it?"

Elder pushed his hat back with his finger and leaned forward. He rested both forearms on the saddle horn and stretched his back.

"Well, Pat — there is something you could do for me."

Patrick regarded him with a skeptical look

"I'd like you to give the boy a job for the

summer. Don't worry about paying him. I just want you to work him hard and help him get his mind right. I don't know any better way of doing that than being horse-back and working cattle — and every other distasteful job that goes along with it."

"Hell, J.D., that's not a problem. We got room in the bunkhouse. Got some pretty good cowboys for him to learn from. And, truth is, we could use the help."

"He's doesn't know much, but he's a tough kid and I expect he'll work hard. You and him have some things in common, and it will do him good to be around you."

"We got a string of horses that will work for him — broke dog-gentle, just right for a kid."

"How about I bring him out next week after school's finished for the summer?"

"Did you talk this over with his mother?"

"I did. She's not sure she likes the idea but, for some reason, she thinks the sun rises and sets on you, so she agreed."

Patrick laughed. "You know she's too good for you, don't you, J.D.?"

Elder smiled. "Yeah, I do know that."

They rode the springs and the tall grass meadows where cows and calves grazed and new babies slept in the shade. The air was warm but not hot and the fresh smell of the mountains made the nightmare of the past weeks seem like a dream only vaguely real. When Patrick chanced to let his mind relax, he gazed upon Elder riding one of Tim's horses and the stark reality of the damage inflicted by General Ike Smith and his company struck back at him with sobering swiftness.

When they spoke, talk was spare. The cadence of the horses' footfalls and the rocking of the saddles caused their thoughts to drift randomly. The sounds of birds and the whisper of the wind and the occasional bawling of a calf quietly drew their thoughts away from the terrible events that had befallen them.

They rode the rest of the day and, when evening came, they shook hands.

For all their benevolent intentions, neither man could have imagined the impact a slightly built child of fourteen would have on them.

FORTY

Elder stood in the kitchen of the Dunn house with Sarah where they waited for Matthew to come down from his room. At the hitch rail out front stood Elder's horse and the Arbuckle horse he brought for the boy. The boy's horse was fitted with a well-used A-fork saddle with a high back cantle and exposed stirrup leathers. It was a cowboy rig with the stirrups shortened but no other concession made for the boy who would ride it.

"What's Matt think about spending the summer working at the Arbuckle?"

Sarah looked up at Elder and smiled in a consoling manner.

"He didn't say much one way or the other, but I could tell he likes the idea of getting out of here for a while."

"You worried about how it will go with him?"

"Of course I am, J.D. I'm his mother. He

knows he can come home on the weekends once or twice a month, so that does help — a little."

"How about you, will you be okay?"

"I'll miss him terribly and worry constantly but, yes, I'll be fine."

Elder looked into her eyes while he searched for the questions she did not ask and the concerns she did not voice. When he did speak, his voice was reassuring. The strength and calmness of it she found soothing.

"He likes Patrick and Pat will do all he can to make him feel at home. He'll treat him like one of the cowboys, and I believe that will mean a lot to the boy. I'll be up there for a few weeks to help with the branding, so I can keep an eye on Matt too."

Sarah sat at the table and asked Elder to sit as well. Her manner was one of some concern as she spoke.

"Matthew asked me to take him out to our place yesterday," she said. "He said he needed some things from there. You can imagine how reluctant I was to go, but Oliver said he would go with us, so we went. Thank the Lord, the place was put back in good order, so it wasn't as bad as it could have been."

"What did he need from there?"

"Just some clothes, he said, and his old hat."

Sarah paused for a moment.

"Then he said he needed something from the barn, so he took his burlap sack with his clothes and things with him and he was gone longer than I thought he should be."

Elder listened and his expression was somewhat strained.

"Finally I called him and he came out of the barn, but I didn't see that he had anything with him. I asked him if he found what he needed. He said no, but it wasn't important, so we left."

"And that was that?"

"Yes, except his mood seemed to be much better on the ride back and has been since then."

"Maybe he's just looking forward to his summer job," Elder offered in the way of explanation.

Sarah turned as Matthew entered the room from around the corner of the stairwell where he stood and listened before he made his presence known. He carried with him the burlap sack filled and tied with a rawhide lace.

"Well, Matt, you ready to go cowboy for the Arbuckle?" Elder asked as he stood.

Matthew looked up at him and smiled.

"I'm ready."

They said goodbye to Sarah. She fought back the tears, kissed her son, and told him to be good and that she would see him in a few weeks.

At the hitch rail, Elder took the boy's burlap sack and was surprised at the weight of it. He looped the lace over the boy's saddle horn on the off side, and then went behind the horse to the near side to help the boy get mounted.

"I can do it by myself," Matthew said when Elder offered him a leg up. He lifted himself up by the stirrup leather and saddle strings until he could get a toe in the stirrup, then he swung a leg over and surveyed his surroundings from his high vantage point. The boy smiled and pulled his hat on tighter. Elder handed him the reins and mounted his own horse. He tipped his horse's nose to the south and when his horse stepped out, the boy's horse did likewise.

Matthew rode unusually easy in the saddle. His manner with the horse was firm and gentle and it surprised Elder, who expected the boy to be less sure of himself. It was a good sign, and Elder smiled as the trail turned and the last sight of the buildings vanished behind them.

"Patrick promised me he was going to work you hard."

Matthew nodded and his eyes scanned the hillsides and swales and the thickets, where the trees grew tall and close.

"You ever brand a calf?"

"Never had a chance."

"Well, they got a bunch of spring calves that we'll be roping next week."

"Will I be helping?"

"If we can get you ready in time, you will. Otherwise you'll end up spending the whole time on the ground crew."

"So what's wrong with the ground crew?"

Elder laughed. "There's nothing wrong with the ground crew. It's just a lot more work and not as much fun as dragging calves to the fire."

"So, what do I have to do to get ready?"

"A couple of things. First off, you need to be able to ride a horse."

The boy looked at him.

"I'm already riding a horse — what's so hard about that?"

Elder looked straight ahead and answered without turning his head to the boy.

"You aren't exactly riding that horse. Granted, you are sitting on him, and granted he is going where you want him to go but, truth is, even if you got off, he would still do that."

The old cowboy let that thought settle with the boy, and then he continued.

"In the branding pen, just like in the cutting pen, you have to be able to get that horse to stop, turn, and back when you ask him. You have to hold a rope and your reins and get a loop built at the same time. Then, on top of all that, you need to toss a head or heel loop and dally up when you get something caught."

The boy looked at Elder and, had Elder been speaking a foreign language, it would have been no less clear to the boy.

"Is that it?"

Elder spat, drew his sleeve across his chin and smiled.

"That's pretty much it — for the first lesson anyway."

"The first lesson?"

Elder nodded.

"It's a lifetime education," he said. "When it comes to horses, you never stop learning. Cowboying is the same way."

"Cowboying?"

"Yep — cowboying. It's the fine art of learning to do all the jobs they can't get a machine to do, and convincing you it's a noble endeavor so they don't have to pay you a lot to do it."

"That doesn't make any sense."

Elder laughed.

"Not to most people, but if you're a cowboy, it makes all the sense in the world."

The boy shook his head.

"Well, I ain't no cowboy and I don't plan on being one, so it's no matter to me."

They rode for more than an hour before either spoke again. Finally, the boy broke the silence.

"So, exactly how do I get my horse to stop and turn and back up?"

Elder appeared to contemplate the question before he answered.

"It's called horsemanship."

The boy laughed a sarcastic laugh.

"So, what does that mean?"

"It means you have to learn everything about the horse first. It also means you'll have to learn some things about yourself. Once you get that part figured, you can start to work on what you got to do to communicate with the horse."

Matthew appeared discouraged.

"If it's that hard, I don't want to do it anyway. What does the ground crew have to do?"

Elder looked at the boy and smiled.

"I'm thinking the ground crew might be just what the doctor ordered for you."

"Good, 'cause I don't care a damn about cowboying or horsemanship."

Elder pulled the brim of his hat low over his eyes, touched the horse with his heels, and they long-trotted the rest of the way to the Arbuckle Ranch in quiet contemplation. The boy harbored grave doubts about his new job. Elder had grave doubts about the boy.

FORTY-ONE

The boy stood in his stirrups and gazed out over the tree tops below as he and Elder topped the last hill and the roof tops of the Arbuckle house and barns came into view. He settled back into the saddle and looked over at Elder, who neither spoke nor acknowledged the assemblage of barns and sheds and working corrals laid out before them in a disorderly fashion that made no sense to the boy.

"Is that it?"

Elder nodded. "Yeah, that's it."

Matthew sat back in the saddle, his eyes wide and his expression one of concern.

"It's a lot bigger than I thought."

"This is just the headquarters place. Back up in there and across that ridge over there are a couple of line shacks."

Elder's hand gesture was broad and sweeping, and no more clear to the boy had he not made one at all.

"What's a line shack?"

"It's a small cabin, just a single room, set way off out there for a man or crew to stay in when they're going to be out there a spell."

The boy looked at Elder.

"I ain't staying in one."

Elder laughed. "Don't bet your last dollar on that."

"Well, I ain't."

"You might want to get a curb on that attitude. These boys here got a low tolerance for nonsense, and I don't think you want to get sideways with any of them."

The boy looked back at Elder.

"It'll do them good not to get sideways with me," he said in a cold and matter-of-fact tone.

The remark caught Elder off guard. He stared at the boy and the boy stared ahead. They followed the road down through the trees and past the first set of corrals. Where the road split to the right, it led to the barns and two log bunkhouses. Elder nudged his horse to the left where it curved away to the main house set among the trees and up from a small creek that ran behind it.

Elder gauged the time to be early afternoon; too late for lunch and too early for supper. He stepped down from his horse and told the boy to do likewise. The boy hesitated, looked about, then swung a leg over and slid down the stirrup leather to the ground. He immediately went to the offside and untied his burlap sack from the saddle horn.

"You need any help with that?"

"No, I got it."

Elder stepped up onto the porch and the boy followed. When he knocked on the door, Patrick's voice echoed from inside.

"The door's open, come on in."

Patrick met them as they entered the cavernous room. The boy looked about as his eyes adjusted to the light. A massive fireplace made of river rocks dominated the center of the room, with its smooth gray stones mortared in place and reaching to the heavily beamed ceiling. The walls, built of exposed logs, stood majestic and imposing. On one wall, an enormous buffalo hide hung hair-side down. Its tanned surface displayed painted figures of warriors upon the backs of charging horses, firing rifles and killing buffalo. It showed mountains and a river. And near the river, there stood many teepees and many horses. The entire panorama circled the hide in earthy colors of ocher, red and black.

Beyond the far wall, in what appeared to

be an extension of the kitchen stood a large table. Matthew counted the chairs: six on each side and one on each end.

Elder and Patrick shook hands and they both looked down at the boy.

"Patrick, you remember, Matt, don't you?"

"Sure do," Patrick said as he extended his hand to the boy. "How you doing, Matt?"

"Good," the boy said as he returned the handshake that he thought was firmer than it needed to be.

"You boys hungry?"

Elder looked down at the boy and then back up at Patrick.

"I don't know about Matt, here, but I'm ready anytime the rest of you are."

The boy did not smile and he did not engage the two men. He solemnly clutched his burlap sack and wished he were elsewhere.

"Let's get you two set up in the bunkhouse. The crew will be in from the lower grazing before long. We'll eat in about two hours."

Patrick led them beyond the first barn and past the breaking pen. A dozen young horses looked up from their hay and watched them from the far side of the small corral next to the breaking pen. The boy nodded toward a cut-off post in the center of the breaking pen. The post was bigger around than he was, and taller than a man.

"What's that for?"

Patrick glanced in the direction of the post and then looked down at the boy and caught his gaze directly in his own.

"It's a snubbin' post. We tie up a colt's head to teach him some respect before we start his education."

The boy did not respond, but he made a mental note of one more thing he did not like about this place.

"Who's riding your colts for you now, Pat?"

"We got a good one name of Ty Riggs, come down out of Canada. He's a bronc peeler and a hard-crusted son-of-a-bitch that can ride the tough ones. Puts a good handle on 'em, but when he gets through with 'em, you gotta ride 'em 'cause they are rough. He is fast, though."

"I know what you mean," Elder replied. "I suppose if you had all the time it would take, you could finish those horses a little smoother, but that ain't always the case."

The boy watched the horses watch him, and he listened to every word the men spoke and tried to understand everything he heard.

"Do you remember No'Ka?" Patrick asked.

"I do," replied Elder. "Is he still riding horses for you?"

"Some. He's getting a little long in the tooth to be getting on those colts, but he picks out the good ones, and when he gets through with them, you got a horse."

They rounded the corner near the first bunkhouse and Patrick nodded to the boy.

"You'll be staying in this one. J.D., we'll put you up in that one," he said, pointing to the bunkhouse on the far side of the branding pen.

Patrick lifted the rope latch and pushed the door open with his boot. The room smelled of smoke and the musky odor of too many men. Matthew stepped in behind Patrick and recoiled at the smell.

Patrick laughed. "It takes some getting used to."

He pointed to the bunk nearest the door with its mattress rolled up and two blankets folded and laying on top of the mattress next to a thin pillow.

"You can take that one."

Elder shook his head and smiled.

"They saved you the best one," he said. "I reckon they did the same for me."

"Why is this one the best?" the boy asked.

Patrick continued walking into the room.

"It isn't. It's by the door, so you get all the cold air. You're also the first one the foreman can reach when he needs help."

"Can I have that one?" Matthew pointed to the one in the far corner with the most privacy.

"No, that's Cal's bunk. He earned it and he's not likely to give it up."

The boy stood with his burlap sack at his feet and a premonition that he would not be here long.

"The woodpile is on the east side of the bunkhouse, and the shitter is out back. Good idea to take a few sheets of one of them catalogs with you each time, just in case you get out there, do your business, and then find out no one left you any pages. It's a two-holer, so you might have to share."

Elder smiled, and the boy saw nothing about ranching he liked.

"So, who brings in the wood?" Matthew asked with a tone that suggested he already knew the answer.

"Last man hired hauls in the wood each night," Patrick said.

"And that would be me?"

"That would be you."

FORTY-TWO

Ty Riggs entered the dining room first. He nodded towards Elder and stuck out his big-knuckled hand. "Ty Riggs," he said. "From up north."

Elder shook his hand. "J.D. Elder. Good to meet you, Ty. I'm here to help with the branding for a couple of weeks."

Elder tipped his head toward the boy.

"This here's Matthew Stanford."

Riggs smiled and his smile was strong and his eyes had the look of confidence that comes with being good at what you do. The boy stood and had his hand extended before Elder mentioned his name.

"They call you Matt?"

The boy nodded.

"Pleased to meet you, Matt."

"Same here," the boy responded with an immediate sense of respect for the hard-edged cowboy that stood before him.

Matthew expected Riggs to take a seat

next to his. When the cowboy ignored the unspoken invitation and walked to the other end of the table to take a seat, the boy took offence. He sat in his seat and looked at his plate while the others talked.

One by one, the seats filled. Talk ran high and the noise level raised to the point Matthew could no longer follow any conversation, so he picked at his food and waited for the right time to tap Elder on the arm.

"Can I be excused?"

Elder appeared surprised. "We got apple pie coming. You want to wait for some?"

"I'm full, thanks."

"There's no formalities here. You can go when you please."

Matthew nodded. "I'm going back to the bunkhouse," he added, as though he owed an explanation anyway.

"I'll check in on you on my way by," Elder said.

Matthew walked down to the colt corral and sat on the top rail, watching the young horses as they lifted their heads and studied him. They had a freedom about them the boy noticed immediately. He saw it first in their eyes. Despite the split rail fencing that separated them from the forests and meadowlands in which they grew up, the horses had an independent air that set them apart from the farm horses Matthew had known all his life.

The boy stepped down from the fence and into the corral, and as he did so, the young horses raised their heads higher with flared nostrils and a heavy testing of the boy's scent upon the wind. Their eyes shown white and alert and Matthew stood without moving, his senses alerted to the change in the horses' attitudes, as they stood tense and on the edge of breaking.

Matthew spoke to them in a quiet, slow voice, surprised at how quickly their posture went from confident to defensive. He sensed not to move, so he stood motionless as he spoke to them.

A stout, dun-colored gelding was the first to extend his nose to the boy and, when the boy extended his hand, the dun snorted, reared, and thrashed out at the boy with deadly intent. Matthew reeled back to the protection of the fence. He rolled under the bottom rail as the dun charged and pounded the ground where the boy stood. Matthew's heart raced and his face flushed red.

"You crazy son-of-a-bitch," he yelled back at the dun from the protection of the corral rails.

The boy's hands shook and when he turned, No'Ka nodded to him from the

373

shadow of the nearby barn.

"I don't think he likes you much," the old Indian said, as he approached the boy.

"No matter, I don't like him neither."

No'Ka placed his hand on the boy's shoulder, edging him back toward the corral.

"Let me show you something about them horses."

The boy wrestled his arm free and turned toward the bunkhouse.

"I don't care nothing about them damn horses."

The old Indian watched him walk away, and there was no smile on the Indian's face.

"Spoiled white kid," the Indian said softly to himself as he turned and approached the corral full of young horses.

Matthew stopped at the corner of the barn, out of sight of the Indian but still able to see him. The Indian slid the gate rails back and entered the pen. He was quiet and confident. The horses raised their heads and their eyes followed him as he walked the perimeter of the pen, paying them no mind, but deliberate in his actions. They moved as a group to the far side of the corral, keeping as much distance as possible between themselves and the Indian. He seemed to ignore them as he walked in their direction. They stood and watched him with less fear, but no less intensity. When he walked among them, and they let him do so, the boy stepped out from behind the corner of the barn.

The Indian positioned himself close to the dun and offered the nervous horse the back of his hand. Matthew tensed in anticipation of the attack he was sure would follow. When the dun stretched his nose out to the hand of the Indian and did not attack, the boy felt he was a witness to some unique power possessed by the Indian alone. No'Ka turned and walked slowly toward the gate, and the dun followed.

Matthew waited for the dun to charge, but the horse only followed the Indian at a distance and regarded him with curiosity. The Indian stopped and the horse stopped. The Indian stepped out and the horse stepped forth in his direction. The boy watched. For all he did not understand about that which he observed, the boy was certain the Indian possessed powers far beyond any of those he had ever seen.

Matthew slipped back behind the barn and walked toward the bunkhouse, his mind reeled with all the things he did not like about this place. He contemplated his low regard for the horses that he did not understand, and he resented the violence the dun displayed in rejection of his gesture of friendship.

The bunkhouse door was open slightly when Matthew stepped onto the single wooden plank that served as a step. He pushed the door open and looked inside before he entered. His eyes adjusted slowly to the dim light inside and, when they did, he saw two cowboys, one not much older than him, settling their gear into the foot-lockers at the end of their bunks.

Matthew stepped inside. The two cowboys looked up and neither spoke as Matthew walked over to his bunk and pulled the burlap sack out from beneath it. He rummaged through the sack and then, without removing any of its contents, tied the sack and placed it in his footlocker.

The younger of the two cowboys closed the lid on his footlocker and stopped at Matthew's bunk on his way to the door. He looked at the boy, sized him up with his eyes, and then extended his hand.

"Name's Lucas," he said.

The boy shook his hand. Matthew felt intimidated by the young cowboy's direct demeanor, and hard-edged look. His firm handshake reinforced the boy's sense that Lucas had a lot more experience than his years would suggest.

"Matthew," the boy said, attempting to sound as grown up as Lucas.

"So," Lucas began. "What brings you to the Arbuckle?"

"I came with Mr. Elder." Then he added for further credibility, "To learn a little about cowboyin' and horsemanship."

"There ain't no money in cowboyin'," Lucas said, as he shook his head side to side.

"Well, it don't appeal to me none, anyway."

"Then why you here?"

"I guess they thought it would do me some good."

The second cowboy stood near the table with his boot set upon the chair and his hat tilted back. He was older than Lucas by about five years, Matthew judged, as he eyed him while he spoke to Lucas.

In the silence that ensued, Matthew directed his attention to the second cowboy and stuck out his hand.

"My name's Matthew," he said, as the second cowboy stood there unmoved and stared at the young boy. Matthew held his hand in suspension for an uncomfortably long time before the second cowboy addressed him.

"Why don't you get your skinny ass back

on your horse and ride back to town if you don't want to be here?"

Matthew dropped his hand and he glared at the cowboy. He gritted his teeth, looked up at the much taller cowboy, and visualized himself with the hammer ratcheted back and looking at the cowboy over the sight of his pistol.

"I don't suppose that's any of your damn business, is it?" Matthew replied.

The cowboy stepped forth and slapped Matthew on the back of his head in a taunting manner meant to demean the boy more than hurt him.

"You're just full of piss and vinegar ain't you?" the cowboy said.

As the cowboy appeared to move to engage the boy, Matthew lunged for Cal. Lucas stepped in between them. With his arm blocking the cowboy's access to Matthew, Lucas stopped the advance and the cowboy looked at him as though his gaze demanded an explanation.

"Come on, Cal, he's just a kid."

Cal and Lucas started for the door, then Cal turned to the boy as Lucas pushed the door open. He motioned toward the stove and the wood box and addressed the boy.

"You best have that box full and the fire stoked when we get back." Matthew glared

378

at Cal. When the door closed behind the two cowboys, Matthew sat on his bed and his eyes filled with hate. He ran his shirtsleeve across his runny nose and then stood before the footlocker with some deliberation.

He lifted the lid, removed the burlap sack, and removed the rawhide lace that bound it. He laid the sack on his mattress and pulled forth the bundle wrapped in a wool shirt. He unfolded the shirt and, when he had the pistol in his hand, he felt his confidence soar. He sighted the pistol on the pillow at the top of Cal's bunk, pulled back the hammer until it clicked twice, and imagined the blast of fire at the muzzle. He gently lowered the hammer and returned the pistol to the wool shirt.

FORTY-THREE

Matthew judged the hour to be late by the length of time he lay on his back. He stared up at the reflection of the fire from the woodstove where the dull orange glow shown against a spot on a ceiling beam and all else was in complete darkness.

He listened to the heavy breathing and the snoring, and he stared at the ceiling to the unending sounds of half a dozen men sleeping in one small room. Some men talked in their sleep and the talk was incoherent and garbled, but it kept on throughout the night and the boy never slept because of it.

He slipped out of his blanket and quietly restocked the stove with wood. He yawned and rubbed his eyes. He stretched, then returned to his bunk determined to sleep. He lay there just long enough to get warm, when the door burst open and Ty Riggs lit the lamp on the small table and slammed the coffee pot against the side of the cast iron stove.

"Let's roll boys. Breakfast is on the table and you're going to need two good horses today, so move it!"

Matthew threw off his blanket and slipped into his trousers and boots. He looked around the room with no idea what to do. He watched the other cowboys as they went through their individual rituals of awakening. Some sat up and stretched, others swung their legs over the edge of the bed, and a few were up, dressed, and ready to go before Matthew could get his shirt buttoned.

They gathered up their spurs and chaps and catch ropes, and were all on their way out the door as Matthew pulled on his jacket and hat and waited, uncomfortably, for some indication of what to do next.

"You ready, Matt?" Lucas asked.

"I think so."

"Come on with me. I'll help you catch a horse and get your rig together. Did you bring your own saddle and rope?"

"I don't have a saddle and I don't know how to rope."

Lucas smiled and looked down at the boy.

"No problem. We'll get you lined out with a decent horse and get you some gear, and go get us some breakfast."

Matthew could not bring himself to give in to the cowboy's kindness, and all he could do was nod.

The sun was a long ways from coming up and, as Matthew and Lucas strode by the colt pen, the cowboy looked down at the boy in the moonlight.

"What do you think of these colts?" Lucas asked, gesturing to the pen where the dun stood.

"I don't think much of 'em."

Lucas laughed.

"Oh, you don't, huh? And why's that?"

"I just don't."

"There's a couple real good ones in there."

"Not that tan-colored one," Matthew added.

"You mean the dun?"

"Whatever you call him."

"Them horses ain't broke yet, but that dun looks to be the best one of the lot."

"Broke?"

"Broke to ride. Until you get 'em broke they ain't worth much. But, get a good one, and get him broke good — then you got yourself a horse."

"How do they break them?"

"Well, ol' Ty, he's a sure enough bronc peeler. He does it the hard and fast way.

Rides them and whups the daylights out of them until they give up. Makes a good horse, but they ain't got no heart. Hard workers — just no heart."

Matthew looked up at the cowboy, still not clear, but with no interest one way or the other. They walked toward the big horse pen where the remuda for the day stood for the selection process.

"Then there's the way No'Ka does it," Lucas continued. "He has a quiet way of working that horse's mind until he has the horse doing everything he wants without the buck and the whippings."

The boy thought back to yesterday, and then he was interested.

"So, does he break the horse?"

"Well, when he finishes with a horse, that horse is definitely broke. In every way, that is, except his spirit."

The boy wanted to ask more questions, but Lucas pulled him over to the catch pen. The sky lightened just enough for the boy to make out the horses in the pen. He watched as, one by one, the cowboys went in, roped two horses each, and led them out of the pen.

"I'm up," Lucas said. "I'll get my two and two gentle ones for you. Wait here."

The boy watched in amazement as the

cowboy walked quietly up to the horses standing with their butts to him, and quietly laid in a backhand loop and pulled out the horses he wanted without disturbing the others. When Matthew saw him pull out the same horse Elder chose for him yesterday, the boy felt relieved.

By the time the sun cleared the eastern ridgeline, the company of cowboys rode well up into the high meadows, crossed many creeks, and traversed several miles of heavily treed forest that surrounded the park lands where mother cows grazed with their babies and herd bulls hid out in the brush.

Matthew found his rhythm with the cadence of the horse's stride and the rocking of the saddle. He looked for landmarks, and when he closed his eyes, he could see General Ike Smith riding ahead and he could feel the eyes of the mulatto searing into the back of his jacket. His eyes snapped open; he could feel his blood rushing and his heart pounding.

He sensed the presence of another horseman and, when he turned to look, Elder reined in alongside him.

"How's it going, Matt?"

"Good."

"I see you met some of the boys."

"I met Lucas and Cal."

"They're both good boys," Elder said.

The boy looked over at Elder and, for a moment, the boy appeared to be contemplating the words forming in his head.

"Yeah, I like Lucas."

Elder looked sideways at the boy.

"And Cal?"

The boy just shook his head.

"I've known most of the crew a while now. Lucas isn't much older than you. But, they're both good boys. Cal can be a little rough until he gets to know you."

"I guess," Matthew said, with no conviction. They rode side by side and finally the boy spoke.

"So what are we doing today?"

"It's a three-day gather, if it all goes good," Elder said. "Today we'll gather everything from the high elevations and move them down to the lower pastures. When we get everything together down below, we'll sort off the pairs and drive them in one group. We'll bring the bulls and dry cows in behind them. We'll work the horses hard, and just hope you don't run out of horse before the day's done."

The boy looked at Elder as if the cowboy had just preached an entire sermon in a foreign language. Elder grinned.

"Just follow along, you'll get the idea."

"I'll get the idea?" the boy said under his breath, as he shook his head and touched the horse with his heels.

FORTY-FOUR

The sun stood high in the sky when they rode upon the first of the high-meadow cattle. In the beginning, they saw scattered pairs and a range bull with its head down. Then they came upon groups of fifty or sixty, with more grazing at the tree line and across the meadows on steeply sloped hillsides.

They rode another hour to the upper meadows. At the top, the cow boss, Ty Riggs, called the cowboys into a circle. He dismounted and cut a short pine branch for a pointer. Riggs then cleared a patch of ground with his boot and sketched out a crude map of the area. He drew lines and assigned positions. He gave instructions and told each man where to hold his cattle if he got them to that point before the others arrived. The men listened and looked out across the endless landscape each time Riggs pointed in that general direction with his stick. They talked among themselves, making contingency plans as they nodded in agreement or argued a point. When Riggs stepped up into the saddle and said, "Let's ride," the cowboys split from the group with a deliberateness that left Matthew feeling alone and confused.

"Ty," Lucas shouted as the meeting broke up. "I'm gonna take Matthew with me."

Matthew grinned and Ty waved his approval as the cowboys rode out in a long line that would soon form a moving wing that spanned several miles across its front.

"Why'd you pick me?" Matthew asked Lucas after they were alone and riding through the thick trees.

Lucas smiled. "Cal paid me five dollars to lose you out here."

Matthew laughed. "He did not."

"Could you find your way back if you had to?" Lucas asked.

The boy's look was stern and serious.

"I reckon I could," he said, and Lucas believed him.

"So how old are you, Matt?"

"Going on fifteen, why?"

"No reason. You just seem older than that."

"I got some miles on me."

"Fourteen years old — couldn't be many."

The boy shrugged, but did not respond.

"So how about you?"

"So how about me, what?"

"How old are you?"

"I'm nineteen." He looked over at the boy, and his expression was serious. "And I got a few miles on me too."

"You like doing this?"

"Cowboying? Yeah, I like it. I don't know anything else."

The boy nodded in the affirmative as though he understood.

They rode down a gradual slope of sweet spring grass scattered about with small white flowers that grew like the hand that put them there did so purely for the beauty of it. They maneuvered the horses between dense stands of buckbrush and the magenta-colored western redbud trees that populated the area and made the going hard.

As they picked their way cautiously through the heavy brush, Lucas reached out and broke off a handful of foliage from the buckbrush that impeded their way. He held his hand in Matthew's direction, and then threw the leaves on the ground.

"The Indians make tea out of this shit. Makes you wish they drank more of it, don't it?

Matthew smiled and pulled his horse up

when Lucas stopped his. The cowboy pointed across the small meadow and generally up toward a heavily treed ridgeline that appeared to run a long distance north to south.

"We're going up there. We can get a pretty good view of this whole side of the mountain. We'll spread out and start our sweep down this way, and we'll push all the cattle we pick up down that way. See where that big jack pine stands between the two smaller ones? You'll want to head straight for that."

"What'll I do if I see some cattle?"

"Just stay behind 'em and yahoo 'em down into that valley and head 'em south. Then wait. I'll meet you down there just below the big pine."

Matthew stood in the stirrups and looked in the general direction in which Lucas pointed. He nodded okay and watched the cowboy turn his horse up the trail.

Lucas waved as he rode off into the trees.

"Keep an eye out for bear."

The boy sat his horse and watched Lucas disappear into the shadows of the trees. When he could no longer hear the footfalls of the cowboy's horse, he looked about with a feeling of foreboding that left his hands shaking. Of all the instructions, the only things he remembered were the thick pine tree between the two small ones, and the bear. He set out for the pine tree.

His horse grew uncharacteristically tense and tossed its head. It bounced on its feet and refused to settle into a walk. The uncertainty of the horse became the uncertainty of the boy and, when it did, the nervous energy of the two bordered on a fight. The boy jerked the horse's head around and the horse took the bit. The horse pranced jogged, and tossed its head with no mind on the job at hand.

The boy gave the horse its head, and it trotted to the east, head held high, and stepping out wildly in the wrong direction. Matthew wheeled the horse around hard, and the horse arched its back and threatened to buck as the boy leaned back on the reins, attempting to regain control of the fractious horse. The boy forced his will on the horse, and the more he did so, the more the horse resisted him.

Matthew felt the explosiveness of the horse building to the breaking point, and he realized he had no control of the animal at all. The horse rolled its eyes and laid its ears back. It tossed its head in an unreasonable manner that jerked the reins from the boy's hand. The boy felt as though he stood with one foot on a narrow ledge and the other on the edge of panic. He snatched up the reins and pulled back and, when he did so, the horse dropped its head, pulling the boy forward in the saddle as it left the ground with all four feet in the air. When it came down, it came down hard, and the boy stayed in the saddle but lost a stirrup.

Fear gripped the boy and his mind raced. He shouted at the horse to stop and pulled back hard on one rein. The horse turned and jigged, and the boy remembered No'Ka and the dun and he immediately pushed the reins forward, took a deep breath, sat deep in the saddle, and looked over the horse's head at the thick pine. As the boy relaxed, the horse relaxed. The boy lightly touched the reins to the side of the horse's neck, and the horse slowly lined up on the thick pine and stepped out in that direction.

The boy let his breath out when the horse settled back into a soft jog. He felt his heart race and his hands shook. For the second time he felt a fear he did not understand from an animal for which he had no regard. And there, for the first time, he began to understand what Elder meant by horsemanship.

Matthew stared across the meadow, high up the slope to the upper ridge where Lucas rode, and when Lucas and his horse appeared from the brush, they appeared as nothing more than dark shadows on the landscape. The cowboy sat straight and easy in the saddle, and he pushed before him sixty or seventy head of cattle. The cattle, the horse, and the cowboy descended the steep slope at a fast trot, and Matthew watched the cowboy with great interest.

The smooth, deliberate movements of the cowboy matched those of his horse and together the man and horse appeared as though one was made for the other, and Matthew experienced his first taste of envy.

The boy nudged his horse forward and it lifted its head; its eyes locked onto the thick brush and rocks just above the trail. Matthew looked, but saw nothing. He touched the horse with his heels when the horse stopped and stood firm. Horse and rider stared into the brush. The brush stood still and quiet, then exploded with a thunderous crash as more than a dozen cows and calves broke for the clearing. Matthew's horse spun and sidestepped, and then charged after the fleeing cattle without being asked to do so. The boy felt himself tilt precipitously in the saddle, then he righted himself and leaned forward as the wind whipped his face. He pulled his hat down tight, gave the horse its head, and galloped to far left of the leaders to turn the cattle toward the big pine tree. When he did so, the cattle turned and finally slowed to a walk. Matthew Stanford sat up tall in the saddle and, for that brief instant, he knew what it felt like to be a cowboy.

He trailed the cattle for a long time, picked up more along the way and, when he saw Lucas waiting at the jack pine with his cattle grazing and resting, Matthew drifted his cattle in with those of the cowboy. Lucas sat leaning back with his right hand resting on his horse's rump as he watched the boy approach him from across the meadow. Matthew sat easy in the saddle, heels down, one hand resting against his leg and the other holding the reins lightly, the way Lucas held his reins.

Lucas shook his head and smiled when Matthew circled the cattle and rode up to him.

"I'll be a son-of-a-bitch." He laughed and grinned. "I sure didn't expect to see you again for a while. And I damn sure didn't expect to see you with any cattle."

Matthew leaned back in his saddle and put his hand on his horse's rump as he sat there. He wanted to laugh and he wanted to weep, but he did neither.

He looked at the cowboy. "Did I do good?"

"You done good."

Matthew sat like that and, as he looked out upon the grazing cattle, he felt as though he had accomplished something great, something he could not describe, and something he could not fully comprehend.

"Don't get too comfortable cowboy, we got a long ways to go yet today."

Lucas sat straight in the saddle and pointed out to the long valley below.

"We'll push these pairs down into the valley there, just let them drift along while you and I ride way up in the brush on both sides and pick up everything along the way."

As he spoke, the cowboy made sweeping gestures with his hand that included the valley and the steep slopes that attended the valley on its east and west sides. Matthew saw the logic in the explanation, and the whole gathering process began to make some sense to him.

"Won't our cattle run off if we leave them to get all the ones up high there?" Matthew asked.

"They'll be okay. Once they're off the hills and in the valley, they'll tend to stay low and follow the meadows around — which is exactly what we want them to do."

The boy nodded, and this time he understood.

"Now the cattle we pick up in the brush will all want to get to this bunch, and we just keep collecting them that way until we got this side cleaned out. Watch for strays. Some of them mommas will brush up with them babies, and it's a lot harder bringing in stragglers."

Matthew visualized everything Lucas said and the more he thought about it, the more sense it made. For everything within him that wanted nothing to do with horses or cowboys, Matthew found himself with a strange feeling of wanting to measure up to some unwritten code he did not understand. The simple act of redefining an imaginary boundary to embrace that which he did not accept, invited an acceptance he did not anticipate.

Cowboying was, by any measure, a thankless job. The men who chose to cowboy seemed to have been chosen by it. The pay was meager, the conditions sparse, and there was no promise of anything better to come of it. But the men who cowboyed did so with a bravado and pride that elevated the position to a level of nobility and gave the impression that to be a cowboy was to have been granted a fraternal privilege attained only by a select few.

Matthew sat his horse and scanned the upper elevations of the slopes for which he was responsible. For everything in him that rejected anything to do with horses and cows, somehow being called cowboy by Lucas made him want to live up to the title. He urged his horse up the trail and, more than anything, he wanted to descend his side of the mountain with every cow, calf, and bull he could find.

FORTY-FIVE

It was late in the day when Lucas and Matthew ran their cattle in through the narrow gap at the south end of the valley to a vast meadow where several hundred head of cattle grazed. The perimeter of the great circle stood defined by the handful of mounted cowboys who rode it in a quiet, clockwise manner.

A wide but shallow creek ran down from the mountains and cut through the valley from east to west. The creek formed a demarcation line where the cowboys would let the cattle drink but not cross. Two men rode the south side of the creek and a third rode the tree line just above them. A flat clearing near the edge of the meadow at the upper end of the creek was set up for the camp. The sun hung suspended half-visible at the distant granite peaks to the west and the warmth of the day gave in to the chill of early evening.

Lucas and the boy sat their horses and watched their cattle join those brought in earlier by the other cowboys.

"How many you think we got?" Lucas asked.

"You mean ours or all of them?" the boy asked.

"Just ours."

"I don't know, I didn't count 'em."

"Riggs is going to ask."

"So, how many do you think we got?" the boy asked.

Lucas looked over at the boy, leaned forward in the saddle, and rested his forearms on the saddle horn.

"Eighty-five cows, seventy calves, and five bulls — give or take."

The boy raised his eyebrows and looked back at the cattle, as though his looking might verify the number. He tried to count the slow-moving cattle and lost count as they milled, changed places, and all seemed to run together.

The boy looked over at Lucas, his brow furrowed and his expression one of curiosity.

"So, how'd you come up with those numbers?"

Lucas smiled.

"The bulls are easy. The rest you have to

watch as they cross a narrow point where you have a tree or a post or rock, or something you can use for a marker. Just count each one that passes that mark. Don't count ahead, and don't count the ones that stop or turn back. Just count the ones that go by your mark. It takes a little practice, but you'll get good at it after while."

"So how good are you at it?"

"Real good — once I count 'em, they stay counted." Lucas grinned and the boy wasn't sure if the grin was one of pride or jest, but either way the boy was impressed.

The boy shook his head and laughed. I don't ever want to be a cowboy, Matthew said to himself. But if I did, I'd want to be like him.

When they stood the horses at the picket line, Lucas swung down easy from the saddle and had his rig off the horse by the time the boy got his feet to the ground. His muscles ached and he stretched his arms to take the tension out of his shoulders that he did not realize was there.

"A little sore?"

Mathew nodded. "A little."

"We 'bout run out of horse today. We'll turn these two in with the remuda and draw fresh ones in the morning."

"How's my other one?"

"He's okay. A little cold-backed in the morning, but once you get the kinks rode out of him, he's good."

"Cold-backed?"

"Yeah — might have a buck or two in him."

"What do I do if he bucks?"

Lucas laughed, but his tone was serious.

"You mean when he bucks. Just stay in the middle of him. Draw back real good on one rein, then let him step out when he settles."

Matthew did not like the sound of any of that and, by his silence, he reaffirmed his dislike for cowboying.

They ate an early supper and, when they spread out their bedrolls, the moon was up and the sky was ablaze with stars. A coyote called to the moon, another answered, and in that dark void Matthew imagined a she-wolf with amber eyes lit up in the night and tracking him in his sleep. He tried not to imagine Ike and Raymond and Sandoval, but all three of them stared back at him from the blackness of the woods. This night, like each night before, would end the same. The boy imagined a shotgun blast and watched Ike explode like mist in a bottle. He saw muzzle fire at the end of the pistol and, when the fire faded, Sandoval faded with it. However, it was Raymond who persisted. He pulled the trigger over and over and over, until only Raymond's eyes remained, then they blinked and they were also gone.

The boy slept a fitful sleep and when he felt Lucas tap the end of his bedroll with the toe of his boot, the boy sat upright, confused, and disoriented.

"Let's go, cowboy."

Matthew rubbed his eyes and looked up at the sky, which was the same sky with the same moon and the same stars he saw when he finally slept.

"I'm ready."

They finished a quick breakfast. What talk there was, was brief and every man there had a purpose. Matthew and Lucas saddled their horses, and Lucas sensed the boy's apprehension as he stood beside his horse and hesitated to mount.

"Just get it over with. He won't blow before you're in the saddle. I'll be right here."

Matthew did not notice the other cowboys as they stopped to watch.

The boy's stomach churned and his hands shook as he grabbed the stirrup leather and hoisted himself up. He swung his leg over the saddle and sat down. The horse stood quietly and the boy touched him with his heels. When he did so, the horse stepped out, then bowed its back, arched as it violently left the ground with all four feet, then twisted and came down hard. When it did, the jolt and the quick turn launched the boy and he lay on his back, with all the wind knocked out of him, but still holding the reins.

He heard laughing and the loud drone of the cowboys' voices as they replayed the ride. Matthew got to his feet, picked up his hat, and stood next to the horse without looking at those who watched.

"Son-of-a-bitch," he said to the horse as he set his jaw and climbed back in the saddle. He pulled the left rein tight and kicked the horse with his heels. At the same time, the horse bowed its back, set for another explosive launch, and the boy doubled his head around and forced the horse into a tight circle. He rode the horse into a trot, with the horse pulling gape-jawed and giving to the pressure as it made small circles around the spot where the boy lay the first time. The boy released the left rein and drew back the right one, trotting the horse in reverse circles until the horse relaxed and settled.

Matthew looked up and, in the dim light of morning, he saw the cowboys as they clapped and cheered. If he had a prouder moment, he could not remember when it was.

"Damn, Matt," Lucas said. "That was nice."

As they rode out, Cal rode up from behind and drifted his horse in alongside Matthew's horse. Matthew looked over at him, and Cal's expression gave no indication as to his purpose. Cal looked at the boy, leaned over, and slapped him on the shoulder.

"Good ride, kid."

Matthew smiled and nodded, and Cal turned his horse back up the trail.

FORTY-SIX

Three more days the cowboys rode the brush and the steep slopes of the mountain, and by the end of the fifth day, the horses had nothing left to give. Riggs totaled up the tally on small bits of paper upon which he made clusters of four lines with a cross hatch for every five he counted. He wet the tip of the stubby wooden pencil on his tongue, recalculated, nodded, and then looked up at the waiting eyes that sat before him like a congregation of supplicants whose fate rested in his hands. He looked out at the cowboys from beneath the brim of his hat and paused a long time before he spoke. The silence that attended the ritual did so with religious reverence.

"Let's head 'em home, boys," he said with great authority.

Whoops and hollers from the cowboys punctuated his proclamation as they whistled and coaxed the enormous herd down country for the long ride to the Arbuckle.

At the ranch they separated the bulls from the cows and calves, and sorted the old, broken-down bulls into the cull-pen. They separated the pairs and ran the calves into the branding pen.

Matthew watched as Lucas, Cal, and what he perceived as the elite of the cowboys entered the branding pen mounted on fresh horses and warmed them up as they shook out their ropes and milled about. The ground crew built half a dozen small fires along one fence line of the branding pen while others sharpened folding knives, and some carried armloads of branding irons from the barn.

Elder walked up behind Matthew.

"I saw you ride that bronc the morning we left. You got a natural feel for a horse."

Matthew looked up at Elder.

"Thanks."

Riggs waved and called to the boy from the high fence of the branding pen.

"Matthew Stanford — come over here," he shouted, loud enough for all the cowboys to hear.

The boy hurried to the branding pen and stood near Riggs.

"I want you to go over to that fire there." He pointed to the fire where No'Ka busied himself.

"We're going to teach you how to brand and castrate."

"Castrate?"

"Yeah, castrate."

The boy looked puzzled, but did not speak.

"Cut the nuts off the bull calves," Riggs added for clarification.

Matthews's eyes widened.

Riggs laughed. "Don't worry, someone will hold them down and show you how it's done first."

Matthew smiled, climbed over the fence, and dashed to his assigned spot.

No'Ka looked at the boy. "You got a knife?"

Matthew withdrew the old folding knife from his pocket and presented it to the Indian in the palm of his hand. The Indian took it, ran his thumb over the blade, and looked down at the boy in a disapproving manner.

"You ever sharpen this?"

"No, sir."

No'Ka reached into the bucket of supplies hung from a hook on the fence, and withdrew a whetstone. He spat upon it and

407

slowly drew the blade across it several times on both sides.

"Give me your arm."

The boy extended his arm to the Indian, and the Indian shaved a patch of hair from it.

"That'll do."

He handed the boy the knife.

"I'll show you how to do the first few, and then it will be your job. Cut first, brand last. Put the brand on the left rib every time. When the brand is done, give the flankers the nod and they'll release the calf and the ropers will drag a fresh one to the fire."

The boy looked up at the Indian. His expression was one of great reverence, as though the Indian possessed many skills that existed far beyond the imagination of the boy.

"Just so you know — I still don't give a damn about cowboying or horsemanship."

The Indian looked down at him with disdain.

"I didn't ask you if you give a damn about cowboying or horsemanship."

By some unspoken declaration, everything happened at once. Cowboys built overhand loops and some built enormous loops they laid on the ground like a trap that snared the hind legs of a calf and stretched it out as the cowboy dallied, took up the slack, then turned his horse and dragged the calf to the fire. The ground crew descended upon the calf and the heaviest man in each crew flanked the calf, left side up. He straddled the neck of the calf and waited for the second man to release the heel catch, then move into position to take the hind legs and push the ground leg forward with his foot as he pulled the top leg back with both hands and held firm.

The Indian nodded at the boy. "Follow me."

No'Ka knelt near the calf, deftly stretched the scrotal sac between his thumb and index finger while he drew the knife blade across it in one smooth motion and the bottom inch-and-a-half of the sac slipped away, exposing the white tissue of the testicles and a ring of blood where the cut was made. He reached up with his free hand, pulled the testicles down to expose them, then pulled one until the connecting tubes and tissue disconnected deep within the animal. He pulled the excess connecting tissues free and repeated the process with the remaining testicle. Matthew cringed, but he watched every movement with complete attention. No'Ka tossed the freshly cut testicles in a bucket and went back to the fire for the branding iron.

Matthew looked at the bucket half-full of testicles then back up at the Indian.

"What do you do with those?"

"Give them to the cook. They'll be in your supper tonight."

The Indian placed one foot on the calf for balance, touched the hot iron to the hide just long enough to burn the surface hair, and to let the calf react to the first sensation of pain. He pulled the iron while the animal kicked and fought the flankers. When the calf settled, the Indian reset the hot iron and leaned on it, sending yellow smoke and the acrid smell of burning hide into the air.

When the Indian removed the iron, he brushed the singed hair aside and nodded to the boy.

"That's how you want it to look — honey brown and not blotched. Leave it too long and the brand will blur when it heals. Take it off too soon and the brand will fade and you won't be able to read it."

They walked back to the fire and waited for the next calf. No'Ka worked the next two and the boy held the knife and fetched the hot iron. When Cal dragged the fourth calf, bawling and kicking to the fire, the Indian looked down at the boy.

"This one's yours."

Two cowboys flanked and stretched the calf, and the boy dropped to his knees and reached for the scrotal sac. He felt between the calves legs, nervous and eager to get the first one right.

Cal's tone was impatient, but his expression was one of amusement.

"Get him cut."

The boy's hands shook and, when he looked up, the cowboys watching him broke into loud laughter that caused the others to turn and look as well.

"That's a heifer," No'Ka said. "No nuts. Get your iron."

The boy looked up at the roper. "Funny, Cal."

When Matthew put the hot iron to the hide of the heifer, the calf kicked, turned, and the iron slipped and blurred the brand. The boy looked up at the Indian.

"Reset the iron and try it again."

The boy did and the new brand appeared passable but, alongside the bad brand, there was no pride in the boy's work, and he walked back to the fire admonishing himself for it.

The next calf went better, but not well. And so the one after that. By noon, the boy had worked nearly eighty calves. His fingers

411

ached, his shoulders ached, and the smell of burnt hair filled his lungs. Cal coiled up his rope, hung it on the saddle horn, and swung down from his horse.

"Time to eat. Come on, Matt — let's get some of them old beans from last night," he said, as he tapped the boy on the shoulder with the back of his hand as he walked by him.

Matthew looked back at the Indian to make sure the invitation included him as well.

"I'll be along," No'Ka said, as he nodded for Matt and Cal to go on without him.

"I don't think No'Ka likes me much," the boy said to Cal.

Cal spoke without looking at the boy. "I don't like you much myself."

Matthew waited for a laugh or a smile but none came, and they walked the rest of the way in silence.

By the end of the day No'Ka calculated the branding would take the rest of the week unless the pace picked up considerably, which it was not likely to do. He and the boy walked back to the barn together, both tired, both satisfied with a hard day's work.

"For a kid that doesn't want to be a cowboy, you did a good job today."

The boy did not respond and, when they

arrived at the barn he cleared his throat, looked down at his boots, then he raised his head, and looked directly into the dark eyes of the Indian.

"I want to rope some calves before we finish," he said, his voice firm with conviction.

"Can you rope?"

"I reckon I can — I just never done it is all."

"Do you have a rope?"

"Yeah, I got the one Lucas gave me before we started the gather."

"Go get it."

When the boy returned he found the Indian standing near an oak barrel set up inside the barn.

"Come here. I set this barrel up for you to rope."

The Indian stepped back and pointed to a spot less than ten feet from the barrel.

"Stand here and build a loop and rope this barrel."

Matthew looked puzzled. He stood on the spot and glanced back at the Indian.

"Anybody could do it from this close."

"Then do it."

The boy made an overhead circle with the small loop, the way he saw the cowboys do it. Each time, the loop collapsed and he was unable to feed it slack to expand it to an adequate size. He repeated the process several times, and each time was unable to build a serviceable loop. In desperation, he threw the loop he had and the loop crumpled at the base of the barrel. Again and again he tried, and each time he failed.

The Indian watched but offered no assistance. The boy threw down the rope and turned toward the Indian.

"Well?" he asked, and shrugged to beg an answer.

"I guess you're just too close to the barrel," the Indian responded with a tone of sarcasm that was not lost on the boy.

The boy picked up the rope and spoke as he turned to leave.

"Just forget it," he said, as he slammed the door behind him.

FORTY-SEVEN

Matthew stopped by the horse pen on his way back to the bunkhouse. He leaned on the fence rails and watched the young horses. He spotted the dun the same time the dun spotted him. The horse snorted and its neck tensed. It tested the air in loud inhalations that sounded both threatening and fearful. The dun trotted lightly to the far side of the corral, its eyes locked onto the boy, and its tail flagged as it circled the horses around him.

The boy walked slowly around the perimeter outside the pen, and he spoke in a soft voice as he closed the distance and approached the horse's position, moving ever closer to the dun. The horse stood without moving, only its eyes tracked the boy as he approached.

The horse pivoted to face the boy, and it extended its nose toward the boy's outstretched hand as he reached between the

rails. The boy talked to the horse in a soothing voice and the horse took one, then two
tentative steps in the boy's direction.

The boy smiled and whispered to the
horse. With no warning, the horse screamed
a terrible scream, reared up on its hind legs,
and pounded the fence rail with its front
hooves, splintering the wood where the
boy's arm had been. The boy recoiled in
panic, his hands trembled, and he was
barely able to pick up his rope. He turned
to leave and saw Cal standing near the
bunkhouse watching.

Matthew ignored Cal as he stepped up
onto the plank board and went inside. He
threw down his rope and lay on his back
with his boots on his blanket.

I hate this place, he said to himself. He
laced his fingers behind his head and lay
there with his hat over his eyes and his eyes
closed, wishing himself anywhere but there.

One by one, the cowboys came in. A few
sat at the table and played cards, others
stood over the coffee pot and some returned
to the privacy of their bunks. When Lucas
came in, he slapped the bottom of the boy's
boots as he walked by without stopping.

"Good day today," he said, with no further
comment.

When Cal came in, he stopped near the

stove and looked over at the boy who remained hidden beneath his hat.

Cal laughed and nodded toward the boy, then announced in a voice too loud for the circumstances.

"Hey, Matt — that little dun horse scare the shit out of you back there?"

Then he laughed and told the story until everybody laughed and poked fun at the boy.

The boy lay there and his emotions converged upon him in a heat wave of hatefulness not even he understood. Matthew jumped to his feet in a rage. He rushed across the floor and stood face to face with Cal.

"You're a son-of-a-bitch, Cal!"

The cowboy's expression turned cold and the silence in the room caused everyone to turn toward the pair. Cal drew back a big-knuckled fist and drove it squarely into the boy's face. Matthew's nose collapsed. Blood spewed forth, soaking his shirt and dripping onto the floor where he stood.

The boy took a wild swing and missed. Cal swung again and his calloused knuckles connected with full impact against the side of the boy's head. Matthew's vision blurred and his ears rang. He turned and staggered toward his footlocker, where he withdrew the burlap sack.

The men watched, and Cal stood motionless, when the boy turned and pointed the cocked pistol at the cowboy. The pistol shook in his hands as he lined the cowboy up in the sights with his good eye and squeezed the trigger.

Before the fire and thunder exploded from the muzzle of the pistol, Lucas caught the boy's arm in an upward motion that sent the bullet spiraling through the wooden shingles above them. Lucas wrestled the pistol from the boy's grip and Cal rushed forth seething with fear and anger.

"Let it alone, Cal."

"The little bastard tried to kill me."

"But he didn't."

Shaken and unsettled, Cal looked back at Lucas as he walked to his bunk.

"Don't give that lunatic his gun back." Cal's voice was unsteady and uncertain.

Lucas walked Matthew outside. Elder, Patrick, and several others came running and stopped when they approached Lucas and the boy.

"We heard a shot. Is everything okay?" Patrick asked.

Lucas nodded. He handed the pistol to Patrick.

"You might want to hold on to this. It

belongs to Matthew."

Patrick looked over at Elder, and Elder shook his head.

"All right, look — everything's okay. We got another big day tomorrow. Go on back inside," Patrick said.

He looked over at Lucas for confirmation and noticed Matthew's cuts and bruises.

"He'll be okay. We'll get him cleaned up and I'll explain everything to you in the morning," Lucas said to Patrick.

After everyone left, Lucas walked the boy down to the barn. They sat on old wooden crates and Lucas looked at Matthew without speaking. The boy stared into the darkness, his eyes void of expression, and his jaw set.

"You know, you could have killed him."

The boy turned his head and looked up at Lucas. There was no remorse about the boy, and the coldness in his voice sent a chill up the back of the cowboy.

"I meant to kill him."

Lucas measured his words with great care, and he waited before he spoke. When he did speak, his voice was soft and deliberate.

"There ain't many good reasons to take a man's life, and if there is, that damn sure wasn't one of them."

Matthew looked directly at Lucas, and the young boy's look was that of an old man

419

contemplating the young cowboy whose opinion was so void of experience as to make it undeserving of a response. Matthew held his gaze and the intensity in his eyes made Lucas uncomfortable and he looked away.

Lucas sat back, watched the boy, and waited for some sign of encouragement or regret or anger, but there was none. He wanted to reach out for the boy, to offer him help, but he had no answers he knew of to help the youngster.

"Look, Matt. Maybe the thing for you to do is just pack your things in the morning and go on back home. You don't want to be here, and you might as well get out before something bad does happen."

The boy nodded in agreement. If he was disappointed or relieved, it did not show.

"I'll go back and get your things and we can make you a bed down here tonight, if you want. In the morning, I'll ride back to town with you and bring your horse back to the ranch."

The boy looked at Lucas and his eyes softened. He held back the tears that threatened to give him away.

"I wanted to rope a calf."

Lucas stood. He walked over to the horse stalls, and leaned back against the wall with one boot up behind him.

"Well, for shit's sake, Matt — do you want to go or do you want to stay?"

"I want to stay."

Lucas started for the door.

"Come on then, you got a lot of fences to mend. You might as well get started and you ain't getting that gun back."

When they stepped through the bunkhouse door, the room fell silent and all eyes followed the boy. He spotted Cal sitting on his bunk near the corner, and the boy walked directly up to him and held out his hand.

"I'm sorry I blew up and tried to shoot you."

Cal looked up at him without rising or extending his hand.

"You can kiss my ass and you best stay out of my way," Cal said, dismissing the boy.

Matthew dropped his hand and glared at Cal. Lucas watched with apprehension. Matthew glanced at Lucas, and then looked back at Cal.

"I said I was sorry — I meant it."

Cal turned his back and ignored the boy. Several of the other cowboys exchanged opinions among themselves, and a few stepped forth to reassure the boy, as though their words accepted his apology on behalf of Cal.

Matthew Stanford sat on his bunk and could not remember feeling more alone.

FORTY-EIGHT

The next morning, Riggs pulled Matthew from the branding crew and told him to help No'Ka work with the young horses. He made it clear there was no time to deal with personal conflicts in the branding pen and he wanted Matthew out of there. Cal refused to work with the boy and Riggs agreed with him.

Patrick and Elder discussed the boy over breakfast. Elder offered to take the boy home, but Patrick suggested they let No'Ka work with him.

"He's a hard-case," Patrick said.

"I know he is. I just hope, for his sake and his mother's sake, it's not too late to straighten him out."

"If he keeps going the way he is at this age, no good can come of it," Patrick said.

"I reckon this is the only chance he's got. I'll do anything I can to help him," Elder added.

Patrick looked across the table at Elder.

"It could have been anyone of us starting out. We were just lucky. Maybe it's up to us to throw a little luck his way if we can."

No'Ka stood in the breezeway of the barn and looked over the collection of ropes, halters, and blankets spread out on the floor. Matthew stepped into the sunlit entryway and let his eyes adjust to the dark room.

The Indian spoke without looking up.

"You didn't bring your gun, did you?"

"No."

"Good."

The Indian paused and looked up at the boy.

"These horses can make you mad. I can't have you shooting 'em."

Matthew looked questioningly at the Indian.

"Cal had no call to pick at me."

The Indian nodded and said, "I want you to remember that when we start on these young horses, and you think they're picking at you."

No'Ka handed an armload of halters and ropes to the boy. He chose a soft, tattered blanket and a stick with an old shirt tied onto one end of it. He turned, walked to the horse corral, and the boy followed.

Next to the horse corral stood a circular pen of solid rails higher than a man's head. The round pen connected to the corral by a narrow alleyway, gated on both ends.

They dropped the gear at the round pen, opened both gates, and entered the corral, where the horses milled in nervous anticipation and moved to the opposite end of the corral.

"Pick one out."

"What do you mean?"

"Pick out the horse you want us to start with."

The boy looked at the dun at the far side of the herd. The horse flagged its tail, snorted defiantly, and tried to lose itself among the moving mass. Matthew wanted nothing to do with the horse that tried to kill him, and he shifted his attention to a quiet gray that stood off to the side.

"The gray one," Matthew said, pointing at the horse.

No'Ka smiled. "Want to start off easy, huh?"

The boy smiled and nodded.

No'Ka tilted his head toward the alleyway gate.

"Go stand over there and let the gray find the gate when I bring him around."

The Indian moved calmly, slowly through

425

the horses, positioned himself between the gray and the herd, and his presence alone drove the gray toward the boy. When the gray trotted close to the gate, Matthew threw up his arms and shouted at the horse to drive him through the open gate. As he did so, the horse bolted and circled back into the herd.

"I didn't tell you to yell at the horse."

"I was just trying to help."

"Then just do what I tell you."

"You told me to run him down there."

"I told you to let him find the gate."

"Then I don't know what you're talking about. How's he supposed to find the gate?"

The Indian walked to the edge of the corral and sat down with his legs crossed. He nodded toward the boy and the boy did likewise. The Indian smoothed a spot in the soft dirt with the palm of his hand. With his finger, he drew a short line and made a dot at one end.

"This is a horse," he said. He pointed to the dot. "This is his head."

He looked up at the boy and the boy laughed.

"That ain't much of a horse."

The Indian ignored the boy and then drew a circle around the horse.

"This is the horse's space," he said, pointing to the circle. "Wherever you put pressure on the circle, the horse will move away from it in the opposite direction."

The Indian put his finger next to the circle and then drew an arrow at the other side of the circle.

"If you stand here," he said, pointing to the circle, "the horse will move this way. The closer you get to his circle, the faster he will move the other way."

The boy's eyes widened and his expression showed great interest.

"So, if I'm here," he said pointing to a random part of the circle, "the horse will go this way?"

No'Ka smiled. "That's right."

The boy contemplated this new information a long time. He leaned forward and wiped the dirt smooth. Then the boy drew the corral, the gate, and made an X where he stood earlier. He drew the horse and he drew the Indian. He pointed to the X.

"When I raised my arms and yelled at the horse, I was pushing on the wrong part of the circle, so he went this way, right?"

The Indian smiled. "That's right. But you did one other thing — you scared the horse. When a horse is afraid, his first thought is to run away from the danger. A horse does not think about it. He reacts. Sometimes he

427

will hurt himself and he will hurt you, when all he wants to do is get away from danger."

"Is that called horsemanship?"

"Maybe for a white man. For an Indian, it's common sense."

No'Ka stood.

"Try it again."

The boy stood at the same spot near the gate and waited for No'Ka to work the gray out of the herd. When the Indian separated the horse from the herd, the gray trotted along the fence line with more caution this time. It looked for an escape route and turned its eyes to the same spot it broke through the first time. As the horse approached the spot, the boy stepped quietly into its path, and the horse adjusted its stride and turned, then trotted through the gate and into the round pen.

Matthew followed the gray and closed both gates, leaving the horse to trot frantically alone along the perimeter of the high-walled round pen from which there was no escape.

FORTY-NINE

Matthew followed No'Ka to the round pen and found a spot outside the high wall where he could watch the Indian through the rails. He leaned on his arms and watched the Indian walk around the pen, holding a rope and seemingly ignoring the horse as he did so.

The horse snorted and raised its head as it moved continually around the perimeter of the fence and looked for a way out, while distancing itself from the man as much as possible. When No'Ka shook out the rope and walked to the center of the pen, the horse stopped and faced him. The horse watched the Indian, its demeanor balanced on a fine line between curiosity and panic. The Indian disregarded the horse while he pulled enough slack through the honda to make a six-foot loop. He held the rope in his right hand and shook out the loop. He picked up two more coils from his left hand,

and then looked up at the horse.

The horse took two steps back and tensed as it prepared to bolt. The Indian walked away from the horse. The horse stopped and faced the Indian with its eyes fixed upon him.

Matthew looked through the fence rails, first at the Indian, then the horse, and back to the Indian. The boy's curiosity ran equal to that of the horse, and they both watched the Indian with eyes that could not look elsewhere.

The Indian turned and walked directly toward the horse, and the horse panicked. Its breathing sounded hard and threatened. It flagged its tail and held its head high as it galloped to the far end of the pen. No'Ka followed the horse with a slow deliberateness that unnerved the horse. The Indian methodically cut off the horse's escape route each time it turned and, when the horse had nowhere else to go, it stopped and faced the Indian. It stood and trembled, and in its eyes, the boy could see a change that now appeared as a confused balance between fear and resignation.

No'Ka spoke to the horse for the first time. His voice sounded soft but not contrived and the horse cocked its head as the Indian spoke. When No'Ka had the horse's complete attention, he took a step backward and the horse moved a single step forward. No'Ka turned his back on the horse and busied himself with the rope.

He stood like that a long time before the horse extended its muzzle and took another tentative step toward the Indian. The Indian stepped away from the horse and the horse followed. He walked across the full diameter of the pen and the horse followed.

Matthew sat mesmerized by the scene playing before him. He watched with great curiosity as No'Ka quit the horse and exited the pen. The boy met the Indian at the gate.

"Why did you quit?"

"He did what I wanted him to do. That's enough for now. He now has one good memory we can work on. We left him in a good place."

"Riggs doesn't do them like that."

"Riggs makes cowboy horses."

"What's that mean?"

"He makes 'em fast and he makes 'em hard."

"What's the difference?"

"My horses work because they want to. His horses work because they have to."

"I never seen anything like that before."

"You ready to try the next one," No'Ka asked.

"I'll try it," the boy responded.

They ran the gray back into the corral and cut out a stocking-footed sorrel gelding with a calm manner. The horse looked like the one Patrick rode, and Matthew figured it a good bet for an easy start. In the round pen, the sorrel ran the fence line and his calm demeanor changed to one of distress and uncertainty.

Matthew carried the rope to the center of the pen and tried to ignore the gelding, but every time the gelding snorted and blew, the boy turned to look and the horse ran off. He looked over at the Indian and the Indian shook his head. Matthew walked back to the gate and retraced his steps to the center of the pen. His unpredictable movements caused the horse to regard him with great caution and the horse ran. The boy walked the pen and ignored the horse, just as he had seen the Indian do.

When the horse turned to the right, the boy cut him off. The horse turned to the left and, again, the boy cut off his escape route. The boy stopped and waited, and the horse turned to face him. The gelding twitched its ears and watched the boy with a wary eye rolled half-wild in its head. The boy disregarded the horse and pretended to busy himself with the rope. Then he turned and took two steps away from the horse and the horse raised its head. The boy stood firm and the horse waited a long time before he took a nervous step forward.

The boy turned to face the horse, and then sat cross-legged where he had stood, and the horse watched him with intense curiosity. The boy avoided eye contact with the horse as he spoke to it.

The boy lifted his eyes but did not move his head and, when he caught a glimpse of the Indian sitting quietly outside the fence line, he saw the Indian nod in silent approval. To the surprise of the boy, the horse stepped forward confidently and extended its muzzle to touch the boy's arm. Matthew sat quietly and the horse stood over him until they seemed to lose interest in one another.

Matthew stood slowly and, as he did so, the horse stepped calmly back a step and watched him. The boy turned and walked toward the gate, and the horse followed. At the gate, Matthew turned at a quarter-angle to the horse's shoulder, and reached out and touched the horse's neck. The horse tensed, it flinched, but did not react as its eyes widened and its nostrils flared.

Matthew extended his hand with the rope hanging loosely in his grip, and the horse touched it with its nose and inhaled deeply several times. The boy stood perfectly still and the horse held its position. Matthew withdrew the rope and the horse jerked back its head when the boy moved the rope.

The boy reached for the gate, but changed his mind and, instead, chose to walk the perimeter of the pen with no regard for the horse. He stepped out and the horse stood firm. When he walked out of the horse's bubble, the horse stepped out to follow him, and Matthew understood exactly what No'Ka described in his drawing in the dirt.

They walked the circle together like that and, when they reached the gate, the boy left the pen without acknowledging the horse, as he closed the gate behind him.

No'Ka motioned the boy over to sit with him.

"Do you know what you just did in there?"

The boy shook his head. "No, not really."

"You communicated with that horse like an Indian."

Matthew looked up at the Indian and smiled.

"Can we do another one?"

"It's almost noon. They'll call us to eat soon. Afterward, we come down and do more horses. There is still much you must learn."

434

■ ■ ■ ■

They spent the rest of the morning talking about the ropes and halters and blankets. No'Ka explained how they would accustom the horses to each piece of equipment and how they would sack them out with the blanket and the shirt tied to the stick. For the first time since Matthew arrived at the Arbuckle, the Indian saw hope in the boy's eyes.

When they sat with the other cowboys at the table, talk ran high and it ran from one branding story to another. Matthew waited and no one asked about, or showed any interest in, the breaking pen. No'Ka did not bring it up and none of the cowboys seemed to care one way or the other. It disappointed the boy that no one showed any interest in the breaking pen and his accomplishments with the stocking-footed sorrel. But his mind reeled with the excitement of getting back into the pen and working with the next horse, and he found himself lost in his own thoughts.

Back at the corral, Matthew was eager to get to the next horse. He and No'ka brought in one, then another and another until they ran the day out.

The following day, No'Ka began the sacking out process with those colts that were ready. The others he started again, and those few that showed no potential he had the boy turn out with the horses that would go to Riggs. "Hard-cases," he called them.

Every evening Lucas spent time teaching Matthew how to handle a rope. The boy roped the blacksmith's anvil on the stump until he never missed. The index finger on his right hand blistered from the friction of the rope and his shoulder ached.

When he laid his head on the pillow at night, he slept with no demons and only the lingering fear they might appear without warning. He awoke early the next morning and dressed in the dark, well before Riggs rattled the door.

During the day, he worked with No'Ka, and in the evenings Lucas drilled him on his roping skills until the young cowboy felt Matthew was ready to rope from his horse.

The Arbuckle cowboys finished the branding without Matthew. The boy pleaded with Lucas, and Lucas promised the boy they would have calves to rope in the sick pens, and Matthew worked hard to be ready.

No'Ka and the boy stood at the corrals and studied the three remaining colts yet to be started, among them the dun. The Indian looked down at the boy.

"You ready for the dun?"

"Ready as I'll ever be."

"Okay, he's yours. Run him in the pen."

FIFTY

The dun charged into the round pen with its eyes filled with rage and its head set high and ready for a fight. Matthew felt nervous and apprehensive, but when he entered the pen behind the horse, the dun's demeanor changed and it trotted the fence line like the others did, but with an air of confidence about it that calmed the boy.

Matthew watched the dun as he attempted to gauge the horse's mood and behavior. To the boy's great relief, the dun's reactions were much like those of the docile, stocking-footed sorrel. There was no fight in its eyes and there was no fear there, only the highly alerted attitude of a horse very much aware of its circumstances shown from them.

The boy envisioned himself sitting in the center of the pen waiting. He envisioned the dun stepping quietly to him to have its head scratched. He could not have been more wrong.

Before the boy reached the center of the pen, the dun rose up high on its hind legs, pinned its ears back, and struck the air in a vicious show of aggression. The boy faltered but did not retreat. He ignored the horse, but his heart pounded and his hands trembled. He walked toward the horse. The horse charged him with bared teeth and front hooves that thrashed the air and reached out for the boy, who spun to the right to avoid them.

No'Ka stood and shouted, "Get out of there!"

Matthew hit the gate at full-stride with the horse not three steps behind him. He had no chance to slide the poles. He turned without thinking and faced the horse, whose eyes were white and vengeful. The boy swung the rope in the horse's face and shouted as he did so. The coils lashed across the face of the horse and the horse slid to a stop and wheeled about, relinquishing the temporary victory to the boy.

Standing outside the gate, the boy's knees quit him and he dropped to the ground shaking.

"I don't think he likes you much," the Indian said.

Matthew looked up at the unsmiling Indian.

"If I had my gun, I'd shoot the son-of-a-bitch."

"Come on."

"Where?"

"Let's go get your gun."

The boy shook his head.

"That's your answer to everything, isn't it? Let's go get it."

Matthew looked down between his boots, took two deep breaths, and then looked up at the horse. His eyes narrowed and he turned to look back at the Indian with an expression of determination that pleased No'Ka.

"So, what do I do next?"

The Indian knelt next to the boy and cleared a spot in the dirt with the palm of his hand.

"You gonna draw me another picture?"

"No. I need a clean place to sit."

No'Ka sat next to the boy and neither spoke.

Matthew's voice was soft, but determined as he studied the toe of his boot.

"What did I do wrong in there?"

"You assumed all horses are the same."

"What do you mean?"

"You went into that pen and tried to do the same thing you did with the others, just because they acted alike."

"What's wrong with that?"

"You knew the dun was different."

"Yeah, well, I didn't know anything different to do."

"Then you need to ask. Think about the horse. Think about what you know about him — then think about what you don't know about him."

The boy lifted his head and looked sideways at the Indian.

"Every horse is the same and every horse is different."

"That don't make no sense."

"They're like people, except easier to understand. The difference between horses and people is horses never lie to you."

The boy looked back down at his boots. He wondered if they were still talking about the horse. The boy absentmindedly bit his bottom lip as he contemplated the Indian's words.

"This ain't about the horse, is it?"

"No, it's not."

The boy leaned back against the fence rails and took a deep breath. He sat like that a long time and the Indian waited. Matthew's voice shook as he cleared his throat and searched for the right words.

"I ain't proud of what I did."

"What did you do?"

The boy turned his head toward the Indian, and his expression was one of suspicious questioning.

"You don't know?"

"They don't tell me much around here."

The boy took several deep breaths as he weighed his thoughts. He clinched his jaw then spoke straight out.

"I killed somebody."

The Indian sat back and nodded, but did not respond. His dark eyes seemed to penetrate the boy as if they asked the question the boy expected was coming.

"You want to hear the whole thing?"

"Yes, I think you need to tell me."

No'Ka placed his hand on the boy's shoulder and the touch of it struck the boy with great reverence as he felt his throat tighten.

Matthew's expression softened and he began to speak as though what he was about to say needed to be said from the beginning. From the morning his father rode out with a broken promise to return, to Raymond's final moments of pleading, the boy spared no details, save the secret cache of weapons that he regarded as his only defense should Ike rise from the dead in his dreams some night. No confessional or spiritual uplifting would help him if Ike should come up from the dead. The guns were his strength, and he entertained no thought of giving them up.

When the boy finished, No'Ka remained silent, and the boy looked up at him awaiting a response. The Indian sat cross-legged with his full attention on the boy.

"Is there more?"

The boy shook his head, but the question made him uneasy.

"No, that's all there is."

"Some horses take longer to figure out than others," the Indian said. "You can work through a lot of problems before you know what they all are, but to fix a good horse, you have to let him find his own way through them."

"Well, that's all there is," the boy said, as though they were still speaking of him.

"That dun horse — he got away with running you off twice. That's not good. It means you have to make up that lost ground just to get even. When you turned on the horse and ran him back with the rope — that was good and bad."

"How can it be good and bad?"

"It's good you stood your ground and made him back off. It's bad you made him see the rope as a threat. But it's done and you have to go from there."

No'Ka reached across and picked up the rope he carried with him, as though the action itself warranted the boy's attention. The boy turned his head and waited for the Indian to continue.

"That dun horse isn't proud of what he did. But — he's not ashamed either. He's just a horse. A horse only knows to fight or run. He did the only thing there was for him to do."

The Indian watched the boy as the boy contemplated the Indian's words. Matthew furrowed his brow and chewed on the end of his thumb as he replayed the dun's actions in his mind.

He looked back up at the Indian.

"I think the dun horse is afraid, that's why it acts the way it does."

No'Ka smiled and nodded.

"If I'm nice to him, he doesn't trust me. If I'm tough with him he's afraid of me. I think I need to break him — the Indian way."

No'Ka stood and the boy stood with him. Matthew picked up his rope and nodded toward the round pen.

"Can I go back in there?"

FIFTY-ONE

Matthew entered the gate into the round pen. The big loop of his rope swung easily at his side as he walked directly toward the dun. The dun turned to face the boy, its ears pinned and its eyes on fire. The boy walked directly at the dun and swung the rope over his head as he did so. When the horse took its first step toward the boy, the boy threw the rope and the dun ducked under it, spun around, and headed for the far side of the pen.

The boy pursued the horse and the horse fled to the edges of the pen. The boy continued the pursuit, as he spoke softly and never let the horse rest. Every time the horse stopped, the boy calmly laid the loop across its back and the horse ducked and ran.

For almost two hours, the boy pursued the horse and the horse grew less determined to run until, finally, the horse turned to face the boy; the boy stopped and watched the horse. He spoke to it, then turned and walked a short distance away. The horse watched him and the boy turned to face the horse and walked closer to it. The horse backed up, but did not turn or run.

The boy threw a loop in the direction of the horse and let the loop drop into the dirt near the horse. The horse snorted and backed, and the boy let the rope lay where it dropped. He spoke to the horse, but the horse's ears were full forward with his attention riveted on the rope.

The boy waited. The horse stepped forward and extended his muzzle toward the rope from a long ways away. When the horse stepped up to the rope, the boy drew it in slowly and the horse stood and watched. The boy picked up the rope and swung the loop as he walked away and the horse followed.

Matthew closed the gate behind him, and No'Ka looked at him a long time before he spoke.

"Why did you quit there?"

"He done everything I wanted. We quit at a good place."

"Do you think he trusts you now?"

"No — but he will."

"What makes you think he will?"

"Well, I don't know. Do you think he will?"

"Trust is a hard thing to understand sometimes. You can't make him give it to you."

"What if he knows I don't aim to hurt him?"

"That's not trust."

"What is it then?"

"I don't know — it's just not trust."

The boy tilted his head in the direction of the Indian. No'Ka nodded toward the horse.

"The horse knows if there is darkness in your heart. I don't know how, but he knows."

The boy dropped his gaze to his boots and fell silent. His look was distant and troubled.

"Maybe I have some in mine."

"Some what?"

"Darkness — what if I do have some darkness in my heart?"

"Then the horse won't trust you."

Matthew's expression softened but the look in his eyes remained guarded.

"I want that horse to trust me."

"Do you trust him?"

"No, I guess I don't. I seen my share of bad."

The boy looked directly into the black eyes of the Indian. There was no give in the boy's expression and the Indian waited.

"I still got their guns."

"Whose guns?"

"From those men I shot — I kept their guns."

"Why do you still have them?"

"Because I haven't slept through one whole night since it all happened."

"Are you afraid?"

The boy dropped his eyes and shook his head.

"I'm not afraid. They can never find where I hid their guns."

"I thought you said they were dead."

Matthew's bottom lip quivered and his eyes clouded with uncertainty as he struggled with deeply buried feelings that threatened to betray his confidence. He looked away, cleared his throat, and tried to speak. But no words came, and if they had they would not have been the right ones anyway. He looked up at the Indian and the Indian simply nodded, then Matthew laid his head on his arms, and his body shook and he wept. No'Ka put a hand on Matthew's shoulder without speaking. The boy trembled and he tried to speak but was unable to do so, and the tears that wet his sleeve were a long time coming. All the while, No'Ka touched the boy's back, and the boy felt no shame or weakness for his tears. He wept openly and, when the words did come, they came haltingly.

"I dream about them all the time. I get so scared I hate the dark and I hate thinking about trying to sleep."

He sobbed. "And I know I'm going to hell."

"Maybe you're wrong about that."

The boy raised his head and wiped the tears on his sleeve.

"Those men are gone. They can never come back. What you see in your dreams is fear. Just like that dun horse — he fears the rope. You know it won't hurt him, but he doesn't know that yet. When you show him it's only a rope he will lose his fear of it and never worry about it again."

Matthew tried to understand, but was not at all sure there was any connection between the rope and his dreams.

"The greater wrong would have been for you to let those men keep killing good people. You took three lives to save many more."

"Are you sure it works that way?"

"Yes, I am."

"You don't think I'm going to hell?"

"No, you were given a job that no one else could do, and you did it."

The boy wanted to believe it was true. He stood there a long time in silence, his eyes staring blankly ahead. No'Ka backed away and neither spoke, but that which was left unsaid lay heavy and burdensome upon them both.

"There's something you don't know."

No'Ka looked at the boy without speaking and the boy looked directly into his eyes.

"There ain't no way out for me."

Matthew dropped his gaze to the ground, moved the dirt with the toe of his boot, and took a long, slow breath before he spoke again.

"When I shot Ike Smith, I did it out of pure hate. I wanted to see him bleed — it felt good to me when he did. When I shot him again and he fell, it made me feel stronger than him — and I liked that too. There was nothin' good in my heart about it. I liked killing him, and I liked the guns."

The softness left the boy's eyes and nothing mattered to him, the horses, No'Ka — nothing. He withdrew into his own thoughts and the Indian neither spoke nor acknowledged the boy's words. The boy's voice dropped to a whisper.

"There was hate in my heart when I killed Sandoval too. I just wanted him dead."

This time the Indian nodded, but still did

not speak. The boy looked back up at him.

"That ain't the worst of it."

The boy stood there with his head down, his shoulders rounded, and his hands crossed. He searched for the right words.

"What I did to Raymond — was no different than they done to the ones they killed. It was every bit as bad. I made him want to die and I didn't let him. And I felt good about doing it."

Matthew's legs buckled and he dropped to his knees. He wept uncontrollably. No'Ka knelt beside him and put his arm across the boy's shoulders; he let the boy cry until there were no more tears. He patted the boy's back.

"It's out now — what's left is up to your God."

The boy raised his head, nodded, and spoke in a very soft voice.

"I swear, if I could undo it all, I would."

No'Ka stood and the boy stood with him.

"It's not up to you. Those things that have passed are gone."

The Indian dismissed the conversation at that, and the finality in his tone brought some relief to the boy, but the boy remained doubtful.

"Here, I want you to have this," No'Ka said as he slipped a beaded amulet on a rawhide lace over his head and handed it to the boy.

"What is it?"

"It's protection."

"What kind of protection?"

"It has great powers from the ancient ones who passed it down in our tribe from a time long before any of us can remember."

The boy took it, removed his hat, and slipped it over his head. He ran his fingers over the soft leather and admired the detail and colors of the beadwork. The boy did not smile and he did not appear convinced, but his eyes filled with gratitude and, beyond that, hope. He held the amulet up to the Indian. His eyes went down to it and back up to the Indian.

"The bad dreams?"

"They're gone — you're done with them."

"What about my guns?"

"You need to tell Mr. Elder about those."

The boy contemplated No'Ka's words, and he squeezed the talisman tightly in his hand. His breathing relaxed. He took a deep breath and released it slowly.

"And what about the dun?"

"You need to fix things between you and that horse."

The next morning, before the others awakened and only the soft, yellow light from the kitchen shone in the darkness, Matthew walked to the breaking pen. In the moonlight, he watched the young horses mill slowly until he found the dun. He entered the pen, opened the gates to the round pen, and slowly worked his way through the herd until he had the dun isolated from the others.

In the same manner in which he had observed No'Ka work the horses, Matthew slowly and methodically cut off the dun's escape routes until it had no choice but to charge bold and defiant through the gate and down the narrow lane to the round pen. Matthew moved in quickly behind the dun, and closed the gates behind him.

Inside the round pen, the dun threw its head back, flared its nostrils and breathed in deep, heavy breaths, testing the air and looking wildly about with eyes that rolled back and its neck arched. The boy stood quietly near the gate while the horse paced the perimeter at a jarring, stiff-legged trot.

Matthew ignored the dun and busied himself at the gate as he attended to imaginary chores that did not include the horse. Then, the boy turned, walked to the center of the pen, and in that half-light of dawn, he sat cross-legged as he paid no mind to the horse and his heart pounded with uncertainty. The dun circled the pen in a frantic display of behavior of a horse balanced on that fine line between panic and fight-to-the-death aggression, and Matthew knew one or the other would prevail.

He did not look at the horse, and the horse kicked up great clouds of dust as it ran a circular path that grew ever closer to the boy on each lap. The boy waited for the crushing blows from the horse's hooves, and his heart pounded harder with each lap the horse took.

From the corner of the barn, No'Ka stood watching with no more confidence than the boy that the dun's unpredictability might end in disaster for Matthew. He knew not to speak and he knew it had to come to this. But the boy sitting in the center of the pen in that dim light, with a charging horse challenging his right to be there, caused even No'Ka to question the wisdom of what he knew he had brought about. It was the boy's time of reckoning with the dun and, in the slowly graying light of dawn, the lines on the Indian's face drew tight about the corners of his eyes in grave concern. He prepared to intervene, but he waited.

The boy began speaking to the dun in soft words No'Ka could not discern, but the rhythm of them was calm and without fear. The boy neither looked at the horse nor acknowledged its presence and, when the horse stopped and turned to face him, the boy spoke to it, turned his head slightly and raised his eyes to those of the horse, and the horse extended his muzzle to the boy. The boy lowered his eyes, turned slightly away from the horse and waited, still talking, but giving the horse no acknowledgment. When he felt the nose of the dun against the sleeve of his shirt, the boy said, "Good horse."

Matthew stood and the horse spun back on its hocks and trotted off. There was no fear in its eyes, but the aloof air of superiority about him remained unmistakable, and the boy turned and walked toward the gate where No'Ka stood waiting.

The boy closed the gate behind him. He and the Indian turned and stood, each with a boot up on the bottom rail.

"I think it's gone," the boy said.

"What's gone?"

"The fear. He ain't afraid of me no more."

"What did you do different?"

"I trusted him."

FIFTY-TWO

Patrick Arbuckle swung his saddle up on the back of a stocky bay horse as J.D. Elder tightened the cinch on his own saddle. At the other end of the hitch rail, Lucas and Cal buckled the bridles on the horses they drew for the tough day of gathering strays that lay before them. No'Ka led his saddled and bridled horse to water, and Matthew followed with the big sorrel assigned to him.

The sky stood clear and absent the stars that adorned its dark canvas an hour earlier. Only the moon hung suspended in its slow descent. The sky along the eastern perimeter backlit the granite peaks that rose above the ranch as the sun began to emerge.

Patrick stood gazing in the direction of the long valley to the north as the other cowboys gathered about him waiting for instructions they knew were coming. With the reins in one hand, Patrick pointed in the general direction of the gap between the mountains with his free hand.

"All we got left out there is about thirty head. They got into that rocky canyon area up-river there. It's not a long ride, but it's rough."

Patrick turned and looked at Cal, Lucas, and Matthew.

"You three take the south fork."

He nodded toward Elder and No'Ka.

"We'll come up the north fork and meet you boys where the river splits up top. If you get there first, wait for us. That way, any cattle we pick up we can drive back together. And watch them damn rocks — they're slick."

"How long you want us to wait there for you?" Cal asked.

Patrick laughed.

"Don't worry about that, us old-timers will be there waiting when you get there."

They rode for the better part of two hours; Patrick and Elder in the lead, followed by Lucas and Matthew, with Cal and No'Ka riding wide in the rear. The river they rode spread through the meadowlands, and ran swift and clear with water from a melting glacier high above the timberline. The air was warm and the breeze that rustled the leaves in the tall aspens blew gentle and steady. Wildflowers attended the banks of the river along with berries and willows that grew there in abundance. A red-tailed hawk soared overhead, riding the thermals that carried it upward on great wings out-stretched and still.

"How's ol' Matthew making it, J.D.?" Patrick asked as they rode a gently sloping trail upwards into the mouth of the canyon.

Elder turned his head toward Patrick and smiled slightly as he spoke.

"You know, putting that boy with No'Ka might have been the best thing that ever happened to him."

"How so?"

"You know me and the boy walk at night after supper almost every night. Well, he said he had some things to tell me. He sounded like a different kid — still a little distant like he can be, but different."

Patrick shifted back slightly in the saddle as though the new position improved his ability to hear.

"He showed me a good luck charm he wears around his neck. Said No'Ka gave it to him. Then he smiled — first smile I can remember seeing out of him. He said he doesn't believe he's going to hell anymore."

Patrick laughed.

"Maybe you and me should see if No'Ka

has a couple more of those."

Elder smiled.

"I've noticed it too, J.D. It just seems like there's more of him here now. You know, there's no one better at bringing these colts along than No'Ka. I suppose he might have the same effect on a boy."

"I sure hope so. I still don't get the feeling he's said everything he wants to say, though."

"You think he's hiding something?"

"I think he could be. We'll see."

At the bottom fork, where the river split, the two feeder creeks ran turbulent and wild. The three young cowboys picked their way upward over river rocks and granite scree that left the horses measuring every step, as the reluctant animals protested the urging of the cowboys to continue forth.

After the first climb, the trail widened out and the going was easier as they made their way up into the trees above the crashing waters below. They rode for more than an hour, stopping only to rest the horses. An hour beyond that, they rode up onto a plateau where the grass grew thick, and a manageable trail fell steeply to a broad, sandy flat where cattle watered, judging by the many tracks that trod the ground around it.

Cal leaned forward in the saddle, calculating the tracks for number and direction.

"Got at least half a dozen not far ahead of us going into that draw past them trees," he said, nodding to the east.

He pulled his horse around and Lucas and the boy followed.

"Don't do anything jerky," Lucas said to the boy.

"What do you mean?"

"Just stay smooth and easy. If you start jerking your horse around up here, you could get in trouble real fast. It's slick and it's steep and your horse could lose its footing."

Lucas looked back down toward the river and the boy did as well.

"It's a long damn way down there," Lucas said.

Cal rode into the trees ahead of Lucas and Matthew and they trotted to catch up. The air was quiet and the noise from the river was no more than a muffled roar with an intoxicatingly soothing sound to it. The tracks of the cattle laid in the soft earth stretched clear and fresh into the trees, and the boys followed them. Lucas and the boy found Cal sitting in the shadows of the trees pointing to six fat heifers grazing like deer in the dark green grass left untouched until they discovered it.

"There they are," Cal said in a whisper. "We need to get around them on the uphill side and see if we can get them moving down river. Make sure they don't break for the brush."

Cal touched his horse with his heels and rode a wide circle to get an uphill position on the grazing heifers. Lucas directed Matthew to a holding position to prevent the cattle from scattering in the trees, and he followed Cal up the steep slope that skirted the heifers' position.

Matthew sat quietly and watched as the two older cowboys gained the high-ground advantage, then emerged from the tree line above the cattle. As they did so, the heifers raised their heads and watched them without moving.

The two cowboys rode a sweeping pattern behind the heifers and, when the cowboys violated the perimeter of their safety zone, the heifers bolted. They charged blindly for the cover of the trees and, as they approached Matthew's location, the boy stood in the stirrups, whistled and waved his hat and they turned. When the heifers reached the steep downward slope to the river, they sat back on their haunches and carved deep parallel tracks where their hind feet dug in but found no purchase.

Matthew spurred his horse onto the trail above the heifers, while the two older cowboys pursued them below on the precarious trail they chose near the water's edge. Cal's horse stumbled, regained its footing, and charged down the rocky trail with Lucas directly to his rear.

Matthew kept the pressure on from above to prevent the heifers from breaking away into the trees and brush, and his trail was no trail at all. The soft ground slid away beneath Matthew's horse, and only the forward momentum of the animal kept it on its feet.

The heifers dictated the pace and they ran heedlessly, like wild animals running for their survival. Matthew reached flat ground first and put the spurs to his horse to out distance the heifers and get them turned up river. The gelding the boy rode was hard and long-legged, and its instincts drove it onward. When they reached a spot a hundred yards ahead of the heifers, the gelding bounced to a stop and the boy pulled its head around and rode at the heifers. Cal and Lucas saw the boy and both cowboys reined their horses uphill to give the heifers room to pass as they turned and retreated up the river.

On the uphill slope, the sides of the heifers heaved as exhaustion drove them to a walk and the cowboys followed, Matthew in the rear, Cal and Lucas riding the tree line above. Matthew felt the sides of his horse billow and contract between his legs. He reached forth and laid his hand on the neck of the horse.

"Good job," he said.

The boy looked up at Lucas and Cal. Lucas nodded and Cal kept his eye on the cattle. The boy watched Cal for some sign of acknowledgement, but none came.

"What an ass," the boy said under his breath.

An hour up the trail, a mother cow, her calf, and a young bull grazed in a small meadow, and they fell in with the heifers as Lucas slipped in behind them and urged them that direction. Matthew watched and he admired the deliberate but subtle actions of the cowboy who always knew where to be at the right time.

When they reached the upper fork, they found Elder and Patrick watching over a dozen strays they picked up along the way. The three young cowboys ran their stock in with those waiting.

Cal shook his head and laughed.

"We'd a been here sooner if all we had to

bring in was old grandma cows like you got here."

Patrick looked across at Cal.

"Well, they weren't old when we got here."

"Where's No'Ka?" Lucas asked.

Elder pointed up into the trees that rose above the river.

"He's after an old bull and a handful of cows that got off up there. You boys go give him a hand, me and Patrick will wait here."

The three cowboys turned their horses up the trail and followed the churned up tracks of the horse and the cows it followed. They rode with an absence of caution and the overcharged energy of their youth. Patrick shouted in their direction to give the horses a break, but they neither heard nor acknowledged his warning.

FIFTY-THREE

Patrick and Elder sat their horses and watched the boys disappear into the shadows of the trees above them. The cattle they held grazed and drank from the swift water of the river, but they kept their distance, ignored the two cowboys, and watched them with uncertain glances when one moved or spoke.

Patrick leaned forward over his saddle horn and stretched his back.

"That kid's going to make a cowboy."

Elder looked up the trail then back over at Patrick.

"I reckon he might. He's got good sense about him."

They fell silent and Patrick watched the river broil and churn over the big boulders in its path.

"You ever learn to swim, J.D.?"

"No. I never took it up. You?"

"No, I never took it up either. I always

wanted to."

"It never had any appeal for me."

"Well, it doesn't have any for me now, either — but at one time it did."

Patrick tipped his head toward the river.

"I never had a desire to swim in anything like that, though."

Elder looked out across the water and back up at Patrick.

"That wasn't meant for swimming."

On the upper trail, the river cascaded white and frothy over boulders and trapped deadfall. The ground around the area lay wet from the spray, and upon it were the fresh tracks of the bull. Cal pulled his horse up sharply and held up a hand for silence.

"Listen."

They cocked their heads in unison. No one spoke. Then, off to their left they heard the low calling of the bull. They waited and, when they heard it again, Cal shouted.

"Let's go."

They rode hard and when they reached a plateau blocked in on three sides by steep granite walls of fallen rock, they found No'Ka with the cattle. The Indian pointed down the trail from which they came. The boys circled, flanked the cattle, and the cattle started the steep climb down.

The bull quit the herd and No'Ka stayed

with him, forcing him generally in the direction of Elder and Patrick. The boys drove their cattle down off the plateau, into the trees, and onto the trail above the river. The cattle wandered onto a precipice above the river and stood in confusion as Lucas and Cal approached them with caution. The wet ground was unstable and the cattle milled at the edge of the rocks. The two cowboys walked their horses cautiously out onto the precipice and urged the reticent cattle back toward the trail, but the cattle refused to move.

Cal looked at Lucas.

"We got no choice. Just take it slow."

Lucas nodded and they moved the horses one step at a time. The cattle milled and the ground trembled beneath them. The cattle inched closer to the edge and when they were near enough to sense the danger, they turned and bolted. When they did, the ground shifted and the entire mountainside seemed to move at once.

Lucas and Cal stayed in their saddles and rode the massive earth slide to the bottom, where it threw their horses onto the rocks and catapulted both cowboys into the crashing water.

Matthew turned his horse down the steep embankment when he heard the earth rumble as it broke loose, and he watched Lucas and Cal drop out of sight on the other side.

When Matthew reached the water, Lucas lay sprawled on his back with his legs floating and beginning to drift into the current. Matthew reached the cowboy, grabbed him by the shirt, and pulled him up onto the rocks.

"Are you okay?"

"Yeah — go help Cal."

Matthew turned and looked downstream to see Cal fighting the roiling water. He turned and watched the two horses charge blindly across the flat and into the trees in a panic, and then he set his own horse in a gallop downriver.

Cal's body turned, rolled, and bobbed below the surface of the water and back up again as the water carried him downstream. The current drove his body into a narrow crevice between two large boulders, where it wedged itself as the water rushed over it. Cal lifted his head and raised one arm as he clung to the sharp edge of the rock that trapped him. He shouted but made no sound the boy could hear. The current pulled him back under and sent him rolling and crashing downstream.

Matthew spurred his horse to keep pace

with Cal as he watched the cowboy struggle to get out of the swift water rushing over and around him. The water swept Cal up onto a sandbar where he rose to his knees and shouted, "Get the horses."

The boy jerked his horse around and whipped it into a gallop over the uncertain footing in pursuit of the runaways.

When Matthew returned to the landslide with the horses in tow, he found Lucas sitting up trying to catch an even breath and Cal stood near him, still shaking.

"Let's go get them damn cows," Cal said with a voice filled with embarrassment, anger, and impatience.

Matthew looked over at Lucas and Lucas shrugged.

When they got the cows gathered and down to the fork with the others, No'Ka was there waiting, but made no comment as to their delay or their wet and muddied condition.

Patrick raised his eyebrows as he assessed the condition of Lucas, Cal, and their horses.

"I expect there's a story behind that," he said as he shook his head.

Lucas smiled and Cal rode out ahead of the herd without speaking.

Down river, where the land leveled and

469

the going was easier, the cattle settled into a steady walk with no hurry about them and the cowboys did not push them. Lucas rode in next to Matthew, who rode alone in the rear. Neither spoke. Finally, Lucas looked over at Matthew and Matthew looked back at him. The cowboy extended his hand to Matthew.

"I just wanted to thank you for what you did back there. Them damn horses would still be running if you didn't catch them."

Matthew smiled, but tried not to. He liked the offhanded demeanor of the cowboys who downplayed everything they did, as though it were nothing more than being a cowboy. And Matthew, very much, wanted to be a cowboy.

The boy grabbed Lucas's hand and shook it hard.

"No problem."

"I think you made a good choice, staying on here."

Matthew nodded.

"I'm glad I did. I just don't know what it is about Cal. I know he don't like me much."

"Well, Cal takes some time to get to know. He's a good man — just a little dodgy at times. He's real good at what he does, and he don't take any nonsense."

"I never gave him any."

Lucas looked at the boy.

"You almost blew his damn head off."

"I know. I don't know what got into me. Maybe I wasn't meant to carry a gun."

Lucas laughed.

"No shit. How many fourteen-year-old kids you ever heard of that carry a gun?"

Matthew laughed.

"None, I guess."

"No, I guess not."

They rode without speaking, and the cadence of the horses' footfalls and the rocking of the saddles had a tranquil affect on the cowboys.

"Now the branding is over, you planning on going back to town right away?" Lucas asked.

Matthew stared ahead, watching the cattle.

"I reckon I won't have a say in it."

"You want to go back?"

"I'd like to stay."

Then he turned his head toward Lucas.

"I ain't roped any calves yet."

Lucas laughed.

"Well, you'll rope more than your share in due time."

Matthew laughed as well.

"I hope to."

Matthew kicked his feet free of the stirrups, stretched his legs, then found the stirrups with the toes of his boots, and settled back into the saddle.

"If they let me stay, I have a lot of work to do with that dun horse."

"The one that tried to kill you?"

"He didn't try to kill me. He was just scared."

"Could have fooled me. I heard he damn near took out a fence rail trying to get to you."

"Yeah, he was pretty scared. I just hope I can get him ready before I run out of time here."

The trail lay flat and gentle where it entered the big meadow. A narrow column of chimney smoke twisted out of the trees and spiraled upwards into a sky filled with soft clouds of many shapes traveling across that great expanse, as though they were put there as a tribute to the cowboys who rode beneath them.

"How about if I talk to Patrick and No'Ka and see if we can keep you around until the end of summer?"

Matthew sat up straight in the saddle.

"I'd like that, a lot."

Lucas nudged his horse forward and, if he had turned in the saddle, the smile on

Matthew's face would have told him much more than the handshake did.

FIFTY-FOUR

Talk at supper ran its course quickly, and when it got around to the landslide, the room fell quiet. Lucas told his version of the story and, as he finished, all eyes turned toward Matthew, who sat near the end of the table between Riggs and No'ka and felt very small.

The boy lowered his head. A voice at the other end of the table spoke out.

"So, tell us what really happened, Matt."

The boy raised his head.

"That was pretty much it."

The cowboys waited, and the silence weighed heavily upon the boy's shoulders. He looked up at Riggs and Riggs looked down at him and waited. He looked up at No'Ka and the Indian waited as well.

Across the table, Cal's voice resonated with startling clarity, and all heads in the room turned toward the sound of it.

"I'll tell you what happened," Cal said

with great authority and an overbearing tone.

Matthew waited for Cal's dismissal of the event; he looked down at his plate and poked at his food with his fork.

"Matthew Stanford stood up to it today. He could have backed off and he could have come up short, but he didn't. If it weren't for him, Lucas and I would still be afoot in them mountains."

Then he looked about the room and added the final compliment that, in Matthew's mind, defined a cowboy.

"The damn kid never lost a cow in the process."

Cal stood. No one spoke. When he pushed his chair back and walked over to Matthew, the boy turned to face him.

Cal stuck out his hand.

"You could have let it go, but you didn't. I want to thank you for that."

The boy took Cal's hand and shook it.

"Are we square then?" Matthew asked.

Cal looked down at the boy's side.

"You're not armed, are you?"

Matthew laughed.

"No."

"Then we're square, Matt."

The silence that followed was absolute. Not a fork moved and not a man spoke as

Cal returned to his seat. He looked about the room. The long silence went beyond the line of comfort and, finally, Lucas spoke.

"In case anybody's wondering, I taught Matt everything he knows." And then he added with a grin, "But not everything I know."

Laughter eased the mood and talk went back to cows, horses, and the weather. One by one, as the cowboys left the table, they found Matthew and slapped him on the shoulder as they passed.

That evening, Matthew and Elder walked in the soft moonlight out past the barn and between the breaking pens. Matthew brought an extra biscuit from the dinner table and offered half to Elder. Elder took it and they ate as they walked.

"Sounds like you had a pretty good day today."

"Maybe the best one I ever had."

They walked and the sound of crickets and tree frogs echoed at them from every direction.

"Lucas talked to me and Patrick before supper."

The boy looked up at Elder and waited for the rest of it.

"He said you might be interested in staying on through the summer."

"I want to learn to be a good cowboy."

"You think you got what it takes?"

"Do you?"

"It doesn't matter much what I think, but I can see you have the makings."

"What does Mr. Arbuckle think?"

"He's seen good cowboys come from a lot less than you have to work with."

"Will he let me stay?"

"He said he'd be glad to have you. He also said he'd put you on half pay so you could earn enough to buy yourself some good gear."

The boy grinned.

"He said that?"

"He did."

The boy's mind raced.

"Do you think it's okay if I stay, Mr. Elder?"

"Look, Matt, just call me J.D. You're making me feel older than I am. I talked to your ma about this before we left and she said if it comes down to it, it's fine with her for you to stay — providing you make it home for a visit when you can."

"That's it, I get to stay?"

"Yes, sir — just like that."

They stopped at the colt pen. Matthew put a boot up on the bottom rail and looked through at the young horses.

"See that stocking-footed sorrel?"

Elder nodded.

"He's a good-minded horse."

The colts milled around and some showed an interest in Elder and the boy, but most did not.

"See the gray?"

Elder nodded again.

"He's good too, but a little skittish at first."

"What about that dun horse?" Elder asked, as he pointed to the fractious dun that disturbed those horses around him.

Matthew backed away from the fence rails and looked directly at Elder.

"He's the best one in there."

They watched the horses a long time before either spoke, and when they did speak, it was Matthew who broke the silence.

"I got something I need to tell you."

"I figured you might."

"I got more guns and I don't want them anymore."

"What guns do you have?"

"All of them. Sandoval's shotgun. Ike's rifle. All their pistols. Bullets — everything."

"Where are they?"

"In my hideout in the barn. I got a secret place behind the horse stall. I'll tell you how to find everything if you want to take it out of there when you go back."

"Are you sure you want to give them up?"

"Yeah, I am. Lucas said a fourteen-year-old kid's got no right to be carrying a gun anyway."

Elder laughed and the boy smiled.

"I'm done with them."

"The guns?"

"Ike and Raymond and Sandoval."

The boy showed Elder the talisman that hung from the rawhide lace about his neck.

"This is all I need."

"This has been a big day for you."

"What day is it?"

"It's Sunday."

"It felt like Sunday."

The boy took a deep breath and let it out slowly.

"You think my pa's looking down at me?"

"I think he is," Elder replied.

"I think so too."

Matthew watched the horses. They were not horses anymore. They were the gray, and the sorrel and the dun. They were each different and all the same. When he watched them move or stand apart from the others, the boy tried to imagine what they were thinking. Which ones were afraid and which ones were hard-cases.

"When are you going back?" Matthew asked, looking up at Elder.

"I'm going to get an early start back in the morning."

"I never talked to anyone before like we talk."

"Well, for what it's worth — neither have I."

"How old are you?"

Elder laughed.

"I'm almost fifty, why?"

"I was just wondering if me and you could cowboy someday when I get good at it."

"Well, you better hurry, because I am slowing down some."

Matthew laughed.

"You ain't slowing down none so I could tell. I seen you rope a lot of calves."

"I suppose I got a few good miles left in me."

Without agreeing on it, they turned and walked back toward the bunkhouses. They got to Elder's bunkhouse first, and he stepped up on the threshold and turned to look at the boy.

"I'll see you at breakfast. I hear No'Ka has a big day planned for you tomorrow."

"See you in the morning, J.D.," the boy

said in his most man-to-man voice.
Elder smiled. "Night, Matt."

FIFTY-FIVE

When Elder rode out that morning, his saddlebags hung heavy with the boy's pistol and his thoughts hung heavy with concern for the future of the boy. He topped the first hill and turned in the saddle for a long look at the Arbuckle Ranch and what he considered to be the last stop for a boy who had every reason to fail. He turned, nudged the horse into a slow jog, and looked ahead to a future for himself that was no more certain than that of the boy.

Elder smiled as he thought to himself. He wants to cowboy with me — that's a good sign for him and me.

J.D. Elder contemplated his circumstances and let his mind drift as the horse maintained a steady pace and, for the first time in a long time, Elder had nothing to do but think. He reconciled himself to the circumstances that befell him, circumstances that brought a woman and a child into his life.

He had no misconceptions of some divine correction of the universe behind his state of affairs, but he could not imagine a worse way for fate to have played its hand, nor a worse time.

He had forgotten what it felt like to be needed. He had long since forgotten what it felt like to need someone. For all that drove him to the monastic life of his choosing, the boy and the woman awakened a part of him he was sure he had laid to rest.

For J.D. Elder, the thought of making drastic changes in his life made him uneasy. At the same time, it revitalized his outlook on people, and he liked the easy way he fell into life with the branding crew. He enjoyed talking with people when he ate, and he liked the idea of being part of something. Maybe just existing was not enough. Maybe people were meant to go on despite the bad turns their lives took. For all the answers he did not have, the one thing he did know was that life had dealt him a new hand and he intended to play it out until the end.

J.D. Elder and Sarah Stanford understood the difficult situation in which they found themselves. Had they been asked, they would not have chosen any of it. As it was, Sarah and the boy had few options, and Elder was a man on the edge of extinction.

Together they had a thin line of hope, and they both grasped it without hesitation. Somewhere in the great order of things, Matthew Stanford stood as the bond of purpose between Elder and Sarah.

Elder knew working on the Arbuckle Ranch would be good for the boy. He had no idea it would do the same for him. As he rode on, he began plans for the Rafter E Ranch with its barns and horses and cattle, and a young boy who, he hoped, would help run it.

By the time Elder caught his last glimpse of the Arbuckle, Matthew and Lucas were saddled and riding the sick pen looking for calves to doctor.

Lucas rode with his rope hanging at his left side and a loop at the ready. Matthew watched and prepared his rope as well.

Lucas nodded toward a calf standing with drooping ears and a dull nose.

"Get a heel catch on the brockle-faced steer there."

Matthew walked his horse up near the rear of the calf, swung a wide loop, then dropped it under the calf. When the calf stepped into it, the boy jerked his slack and the calf walked out of the loop and disappeared into the herd.

"You didn't release with your left hand

quick enough. Your loop died before it made a good trap and the calf just walked out of it," Lucas said.

Matthew reeled in his rope and rebuilt the loop.

"Leave a little spoke on it so you got some rope to work with once you toss your loop."

The boy nodded, and Lucas pointed to another calf.

"Try the red one there."

This time, Matthew rode up, found his spot, swung a wide loop at an angle over his left shoulder, made an arc that allowed the loop to stay open as it dropped under the calf, and stood there while the calf trapped its hind legs as it moved away from the horse. Matthew jerked his slack, and this time the loop closed around the calf's legs and tightened as the calf moved forward. The boy dallied and pulled back the reins. With the rope set, the boy backed his horse and stretched out the calf as it stood with his front feet on the ground and its hind legs in the air stretched out behind it.

"Good shot," Lucas said as he dismounted and treated the calf.

When he finished, Lucas held the calf down with his knee and asked the boy to step his horse forward. The boy did, and Lucas pulled the rope loose and let the calf go. Matthew pulled in his rope and coiled it as he went. Lucas caught his horse and rode next to the boy.

"What do you think?" Lucas asked.

Matthew nodded and smiled.

"That felt good. Can we do some more?"

Lucas laughed. "Yeah, we have to check everything in here."

Matthew missed the next two, but found his rhythm and started catching both heels on almost every throw. They finished out the day, and that night Matthew lay awake a long time looking at the ceiling in the darkness and replaying every loop as he rolled the talisman between his fingers, unable to think about anything but cowboying.

The next morning at breakfast, Riggs sat across from Matthew. Halfway through his eggs and steak, he called out to the boy.

"Hey, Matt, how would you like to ride with Cal today? It's a full day of riding and checking the cattle in the south meadows."

Matthew looked down the table at Cal. Cal winked at him and nodded.

The boy looked over at Riggs and grinned.

"I'd like that just fine."

"Don't you boys stop for a swim up there," said an anonymous voice at the other end of the table.

Cal shook his head and laughed. "Well, I damn sure won't."

Then Cal looked at Matthew.

"You ain't bringing your gun, are you?"

Matthew laughed a long time and just shook his head.

Cal and the boy rode side by side, and talk was spare when there was any talk at all. Matthew watched the cowboy watch the cattle, and he watched him scan the tree line.

He liked the cowboy way of doing things and Cal, especially, had an air about him that went from lighthearted to serious as circumstances dictated. The boy saw Cal as hard, competent, and reliable. Things he did not see in the men in town who were merchants and bankers and had no calluses on their hands.

From his spurs to his hat, everything about Cal said cowboy. As lowly a job as others thought that to be, it was exactly what Matthew wanted. Cal settled back in his saddle and the boy took the opportunity to break the silence.

"How long you been cowboying?"

Cal looked up as though the answer hung suspended above him.

"I left home when I turned fifteen. Riding

a broken down plow horse my dad give me. Got my first job at a feedlot in Kansas."

"You started right out as a cowboy?"

"No, I was a shit shoveler. But it was cowshit, so I started pretty close."

Matthew laughed.

"Is that the truth?"

"Most of it."

"What part's not true?"

"The part about the horse. My dad didn't give him to me. I just took him. The old man was drunk the day I left, like he was every day before that. My ma died when I was about your age — maybe a little younger."

"How did you end up on the Arbuckle?"

"Tim Arbuckle — he was Patrick's brother. He found me working at a feedlot in Abilene. I was seventeen and I was about fed up with the feedlot. He offered me a job and I took it. Been here ever since."

"You ever plan on leaving?"

"No — I don't plan on it."

"I guess I got a job here too. Half pay's all I'm worth right now."

"I heard that. They say you'll make a cowboy."

The boy nodded and they rode the length of the first meadow in silence. Cal spoke up first.

"They say you had a hard go of it."

"Maybe."

"Maybe?"

"When I think back on it — I might have been lucky."

Cal's expression begged the question, and the boy responded accordingly.

"They could have killed me."

"Yeah, I guess that's lucky all right."

Cal paused as though he were pondering the whole of it.

"You know, if they killed you — I might still be walking. So, I guess we both got lucky on that one."

Matthew laughed.

"Yeah, we did."

The boy pulled on the brim of his hat.

"Do you believe in predestination?"

"I can't say I do — I never seen one."

The boy laughed again.

"It means that some things happen because they were meant to — it's in the Bible, I think."

"I never gave it much thought."

"Me neither, up till now."

"That's a little deep for me," Cal said. "But I can see how some things might look that way."

Matthew let it go at that.

"I used to think you were an ass," the boy said.

Cal laughed.

"What do you think now?"

Matthew tipped back his hat and laughed.

"I think you probably still are."

"Well, I used to think you were a lunatic."

"What do you think now?"

"I'm pretty sure you still are."

FIFTY-SIX

In the mornings, the chill in the air accompanied the coming of fall and suggested an early winter. The leaves on the aspen trees turned gold and yellow, blew across the corrals, and piled against the barn walls. Work on the ranch changed. A few of the itinerant cowboys had already packed it in and headed south for winter work. The permanent crew brought in hay and stacked it high in the barns. They fixed broken fences and repaired long overdue damages to the bunkhouses. They shipped out the yearlings, and the mother cows carried their summer fat, waited for spring calves, and the beginning of a new cycle.

Matthew and No'Ka finished off the young horses. The dun proved to be more of a challenge than either expected, but when they ran the hard-case colts in with the others for Riggs, they held the dun out.

The boy worked with the dun every day

and promised to come back the following summer to finish him, if he had to. No'Ka understood the boy's refusal to quit the dun, and he promised Matthew he would hold the horse for him.

The boy and the Indian walked to the breaking pen after supper one evening when the night was clear and there was frost in the air. On the far side of the pen stood the dun, alone and defiant.

"So, how long are you staying?" No'Ka asked.

"Mr. Arbuckle told me I'm done on Friday."

"What about next year?"

"I'm coming back. We shook hands on it."

The boy watched the dun.

"He sold me a saddle and a bridle."

"How much did that cost you?"

"I still got a dollar left."

"You still got four more days to work with the dun before you go."

"I know — it ain't much, is it?"

"No, it's not, but you have come a long way with him."

"Will you work with him for me some this winter if I can't get him done?"

"I'll do what I can. It's not easy working a horse when the weather turns."

"I hate to see him go backwards with me

being gone and all."

"Sometimes the slow ones don't make it — time works against it."

"Do you think he's a good horse, No'Ka?"

"I think he can be a good horse. He's got a good mind, good feet, and he's built right."

No'Ka appeared to be in deep thought.

"Anyone riding back to town with you Friday?"

"I'm going alone."

"You want company?"

"You'd ride with me?"

"Yes, I would. You're one of the few white men I've met that was worth anything."

Matthew laughed.

"You got a lot of white friends here."

No'Ka smiled.

"Yes, I do."

Matthew pulled out the talisman and held it in the palm of his hand for the Indian to see.

"I ain't had a bad dream since you give me this."

"You know it had nothing to do with that, right?"

The boy nodded. "Yeah, I reckon I did, but I keep it close just the same."

"If you lose it, I have more."

Matthew's expression wavered between

surprise and disappointment.

"You didn't think I'd give all my protection away, did you?"

Matthew smiled.

"No, I guess not. I'm keeping this one anyway — I know this one works."

For the next three days, Matthew spent every daylight hour with the dun. At night when the moon was up, he stayed with the dun and spoke to him, and handled him. He saddled and bridled the horse, and every night he prayed.

His last night at the Arbuckle, he sat with the cowboys in the big bunkhouse, where they all gathered. To a man, each one shook his hand and said, "Good riding with you." Riggs told him he wanted him in the roping pen next fall, and when Cal approached him, they just shook hands and exchanged no words, for all they had to say had been said. Long after the others left, Lucas and the boy sat in the dim light of a single oil lamp with the wick burning short.

"What time are you heading out in the morning?"

"First light. No'Ka's coming with me."

"Taking your saddle with you?"

"It'll get me through the winter."

"You done real good here. No one expected you to last a week."

"What did you think?"

"I gave you three days."

"What did No'Ka think?"

"He never said, but I think he had you pegged. Otherwise he wouldn't have wasted any time on you."

"He's a good man."

"I've known him ever since I got here. I never heard any bad said of him, ever."

"Will you be here next year?"

"I reckon I will, if I don't get restless."

"I hope to see you then."

"Same here, Bud."

In the morning, Matthew and No'Ka started on the trail before the moon set. The air was cold and the breath from the horses billowed out in great white clouds that made it feel colder than it was. The burlap sack the boy came with hung over his saddle horn, and all it contained was the clothes he owned. He sat straight in the saddle with an air about him that appeared somewhat hard, but capable. He wore his hat with authority. He rode deliberate, but not arrogant.

When they reached the top of the first rise, Matthew turned and looked back. A light shone from the kitchen in the house and another from the barn. He could neither see people nor hear any sounds but, in his mind, he was still back there and it was all very real to him.

"You going to miss the place?"

Matthew turned.

"Yeah, I am."

At midday, they stopped to water and rest the horses. No'Ka retrieved dried beef and biscuits from his saddlebags. Matthew hobbled his horse, slipped the bridle from its head, and hung it from the saddle horn. He sat on the grass in the sun with No'Ka and they ate.

"What's next for you?"

"My ma and me need to find a place to live."

"You got any ideas on that?"

"I think Mr. Elder, I mean J.D., is going to help us with that. Probably go back to our place."

"Are they going to get married?"

"I reckon they will."

"How do you feel about that?"

"I guess I feel good about it."

No'Ka smiled.

"I don't suppose it matters, does it?"

"I don't think it does."

When they rode up on the crest of the last hill and looked down upon the small town, for all appearances, nothing had changed. The comings and goings of Ike and Raymond and Sandoval, the search parties, the U.S. Marshal, all the deaths — none of it made a lasting impact from what they could see.

"It's kind of sad, ain't it?"

"What is?" No'ka asked.

"That so much happened down there, and today it looks like nothing at all."

"It's the way of things. In your Bible, it says, 'all things will pass.' My people have known that forever."

"All the same, it seems sad to me."

They shook hands and No'Ka turned back down the trail. Matthew watched him until he could no longer see him or hear the sound of the horse's hooves upon the hard ground. He watched the empty trail a long time before he turned and rode the rest of the way into town.

Matthew rode directly to the Dunn house. He stopped at the hitch rail, took a deep breath, reached down and patted the horse's neck, then sat there and waited while he collected his thoughts. So much had happened since he and Elder rode out to the Arbuckle. Things changed. He changed.

Now he wondered if he could adjust. He looked up the street and he looked at the familiar buildings, but there was no bunk-house, no breaking pen, and no cowboys saddling their horses. He put his hand on his rope. He liked the feel of the coils and the leather keeper strap that held it against the saddle. He rolled the reins in his fingers and he watched the horse's ears turn, one back one forward, as it took in its new surroundings. He looked back over his shoulder in the direction of the Arbuckle and contemplated turning his horse back up the trail. Instead, he chose to sit his horse as he pondered thoughts too complicated to reconcile.

His horse jumped when the front door of the house burst open and Sarah Stanford rushed forth onto the porch with her hands to her face and tears running down both cheeks. Matthew smiled and kicked his right boot free of the stirrup as J.D. Elder stepped out with a hammer in one hand and a bag of nails in the other. Elder set the hammer and nails by the door, then stepped down to stand at the shoulder of the boy's horse.

"Well, I'll be damned," Elder said, as he reached out to pat the horse on the shoulder. He looked up at the boy and his expression was one of surprise and admiration.

"I see you got your dun horse broke."

Matthew swung his leg over the saddle

and stood before Elder with the reins in one hand and the other hand hung over the saddle horn. His manner was direct and his demeanor, polite and unassuming.

"We didn't break him — we just helped him find his way."

EPILOGUE

Matthew never saw Lucas after that summer. They told the boy Lucas rode south in the spring, and a few said they ran across him one place or another over the years, but no one knew for sure. Matthew stopped waiting to hear from him.

Ty Riggs died early that winter when one of the young horses he rode ran him into a bog, where they found his body and that of the horse two days later.

Cal took over the foreman's job in January. His friendship with Matthew continued for the rest of their lives. Cal never left the Arbuckle.

Most of the regular crew stayed on, but a few drifted after the itinerant cowboys left in the fall. Each year a few of the older cowboys left and new ones took their places. Some returned off and on and, eventually, even they disappeared.

Patrick Arbuckle married and raised a

family, and never left the mountains.

No'Ka stayed on and quietly trained his horses, and each fall he and Matthew packed in to the high country to hunt and talk of horses. The year No'Ka died, Matthew collected the Indian's ropes, halters, and blankets and returned them with the body to the reservation where his passing was celebrated with great honor. Matthew never stopped wearing the beaded talisman.

Elder abandoned his cabin and bought five sections of land adjoining the Stanford place. He and Sarah married the following year. They lived out their lives on the Rafter E Ranch they built with the help of Matthew.

The Dunn place stood vacant and was never re-occupied.

They buried Clarence on a grassy hill overlooking the place he fished on the river. They marked the grave with a simple wooden cross and, by the following spring, there was no sign he had ever been there.

The bodies of Ike, Raymond, and Sandoval lay buried in unmarked graves in a remote corner of the same cemetery in which Milo Dunn, his wife, and the remains of Pastor Stanford were laid to rest. No one ever visited the unmarked gravesites.

The town never grew, and eventually they

abandoned the jail and the sheriff's office.

Matthew Stanford rode the dun horse until it grew too old to travel. Matthew continued to cowboy, for it was all he was ever meant to do.

ABOUT THE AUTHOR

D. B. Jackson is a previous resident of the Big Sky country of Montana. He and his wife, Mary, reside on their ranch near Oakdale, California, where he is involved in the registered Angus cattle business and is a full time writer.